Mitterhal's Post

Published by the Piscataqua Press
An imprint of RiverRun Bookstore
142 Fleet Street | Portsmouth, NH | 03801

www.riverrunbookstore.com
www.piscataquapress.com

ISBN: 978-1-939739-46-9

Printed in the United States of America

Mitterhal's Post

By R. E. Nelson

Acknowledgments

Titia and Gijs Bozuwa, for the gardens, the workshop and the workshops, the dinners, the readings, the olives, the purpose, the cheer, the home.

Elizabeth Barrett, editor, for the uncensored encouragement and spot-on analysis that made a writer out of me.

Connor Nelson, my son, for the reason to get up.

Mark Polakow, friend and life brother, for fleshing out Part One.

Bob and Dorothy Nelson, for doing what parents do and more.

Pastor Mary James, for the sermons.

Jeff Knight and Terry Colligan, for keeping me busy.

Ken Cereghino and Professor David Fairchild, for the philosophical input and perspective.

Robert Kneeland, for uncompensated time in the recording studio.

Amy Pinhero, for Enyalda.

The First Congregational Church of Wakefield, for being there.

Last but not least, I acknowledge the unyielding force that compelled me to write this book. Thank you.

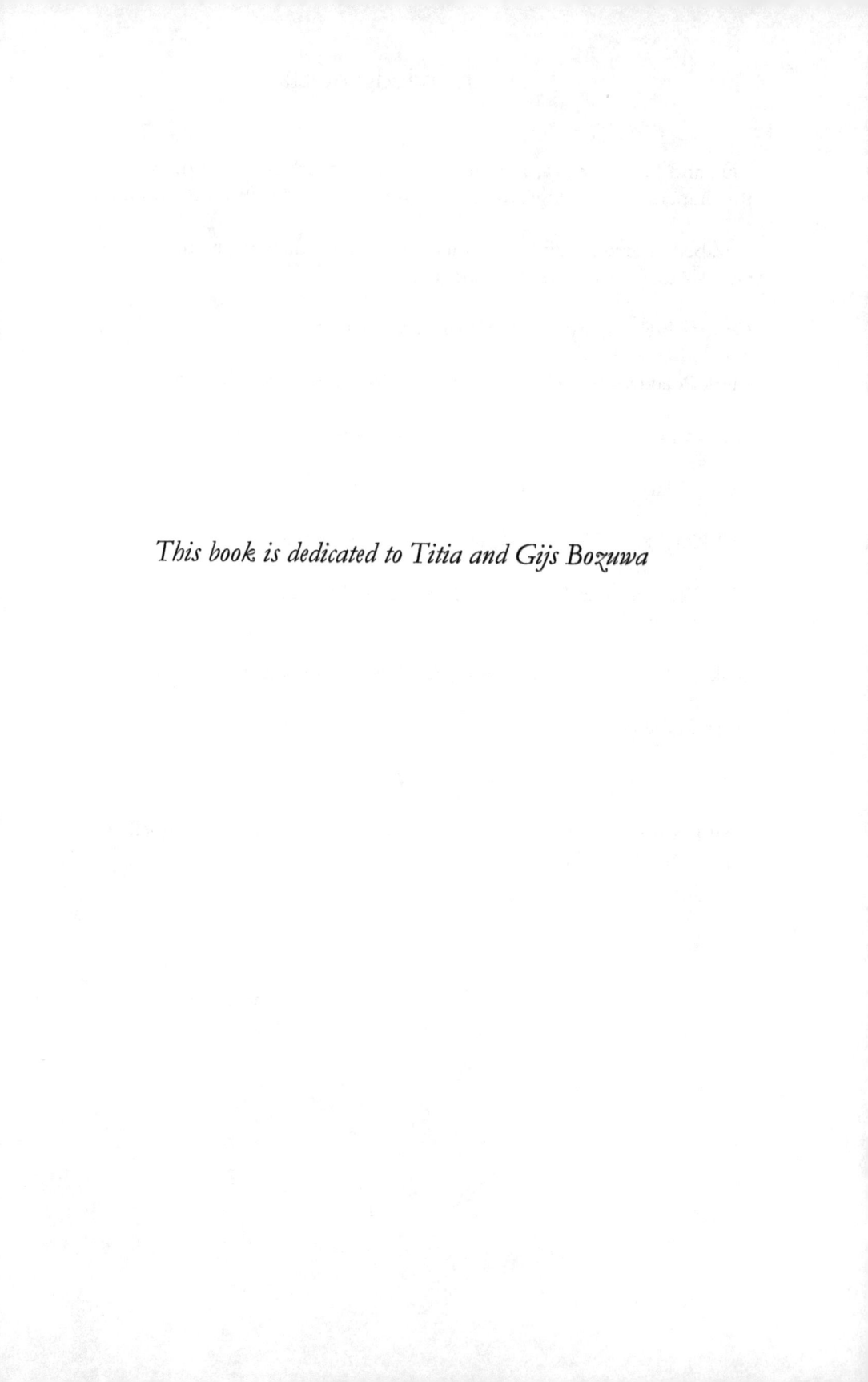

This book is dedicated to Titia and Gijs Bozuwa

There is a very remarkable inclination in human nature to bestow on external objects the same emotions which it observes in itself, and to find everywhere those ideas which are most present to it.

—David Hume, Scottish philosopher, 1711-1776

Contents

Prologue:
The Battle at Spaulding Pass

The first hint of dawn gave shape to the shadowy mountains in the east. Colonel Cornelius Mitterhal sat on his warhorse smoking his pipe, his spyglass fixed on the herd of wild goats that floated like ghostly sentinels high up on the ridge. "Have patience, my friends," he said to them. "You will have your pastures back once our business here is done."

Behind the colonel, his army stood. Two thousand men shrouded in the mist of an alpine meadow, their faces chiseled like the rocky clefts that loomed about them. A commanding silence hovered over the pass as they awaited their leader's word. Even the horses kept still, their heads high to the withers, preparing in some horse-like way for what they would be called upon to do. In time their ears perked to the advance of a one-legged rider galloping up the misty slope. Lieutenant Uryan McFadden cut through the field of lupine on his warhorse, wasting no time to deliver his message.

"They have rejected our terms, sir."

Cold and neutral, the colonel took a moment to process the news. A twitch flickered like a candle flame over his right eyebrow. Calmly, he raised his war scope and aimed it back on the goats on the ridge. Above them he spotted the white belly of an osprey circling high in the dawn's light. Faith hovered in the wind.

"So they have," he said as the smoke curled out of his pipe. Resolved,

Mitterhal lowered his lens and turned back to McFadden. "At least history will not accuse us of turning a blind eye to diplomacy. Are the pipers in position?"

"Yes," McFadden answered.

"Good. Ready your talon, Lieutenant."

Mitterhal tugged the reins of his horse. The disciplined war steed spun on cue. He rode forward to address the troops, weaving a thin thread of smoke through the ranks of cavalry, archers, and musketmen. The embers in his pipe burned hot in contrast to the cool gait of his mount.

"The time for battle is upon us," he announced in a voice that echoed off the crags. "The bear has come to ravage the hive. Behind this pass lies your treasure. Your land. Your families. Your way of life!"

He paused to let the weight of his words set in. Every eye was on him. Eyes that radiated confidence and purpose—qualities he had fostered during their training and throughout the war.

"I will not mask the truth. For every one of you there are ten of them. The Toriceans bring cannons and guns that we cannot match in open battle. But I will also tell you this. That our Fatherland's bear has grown fat and clumsy in its arrogance. When the wulfweed burns, you and your foe will be wrapped in smoke. That is when your training will become crystal clear."

Mitterhal nudged his horse into a trot, passing back through the front line where Lieutenant McFadden held position next to the banner of the Three Havens. There the colonel faced the insignia woven into the tattered fabric—three crossed stalks of lupine, the mountain flower, flapped boldly in a border of blue. He peered down into the pass to better read the details of the wind. Long he listened until a raven's call drifted up the misty slope, assuring him that the music would carry well.

Satisfied, he returned his attention to the troops. "The pipers are in position. At all times you must trust in your training and listen to the music that surrounds you. That is where your advantage lies. Chant the codes and you will remain united in the smoke. I assure you that your enemy will not!"

He nodded to Lieutenant McFadden, who closed his eyes and began the mantra. An archer positioned on a nearby precipice acted on the signal and launched a fire arrow high into the mountain pass. Within seconds, the distant drone of a single goat-hyde pipe pierced the mist that rose out of the valley.

"Remember, lads," the colonel resumed. "It is not the sting of the bee that disheartens this bear. It is the sound of the swarm in its ear that drives it mad. Go now. Defend your hive and listen to the music. Sing. Sing to the Mountain! Sing to your hearth and home! A soul will never get lost if it leaves the world in song!"

Prologue

Volleys of fire arrows flew into the dawn's light, triggering a symphony of pipers to answer from their hidden aeries. The men joined in the war chant led by McFadden. Cornelius Mitterhal held back on his horse, watching his troops descend into battle. He rekindled his pipe in the wake of their spirited verse, paying scrupulous attention to the direction in which the smoke drifted. Alone he remained, silent and still, until McFadden's cavalry veered from the march and galloped west across the slope. With his order underway, Mitterhal patted the shoulder of his warhorse and began the arduous climb back to his command post on the ridge.

Far down in the vale, the enemy's march halted as the eerie blend of pipes and song emanated out of Spaulding Pass.

Part I
On the Roof

1
Light on the Haven

Cornelius Mitterhal lived alone in a vacated manor on Cotton Crown Mountain, which overlooked a vast lake to the south and west. The Old Mitt, as he was often called, was an odd man. He never left his property after the war. And when he was not tending to his goats or beehives, he would climb up an oak ladder to his slate roof, upon which he had built a modest wooden platform. The lookout straddled the roof peak next to an old weather-beaten chimney. Old Mitt spent countless hours manning his post, gazing across the alpine pastures and out into the Haven.

It was a still summer evening, the sun setting over Lake Lakwynn. Cornelius Mitterhal sat with his back against the chimney, smoking his pipe and watching the shiny brass gears of his Toricean music box go round and round. Every turn of the hand crank released another wave of soothing music. He had a special affection for the little blue box, even though it had been crafted in the land of the enemy. Only a year had passed since his return from the war, and somehow he had managed to pardon the melodious toy of the crime. Or maybe he'd just forgotten. Regardless, it had become his habit at this time of day to smoke his pipe with his precious blue box and sing to the music. It was his way of watching the realities of the day melt away into the mysteries of the night.

The sunset was more magnificent than usual on this particular evening. Mitterhal assessed the view from his vantage on Cotton Crown Mountain. Far below, the city of Wulfhaven glistened on the harbor's edge. Beyond Wulfhaven, to the north, the Awshaw Mountains loomed out of Gwyntahlynn like a ring of dark guardians, shielding the Pemihawynn River from the blaze in the western sky. Farther up the coast, the harbors of Tufthaven and Multynhaven radiated a fiery mix of reds and yellows that challenged Mitterhal to delineate where the Three Havens ended and the heavens began.

"Mark my words," he said aloud. "Just when you think you've seen it all, a sunset like this comes along and puts you right back into your place."

Awestruck, he reclined against the chimney and nestled deep in the Haven's light. The sight inspired him to turn the crank once again and sing to the enchanting tune.

Celebration, song and dance
See the wagon's ponies prance
Beneath my tapestry receive
Your mother's blessing.

A voice joined in harmony—similar to the colonel's, but not quite. Barely audible at first, more like an echo. When he finished the verse, he lifted the box but saw nothing, just the bottom. He opened the lid wide but heard nothing, only the passing of a breeze through the gears. With a shrug he went back to turning the hand crank. No sooner did the music begin when the voice returned, only it spoke rather than sang.

"What is sunset?" it asked, distinct and present.

Mitterhal, never a jumpy man, closed the lid of the music box and turned around slowly. "What did you say?" he asked, casting a hard look at the bricks of the chimney.

"The sunset," the chimney answered. "You said it puts you in your place. What is it?"

The colonel dragged long and deep on his pipe. His right eyebrow twitched; such was the case now and then. Definitely a male voice, he decided. After exhaling the smoke, he opted not to encourage the delusion. Rather, he gulped down a spoonful of honey from a mason jar that he kept in an old weathered crate. He then reopened his blue box and spun the brass handle again.

"Why will you not answer?" the voice asked from out of the bricks.

Mitterhal held his tongue and spun the crank harder. The tempo of the music increased. He watched the gears go around while the chimney repeated its plea. Still, the willful old warrior held his ground. To answer the question was to admit that the chimney had actually asked it, something his war-hardened mind would not concede without a fight. The gears in his blue box spun like tops at a fair and drew his focus ever inward. In a last ditch effort to squelch the foolish spell, he put down the box and aimed his war scope at the crimson shores. With his lens set on the sunset's glow, he submitted his own plea to the fading light on the Haven.

"I am tired of this war, Marcus. Tell me more about your merciful God. I would like to know where he stands on the issue. Does he even care? When you preach to my men about his light on the Haven, they listen. Does he?"

"War is an earthly event, Cornelius. Like a storm or a wildfire, it will run its course. It is part of our Great Father's plan, and as such he will not meddle in our politics. Yet I believe he keeps a place ready for those who hold true to their faith. Be it in heaven or on earth, your men will know his mercy."

A trickle of smoke rose out of the chimney and choked the colonel from his trance. Defiance gave way to wonder. For the life of him, he could not remember stoking the fire that day. He assessed the breeze that blustered up the valley, attempting one last logical explanation. Could a rogue gust have stirred up the soot in the chimney's flue? Perhaps, but not likely.

The sun sank into the lake, leaving a faint streak of scarlet on the clouds. At last, his gaze softened and he surrendered to the notion of a talking chimney.

"Very well then," he said, leaning against the bricks. "If you must know, I will tell you about the sunset."

So began the friendship between Colonel Cornelius Mitterhal and his chimney.

2
Purpose in the Puff

During the war Cornelius Mitterhal would gather his men for a chat on the eve of battle. These chats had a peculiar quality in that they were the one time when he would relax his authority and allow his troops to speak whatever was on their minds. More often than not, the subjects raised had little to do with war. The men's faith in the colonel freed their minds to explore other matters. In fact, it became somewhat of a tradition at these times for the more seasoned warriors to interrogate their commander on the softer subjects of life. If for nothing else, it provided a calming diversion for the men. Woven within his answers, were the threads of inspiration that many took to their graves.

One day at dawn the Old Mitt climbed his ladder with a bucket of mortar and a clinking leather pouch filled with tools. At the eave he stepped onto another ladder that lay flat on the slate shingles and extended to the ridge. A sturdy hook at the peak kept it from sliding. From the hook he walked the ridge, straddling both sides with his feet. He was careful not to lose his footing on the morning dew that had yet to evaporate off the slate. Eventually he made it to his watch post.

"Good morning, Colonel," the chimney said.

The staging planks creaked as the old man stepped from the roof ridge onto his platform. "Good morning, Chimney." He pulled a narrow metal object out of his tool pouch.

"What do you have in your hand?" asked the chimney.

"It is a mason's pointing tool. It is used to pack mortar between bricks and stone. When I'm done, you will be as good as new."

Mitterhal sat on his tin bucket and prepared to repair the old chimney. He hummed a melody while he packed his pipe with a dash of the lupine leaf that grew wild in his goat pastures. Before loosening the mud, he removed the blue music box from his vest pocket and set it carefully on the platform next to his pouch. No sooner had he put the trowel to the mortar than a buzz circled his head several times before landing on the blue box.

"Well, hello there, little fellow," he said, raising a bushy brow. "And what gets you up so early in the morning?"

The honeybee crawled across the music box, exploring its every detail. The colonel watched with interest. "I am afraid you will not find any nectar in there, my friend. You will have much more success in the meadow."

The bee buzzed off the box, as if comprehending the suggestion, and passed through the colonel's pipe smoke before disappearing into the pasture.

"Colonel, who were you talking to?"

"Nobody," Mitterhal said, gazing at the glossy blue enamel. "Just a bee that mistook my music box for a flower. An honest mistake."

"Are you going to open the blue box today?"

Mitterhal looked at the box. "No, not today. I know the tune by heart. I think it's time to put it back where it belongs."

"Why did you bring it then?"

"I don't know. Habit, I suppose."

"Colonel?"

"What now?"

"Who is S. Harthmocker?"

"Nobody of importance. Why do you ask?"

"His name is embroidered on your tool belt."

"Well, then I would have to assume he was a mason. Wouldn't you say?"

"That would make sense," the chimney said.

"Good. You are full of questions this morning, my friend. I suggest you pace yourself. It's going to make for a long day if you keep this up."

The morning moved on without further fuss. Mitterhal went back to his work and sang the old melody unaided by the box. He delved deep into his task, filling the voids of silence with smoke and song. His voice, though gritty and gruff, kept in perfect time with the scraping of metal on masonry. The chimney remained silent for its part, wrapped in a cloud of contemplation.

Mountain lupine in full bloom,
Flowing blue on meadow's tide.
On yellow wagon you and I,

5

To the Haven we will ride.
Upon arrival at lakeshore
We will open wagon's door.
By the fountain we will be
Blessed in love eternally.

From the fountain we will cross,
Love's reflection on the lake.
Wagon carry us away
Sea of crimson in our wake.
And in the moonlight's subtle glance,
We will watch the ripples dance.
From our wagon we will see,
The land we love, the love we leave.

"Colonel?"

"Yes, Chimney?"

"What is love?"

Mitterhal squinted and took a deep puff from his pipe. He was not particularly fond of the subject. "Love is something that occurs among the living. Why do you ask?"

The chimney remained quiet for some time. The colonel had gone back to his work before it answered. "I hear it in the song that you sing. While you were fixing my bricks I felt something strange and wondered if it was the love that you sing about."

The comment, though innocent, vexed the colonel. The conversation was not going in the direction he wanted. "It is an old ballad that I sing to pass the time and nothing more." He stirred the mortar in the bucket. "Do not put so much thought into it."

Smoke churned out of the chimney. "Colonel?"

"What now? Can't you see I'm busy?"

"Is it only the living that can have love? Can I have love as well?"

The old man inhaled long and deep on his pipe, giving ample time for the smoke to permeate his lungs. In spite of all effort to the contrary, he could not ignore the growing sense of responsibility he felt for the happiness of his inquisitive friend. Even a talking chimney, as odd as it seemed, deserved love. Alive or not, to deny it something so basic would not only be cruel, but fundamentally insane. At last, he exhaled and answered.

"By every sensible law that governs this world, you should not even exist as you do, yet you do. To that I have no answer. But given that things are as they are, I will say that yes, even you, Chim, can have love."

The smoke had barely dispersed when the chimney beckoned yet again. Mitterhal refused to respond. He had had enough love nonsense for the day. Rather he dragged on his pipe and sang the old melody even louder to drown out the interrogation of his persistent friend.

"How do I know when I have love?"

No answer.

"Colonel?" the chimney pleaded.

Still, no answer. Round after round Mitterhal recited his verse, ignoring the chimney's amorous thirst. Every stanza sent him deeper into a trance, until at last the song faded and he slipped away to a forgotten time and place.

"Remember this day, lads! When the mighty Jeziah stepped out of the ranks on the eve of his big dance with the bear to ask what love is. Far be it from me to deny our chief cipher his lesson. Perhaps it is a question we all should consider. I would start by laying down your muskets and giving a good hard look to the pass you defend. What do you see? Hear? Smell? Listen to the bees, the buzz around you. Think about what inspires them. What draws them to the gahenya? Yes, the blue beauty, of course, but there is more to it than that. It is their devotion to the hive, where their true treasure lies. Without that they will not bother with the blossom, no matter how tempting. Take away their hive and you take away their drive. Remember that when you fire your muskets."

"Colonel, are you still there?"

Cornelius Mitterhal opened his eyes and laid down his trowel. He removed the spent pipe from his mouth and glared at the newly pointed bricks. "Love is the power that puts purpose in your puff! Now be silent so I can work in peace."

The chimney stayed quiet. Whether or not it comprehended the colonel's explanation remained a mystery. But if residents in the nearby highland village of Cotton Crown had been observant, they would have noticed a steady stream of smoke rising over Old Mitt's manor that afternoon and into the evening.

3
Commemoration Day

Every year in early summer the lake port of Wulfhaven put on a celebration to commemorate the emancipation of the province. For three years Colonel Cornelius Mitterhal observed the event from his lofty post on his rooftop. From his vantage he could view the fireworks launched over the lake and feel the percussion of distant cannons. Sometimes, if the wind blew just right, he could hear the faint drone of goat-hyde pipes wafting up the valley from the fairgrounds.

It was morning on the mountain, a day to embrace. Silver dew sparkled on the rooftop. The colonel stood on the edge of his platform, spyglass fixed on the black dots that swarmed the fairgrounds on the outskirts of Wulfhaven. The dots were celebrating something, that much he knew. It happened every year at this time when the gahenya blossom came into bloom. He was glad not to be part of the festivity, but looked forward, nonetheless, to the fireworks that would come later.

"Colonel?"

"Yes, Chim?"

"You spend a lot of time up here."

"Your point?"

"None really. Just an observation."

Smoke fogged the lens. "Well then, congratulations."

"For what, if I may ask?"

Mitterhal's Post

Mitterhal squinted back into the scope. "For being the most observant smokestack on this side of the Haven." Masses of dots were leaving the fairgrounds.

"You mean there are others like me?"

The colonel shook his head. The chimney just didn't get humor. It was an irritating quirk that made jesting with it impossible. Again the lens fogged. "You exhaust me, Chim."

"My apologies, Colonel. What can I do to stop exhausting you?"

"You can start by laughing once in a while. Stop taking things so seriously."

Smoke curled out of the chimney's top. "Laughing... What is that?"

"What do you mean, what is that? It is as basic as breathing. It gives power to your puff."

"I thought that was love."

Mitterhal choked on his smoke. "You are impossible, Chimney," he said after a bout of gritty coughs. "Let's just call it a celebration and leave it at that."

The chimney remained silent while the colonel finished clearing his lungs. He raised his war scope between hacks to keep a tally of the dots. Something wasn't right. Why were they leaving the fairgrounds so early this year?

"Colonel?"

"What is it, Chim?"

"Will you show me how to laugh?"

"That will be a lesson for later. We have more pressing business at the moment. Tell me what is happening down by the harbor? Hurry!"

"The shadows of the clouds are moving across the Haven."

"No. No. The people—what are they doing?"

"They appear to be leaving the fairgrounds and making for the road that ascends this mountain."

Mitterhal pressed his palm to his temple in an effort to steady the twitch over his right eyebrow. Quickly he reached for the mason jar and slurped a mouthful of honey.

"Are you all right, Colonel?"

"Quiet, Chimney, I need to think." He wiped the sweet mass off his lips. "They must be making for the village. This is unexpected. Strange. Unprecedented." Dazed, he sat down on his bucket and pressed his back to the chimney. His jaw began to quiver. "Keep watch on the march, Chim," he said, honing in on the distant drone of the goat-hyde pipes.

Shortly thereafter his trembling chin came to rest on his chest. He remained as such, only vaguely aware of the chimney's shadow creeping across the weathered gray planks of his platform. With his mind so engaged he hummed a melody, accompanied by the mountain breeze that strummed the stalks of gahenya on his pasture.

9

Look to the mountain goats
They guard the way
Sail to the Haven's coast
We sing today
Hail Gahenya, Maha gaila

Peace to our land unveiled
By a talon strike
Wind on the lakehawk's tail
Today we fight
Hail Gahenya, Maha gaila

Climb her Highland Dome
Breathe in the air
Sing to hearth and home
The tune we share
Hail Gahenya, Maha gaila

"Colonel, I do not believe the procession intends to stop at the village."

Mitterhal twitched; his head snapped up. The shadows on the rooftop were gone. Looking beyond the eave, his unaided eyes spotted the yellow pony-drawn wagon that led the parade up the carriage road and through his south pasture. Behind it advanced an army of skirts that extended clear back to the upper village, hundreds of women and children waving flags and marching in pace with the goat-hyde pipes.

"Why didn't you say something sooner?" he asked the chimney. "It is nearly noon!"

"Forgive me, Colonel. You were singing with the music. I did not want to be rude."

The pipes carried loud and clear over the rippling fields. Mitterhal scanned the gahenya in search of his goats. Where did they go? He spotted them to the north on the steep slopes beyond the high pasture. The displaced herd had congregated on the rocky outcrops below the mountain's towering peak.

"Have no worries, my friends," he said, repacking his pipe with a pinch of the highland herb. "You will have your pasture back once the fuss is over." He shot a stern look to his chimney. "Chimney, I will handle the matter from here. Do not make a sound. Do you understand?"

"I do."

"Good."

The Old Mitt relit his pipe. He stood on the edge of his platform, arms crossed at the chest in standard military fashion, watching the yellow wagon advance through the wild lupine. Eventually, the wagon breached a gap in his fieldstone wall and entered the courtyard. A score of kilted pipers marched by its side, their music droning on. The plumed ponies drew to a halt near a hedge of laurels, within a shout of the manor. The procession funneled in behind, bustling the grounds with life.

Tall banners were raised in the courtyard amidst carts laden with pies and pastries. Mitterhal monitored the activity without smile or word. He saw children and ladies—lots of them. Where were the men? The proportion seemed skewed.

One of the pipers blew a single high note and the music stopped. A stately officer holding a long wooden voice horn stepped out of the yellow wagon and strode to a podium set near the hedge. He adjusted one of many sparkling medals that dangled on his chest before raising the voice horn to his mouth.

"Hail, Gahenya!" he announced, facing Mitterhal and bringing all to order. "We trust you are well, sir. On behalf of the good people of the Three Havens and all free Lakwynnians alike, we wish to honor you for the peace that you have brought to our province."

Mitterhal eyed the decorated spokesman. There was something hauntingly familiar about him, his voice … his posture … his uniform … Obviously a man of importance. The colonel looked to the line of stone-faced pipers positioned around the yellow wagon. A banner rose out of their midst. Three crossed stalks of the mountain flower stitched on a border of blue.

"Who are you?" he finally asked, looking back to the master of ceremony.

The simple question had an unnerving effect on the officer. The epaulettes slumped on his shoulders and his chest deflated. "I am Captain Marlin Barleycopp, sir, of the Haven Guard. I was your …"

"You were my what, Captain? Speak up."

Captain Barleycopp lowered his voice horn and wiped his face with a sleeve. A heavy hush settled on the crowd as all waited for his reply. He took a deep breath and lifted the voice horn once again. "That is not important, sir. What is more important is that we celebrate the sovereignty of our land and that you are properly recognized for your service to the province."

Mitterhal grimaced and turned his back on the apprehensive mass of onlookers. He raised his war scope and studied the goats upslope, so ghostly white against the outcrops. A child's giggle drew him back. He swung his lens in search of the source. He spotted her alone, skipping by the rock wall near his beehives, whispering to the wild flowers—a young girl. Like a babbling brook in a spring thaw, her giggles tickled his ears, drawing a long dormant smile out of his scowl. So charmed, the colonel returned his attention to the master of ceremony. "Tell me, Captain. Has there been a death?"

11

Marlin Barleycopp shifted uneasily and adjusted his regalia. "A death, sir?"

"Yes, a death! You have marched up this mountain to tell me about a celebration, but it feels more like a funeral to me. A celebration is meant to be a joyous occasion, is it not?"

Visibly rattled by the challenge, Barleycopp fumbled for the right words.

"Is it not, Captain? The question is simple."

"Eh … I … Of course, sir."

"Why then are you standing in the middle of my courtyard like a peacock plucked of its plumage?"

A wave of chuckles rippled across the crowd. Barleycopp snapped out of his malaise. Even the rigid line of pipers eased their stance at the colonel's humorous jab at their captain.

"Forgive me, sir," the captain said, playing up to the insult. "I seem to be a bit out of practice at this business."

The Old Mitt scanned the gathering; his sharp eyes pierced the crowd. Nobody escaped his scrutiny. "I do not want your apology!" he bellowed. "I want you to simply do as you say. If this is indeed a celebration, then make it so. That goes for all of you. Otherwise I will have my afternoon nap."

Captain Barleycopp jumped on the order and spun around to address the crowd. His medals sparkled in the sun. "You heard the colonel." He raised his voice horn straight to the sky. "Let the celebration begin!"

An explosion of cheer shook the mountain.

"That was a fine speech, Colonel," the chimney said as the applause faded and the music resumed. "I think they liked your comment about the peacock."

Mitterhal returned to his post next to his charmed friend and assessed the celebration. Slender young women spun in circles to the haunting tones of the kilted pipers. Flags and banners flapped in synchrony to the mountain breeze. Flocks of cheering children liberated from their mothers' clutches assaulted the horse carts of pies and pastries. Even the plumed ponies hitched to the yellow wagon appeared to prance in their harnesses.

"I suppose it was," he finally said. "It is an old skill I forgot I had."

"Why did all these people march up the mountain to honor you?"

The twitch returned. "I honestly don't know, Chim," he said, looking back to the goats. "They seem to have me confused with someone else, a war hero of some sort, by the sounds of it."

"Another colonel?"

"Apparently."

"Shouldn't we inform them of the mistake?"

"No, Chim. They came to celebrate. No sense deflating their spirits now. They will figure out their blunder soon enough."

"I don't mean to be troublesome, Colonel, but it does not seem right for us to enjoy the celebration if it was really meant for someone else."

Mitterhal, wary of the chimney's point, directed his spyglass over the thatched roofs in Cotton Crown Village, then far down the mountain to the distant church steeple that sprouted out of Wulfhaven. Finally, he set his lens on the treeless peaks that loomed high over the shoreline across the harbor. "What difference does it make so long as the people are happy?" he whispered.

A wisp of wind spun the smoke into a fleeting halo around the rim of Mitterhal's goat-hyde hat. "I suppose you are right," the chimney said. "If I may ask one last question, what do you think the other colonel did that made these people so eager to celebrate?"

Mitterhal waved his hand to clear the smoke. "That is not a subject for the rooftop, Chim."

Time itself smoldered in the ash as the last charred seeds of amnesia crackled in the colonel's pipe.

"Angels? Why do you ask me, Captain? That is a question for Poulakis. So much of what goes on in this war is a guess to be sorted out later. If you ask me, the men are hearing their own voices. It is not uncommon in the heat of battle when the codes are chanted."

"Sir, the men are reporting the same harmonies when the pipes are played. If the voices are delusions, shouldn't the report be different for each man?"

"What are you trying to say, Marlin? That we are singing with angels? This is a war we fight, not a fairy tale. If we tell the men that the music is the work of the Father, what will happen to the morale of those who fight for the Mother, and vice versa?"

"With all due respect, sir, what will happen to the morale of all the men if we tell them they are delusional?"

The shadows had long stretched east over the celebration when the chimney sounded its second alert of the day. "Colonel, we appear to have a visitor."

Mitterhal opened his eyes and nearly swallowed his pipe. The young girl he had spotted giggling by the stone wall had managed to climb his ladder. Stunned, he watched her scamper across the roof peak and onto his platform. In her hand, somewhat mangled by the journey, was a pastry. She stopped in front of him, still as a garden statue, offering her gift with her eyes hidden behind a tangled veil of red locks. She could not have been more than nine years old.

A voice shot across the roof as a boy topped the ladder. "Enya! Get over here now. You have really done it this time, young lady."

13

The adolescent charged across the ridge to apprehend the girl. She grabbed the colonel's hand before the boy reached the platform and shoved the pastry into it. Then, sweeping the hair away from her eyes, she whispered something to the chimney.

"Forgive me, sir," the boy said, running across the platform and taking hold of the young girl's arm. "My name is Adman and this is my sister Enyalda. She was kicked by a horse last year and hasn't been the same since. Now she just whispers to things and nobody knows what she says. I will bring her down right away."

The boy, on the verge of manhood, stood tall and proud. Something about his manner taunted Mitterhal's memory. "Take your time, lad," he said. "There was no harm done. The horse's kick did not break her feisty spirit, but a fall off this roof will."

Adman nodded and proceeded to lead his sister across the roof ridge. The colonel remained still until he saw them safely on the ground amidst the wide-eyed crowd that had gathered in the backyard. Adman peered up to the platform and held a salute. "Thank you, sir. Thank you for everything." He clenched his right fist and pressed it to his chest. "Hail, Gahenya!"

The colonel made a motion to return the salute, but then looked down at his sticky hand as if it held some long-lost secret. After a pause he simply held up the pastry. "Enjoy your country and your land, young man. But most of all, enjoy your family." He took a bite from the treat and returned to his post by the chimney. It was time to rest.

4

The Rabbit's Peace

The Haven Guard had a term for a perfect kill. They called it a *talon strike*. Such a strike was clean and quick, a corporeal act in which the enemy was mercifully dispatched. The realities of combat did not always conform to this objective, yet Mitterhal insisted his men make every effort to achieve it when called to battle. Few in the Haven Guard strayed from this code. Those who did felt the heat of his command.

"That was a terrible moment for the rabbit," said the chimney.

Mitterhal watched the osprey sail away with its prize, his scope locked on the noble bird as it descended toward the harbor. How unusual, he thought, for the fish bird to venture this far from the shoreline for a taste of what the alpine pasture had to offer. Only moments before, the rabbit had dashed across the lower south field. The osprey swooped down and struck with deadly precision. The drama was over almost as soon as it began, the rabbit quickly dispatched in the talons of the hungry bird.

"Why do you say that, Chim? The moment could be worse for the lakehawk."

The chimney kept silent for some time. A steady breeze came up the valley, dispersing the smoke that rose out of its top. "Forgive me, Colonel, but I do not see how the lakehawk could be worse off than the rabbit in this case."

Mitterhal lowered his lens and left the osprey alone to dine on its lunch.

"The rabbit has been relieved of its struggles. The lakehawk must continue to fight for survival."

"But, Colonel, isn't it better to live and fight than not to live at all?"

"You would think so, Chim. But all life ends, just like any battle. It's how you conduct yourself that makes the real difference. The rabbit ran hard but was defeated, and for that will be rewarded with the peace that comes with knowing there is no longer a reason to run."

The old man nodded and cleaned out his pipe with his silver soot scraper. He was pleased with his insight and wanted a fresh smoke to celebrate the occasion. The chimney, on the other hand, did not seem as content with the answer.

"Colonel?"

"Yes, my friend?"

"Where does the rabbit go to enjoy this peace?"

"I don't know, Chim. That would be the answer to all answers. My guess is that it goes to wherever it was before it was born."

The chimney did not respond, which the colonel found unusual. These kinds of discussions typically made the chimney quite chatty. The silence became eerie, even for the colonel. At last he could no longer bear it and was forced to make a rare show of compassion.

"What is wrong, my friend? You seem troubled."

The chimney started to say something, but hesitated.

"Come on, Chim. Have out with it."

A black haze hovered over the rooftop. "I was not born, Colonel. I was built. How will I ever achieve the rabbit's peace?"

Mitterhal's brow twitched as he lit his pipe and scanned the horizon. The question rolled in his mind like the waves of white clouds over the lake. The incoming cold front compounded the pity he felt for his friend. How could the one companion he had in this world be so isolated from everything else? A deep sadness set in. Not just for the chimney, but for the rabbit as well. Had the feisty creature escaped its fate, his conscience might have been spared. But the lakehawk's talons had held fast, and to that his sorrow clung. In the twitch of awareness, he wiped away a single tear that rolled down his sun-scorched face.

"Are you all right, Colonel?"

The noonday sun beat down on the rooftop. Woozy, Mitterhal put one hand to the bricks, but to no avail. The grand mal seizure struck fast and drove him hard to the planks, leaving his thoughts with nowhere to go but back.

"Where to begin? So much to say, so much not to say. What is your assessment, Marcus? Are the men ready to sing?"

"They are ready, Cornelius. I see it in their eyes. Heart, body, mind, and soul. Their song will be heard, whatever their faith."

"Good. Then at dawn they will sing. Some to their Mother, some to their Father, it makes no difference. That is where they will find their peace. Thank you for your service, Marcus. Go back to the abbey now. You will be needed there."

"Colonel, the lakehawk has returned to the mountain."

Mitterhal awoke lying face down on his platform with a terrible headache. It was late afternoon; the blood on his forehead had long dried. Without saying a word he picked himself up and brushed the dust off his vest. He looked long at the chimney before stepping off the platform and shuffling along the roof pitch to his ladder. When he got to the eave, he grabbed the top rung and turned around before making his descent. A winged shadow whipped across the rooftop. High overhead the osprey hovered on a thermal.

"Chimney."

"Yes, Colonel?"

"You will have the rabbit's peace. I give you my word on that."

5
Whispers in the Leaves

A tree grew within a stone's throw of Mitterhal's house—a Torican beechwood. It was unlike any other tree on the mountain. Its leaves were deep crimson and its bark a weathered gray. Planted by the first Toriceans who migrated over the mountains from the south, the beechwood was old, very old. Its canopy consisted of an immense network of branches, some of which were the size of mature trees. The largest of these limbs extended toward the house, almost touching the colonel's rooftop.

An easy breeze blew across the pasture and rustled the leaves of the old beechwood. The lupine had just come into bloom, heralding another summer on the mountain. Cornelius Mitterhal drew deep on his pipe and then watched the smoke wisp away into the canopy of his towering neighbor. His thoughts meandered like the mountain goats that grazed on the tasty blue blossoms of the gahenya. Was it the second or third season, he wondered, since the valley folk had come to visit?

"Colonel, do you ever get the feeling you are being watched?" the chimney asked.

"Only by you," the colonel answered, snapping out of his daydream. "Why do you ask?"

The chimney lowered its voice to a whisper. "I think the tree with the red leaves is watching us."

Mitterhal looked to the beechwood. "Really? What makes you think that?" he whispered back.

"I've been hearing voices coming from it. Whispers in the leaves."

Balance teetered on edge; the colonel sighed in concern. Not for himself, but his friend. Whatever the cause, the chimney's senses had become compromised—a condition that could spiral out of control if left unchecked. The painful truth had to be addressed.

"Chimney, I am afraid I have bad news for you," he said with as much sensitivity as he could muster. "You appear to be suffering a delusion."

"Delusion? What is that?"

Mitterhal had never been one to sugarcoat an unpleasant report, though for the sake of his chimney he tried. "It is when your view of the land does not match the land in your view."

"I do not understand."

Agitated, the colonel yanked the pipe out of his mouth. "Well, for one thing, trees do not talk. They do not have the mouths to do so. Nor do they have the eyes to do any kind of watching. You are delusional, Chim. It is your own voice that you are hearing. The sooner you accept that, the better off you will be."

"But the whispers seem so real."

"Of course they do! If they didn't, they wouldn't be delusions, would they?"

Silence followed. Mitterhal regretted his harshness. In truth, he was deeply concerned for the well-being of his friend. He looked high to the ridge, wondering what could possibly be the cause of such disorder.

Snap!

Out of the blue, shots fired from behind. He jerks back to a field of lupine gone to seed. Smoke carpets the land—the reek of tar and death in the air. He shakes his head to shed the vision, but it sticks like soot on brick. Cannons blast from the village, spraying fire on his goat herd. No, not goats—men. Men on horses, men on foot, some down, some up; all of them chanting, even those who lie dying in the field. The peacock with the war medals strides out of the smoke. "There will be no white flag, sir!"

The last call of the goat-hyde pipes fuse together in a single tone …

"Colonel, did you hear that?"

In a blink the smoke was gone, and so were the men. The goats were grazing happily on the lupine once again. Mitterhal gulped a scoop of honey before speaking. "Hear what?"

"The voice. It whispered in the leaves again. What should we do?"

The old man wiped the sweat off his forehead with his shaking hand. "We shouldn't do anything, Chim. Just listen. It is all we can do at this point. My guess is that your own voice is trying to tell you something."

The sun began its fiery descent into the lake. The colonel's gaze grew

19

heavy, drifting over the molten sea.

"Colonel?"

"Yes, Chim."

"Where is my mouth?"

"Your what?"

"My mouth. The place where my voice comes from."

Strange question, Mitterhal thought, but fair. "I don't know," he said after a ponderous search of the structure.

"I was afraid you would say that. That makes me a delusion, just like the tree, doesn't it?"

The wind changed direction. Mitterhal buttoned his vest to keep it from flapping. The chimney's deduction was sound; he had to admit that. But then again, this was a talking chimney he was dealing with, one that had somehow managed to defy the most fundamental laws of logic. To trust its reasoning was a paradox in itself. The chimney's smoke, on the other hand, was real. There was no denying that. He watched the ethereal plumes wisp away over the goats grazing in his south pasture.

"No, Chimney, that is not the case at all. There is a difference between believing a delusion and being one. Your imagination has got the best of you, that is obvious, but your thoughts are real. I assure you that we would not be having this discussion if it were otherwise."

"But, Colonel, I do not have a mouth. How do you hear what I have to say?"

Stumped, Mitterhal rekindled his pipe and thought hard on the matter. To even suggest that the chimney had a mouth seemed ludicrous. What could he possibly say that would not come off as an out-and-out lie? The chimney was naive but not stupid. The sky over the lake had turned to rust by the time the answer came to him.

"Listen to me, Chim. Just because you can't see your mouth doesn't mean it isn't there. Look at me, I can't see mine either, but I know I've got one." The old man peered down the length of his nose, attempting to pin-point the location of his lips. With each attempt his white handlebar mustache flapped like a seagull's wings on his puckered face.

A barely audible giggle trickled out of the beechwood. Mitterhal shot a quick glance at the ancient tree, his mustache still flapping.

"How do you know for sure that you have a mouth if you cannot see it?" the chimney asked.

Mitterhal dragged deep on his pipe and blew a smoke ring that twisted over the rooftop. "I can see the smoke that comes out of it when I exhale," he said, watching the ring dissolve. "That is evidence enough."

"Evidence?"

"Naturally," the colonel said, becoming bolder by the minute. He put both hands behind his head and cleared his lungs with a fresh breath of mountain air. "Smoke has to come from somewhere, doesn't it? It can't just seep out of the top of my skull."

"I blow smoke as well," the chimney said.

Mitterhal slapped his leg. "Well, then, there you have it. Congratulations, Chim, you found your mouth. Now maybe we can get on with this sunset without so much worry nonsense."

Mitterhal leaned forward and launched a sortie of smoke rings off his platform. It was a relief to have skirted the issue. His gaze relaxed on the soft-colored haloes that hovered over the Haven. A good nap was imminent.

"Colonel?"

"Yes, Chim?"

"What does white flag mean?"

He yawned. A beautiful song tickled his ears from the leaves, like the piping of a distant flute, or the call of a dove. He was not sure. In either case, he was too tired to investigate. "It means give up," he said, already slipping into a peaceful slumber.

The eyes of the old warrior sank with the sun as he fell asleep to the enchanting whispers of the beechwood's lullaby.

6
The Fifth Flue

There was a well-kept secret among masons in the Fatherland that a nobleman's chimney served as more than just a smokestack. Less of a secret was the custom of a master mason attending the funeral of a nobleman so that he could become acquainted with the heir of the recently deceased. Most folk never questioned the formality, passing it off as the mere observance of a bygone tradition. Only the most savvy of lore masters were privy to the true purpose of the visit.

An unaccounted space existed in the masonry between the fireboxes in the center of Mitterhal's chimney. It was a flue of sort, designed for the passage of air, though unlike the other four flues, it did not blow smoke. Rather it continued downward through the core of the chimney, along a series of metal rungs, into a sizeable vault buried below the basement of the manor. The only access to the chamber was through a porthole hidden in the root cellar by the footing of the chimney. Mitterhal knew exactly where the portal was, though only once did he ever descend the metal rungs to confirm his suspicions.

The summer had peaked; the pastures swelled in growth. Blissful silence settled on the land. Mitterhal savored the peace, the simplicity, the lack of obligation. It all flowed together into an easy routine of self-reliance. Boredom was never an issue; the chimney saw to that. Every now and then, however, a subtle pang of loneliness crept into his perfect world and muddled his musings. Not in an obvious way, more like the vague sense that he was missing something. Usually he simply smoked the feeling away by adding a pinch of crushed gahenya seed to his pipe mix, and then cutting it down with a spoonful of honey. Though even that had its price.

"Colonel?"

"Yes, Chim?"

"I have been thinking about my mouth lately."

"Really. And what does your mouth have to say about that?"

"It ... I have counted five passages that lead up to it."

"Yes, that is quite normal for a chimney of your size. They are the flues for your fires. Nothing to worry about, my friend."

"I am not so much worried as curious. Why do I have so many?"

"This is a large house, Chimney. It takes more than one firebox to keep it warm."

"How many fireboxes do I have?"

Mitterhal paused to do the tally. There were the two downstairs in the hearth room, set perpendicular to each other in the main stack. The smaller of the two—the beehive oven—smoldered day and night, regardless of the season. The other he used in the dead of winter when he huddled in his leather chair, wrapped in blankets. Two more fireplaces shared the same stack on the second floor, directly above the hearth room. Those fires were never lit, for he rarely went upstairs. Occasionally in the summer, if the night was stuffy beyond bearing, he would dare a sojourn to the first bedroom at the top of the stairs where he might catch a breeze through the opened windows. But for the most part, he spent the majority of his nights downstairs in the leather chair.

"You have four fireboxes, my friend," he said after the count.

"Only four? But I have five flues."

"True, your fifth flue serves another purpose."

"What purpose is that?"

"I am sorry to say that I cannot tell you, Chim. I have sworn an oath of secrecy."

"A secret, how exciting. If I may ask, who told you the secret?"

"It was something I learned in the Fatherland."

"Where is that?"

"Far away to the south."

"Did you like your father's land?"

"At times," Mitterhal said with a smile. "Like any land, it had its good days and bad."

"What about your father? Did he have his good days?"

The smile disappeared at the sudden flash of swinging black boots. Quickly he scooped a spoonful of honey out of the mason jar and swallowed it, leery of the turn in conversation. "I don't know," he said guardedly.

"Why did you leave his land?"

"I did not leave it, Chimney. I returned to it." Mitterhal stood up and extended his arms to the distant harbor. "What you see before you is, or I should say, was his home. The Haven. Everything: the lake, the mountains, the city below, even the sky above. This was the place that he loved."

"I am confused, Colonel. How could this be your father's home if his land was so far away?"

Another twitch, more pronounced. The chimney's voice sounded muffled, like water in the ears. Mitterhal shook his head to shed the echo. No good. A smoke was in order. He packed his pipe with a pinch of the seed and set it to light.

"Are you all right, Colonel?"

"I am fine, Chim." He inhaled long and deep, holding in the smoke.

"You are making a lot of evidence," the chimney said after the colonel exhaled.

"What?"

"Your smoke."

"Oh, that. Well, such is the case now and then. What do you say we change the subject and enjoy this lovely day?"

"By all means, Colonel. Would it be too much to ask you to make those smoke rings again? I love watching them float over the harbor."

One by one, Mitterhal unleashed his rings. Like a chain of silver links they stretched beyond the roof. He watched them dissolve into the Haven, an ethereal cord unfolding. Back, back, back he went, chasing the circles further than ever before—before the war, before the wife, before the musket, and even before the trowel. To the very beginning, when the blue box played in his lap and his mother's soothing words were forever encased in its melody.

Cornelius, my love, listen to my song and worry not to why I sing it. Always know that I am with you. Never waver from that thought. I am your mother. Hear me in your dreams. Neither life nor death will sever that bond. On yellow wagon you and I, to the Haven we will ride.

"Colonel, I do not mean to ruin your nap, but I think you might want to see this."

Mitterhal opened his eyes to an excruciating headache. He removed the handkerchief from his vest pocket and wiped the streams of saliva off his face and shirt. Refolding the cloth, damp side in, he returned it to his pocket. A beast snorted below. He peered over the roof's edge. Of all things, a draught mule stood in the courtyard, harnessed to a hefty farm cart full of young people, all peering up toward the rooftop. Every one of their shadows listed to the east. Where had the morning gone? Next to the mule, a young lad on a horse held a salute, the same lad who had climbed the ladder to fetch his little sister during the celebration on the mountain. Adman, he recalled.

"Hail, Gahenya, sir."

Mitterhal, still groggy, saluted with his pipe, not quite ready to speak.

"With your permission," the lad continued, "we would like to tidy up your premises. Just a little maintenance: trim the hedges, cut the grass, weed the gardens. Those sort of things. We'll be done before you know it."

Mitterhal grimaced at the pain in his head. He reached for the mason jar in the crate. After slurping a spoonful of honey, he waited for the throbbing to subside.

"Colonel, I think they are waiting for you to answer," the chimney whispered.

"Let them wait, I did not invite them."

A young boy with fire-red hair stood up in the farm cart. "What's your answer, old man?" he shouted. "We don't have all day."

Adman charged the cart. "Shut up, Donny. I told you I would beat you silly if you acted up and I mean it."

"Go beat yourself, brother," the boy said. "I'm just gettin' things done."

The outburst inspired Mitterhal to rise from his bucket and make himself presentable. "Do what you will," he announced while buttoning the top two buttons on his vest and sizing up every face in the farm cart. "Take the hedge trimmings to the fire pit by the beehives. The cut grass goes in the outbuilding behind the manor. Make sure you latch the doors when you leave or the goats will get in."

"At once, sir," Adman said. "Oh, and one more thing, sir." He nodded to a pretty young woman in the cart, who immediately stood up and adjusted the busty folds above her snug-fitting corset. "This is Serena Schonhauser, the barmaid at Crown Tavern. We thought we'd send her in to change the linens and do a little housekeeping around the manor. Madam Hornpout, the tavern's keeper, also sent us up with a bushel of turnips to put in your root cellar."

"How wonderfully thoughtful," the chimney said.

Mitterhal spun around and glared at the bricks. "I don't recall asking for your opinion. Spare me the running commentary."

"I am sorry, Colonel. Times like these I can barely contain myself."

"Well, you better start!"

The command blared off the rooftop and jostled every sickle into action. The busty barmaid was already through the door by the time the Old Mitt knew what had happened.

The gang of villagers worked late into the afternoon—mostly boys but a few girls. Mitterhal monitored their progress from his platform, smoking his pipe and slurping his honey. Adman did more ordering than work. He was especially bossy to the mouthy red-haired boy named Donavon, apparently his brother. He and several other smaller lads were ordered to rake the cuttings into neat piles, which the older youths loaded into the mule cart. To the left side of the cart went the laurel clippings; to the right went the grass. The colonel, for his part, remained glued to his bucket, until a terrible shriek compelled him to rise.

Out from the fresh clipped shrubberies leaped a little girl in hot pursuit of a beefy lad with an armful of uprooted flower stalks. She caught up with him just prior to the cart and appeared to crawl up his back. She must have bit him too, for he fell to the ground and let out a shout that made the draught mule jerk in its harness.

"Oh, my," said the chimney. "What an unpleasant noise."

"Quiet," the colonel said, intrigued by the turn of events. His gaze froze on the girl's bright red locks. Where had she come from? Surely he would have noticed her when they arrived.

"Colonel, I think that might be the girl who gave you the pastry."

Adman was quick to step into the scuffle, which confirmed the chimney's suggestion. "Enya, what in the world are you doing?" He grabbed her shoulder and pulled her off the back of the writhing lad.

Free of the assault, the boy got up and pointed at her. "You're as crazy as they get!"

Donavon suddenly charged from behind the cart and rammed his shoulder into the gut of the beefy lad. Both went down, locked in arms. Several of the older boys stepped in to break up the grapple.

Finally subdued by Adman, Donavon seethed in the clutch of his older brother. "Don't you ever call her that again, Angus," he said to the other lad.

"I was just doing my job, Donny. Your brother told me to clear the beds. I didn't even know she was there. She just came out of nowhere and attacked me."

The girl broke down in tears and ran out of sight below the eave of the manor. But not before picking up every flower stalk that lay strewn on the ground.

By evening the work was complete. Mitterhal watched the draught mule amble past the pile of hedge clippings left at the smoke pit by the beehives. Spyglass out, he tallied the passengers in the cart as they rolled past the goats in his south field, back to the village. He accounted for all but the girl.

"The yard looks wonderful," the chimney said.

"It does indeed." The colonel lowered his scope and eyed the bricks suspiciously. "Tell me, Chimney. What did the little girl whisper to you that day when she climbed up the ladder with the pastry?"

"Forgive me, Colonel, but I cannot tell you. I have sworn an oath of secrecy. I hope you understand."

Mitterhal retracted his war scope and prepared to descend for the night. "I do, Chim. Good night, my good friend."

7
A Visit at Dawn

The Toriceans who pioneered the Haven were of a hardy stock and well received by the tribes native to the region. Independent in nature, they valued freedom over wealth and embraced the challenges of mountain life. As such, the first seeds of fellowship were sown with the Gwyntahmahoma, which gave rise to a society unlike any other in the lake province. For generations the two cultures prospered in peace, sharing customs and knowledge, until even their theologies began to merge.

The Gwyntah believed that the Great Mother embodied the land and by her grace they were granted the gift of life. The Toriceans believed the Father governed all life from his lofty post in the heavens. As time went on and generations fused in blood, some suggested that the Great Mother and Father could meet halfway on the heavenly peaks of a mythical mountain, from which they would join in harmony and sing their blessings upon creation. It was a timeless place between day and night, where the land and sky became one, and life and death were hallowed by voices and visions. Some called it the Highland Dome, the Great Mountain Montayega. And though its precise location was shrouded in fable, a select few held fast to the creed that the sacred height could be attained by those of pure heart, mind, body, and soul, who climbed the highest peaks on the Haven's coast and whispered to the wind.

The robin had yet to alert the mountain of a new day when Cornelius

Mitterhal approached his ladder, cautiously counting his steps in the dark. The subtle rhythms of dawn were long familiar to him. Though the passage of his days on the rooftop were somewhat blurred by routine, his senses were most acute in the darkest moments just prior to sunrise. He savored this time, much like a sunset only different. With dawn, like dusk, came peace, but at the expense of awareness. Awareness that had obscured the line of delusion and drew him up his ladder every day to the highest point on his rooftop.

This particular dawn was different. What was it? The crickets. Yes, that was it. There weren't any, at least none that he could hear. Mitterhal stood stiff at the base of his ladder, his right foot propped on the lowest rung, contemplating the unnatural silence. Near the trunk of the old beechwood he heard a click. Had the crickets been active, he might have passed it off as a falling twig. Yet something in the metallic tone compelled him to step off his ladder.

"Who is there?" he called in the direction of the beechwood.

A dark figure advanced. Something long and narrow protruded from the wraith-like shape. It stopped within a cannon's length of the old man. "Musketman Willis Hume of Tufthaven, reporting for duty," said the shadowy form.

The voice had the timbre of a lad who had seen combat and was no longer inhibited by the insecurity of youth.

Out of instinct, Mitterhal crossed his arms at the chest to assume command. "State your purpose, soldier."

"To kill a coward and a traitor to his men," came the quick reply, followed by another step forward.

Mitterhal squinted in the shifting darkness. *So this is how it ends*, he thought. In the tinted pre-dawn light, he knew he was looking down the barrel of a musket. "I see. And on whose order do you act?"

The shadow froze. "That is not your concern."

"Not my concern? Lad, you've got the working end of your musket so close to my face, I could smoke it. If you're going to kill me, then at least tell me my accuser. Every man's got a right to know that."

"He's got a valid point," the soldier said. "What difference does it make what he knows once he's dead?"

Mitterhal scanned the shadows in search of whomever the musketman was talking to.

"Of course I plan to do it," the soldier said in response to the silence. "I just think the execution should be clean and quick. He is the colonel after all, even if he is a coward."

Seeing and hearing no one else, Mitterhal reached for his pipe and flint box. The lad's judgment was clearly compromised. If today was to be his last day, then a smoke was certainly in order. His only concern, oddly enough, was for the chimney. The loneliness would be unbearable for it. He mulled over his good friend's woe while he waited for the musketman to settle on an answer.

"By order of Musket," the soldier declared, "you are hereby sentenced to death for the cowardice betrayal and slaughter of your regiment at Spaulding Pass. If you have a last word, speak it now."

Mitterhal ignited his flint box. In the flash, he saw the face. A young face, as expected by the voice, smooth-skinned and stern beneath a tattered war cap. The eyes, however, he did not expect. They were sharp and confident yet conflicted, betraying a hint of regret for what had to be done. The colonel thought back to the initial click. Had he heard one or two? The difference was significant. For better or worse, Mitterhal decided he had heard only one click.

"Listen, lad, standing there in the shadows with your lock half-cocked, telling me you take orders from a talking musket, is no way to conduct yourself. If you're going to kill me, then do it right. Set your hammer proper and be done with it."

Mitterhal listened as the soldier made a last appeal to the stock of his musket. "But he doesn't act like a coward. How do we really know it's true? ... Yes, I suppose you're right. A traitor is still a traitor."

Resolved, the soldier addressed the colonel. "By your command, sir, I will see to your order."

A hushed snap split the darkness. Mitterhal's legs went limp. He heard the wake-up song of a robin just as the ground came up to greet him.

"Captain! Have the first line on the east flank fall back to the third, musket ready."

"If I may suggest, sir, the ranks from Tufthaven have already sustained three rounds of cannon fire. They would stand a better chance at close range charging with bayonets."

"No, Marlin, we must lure the bear past the bails. The winds will shift once the sun hits the slopes. The rising thermals will draw the smoke into the hollow. That is the plan."

"To what end, sir, if there are so few left to engage them in the smoke?"

"We must do everything we can to insure the impact of the cavalry. McFadden's charge will deliver the sting. The loss of our good men on the lines is unavoidable."

"By your command, sir. I'll have the pipers on the east ridge sound the order."

Dawn had long passed by the time the colonel stirred. Rays of sunlight beamed over the mountain and churned up the mist in the valley below. Morning dew sparkled everywhere. Still groggy, Mitterhal unfolded his handkerchief and patted the dew off his face.

"Good morning, Colonel. Are you feeling better?"

Mitterhal jolted. "I'm on the rooftop," he said, more to himself than the chimney. Quickly, he peered around the bricks and over the eave, down to the trunk of the beechwood. The musketman was gone. He reached for the pipe in his pocket before realizing it was still in his mouth, spent of all its contents.

"Did you expect to be somewhere else?" the chimney asked.

"How did I get here?"

"You climbed up the ladder as always. You were not in a good mood, though. I am glad you are feeling better."

Mitterhal kept his eye fixed on the burly trunk below. "Listen to me, Chim, I have something very important to say. Something you may not want to hear but you must. A day may come when I no longer climb up this ladder."

"What do you mean?"

"What I mean is that there is a limit to my time in this world. I am not made of the same stuff you are."

"Like the rabbit?"

"Yes," said the colonel, "just like the rabbit."

A light breeze picked up, drawing the colonel's attention down the valley where the morning thermals simmered in the mist. A low-lying cloud hovered over the lake like the aftermath of a great battle. He thought to ask the chimney what it had witnessed at first light, but then thought better of it. The question would only spur more questions. The musketman's visit was best kept a secret—at least for now.

"Colonel?"

"Yes, Chim?"

"When you find the rabbit's peace, who will I talk to? You are the only one who hears what I have to say."

The colonel swallowed down his honey while he struggled over the question. The breeze continued to comb the pastures. The answer came on the waves that rippled over the gahenya.

"The wind," he whispered. "You must learn how to speak with the wind. Then you will never be alone."

"What should I say to the wind?"

"Whatever you want so long as it's true. If you say it enough, the wind will learn your language and speak back." He dipped the end of his pipe into his smoke pouch. "Then you can have all kinds of fascinating conversations. More than you'd want most likely."

"Colonel, I think that even with the wind as my friend, I will still miss you."

Mitterhal wiggled on his honey bucket, pondering how to address the chimney's mushy sentiment. His friend needed hope more than anything else. Even a sappy smokestack deserved that.

"I'll tell you what, Chim, why don't we make a deal?"

"A deal? What is that?"

"It's an arrangement. A promise between two people ... eh, parties."

"What promise is that?"

"I propose that whichever one of us finds the rabbit's peace first shall do everything in his power to remember the way back so that the other may follow. How does that sound?"

"That sounds wonderful. Except, how will the one who finds the rabbit tell the other where to go?"

"Well, that's easy. We'll send a message."

"But how will the message be delivered?"

"By a messenger, how else?"

"But who will—"

"Chimney, have you not heard a single word I've said? You are thinking with your bricks! Use your ... eh ... hmm ... whatever else it is you might think with. The answer is obvious."

A current swirled across the rooftop and carried the smoke away to the grazing goats.

"The wind?" the chimney whispered.

"There you have it. Now you're thinking. We will use the wind as our messenger. So what do you say? Do we have a deal?"

"Yes, Colonel, we have a deal."

With their arrangement in order, the colonel fired up his pipe and returned to his surveillance of the Haven. The morning mist had lifted and the sky over the lake promised a clear, easy day. The soldier's visit at dawn already seemed like a distant dream. Inhaling long and deep, Mitterhal leaned his back against the solid bricks and assigned his worries of the morning to another day.

8

The Yellow-Winged Wagon

Pastor Marcus Poulakis was a no-nonsense reverend, a man who commanded respect. In everyday practice, though, his hard edge was tempered by the genuine love he held for all things great and small. He had come to the Haven as an infant and was taken in by the monks at Wulfhaven abbey. Headstrong from the start, his tireless attention to practical matters inevitably earned him a place among the top decision makers in the Three Havens. His service during the war ministering the Haven Guard only further cemented his legacy in the province. Yet for all his political clout, he insisted on retaining the title of pastor.

The day began as any other. Cornelius Mitterhal climbed his ladder without thought or care to the world's events, looking forward only to a good smoke and another day on the roof with his friend. A year had passed since the visit of Willis Hume. He looked to the beechwood on his way up. The deep red leaves had already begun to rust. How strange for them to change so early, he thought. But it had been a dry summer, the kind of season that saps the life out of the land.

At the eave, the chimney hailed him from the peak. "Hurry, Colonel. Come see. It is snowing color on your pasture."

The old man scurried up the backside of the roof, intrigued by the chimney's enthusiasm. What could possibly have stirred such excitement in the stack of bricks? Getting to the top, he peered over the roof ridge. Indeed, millions of "snowflakes" floated up and down over the pasture on bright yellow wings of light. He stared into the glittering field, twisting the tips of his handlebar mustache. From the ladder hook he carefully maneuvered across the ridge and onto his platform.

"Those are not snowflakes, my friend." He lit his pipe and drew in a breath. "Look closely. You will see that the flakes never touch the ground. They are living creatures. Butterflies, they are called by my kind."

"They never stop moving."

"Yes, they are happy little buggers, aren't they? This is a rare show, indeed. Only a handful of times have I seen the Vahegan Butterfly appear in such numbers. They're quite a mystery really. They love the gahenya, but only when the meadows are parched. You will not find them like this when the land is lush. Enjoy the show while you can. The yellow-winged wagon will not stay long."

"What makes the butterflies so happy?"

Mitterhal assumed his post on the bucket. The question seemed innocent enough, though with the chimney he was never quite sure. "I don't know, Chim, I am not a bug. But if I were to guess I would say it is because they have good reason to get up. They have spent the entire summer wrapped in the gahenya like cigars on a stalk."

"I wish they would stay forever."

"Why is that?"

"They make me feel light, like I could float off the rooftop."

Mitterhal's pipe jiggled as he imagined the chimney's bricks sprouting wings and fluttering off into the pasture amidst a flurry of butterflies. "I do not think that will happen in this world, my friend. Besides, if you did that, then with whom would I talk? My honey bucket?" He glanced down between his legs and chuckled. "I don't expect the conversation would be nearly as interesting."

The chimney remained silent while the colonel enjoyed the alpine show, seated on his rusty tin bucket. Even the mountain goats that grazed on the scorched meadow grass along the dried-up rills appeared more playful than usual. He watched them leap into the air after the butterflies, dancing in the symphony of quiet sound that surrounded them.

"Colonel?"

"Yes, Chim?"

"Could it happen in another world?"

"Could what happen?"

"Could I float with the yellow-winged wagon forever?"

Mitterhal added a pinch of the crushed bean to his pipe to aid his consideration of the question. "I suppose it is possible," he said, squinting. "But I would be careful about what you wish for."

"Why is that?"

He spun around and cast a hard look at the bricks. "Do you think you would be as happy watching the butterflies if you did not know what the pasture was like without them? Too much of a good thing can be a bad thing. They will be gone before you know it. Thank them for that." With conviction he went back to watching the pasture. Doing so, he spotted a black speck moving upward through the glittering field of amber. His right eyebrow twitched. Something was wrong. Quickly, his shaking hand went to his spyglass.

"Colonel, why do we not have many visitors?"

The scope stopped on the speck. "There was a time before our first sunset together that I had many visitors," he said while adjusting the lens. "More than I cared for really. It affected my peace. They all wanted to talk. I just wanted to enjoy the view."

"What made them stop coming?"

"I drew the line when the pastor came to visit. He took it upon himself to give me a lesson on the hereafter."

"What did you tell him?"

The mix in his pipe glowed red. Hot smoke fogged the lens. "I told him I would give him a lesson of my own if he didn't take his nonsense somewhere else."

"I see. If I may ask, what did the pastor wear?"

"A robe, Chimney. Why on earth would you want to know that?"

"What color was the robe?"

"What has that got to do with anything? This is getting irritating."

"Was it black, Colonel?"

"Yes, it was black. Black as the soot on your bricks. What has got into you?"

The chimney's report arrived like an arrow, straight and to the point; the only way the colonel would have it. "Forgive me for irritating you, Colonel, but there appears to be a man in a black robe walking through the butterflies."

Mitterhal lowered his war scope and dropped to his knees, doing his best to retain his balance on the platform.

"Say your peace, Marcus, but be quick. We are on the move."

"You are making my job impossible, Cornelius! You ask me to prepare your men for the afterlife, yet you insist on perpetuating this myth of a Highland Dome."

"Afterlife? Is that why you think you are here, Pastor? Many of these lads are marching to their deaths and they know that. What they will soon discover is their business. You are here to feed their faith while they live, to assure them that their sacrifice will not be in vain. That is the task I've asked of you."

"And how exactly am I to do this when all they talk about are talons and rabbits and mountain goats the size of oxen that graze on endless fields of gahenya? I cannot lead the men in prayer if their hearts will not listen."

"This is war, Marcus! The men need a vision. Something to rally on with sights and sounds that are relevant to the land they defend. Floating with angels in some faroff place in the sky does not inspire the fighting spirit. If your prayer cannot accommodate for that, then for the sake of the Haven I suggest you have a chat with your all-mighty Father and figure out a way to make an exception!"

Pastor Marcus Poulakis ambled over the colonel's stone wall with surprising agility for an old man. He strode into the courtyard with his holy staff in hand, sweat streaming down his bald forehead to his enormous, bushy eyebrows. What he lacked for hair on the top of his head he made up for on his cheeks and chin. A gray beard extended out and downward, nearly doubling the length of his face. Not until he was exactly in line with the colonel in the center of the courtyard, did he look up.

"How are you, my good friend?" he called. "I had a meeting in the village and saw your fields full of new life. It inspired me to take a walk long overdue."

Mitterhal opened his leaf pouch. He tapped the end of his pipe on the chimney's bricks several times to clean out the ash before dipping it into the leather sack. Long he looked into the bowl while he pressed the leaf within it. His motions were unhurried and precise, refined by years of repetition. "You mean old life in a new form, don't you, Pastor? What makes you think you are any more welcome now than you were before?"

Marcus stooped and picked up a handful of dirt. The waterless grains slipped through his fingers into a cloud of dust. "You have always been one to get to the point. I will spare you the sermon if that is your wish. My reason for this visit is entirely practical."

A cluster of wings fluttered by the eave. Mitterhal blinked at the yellow tracers, and then returned his bloodshot gaze to the courtyard. Warily, he crossed his arms at the chest, squinting at the pastor's glistening bald spot. He knew that veiled in the shade of that shining temple were a set of eyes as sharp as talons. Eyes that when put to it, could tear into the fabric of a wayward soul with striking efficiency, yet in the next glance deliver peace and comfort to those who had suffered their darkest hour. He also knew that the holy man's attention to practical matters would most likely be sound, and worthy of a listen.

"State your purpose, Pastor. But keep your preaching out of it."

"As you wish. We are in a drought, Cornelius. The land is parched as you can see. Crops have failed on a wide scale throughout the province. We cannot depend on shipments from the south. There will be famine in the Haven this winter if steps are not taken now. I have called on all highland villages to stock their gahenya. Your pastures are rich in lupine. I ask that you grant permission to the villagers to harvest your fields."

A long moment passed while Mitterhal pressed more leaf into his pipe. "The seed of the wulfweed can do more harm than good. You should know that, Pastor."

Marcus tossed the remainder of dirt out of his hand and looked at the goats that had congregated along the fieldstone wall. He spoke with the authority of a father who must do what is best for his children, even at the expense of his own principles. "I am aware of that, Colonel. There are methods for extracting the poisons."

"Those are pagan methods," Mitterhal said. "I would not expect a man of the cloth to approve of such practices."

"These are desperate times, Cornelius," the pastor said, his rising voice slicing the air. "Lives are at stake. It is the will of our Great Father. If we are to—"

"I thought you were going to leave your deity out of it."

Marcus's face flushed red, more than the hot sun warranted. "I agreed to no such foolishness. I said I would spare you the sermon. There is a difference. This is life and death. You have a responsibility, Colonel."

"Responsibility! Is that what you have come to preach?"

A voice interjected from behind. "Colonel, may I make a suggestion?"

Mitterhal turned his back on the pastor and glared at the chimney. "Quiet."

"I will not be quiet," Marcus said from below. "Not on this matter."

"Colonel, I think I have a solution to the problem."

"I said quiet! Go back to blowing smoke."

A curious lapse followed in which the pastor puzzled over the comment. "I am afraid it is not me that is blowing smoke, Colonel." The venerable clergyman took a deep breath and began again. "If you want your damned isolation, you can have it. All I ask is that you face me and tell me that you are willing to let good people suffer in a land that you fought to save. If you can do that, then you will surely be rid of me."

"Colonel?" said the chimney. "I do not mean to nag but—"

"But what?" Mitterhal said, seething at the bricks. "What do you want from me?"

"It is not what I want. It is what our Great Father wants."

The pastor's words echoed over the field, raising the horns of the goats. Mitterhal froze. The three-way conversation had become impossible to manage. Stubbornly silent, he sat on his bucket like a land mine in a placid field ready to blow.

Not a word was exchanged for the remainder of the morning. Marcus knelt in the dust to pray while the goats stood behind the wall, cast in eerie poses. Even the wind seemed to mind its manners, quiet and still, only the hushed swish of a butterfly's wings.

The chimney's shadow had long shifted to the east when Mitterhal blinked out of his trance. "You are fortunate, Pastor. I happen to have a friend who is much more understanding than I care to be. You can tell the villagers they may take the lupine so long as two conditions are met. The first, that one third of the harvest be sent across the Haven as compensation to the tribes for the use of their knowledge. And second, that not a single seed be taken until the last of the Vahegan leaves the pasture."

Marcus lifted himself up by his staff and wiped the dirt off his knees. He made a sign of blessing, directed toward the sky. Calm and composed, he appeared more a diplomat than a clergyman.

"Bless you, Colonel. Your gift will be well received. Though I have concerns regarding your first term. The tribes are leery of visitors these days. Delivering the harvest to the Gwyntahmahoma will pose a challenge."

"You will find a way, Pastor. Lives are at stake. I believe those were your own words. Even your Great Father would agree to that. Now go. And take your blessings with you. All this jibber-jabber is upsetting the goats."

The pastor wiped the sweat that rolled down his cheeks. Or were they tears?

"As you wish," he said solemnly. "Farewell, my good friend."

Mitterhal strode back to his post and sat on his bucket, intent on silence. He spent the remainder of the afternoon watching the pastor shrink back into a black speck in the south pasture.

"Colonel?"

"What is it, Chim?"

"I think you made the right choice."

"Be quiet. I just want to watch the butterflies."

9
Butting Heads

A herd of mountain goats had migrated to the Old Mitt's pastures in the first spring following the war. This was not unusual, at least not initially. The wild breed was known for its love of the gahenya blossom. What was unusual was that the herd lingered long into the autumn rut, even after the mountain flower had gone to seed and became unpalatable. The curious exodus became a hot topic in the gossip circles throughout the Three Havens. The locals in Cotton Crown Village insisted it was Old Mitt's wild mountain honey that had lured the beasts away from their highland haunts.

It was autumn, crisp and clear, the kind of day that plays tricks on the senses. The sky was laced in sterling silver and the mountains swathed in color that splashed off the lake. Mitterhal manned his post with his spyglass fixed on the wild goats that bounded about the steep knolls to the north. Hard to imagine that only a year ago the pastures had been scorched by drought.

"Chimney, wake up. You are missing a spectacular show."

An easy gust of wind sailed over the grassy slopes in the south pasture and funneled into the chimney's flue, creating the closest semblance of a yawn for the wistful structure. "What is it you wish of me, Colonel?"

"Look. Look to the north."

Crack!

Horn on horn, the collision echoed downslope like a cannon shot. It happened every year at this time—the ramming of the goats. The males seemed extra vigorous this year; a sharp contrast to last season's pitiful performance following the drought.

"Did you hear that, Chim? A shot like that would bring a bear to its knees. What say you?" Mitterhal fidgeted with the rim of his scope while he waited for the chimney to respond, a response gratingly slow in the making. "Chimney. I said, what say you to the boom?"

"Not much, Colonel. I am afraid my attention was on the rabbits in the south pasture."

"Rabbits? How can you watch rabbits at a time like this?"

"I like them. They are peaceful."

"Yes, yes, of course, but you can watch the little furballs anytime. The goats go into rut only once a year."

"My apologies, Colonel. But if it is all the same to you, I would prefer to keep watch on the south pasture."

"You are a puzzle, Chim." He glanced southward and spotted a crippled yearling grazing alone in the field grass amidst the rabbit burrows. A raven had perched atop a weathered white boulder not far from the goat. "Hmm, how curious," the colonel said. "Little Three Legs is staying clear of the herd."

Crack!

Mitterhal swung his spyglass back to the north.

Old Smoker—a sure-footed veteran of the slopes—waited for the next challenger to arrive. Out of the ranks came a stout buck. The colonel leaned forward on the edge of his bucket. He had been looking forward to this matchup all year, wondering how the herd leader's clever techniques would fare against such a powerful young specimen.

Even the chimney expressed an interest. "Colonel, why do the goats butt heads?"

"Be quiet! Do not distract them."

Crack! The battle unfolded. Old Smoker held fast to the high ground, though he appeared to favor his left flank. Another hard hit brought a stunned pause to the melee. The colonel spared a moment to address the chimney's question. "It is the season of love for the goats, Chim. They are battling for mates."

"Colonel, if I may? It seems there should be a more sensible way for the goats to put the purpose in their puff. Are you sure you did not mean the season of love's opposite?"

Mitterhal sneered at the bricks, astounded that his friend would downplay such a long-standing tradition. "And what would you know of such things?"

"I do not mean to be contrary, Colonel, but the love that you sing about in your song does not match the behavior of these goats."

The colonel sprang from his bucket, sensing his authority challenged. Smoke fumed out of his pipe. "You are a structure made of brick and mortar, Chimney. Know your place."

Dead silence followed, and with that came regret. Mitterhal had crossed a line and he knew it. An obscure line perhaps, but one that bordered on betrayal. His regret spread like a rash on his conscience, making it impossible to concentrate on the excitement upslope. What a fool. Guilt festered and took him to a place he dreaded to go. How was it, he wondered, that he could spend a lifetime fostering confidence in the hearts of the living, only to sink to the point of degrading a true friend whose devotion had never once wavered on the rooftop?

Crack! A flash of memory escaped his lightless vault.

"Spar hard with the men, Uryan. Challenge them to love what they are fighting for. That is your task. If they train with purpose, they will fight with purpose. The bear will not expect a charge of this nature."

"How is it, sir, that you know so much about the bear? The way they think, their maneuvers, their tactics, their routines, everything. Almost as if—"

"As if what, Lieutenant? As if I were one of them? Is that what you mean to ask?"

"Your pardon, sir. I am out of line."

"Not really. Your insight serves you well. But that is talk for peacetime. We have important work ahead of us. Our strength is in the herd, Lieutenant."

"Absolutely, sir. And the herd will be ready."

Mitterhal awoke with a terrible headache. Old Smoker was still at it on the slopes. Another challenger had arrived.

"Forgive me, Colonel. I should not pass judgment on the living if I am not of the living myself."

"You are not the one that needs to be forgiven, Chimney. I was caught up in the excitement of the moment. Do not belittle your opinion on my account. It carries more weight than you know. Maybe it is time for you to give me a lesson. Tell me, my good friend, where does your heart go on this matter with the goats?"

"If I were of the living, and had such a heart, I believe it would go to the rabbits that give company to the crippled yearling in your south pasture."

Mitterhal aimed his scope to the south just as the young three-legged billy made an awkward bound toward a rabbit. The raven circled low over the chase, sweeping the field with its shadow. The old man watched, heedless of the ramming goats to the north. He could not help admiring the little creature's tenacity in spite of its ill-fated condition. With his heart so disarmed, he locked his spyglass on the yearling's clumsy pursuit of the rabbits.

"Did you ever have a mate, Colonel?"

41

Back and forth the war scope swayed. "Yes, I believe I did once," he said, hypnotized by the chase. "A long time ago, far away to the south … in a place I thought was my home." His focus switched to the raven's shadow that swept the grasses.

"Did she put the purpose in your puff?"

Around and around the shadow went. Big circles, little circles, sometimes high, sometimes low. "I don't know, Chim. She was a princess of some sort. Yes, that's right, I see her now. Raised in royalty. I was young, strong, eager to impress. Our union offered promise."

Crack! A skull-crushing collision on the north slope broke the spell. The colonel spun around and set his scope on the last of the challengers that staggered down the knoll, its head bowed in defeat. Old Smoker stood alone, holding the high ground, exhausted in victory, even as he eyed his harem below.

"Colonel, did you have to butt heads to attain your mate?"

Mitterhal smiled at the chimney's childlike question. How merciful that his naive friend was spared the challenges of the living. "No, Chim, I did not have to butt heads to get her. I butted heads when I got her."

No more was said on the subject. In fact, no more was said at all. The colonel simply fired up a smoke and waited for the day to pass. When twilight came, he watched Old Smoker wander into the cedars with his hard–won harem. The rut winding down, winter was soon to follow.

10
The Pilgrim's War Hymn

The Guard had a saying: "Even a bear will dance if you teach it to sing." Music was a staple for a soldier, or so the colonel said. Like rations or clothing or ammunition, it was essential to a troop's success. To wage war without it was akin to charging naked into battle. The colonel had another saying along the same vein that spoke less to the heart and more to the soul: "When all else fails, sing." Mitterhal rarely used it. But when he did, it was heard by all, friend and foe alike.

It was in the middle of the night, the main hearth room, the only warm room in the manor. Cornelius Mitterhal awoke to a jarring knock at the front entry. A wintry gale had sprung loose the latch on the wooden storm door and battered it against the exterior clapboards. At first he ignored the knock, thinking the wind would eventually slam the door back into position. Wide-awake, he stewed in his leather chair, draped in a wool blanket. At length he got up to rekindle the coals in the dying fire. The leather in the chair squeaked at the shift of inertia.

Up at last, he decided to secure the storm door. A soft glow radiated from the hearth room as he crossed the adjoining parlor. His candle illuminated the hard lines of frost on the windows. In the parlor he placed the candlestick atop the newel post at the foot of the staircase and waited for the knocking to stop. A thin sheen of ice had congealed on the dead bolt of the main door. The wind quieted and Mitterhal slid the bolt back, pressing down on the latch to open the door.

Swish! The door blew open and thrust him back to the newel post. He landed with a thud on the third step, next to the snuffed-out candle. What followed had the air of a dream, though the icy gale that howled through the entry could have woken the dead.

A man-sized creature covered in snow and fur charged over the threshold with musket drawn. A bayonet was mounted at the end of the gun, the tip of which came to within a hair of Mitterhal's nose.

"Good evening, sir. May we come in?"

The creature's voice was human and somewhat familiar.

"What do you want?" Mitterhal asked.

"I want to come inside. It is cold."

"You are inside," the colonel shouted, his adrenaline rising. "In case you haven't noticed, you've got your damn stinger buried in my moustache."

The eyes blinked in seeming surprise. Quickly he retracted the weapon. "Sorry about that, sir. Musket gets carried away sometimes."

Mitterhal stood up and swept the snow off his vest. He squinted at the camouflaged face. It was the lad with the talking musket—Willis Hume of Tufthaven.

"Very well, soldier. Close the door behind you and get yourself to the fire."

At the hearth Mitterhal stabbed at the coals with his iron poker and set another log on the fire. The young musketman stood next to a crate full of tinder, watching the sparks scurry up the damper. Streams of melted snow trickled off his bulky overcoat into an ever-widening puddle on the floor. The thaw exposed a hefty collection of rabbit pelts that dangled from his combat pack. Mitterhal returned to his chair and fired up a smoke. The pungent scent of the wulfweed wafted around the hearth.

Willis propped his musket and powder horn against the hearth wall and loosened the harness on his pack. The pack collapsed to the floor into a musty heap of buckles, straps, and fur. Relieved of his burden, Willis kicked the crate closer to the fire, set a half-split log over the top of the box, and sat on it. He leaned forward, extending his hands toward the heat.

"You smoke the gahenya," he said, sniffing the air. "Back at base camp I stoke the cooking fires with it. The whole plant, roots, stems, leaves, and all. I've never known anyone crazy enough to put it in a pipe, though. Not even my brothers would do that."

Mitterhal launched several smoke rings that rose to the ceiling and spread across the plaster. "It's not the leaf that gets you, lad. It's the bean you got to watch out for."

Willis removed his overcoat and continued to bask in the heat. "My brothers like the smoke. It gets them chanting the codes. Sometimes my father will accompany us from atop the east ridge. We love it when he plays his pipes."

Mitterhal withdrew his gaze from the ceiling. The soldier, having shed his gear, appeared much more lad-like. Youthful stubble mottled a lean face that, despite its scabrous veneer, retained a hint of innocence. Pinned to the center of his cap, just above the visor, sparkled a silver crest—three crossed stalks of the mountain flower.

"Where is this camp you speak of?" he asked.

"It is a four-day march from here, to the south, in a pasture that overlooks Spaulding Pass. My brothers say the pass is the only way the bear can reach the Haven now that its fleet is gone. My father mans his post on the ridge to warn us of their return. In the meantime we sing war hymns to pass the time."

The lad's story in combination with the wulfweed had a feverish effect. Mitterhal's thoughts rolled back to the year when the yellow wagon had led the parade up the mountain. It was sovereignty and peace the people had celebrated; he was certain of that. If so, why then would the soldier and his brothers still be mobilized for battle? The story didn't add up. Conflicting facts tugged at the colonel's censored memory.

"Are you all right, sir? You don't look well."

"Your brothers ... Why are they still there?"

"They await your word. That is why I am here. They will not leave their posts until you give the order."

Dizziness. Clammy sweat.

"I don't know what you are talking about," Mitterhal said, reaching for his handkerchief. "You must have me confused with someone else."

"You don't remember, sir? How could you not? My brothers trusted you. A soul will never get lost if it leaves the world in song. Those were your last words to us. You've got to remember that at least, don't you?"

"I remember no such nonsense. You are making a sad mistake."

"But it was you who told us to sing. You showed us the way to the Highland Dome."

"Nonsense!" The colonel wiped the saliva off his face. "You are delusional."

Willis twitched and looked to his musket against the wall. He blinked rapidly. Suddenly, his eyes appeared cold and black, lifeless and penetrating. "Musket doesn't believe you. It knows you are lying, that you really do remember everything and are refusing to face the charge of your treachery."

In one smooth motion Willis snatched his gun and pointed the bayonet at the colonel's midsection. "Musket will count to three, sir. If by the third count you still don't remember, then you will die a traitor's death. One ..."

Mitterhal knew the wound would not be fatal—initially that is. An impalement to the gut would render him immobile yet conscious, followed by a slow, draining journey to death, during which he would have all kinds of time to contemplate his crime. He looked to the rabbit skins that shrouded the combat pack on the floor. What if the lad were right? What if he were, indeed, a traitor? He made a genuine effort to remember something, anything, about the war, but all he could focus on were the rabbits and the deal he had made with his chimney. It was not death he feared so much as the failure to honor a promise. Whatever the afterlife had in store, it could not be much for a turncoat, and certainly not the place to invite a friend. The chimney would be forever damned to a state of purgatory on the rooftop, never to know the rabbit's peace.

"Two ..."

The heat riffled his tattered memory. Sweat beaded on his face. Still nothing. It was like scanning the fog with a cracked scope. If only he had more time to think. Even a lie could be justified for the sake of his chimney, but that was a skill he had never mastered.

"Three."

"Wait!" he said.

The musketman appeared relieved. "You remember now?"

"No, lad, but I have something for you to remember." Mitterhal rose from his chair, knowing he would never rise again under his own power. "You can ream a rag up that musket of yours. It should never hurt to be a chimney!"

The boy's eyes flared in the fire, followed by utter blackness.

"Sir, my apologies for the interruption, but there is a personnel matter within the ranks that I would bring to your attention."

"What is it, Captain?"

"One of our herald bearers from Tufthaven insists on fighting on the first line with his brothers. He refuses any other order."

"Why do you bring this to me now? This is war, Marlin. You know the consequence of insubordination."

"He's just a boy, sir, and—"

"And what, Captain?"

"Well, sir, it's a bit complicated. He's the youngest son of Johan Hume, my best piper. Johan stands by his son's decision."

"Johan Hume ... His company has been deployed to the east ridge, has it not?"

"It has."

"Does the lad know the codes? Can he sing under fire?"

"He is green, but as the son of Hume, I would expect so."

"Go to my tent, Captain. Give him my musket and tell him to join his brothers."

"Sir, you've had that gun as long as I've known you."

"And have I used it? Are there any other issues?"

"No, sir."

"Then do as I say and have the pipers ready. I want the mountains to sing when the wulfweed burns."

Mitterhal awoke to the soldier's war hymn. The musket was back against the wall next to the powder horn. Willis held the dismantled bayonet in his left hand and a honing stone in his right. The young soldier seemed lost in a trance as he stared into the fire and sharpened the blade.

There's a rabbit in the Pass
Yes there is, yes there is
Bleeding in the grass
Yes it is, yes it is

The colonel shifted in his chair, promptly ending the soldier's lament.

"Sorry to rattle you, sir," he said, placing the bayonet next to the musket. "I had to absolve you of the crime. The only way to do it was to convince Musket that you really are crazy." Willis held the honing stone close to his mouth as if to whisper a secret. "I think we may have succeeded."

Mitterhal closed his eyes to ease the throbbing in his head.

"What does it feel like, Colonel?" Willis asked.

"What does what feel like?"

"Facing a traitor's death."

"In all honesty, I found it unnerving. It drew attention to unfinished business I have with a friend."

"Tell me more about your friend."

Mitterhal shot a look at the musket against the bricks. "Why don't we start with yours?"

"Mine?"

"Your talking gun."

"You mean Musket?"

"Yes. You seem to put a lot of stock in what it says."

"I suppose I do. I owe my life to Musket. It's a funny thing really, owing life to something that is meant to take it. The first time was on the firing line with my brothers. I could barely see a thing. Everything was so black. I could still hear the pipes on the ridge though, even in the smoke, like they were right there next to me. I sang to them just like Father taught me. Then the tune changed. I heard hooves and song from all sides. The cannons stopped. After that it all got quiet, like a dream with no sound. I had no idea where I was. That's when Musket spoke. 'Get up,' it said. 'Get up and climb.' I didn't know what else to do, so I obeyed. I climbed upward through the blackness until I could climb no more. After that I don't remember much, only that when the darkness cleared I was on a sunny ridge somewhere far in the mountains, surrounded by goats. The big ones that you told us about." A sorrowful look came over Willis. "I don't like killing mountain goats, sir. They're not at all like the ones on the Schnite's farm. They are wise to our ways. But I had to. Musket told me to do it. I was so hungry. I haven't shot one since. I stick to rabbits now."

A red-hot ember snapped out of the fire and landed on the fur-laden combat pack. Out of habit, Mitterhal reached for his smoke pouch. The soldier's song came to mind as he watched the spark slowly suffocate on the dampened pelt.

"I see," he said, giving the pouch a second thought. "And that's why you sing about bleeding rabbits I presume."

"Oh, that. It's just a song I've been working on, a war hymn for my brothers. When I made it back to the pass, everyone had left except them. They waited for me, knowing I would return. They love to sing. I wish I could sing like them. They really like my song but they say it needs more work."

Mitterhal put both hands in his lap. "From what I've heard so far, I would have to agree. A war hymn needs to inspire the fighting spirit. A bleeding rabbit is a pitiful sight. You need to pick it up."

"But the verses need to be true. You told us that yourself. Otherwise it's just a waste of breath."

"I don't recall ever saying such a thing, but you are right, a good war hymn should speak true to a soldier's soul. That being said, there's nothing wrong with giving the rabbit a little boost. It needs a reason to get up. Something to rouse it out of its sorry state."

"There is a wolf in my song."

The colonel's brows went up. "Ah yes, a wolf, that will certainly inspire the rabbit to move. Let's hear it, sing me the verse."

Willis looked to the floor, appearing embarrassed. "I'm sorry, sir, I can't do that."

"Why not? You sang about the rabbit without problem."

"But I didn't know you were listening."

"What difference does that make?"

The lad's gaze rose sheepishly from the floor. "I can't sing to an audience unless there is a gun pointed at me."

"Well, I've never heard of such nonsense. How can you expect to be a hymn smith with that kind of thinking?"

"I can't help it, sir. It used to be no problem for me, but everything changed after Spaulding Pass."

Willis reached for the musket. With uncanny efficiency he removed the ramrod from the sleeve at the base of the barrel and reamed a slug down the muzzle, then slid the rod back in its place and filled the firing chamber with a quick tilt of the powder horn. Setting the lock to its half-cocked position, he handed the gun, stock first, to the colonel. It all happened within seconds.

"Take it, sir, I really want you to hear my song."

"Well this is just—"

"Please, sir. It's the only way."

"Very well." Reluctantly, Mitterhal grabbed the gun. The grip felt familiar, perfectly balanced in his hands. It was a Toricean flintlock, a finely crafted weapon. He got up from his chair, scanning the letters engraved in the brass inlay of the housing—*Gen Simon Harthmocker*. Stirred by the name, Mitterhal set his eye to the sight.

"All right, lad, let's hear it," he said, pointing the muzzle at the soldier's head.

Willis remained quiet, neither word nor verse.

"What now?" the colonel snapped, irritated with the delay.

"Your lock, sir. It's half cocked and your finger is not on the trigger."

Fed up with the charade, Mitterhal drew the hammer back to its firing position. "There you have it. The stage is yours. Now sing the damn song or I'll blast you for real!"

Willis closed his eyes. His voice rose in answer to the threat, backed by the crackles of the cackling flame.

A wolf is in the wood
Yes it is, yes it is
Hunting in the wood
There it is, there it is

His eyes opened. "What do you think, Colonel?"

"Good, good. Go on. Don't stop."

"That's all I've got so far."

"That's it?"

"Yes."

The colonel lowered the gun. "Well, it's not bad, but there clearly needs to be more. So far you've got a bleeding rabbit and a hungry wolf. You need to sing about what they're up to. Something has to happen."

"I know why the rabbit bleeds, sir."

"Let's hear it then. Put it in song."

Willis waited for the colonel to take aim before closing his eyes again.

There's a hawk above the ridge
Yes there is, yes there is
The rabbit's whiskers twitched
Yes they did, yes they did

The colonel clenched the gun tighter. "A hawk, very good. Talons of justice. Now you've got yourself a war hymn. The plight of your rabbit doesn't seem so hopeless anymore, does it? Go on. Tell us more about the wolf. Does it get the rabbit?"

"It doesn't want the rabbit," Willis whispered, opening his bloodshot eyes and staring into the loaded barrel.

"What?"

"It wants to protect it."

The gun came down again. "And why would a wolf do that? Especially a hungry one. Your hymn has to be believable. Otherwise it will lose its punch."

"But it needs to be true. I can't sing about a wolf that eats a rabbit that it would rather protect."

Mitterhal took a moment to ponder the point. "True," he finally said. "But if you want your brothers to take your song seriously, the beast better have a damned good reason for bypassing an easy treat."

Willis looked into the fire. "It does, sir."

"Let's hear it then." The barrel went up.

There's a fire in the field
Yes there is, yes there is
Smoke rises in the field
There it is, there it is

Silence, dark and still. A deep breath penetrated the shadows, giving life to the lifeless. Everything, from the soot-stained pewter on the fireplace mantel to the patterns of stress cracks in the chimney's masonry seemed to pulse with awareness. All the while the war hymn remained suspended in verse, dangling precariously close to completion. Even the embers ceased their popping, as if to eavesdrop on the soldier's song.

Mitterhal held steady aim on the silver crest over Willis Hume's visor. The emblem, in all its sparkling beauty, haunted him. How many times had he looked into the steadfast eyes of men who bore that same insignia over their brow? How long had it been? Five, six, maybe seven years? No, it couldn't be. The lad would have only been a boy. What kind of madman would send a child to the front lines? The mere thought consumed him. And so, at an utter loss, Mitterhal resorted to the only course of action that made sense. He sang.

Wolf ... leaps over rabbit
Wolf ... burns in the meadow
Wolf ... cries to the mountain
Talons fall from the sky

Mountain flower
Burns on the seed of air
Cinders shower
Ash on the hare

Willis blinked and looked to the windows. Dawn's glow mounted in the frosted panes. He knelt down and hoisted his pack back onto his shoulders. The cluster of pelts swung in unison. "Thank you, sir," he said, smiling for the first time that night.

The action snapped the colonel out of his own spell. "Where do you think you're going?" he asked, still pointing the gun at the lad's head.

"It's dawn, sir. I have to get back to Wulfhaven to feed the goats. Master Schnites will wonder where I've been. He is very good to me and I don't want to disappoint him."

"Wulfhaven? What about your brothers? I thought it was to the pass that you return."

"Not in the winter, sir. The bear will not march in the cold months. My brothers insist that I use the downtime to gather tidings from the Haven. I will report back to them in the spring when the gahenya blooms. They call me their Little Pilgrim." Resolved to his task, Willis tightened his straps and set the powder horn around his neck. He looked to the musket expectantly.

Mitterhal disengaged the lock and handed it back to Willis. "You've got yourself a good gun, lad. And a good song. Your brothers will be proud of you."

Willis took the musket and strode to the door. When he got there he put one hand to the latch and made ready for the cold. The other hand remained clenched tight around the stock of his musket. Abruptly, he turned and saluted. "Musket knows that you are not a coward, sir, or a traitor. And that you might not even be crazy. Hail, Gahenya."

In an instant Willis was gone. Mitterhal returned to his seat, where he found a single rabbit pelt on the floor. He picked it up and settled back into the lonely folds of his leather chair. The fur remained nestled in his lap as he drifted off into the frosted light of a new day.

"Journey well, Little Pilgrim ..."

11
A Reason to Get Up

War had its way with the colonel, not in body but in mind. The rooftop was the one place he could rest despite the laborious climb to get there. It had everything he needed: a glorious view, wonderful ventilation, and a solid friend to lean on. The chimney, for its part, remained remarkably resilient to the forces that acted on it; never budging in the mountain gales, nor withering in the hot sun, nor curling up in the ice and snow. It was a quality that Cornelius Mitterhal found most admirable.

The chimney, for all its stamina, did have a soft side. The colonel tolerated this to a point, though at times his friend's tender fascination with the living became tedious. So much so that not even the wulfweed could do its work. Nevertheless, discussing issues of life with the chimney enabled him to retain a connection with a world he might have otherwise forsaken.

It was a lonesome day. The winter sky cast in dull gray lay heavy on the mountain. For several weeks a numbing chill had kept the colonel away from his chimney. The visit of Willis Hume had taken its toll as well. Isolated in the confines of his manor with nothing but a war hymn to pass the time, Mitterhal slipped into a state of despair. And though he would be hard pressed to admit it, he desperately missed the companionship of his good friend on the rooftop. The time had come to end the gloom.

The wind whistled through the rungs of his ladder as he labored upward. From the eave he began the exhausting trek up the roof through knee-deep snow to the peak, slow and spiritless. At the platform he found the chimney half buried in a drift. He exposed as many bricks as his strength allowed, then leaned back to rest in his snowy bed.

"Colonel, shouldn't you be wearing a jacket?"

Slowly he opened his eyes. "Why would I need that?"

"It is very cold today."

A chickadee landed on the wind-swept verge, infringing on the chill with a chirp. The colonel studied the tiny bird at length, noting the black cap on its head, which tilted this way and that over its fluffy white down. Such a remarkable little creature, he thought, to exhibit such zest in the cold. The old man tipped his hat to the bird and then set his gaze to the distant dale.

"And how would you know what cold is? You are a chimney. Now let me be. I need rest."

"As you wish, Colonel. But before you nap may I share some thoughts I had while you were away?"

"Very well, if you must. But be quick. I am very tired."

"I have been thinking about life lately."

"You don't say." The colonel watched a second chickadee flutter by the eave. "And what did you come up with?"

"I am not quite sure."

Mitterhal drew out his flint. With great effort he shielded his pipe and sparked the potent mix within. The warmness felt good on his bare hands. "Well, that just about sums it up, doesn't it? It's been a wonderful conversation, Chimney. Your insights never fail to astound me. Good-bye, my good friend."

"Where are you going, Colonel?"

"Please, Chim, it's time for me to rest."

"But I'm not ready for you to leave yet."

Mitterhal shut his eyes. The shivering stopped. Tired—so tired. "Nothing lasts forever," he whispered, barely coherent.

"But where—"

"To the Mountain ..."

Something fluttered past his pipe. Wings? A winter's song tickled his ear. A symphony of quiet sound.

Swish. Fresh air on the face, a rush of color. Millions of butterflies like snowflakes, floating up, down, never touching the ground.

Ah, yes, happiness at last. The breath of trees on my wings—so fragrant, so clean, so high on the Mountain. So free to ride the meadow's tide, down to the fountain, over cedars, pines, and firs. To the Haven on a yellow wagon I ride!

"Hello, Cornelius."

"Marcus? What are you doing here? You have wings."

"I do indeed, as do you. This is quite a dream you are having. An unexpected pleasure,

I must say. You were always so grounded during the war."

"You look ridiculous, Pastor."

"This is your dream, not mine. I'm just here to deliver the message. It is your decision whether to go up or down with it. You promised the rabbit's peace to your friend on the rooftop. It would serve your family well to honor it."

"I have no friends or family."

"I beg to differ, Colonel, but that is for you to decide. I must flutter-flutter-flutter. It seems a pastor's job is never done."

"Where are you going, Marcus?"

"To the Haven, where else? Lives are at stake. I believe those were your words. Farewell, my good friend."

A hand on the wing, a shake, a voice. "Get up, you old fool!"

Mitterhal pried open his eyes. So brittle, so painful. "Who's a fool?" he muttered through frozen lips.

Smoke piped out of the chimney and rolled over the hoarfrost on its bricks.

"I'm sorry, Colonel, did you say something?"

"No, but you did. I don't like your tone."

"I'm not sure what you mean. I have been busy thinking."

"Thinking?"

"Yes. I was thinking about happiness."

Mitterhal shuddered in the snow to shake off the delirium. A sortie of snow devils swept the pasture. He counted the whirlwinds to help center his thoughts. "Happiness?" he grumbled. "You woke me up to talk about happiness?"

"I was hoping you might clarify a point. Something you said when the butterflies came to visit us on the mountain."

The colonel snapped his arms in the snowdrift to better regain the feeling in his hands. His fingers began to tingle. "Of all times, Chimney … That was three years ago. I see no reason to revisit that now."

"Yes, but after thinking about it, I found a flaw in your reasoning."

The colonel scowled and reached for his flint box. The chimney seemed unusually assertive. Bordering on insubordination, in fact.

"Really. Have you considered that three winters of ice and snow may have cracked more than your mortar joints?"

"I must confess that I have not. But if I may, you said happiness is having a reason to get up. After thinking about it, I believe that happiness is having a reason not to get up."

Mitterhal dragged deep on his pipe. The hot smoke thawed the rime on his mustache. What could possibly have possessed the chimney to make such an outlandish statement? The more he thought about it, the more the circulation returned to his limbs.

"I fear you have been puffing too much pine pitch, my friend. A person with no reason to get up is a person without purpose. And that can hardly be described as happiness."

Another pause. "I do not have a reason to get up."

"That's it!" the colonel roared. "I've had enough of this." In one great effort he forced himself out of the snow. "You have no reason to get up because you can't get up. You are a chimney, Chimney! And chimneys don't get up!" The blood once again ran hot through his veins.

The wind settled down, eerie and still. Hot embers sizzled on the white. Even the perky little chickadees kept their beaks shut.

"But I am not the one that is unhappy."

Happiness held hostage, the colonel chewed on his pipe. For the life of him he could not remember ever feeling so stumped. It impressed him, in an odd way, that a chimney of all things could exhibit such flare on the topic. Nevertheless, with his pride at stake, he knew he had to end the conversation before the fix got worse.

"Happiness is not having to listen to the senseless ramblings of a talking chimney!" He spun around to seethe at the view. Doing so, he spotted two youngsters hurrying through the courtyard and around the snow-covered hedge of laurels. The sight enraged him. Not so much that they had trespassed, but that they had witnessed his humiliating defeat. "What do you think you are doing?" he shouted.

One of the boys stopped in the courtyard and sneered at the rooftop while the larger one lumbered over the wall and continued down the snowy slope. The lad in the courtyard removed his mittens and packed a snowball. Frozen clumps of ice dangled from his tangled red hair.

No hat, Mitterhal noted. How odd on a day like today.

The missile came in fast and straight. He ducked just in time to avoid the headshot. The lad's snowball exploded on the bricks.

"Next time wear a jacket, you old fool!" the boy shouted, then dashed over the wall to join his cohort.

The fiery words echoed long in the colonel's mind. He watched the two lads scuttle away until they vanished in the white. At last, the chimney broke the silence.

"I am sorry for ruining your nap, Colonel."

Mitterhal turned. Remnants of the frozen missile still clung to the bricks. A trace of color drew his attention downward. There on the platform, half buried in the drift, lay a finely woven wool hat. He picked it up and noticed fresh footprints next to it.

"There is no need for apologies, my friend," he said, scanning the tracks across the roof ridge to the ladder to the eave. "I think it is time to get down and warm up a bit. Keep watch on the Haven, Chim. I will see you in the spring."

12
Ice Out

The *Lyssia* was a massive galleon built by Toricean shipwrights from the south bay of Lake Lakwynn. She had a sleek design in spite of her initial function as a cargo ship. Her high, rounded stern overlooked the main deck, out of which sprouted three towering masts. Mounted just below her prominent bowsprit and clad in sterling silver was the figurehead of a beautiful girl—a mythical lake spirit alleged to protect the souls of all who set foot on the *Lyssia's* vast deck and sailed the lake with pure intent.

For generations her majestic white sails served as a harbinger of prosperity. Traditionally *ice out* was declared in Lakwynnia when the lake thawed and the *Lyssia* set sail from her homeport in Altomar to circumvnavigate the newly opened waters. It was an annual event that stirred tremendous celebration throughout all the ports in the province. The Three Havens, in particular, went to great lengths to welcome the *Silver Girl*—as she was also called—with an extravagant show of festivity. Not until tensions with the Fatherland escalated and the great ship was refurbished with enough firepower to raze a small city, did her arrival lose its luster.

Spring at last. Songbirds fluttered every which way, enlivened by the thaw. Cornelius Mitterhal hummed his favorite melody as he approached the ladder. He placed his foot on the first rung and looked up to assess the climb. The roof seemed a little higher this year, but no problem. The cold days of confinement were over. That was all that mattered. So inspired, he began the ascent accompanied by a chorus of chirps. Upon reaching the roof ridge, he scanned the view and grinned. Rays of sunlight had just cleared the mountaintop and touched down on the harbor below. Clouds of vapor rose off the pockets of snow that still clung to the slopes. Like a newborn fawn testing his legs, he walked the length of the roof ridge to his lookout.

"Welcome back, Colonel," the chimney said when he'd taken three steps onto the platform. "I am happy to see you. It was not the same up here without you."

The old man put his hand on the bricks and was promptly greeted by the sweet scent of new life that blossomed out of winter's decay. He peered at the pastures and then took his seat on the bucket that he had tied to the crate last fall. "It is good to be back, my friend," he said, taking out his pipe and preparing a smoke. "And how did you fare this winter?"

"I was very lonely at first, but I followed your advice and spoke to the wind. It learned my language, just like you said it would."

"Really?" he said, amused at the notion. "And what did our good friend the wind have to say?"

"It said a lot, but I do not think I can tell you in words. The wind does not have a mouth like you and me."

"I see. Perhaps you could paraphrase?"

"I will try, Colonel, if it pleases you. From what I can best describe, it used my own evidence to speak."

"Evidence?"

"Yes, my smoke. The wind blew my smoke. At first I thought nothing of it. I was just happy to know that you were safe and warm under the roof. But then I started seeing shapes and patterns that reminded me of our time together: the butting heads of the goats, the lakehawk and the rabbit, the crippled yearling that danced under the raven's shadow. The shapes never made a sound but they seemed so real. After that I did not feel alone."

Mitterhal smiled. As absurd as the chimney could be at times, its view of the world was contagiously refreshing. He leaned back against the bricks and watched his own smoke blow in the wind. If an imagination was all it took to keep up the morale, then so be it.

"Well, it is good to see that our theory worked then. Now we know we've got nothing to worry about. So long as the wind blows, of course."

He tilted back his hat and scanned the lake. Something caught his eye—a speck on the horizon. Quickly he returned his attention to the pasture, pretending not to have noticed.

"Colonel, there appears to be something floating on the water."

"Nonsense, Chimney. It's too early for that."

"Perhaps you could verify it with your looking glass."

"I said nonsense."

"But Colonel, I—"

"Very well." He drew out his war scope. After several sweeps of the broads, he locked on the speck and adjusted the lens. Three square sails sprouted like tiny white blossoms on shimmering glass. Reluctantly, Mitterhal lowered his scope. "You are right, Chim. The thaw came early this year."

"What do you see?"

"I see a warship."

"A warship?"

"Yes, now you must be quiet. I need to concentrate."

"Is there a problem, Colonel?"

"Nonsense. Now be quiet."

"Colonel?"

"What is it, Chim?"

"I am glad we have nothing to worry about."

"Right. Now I insist that you be quiet."

"Colonel?"

"What, Chim? What!"

"Is there war in the Haven?"

"Of course not. Now if you don't stop this nonsense, I am going to dump my honey bucket down your stack."

"But, Colonel, why does the warship arrive when there is no war in the Haven?"

The scope went up again and swung like a jib boom to the ring of white-capped mountains across the harbor. There his vision sailed away through the wisps of wulfweed that shrouded his lens.

"Repeat command, sir?"

"I said full rudder right, Captain. Ready the cannons!"

"That will take us to the bridge."

"Correct. I want every piper on deck. Not a note is to be sounded until the ciphers begin their chant from the shoreline. Jeziah knows the codes."

"Sir, this action has not been authorized. General Rankwall will—"

"The general has authorized us to recruit the Gwyntah. He did not specify how we do it. Promises are nothing but empty words to the tribes. It is our actions they will trust. The wolves will hear the Silver Girl sing and know our purpose. They will follow her song to where the lake and sky become one."

"Forgive me, Colonel. I did not mean to waver."

"Listen to me, Marlin. You are captain of the goat-hyde pipers for good reason. Your integrity is sound, as was your question. I would expect nothing less. Now ready the cannons! We have a bridge to raze."

A songbird chirped incessantly in the beechwood.

"I'm sorry, Colonel. Could you repeat that?"

Mitterhal opened his eyes. The morning shade had left the platform. He shielded his face from the direct sun and picked up his war scope, which had rolled against the crate. "What are you talking about? I didn't say a thing."

The bird stopped chirping.

"I don't mean to be argumentative, but you did. You said my question was sound."

"Please, Chim, let it rest. What you ask is complex."

"By all means, Colonel."

Mitterhal looked to the harbor, surprised to see that the ship had dropped anchor just offshore of port. It seemed only seconds ago that it was out in the broads. He sniffed the sweet fragrance that wafted out of the chimney. "What's that smell?"

"What smell?"

"The smell coming out of your stack."

"I am sorry, Colonel. Is it offensive?"

Mitterhall looked to the tree. He thought he heard a giggle. "What was that?"

"What was what?"

"Don't give me that, Chimney. You're up to something. I'm no fool. Blow your incense somewhere else."

Again the giggle.

"That's it! I've had enough." The colonel rose off his bucket and squared off at the tree.

"Who are you talking to, Colonel?"

Mitterhal stared into the budding branches of the beechwood. Not a chirp, chip, or chuckle came from them. "That's better," he said, going back to his bucket. "Now, where were we, Chim?"

"I believe we were talking about the warship, but you said it was complex."

"I see." He leaned back against the bricks. "Well, perhaps we could talk about the bridge then. There's nothing complex about that."

"I would like that."

"Good."

More silence—long and grating.

"Well?" said the colonel.

"I'm sorry, did you say something?" the chimney asked.

"Yes, well … No, not really. I mean, yes … in the sense that I'm waiting for you to say something."

"What would you like me to say?"

"That's up to you. Surely you must have something to say about the bridge. You only look at it every day."

"I am not sure what you mean."

"For goodness sake, Chim. Look to the north and east of the ship. What do you see?"

"I see a circular range of mountains across the harbor."

"No, no. Not so far. Look to where the harbor narrows and is fed by the river."

Mitterhal peered through his scope. From the far east bank he tracked the network of trusses that spanned across the water along a series of towering stone pylons.

"Oh, that," the chimney said. "I never realized it was a bridge. Nobody ever uses it."

The lens stopped on the tangled wreckage of beams, girders, and stonework halfway across the harbor. Splashes of sunlight reflected off the twisted metal rails. "Well, there you have it. Now you know," the colonel said, suddenly somber.

"Colonel, now that you point it out, I feel pity for the bridge. It seems so alone and broken. Why doesn't anybody fix it?"

"Not all things serve the purpose of their intended design, Chim. Sometimes the finest quality of something is best observed by what it doesn't do."

"That sounds awfully complex. Are you sure we should be talking about this?"

A bird chirped in the beechwood yet again. Mitterhal blinked and retracted his scope. Warily he peered around the corner of the bricks.

"Colonel, if you don't mind me asking, what are you looking for?"

"What I am looking for and what I am looking at are two different things."

"Oh, a delusion, how exciting," the chimney said. "Can I help you find it?"

"What exactly do you mean by that?"

"Nothing really. Only that it might be fun to match your view of the tree with the tree in your view."

"Yes, well, do us both a favor and keep your watch on the Haven where it belongs."

"Of course, Colonel. I love how the harbor turns the mountains upside down when the sun shines on them."

Ensnared by the reflection, Mitterhal drifted away. He didn't say a word for the rest of the day. Eventually the mountains melted into sunset and the lake and sky became one. With darkness came rest. The bridge and the warship faded in a dream.

13
Music in the Night

To call the Haven Guard a militia was an understatement. The men were indeed fighters, trained to kill, yet it was their resourceful tactics that set them apart from other forces in the Lakwynnian army. Most noteworthy was their innovative use of goat-hyde pipes to dispatch commands on the battlefield. The men were trained not only to listen but to chant as well, serving a dual function of relaying vital information in addition to sustaining unity. Every combat unit in the guard was deployed with a company of field ciphers, whose task—in addition to fighting—was to listen to the pipers and decipher the command codes in their melodies. They in turn would relay the instructions to their unit commander, who would authorize the ciphers to chant the encoded message to fighters in the field. In this way commands were dispatched quickly and effectively over long distances, even when visibility was compromised. It was a link that Cornelius Mitterhal orchestrated with deadly effect.

An even more specialized breed of fighter existed within the Guard. Masters of stealth and proficient at the kill, they were the men for whom the talon strike was named—guardians of the music, protectors of the link between Mitterhal and his troops. Loyal as they were lethal, they provided safe passage for the pipers behind enemy lines and protected them once they established their positions and the music began. To this task they were fiercely committed and held no rank within the conventional chain of command. As such they were simply referred to as Mitterhal's wolves.

Cornelius Mitterhal awoke to the light of the hunter's moon filtering through the distorted panes of his bedroom window. He clutched at his shoulder and turned over in his bed to shield his eyes from the light.

"Wake up, sir," whispered a voice not far from the bed.

Mitterhal jolted up to face the intruder. A dark shadow sat in the nearby chair. He did not see a face but could feel the eyes on him. The moonlight split the shadow in half and revealed the familiar musket on the soldier's lap. "So you're back," the colonel said, propping himself up against the headboard. "Your arrivals are becoming much more civil."

"You have secured Musket's trust, sir. We are not here to test you. We have come to warn you. The wolves have crossed the Haven. They will be here soon. I am sorry, sir, I think I may have told them too much. They are coming to release you."

"What are you talking about, lad?"

"I have bad tidings from Gwyntahlynn. Their scouts have reported suspicious activity in the Awshaw mines. Plans may be underway to rebuild the Silvermine Bridge across the Haven."

With a sudden jerk, Willis Hume sprang up from the chair and held at gunpoint the shifting shadows on the wall.

"My brothers will be very upset." He swung down the barrel and took aim at who knows what. "It was our father's song that was played on the *Lyssia* when the bridge was destroyed. We cannot betray the wolf. The wolf protected the rabbit."

Mitterhal threw off his blanket and sat on the edge of his bed. "That is all very profound, lad," he said, adjusting his nightcap. "But before you blast a hole in my floor, why don't we stick to the facts that have spurred you to wake me up in the middle of the night. What exactly did you tell them?"

Willis released the firing lock and resumed his seat on the chair. "I told them that you helped me finish my war hymn. I wasn't going to sing it at first, but their scouts threatened to kill me. Once they heard it, they withdrew their guntocs and took me to their chief."

"Very well then, but I still don't see why this would provoke their chief to issue his wolves."

"I told him everything, sir. Even how you put the wulfweed in your pipe, and the white foam that comes out of your mouth when you faint. He summoned his shamans and had me repeat the account to them. They asked me a lot of questions. Where and when it happened and what you said when it did. They spoke entirely in their own tongue after that. *Kulu ah shahanah*, they kept on saying. I asked the translator what it meant and he said, 'Shadow of raven.' He said you are waking from a great sleep and would need assistance. I think that is why they have sent their howlers. Musket is concerned for your safety and thought we should warn you of their arrival."

"You told their chief that I fainted? What possessed you to say such a thing?"

"It is true, sir. Musket as my witness, I swear it. Once at your ladder and then again at your hearth. I had to tell him. I could not lie. My brothers warned me not to jest with the wolves, and above all never to lie."

Mitterhal looked to his window. The moonlight fell stark on the splintered panes. "You were wise to do so. Your brothers' advice most likely saved your life."

Willis rose again from the chair; he kept his musket tight to his chest. "I must leave, sir. The wolves are coming. They do not know that Musket and I have come to warn you."

"Where are you going, lad?"

"Back to the pass. I must tell my brothers about the bridge right away. They will know what to do."

Like a fleeting dream, Willis Hume stepped out of the moonlight and vanished in the doorway. Alone in his room, Mitterhal remained upright in the bed, wide awake, staring at the shadows on the floor. In time he got up to fetch a jar of honey and settle his thoughts on the rooftop.

A dispirited cloud hovered over the chimney as the colonel stepped onto his platform with the jar of honey in hand. After sitting on the bucket, he dipped his pipe into the jar, using the stem as a spoon. Gloomy still, he licked off the sweetness and prepared himself a smoke by the light of the hunter's moon.

"Another dream, Colonel?" the chimney asked.

"Something like that, Chim."

The chimney's smoke wafted through the moonlight, casting wraithlike shadows on the bricks. "Is there something I can do for you?"

Mitterhal leaned against the solid masonry. "You are doing it," he replied, lighting his pipe.

The moon eventually retreated behind the clouds and a chilling cry echoed across the pasture, snapping the colonel out of his mood.

"What was that noise?" the chimney asked. "I have never heard anything like it."

Several more cries sounded in the knolls.

"Ah, yes, wonderful, isn't it?" Mitterhal said. "I have not heard the wolves sing on this mountain since I was a boy."

"Their song makes me feel strange, Colonel."

"How so, Chim?"

"Like I might lose something."

Mitterhal's brow twitched. "Yes, I can see how you might think that," he said, musing over the mournful wails. "You are hearing the wolf's pain,

Chimney. That would be sorrow that you feel."

"Sorrow?"

"Yes, it is a condition that afflicts the living. In the case of these wolves, I suspect that they cry for the loss of their love and land. Their homeland once ranged from these mountains right down to the lake. In fact, the city in the harbor below was named after the spirited beast."

The moon struck the low-lying mist on the Haven, creating the effect of a soft white blanket on a child's bed. The colonel shook his head to shed the sliver of awareness that penetrated his thoughts. His eye still twitching, he gazed at the mountains beyond the shrouded harbor.

"My mother would sit with me late at night when the wolves howled. 'Wake up, my boy,' she would say. 'Wake up and listen to the music.' It is one of the few memories I have of her. There were many more wolves back then. To hear them all at once was like listening to a symphony. It is a shame they have gone."

"Why did they leave?" the chimney asked.

Mitterhal shook his head again. "One too many letdowns, I suppose. It is a curious custom of my kind that we name the lands in which we live after those we have oppressed to seize it." His body quivered as another sliver pricked at his awareness.

"Sir, Gwyntah longboats have landed in Wulfhaven. They have brought their war drums. Gwyntahpynn Choroqua sends message that his warriors await your command at the docks. They call you the Mahocpynn."

"Have Jeziah assemble the ciphers at the fountain, Captain. You and your pipers line the promenade in single-file procession, facing the harbor, ready to play. Send for McFadden. He and I will walk the docks."

"Sir, what of an armed escort?"

"No, Marlin. Tonight we lay down our guard and celebrate life. We will sing with the wolves."

"Of course, sir. And the tune?"

"The piece you did on the Silver Girl will suffice."

"Colonel, I don't think I like sorrow."

Foam bubbled out of the colonel's mouth. He grimaced at the comment. So painfully obvious. "Of course you don't, Chim. Nobody does. That is its nature. But if you want to understand my kind, then you must know sorrow. You must live it and breathe it until it pulverizes the very mortar in your joints and reduces you to nothing more than a heap of rubble. Then and only then, when you have nothing left to lose, will you become aware of what it means to be alive."

Gravity pressed heavy on the rooftop. The colonel used his handkerchief to wipe the foam off his face.

"Forgive me, Colonel. But if it's all the same to you, I think I'll just remain a chimney."

Mitterhal glared at the bricks watching the shadows of the beechwood's branches dance on the moonlit facade. *What a silly comment*, he thought.

The tremors began again, only they felt different this time. Not quite as dismal. Rather, they tickled his chest and torso. He put his hands on his stomach. No good. The spasms escalated. The chimney's silly comment kept on repeating in his mind. At last he opened his mouth to release the pressure within. So it happened that for the first time since his return from the war, Cornelius Mitterhal laughed.

It was a deep, good, hearty laugh. The kind that brings light to dark places and soothes a soul of sore wounds. The chimney, for its part, remained stoic while the colonel carried on, holding his belly and slapping his knee. In time, the old man wiped the drool off his chin and praised his steadfast companion.

"Thank you, Chim. I have not heard a gut-buster like that in a long time. For one who is not considered among the living, you have a rousing take on life. It would do a world of good for more of my kind to talk to their chimneys."

He took a deep breath and gazed up into the heavens. Starlight sparkled off the silver buttons on his vest. He smiled at the chimney's smoke that drifted overhead. "You're awfully quiet, Chim. What's on your mind?"

"I am sorry, Colonel. I was just thinking about that noise you made when I told you I wanted to remain a chimney."

"Oh, that. It was just laughter." The colonel chuckled again. "Certainly nothing to get gloomy over."

"I thought so. If I may ask, what caused you to celebrate?"

"Celebrate?"

"Yes. On the day that the other colonel was honored for his service in war, you called laughter a celebration. I am curious what you were celebrating just now."

Mitterhal's thoughts raced back to the year of the parade, when he spotted the spirited little girl giggling among the wildflowers. "I suppose I did. If you are going to hold me to that, then I would say life."

"Life?"

"Yes, life. Laughter is a celebration of life. There you have it."

"I like that definition, Colonel. May I laugh with you?"

"There's no need to ask, Chim. You simply do it. If you feel like laughing, then by all means do so."

A deep, haunting tone emanated from behind the chimney. Mitterhal probed the bricks in search of the source. It sounded more like the bass drone to a tribal chant rather than an expression of mirth. "Chimney, what on earth are you doing?"

"I am laughing, Colonel."

"By the light of the Haven, you're going to raise the dead if you keep that up!"

"Forgive me, but I am afraid I cannot help myself. It feels too good."

More wolf cries ascended to the roof; only this time they were accompanied by the deep drone of the chimney's laugh. The ensemble went on throughout the night and into the morning, orchestrated by an ancient drive. All the while, Cornelius Mitterhal smiled at the shadows that prowled about on his rooftop while he sipped his honey and listened to the music.

14
Sweets and Cinders

Few sights lifted the spirits more than the mountain lupine in full bloom over the highlands of the Three Havens. From the eastern shores of Lake Lakwynn, one could peer up into the Awshaw Mountains and imagine the landscape flowing blue on a meadow's tide. It was a floral spectacle that heralded the coming of summer.

The natives called it gahenya, or seed of air, and believed that the roots of the mountain flower were nourished by the wind. Prized not only for its beauty, the unique highland strain also possessed a host of properties that were of special interest to the tribes of Gwyntahlynn. The pea-sized seeds in the lupine pods, though rich in sustenance, were consumed only after careful steps were taken to remove their toxins. Harvested in autumn at the peak of potency, the bright yellow lupini beans were soaked in a solution that leached them of their poisons, after which they were mashed into a nutritious paste. Those foolish enough to consume the raw lupini without paying strict attention to this procedure were subject to a host of illnesses that ravaged both mind and body, thus giving rise to the highland flower's more ominous name—wulfweed.

Fall had come. Cornelius Mitterhal hummed his favorite melody as he stepped onto his platform with a wicker basket draped in a blue velvet cloth. He placed the basket next to the wooden crate by his tin bucket, then stretched out his arms and inhaled the crisp autumn air.

"Good morning, Colonel," the chimney said. "You seem to have a good reason to get up today."

"I do indeed, Chimney." He sat on his bucket and covered the dingy crate with the blue cloth. He placed various items on each corner to hold down the cloth in the wind: two clay plates, a peppermill, and a mason jar full of sun-dried tomatoes. "I think it is time for you and me to have a picnic, my friend." One by one Mitterhal unpacked an array of surprises. Fruit tarts, goat cheese, plump cherries, two large boiled turnips soaked in butter, and a loaf of fresh-baked pumpernickel bread were but a few of the tasty treats he neatly arranged on his cloth-covered crate. When all was just right, he packed his pipe and fired up a smoke.

"Colonel, where did all this food come from?"

"Funny you would ask that, Chim," he said, looking suspiciously at the bricks. "That is exactly the same question I was going to ask you. I found this basket by your hearth at sunrise and thought you might be able to offer an explanation of your own."

"My watch was on the Haven, as always," the chimney replied, though somewhat hurriedly.

Mitterhal held his tongue, sensing the defensive shift in his friend. He knew better than to pry. Years on the rooftop had long laid bare the folly of trying to force out the truth. To do so would only cause the chimney to feign ignorance and retreat behind a veil of childlike innocence. No, the question would have to wait for now.

A rogue wind rumbled off the summit. Mitterhal battened down his goat-hyde hat in preparation of the gust. The tides of the sky had changed and the casual flow of summer was gone.

"So be it, Chim," he said, returning his attention to the festivity at hand. "To celebrate our picnic I thought it fitting to offer a contribution of my own." He removed a golden glass jar from his vest pocket and proudly held it aloft, just as the brisk highland draft delivered its message of winter's imminence. "Ah, yes, wild mountain honey," he said, keeping his other hand planted on his hat. "The best of the best. It has been a bountiful summer for the bees and they have been most charitable with their treasure this summer." His mustache flapped as he appraised the jar.

"Why were the bees so friendly?" the chimney asked.

"Friendly?" The colonel looked sternly at the bricks. "That is hardly the word I would use to describe the feisty little buggers. In fact, they can be downright nasty. Convincing them to give up their honey requires careful diplomacy." He paused, spellbound by the prisms of light that dashed across the bricks with the slightest turn of the honey jar. Long he reflected on the tactics he had used to persuade the wild swarms to take up residence in his makeshift bee boxes—and the stings he'd endured once he had. "After years of fuss, Chimney, the bees and I have settled on an arrangement that works for all of us. It is very simple really. I give them what they want and they give me what I want."

"What do you have that they want?"

Mitterhal removed the pipe from his mouth and held it next to the jar of honey. The shadows of pipe smoke swirled amidst the glass. "They like to smoke the wulfweed," he said with a grin.

"But, Colonel, bees do not smoke pipes."

"No, they certainly do not. And that is exactly why the arrangement works. I give them all the smoke they could possibly want and in return, they give me what I want. Even then I only take the sweets from the upper crates. Deal or not, they don't like it if you get pushy with their queen. The sting of a bee is very convincing. It has only the one to give, after which its life is spent. To feel the sting of many is an even harder lesson."

Smoke churned out of the chimney. "Colonel, I cannot help wondering why a bee would do such a thing if it knows it is going to die."

"Trust me, Chim, even a bee is no fool. It will only commit such an act if it believes its hive is in imminent danger."

"The hive must be very important to the bee."

"Very much so." The colonel looked deeper into his jar of honey. "It is the place where its family resides. As such, it will defend it at all cost, even at the expense of its own life." He raised the jar into the direct sun, casting splintered rainbows on the smoke.

The light transfixed Mitterhal again, and he spent the rest of the morning chasing colors on the rooftop. So engrossed he became, that he forgot about the picnic. The goat cheese had long oozed into a formless mass by the time the chimney steered him away from his play.

"Colonel, this has been a wonderful picnic. Thank you for including me. Maybe next time we can invite company. I would love to meet the bees."

Mitterhal pressed his fingers just above his ears and behind the eyes. He had a terrible headache—a real splitter. "I'm afraid they are not the picnicking type, Chim. They stay to their hives when they're not out working."

"Maybe we could invite the goats then. Do you think they would find the time to leave their hives?"

"No, Chim, I don't." He reached for a cherry and dipped it in the honey jar. Honey. Yes, that was the key. It cut the headache every time.

"Why not?"

"For one thing, goats don't have hives. They have herds."

"What is the difference?"

Mitterhal chewed on the cherry while he entertained the thought. "Not a whole lot, really, when you get right down to it. Only structure, I suppose. In principle they both serve as places for their families to thrive. Safe havens, if you will."

"Safe havens?"

A subtle hum came out of the beechwood, like a whisper with a tune. The colonel spit out the pit. He watched it roll down the slate and over the eave.

"Colonel, I think I figured out why you spend so much time watching the Haven."

"Really, and why is that?"

"I think the Haven might be where your hive is."

"A fine thought, Chimney, except for one thing. I do not have a hive, I am not a bee." His gaze shifted to the mountain goats that bucked about on the grassy knolls to the south; the first signs of rut were coming into play. Soon they would be putting their skills to the real test on the steep slopes of the north pasture.

"Maybe the Haven is where your herd is then," the chimney said.

"I do not have that either. I am not a goat."

"What about a family, Colonel? Do you have that?"

The question was simple. Why, then, wasn't the answer? He felt it knocking at his memory. A family. The mere thought made him twitch. He needed a smoke, something to keep the door shut. Damn the chimney! Bad word. Where's the pipe? Dizzy … Too late. The door creaked open.

"Permission to speak freely, sir?"

"Has it come to this, Lieutenant, that you need consent for such a thing? Speak your mind as always."

"The men will charge a storm of hornets if you ask them, as will I. But with all respect, the wulfweed is in seed. Once the bales are lit, we will all be subject to the sickness."

"You are the heart of the guard, Uryan. Yet bravery alone will not win this battle. There is no sign of Rankwall's reinforcements, nor is there word to explain his delay. We are very much alone and the bear is hungry. Our only hope is in the smoke. If we are going to charge into its jowls, then let it be under cover of the Raven's Shadow. The bails have been saturated in tar and set at twenty-pace intervals along the east flank. The wolves will ignite them once the signal is sounded. You and the cavalry will await the pipers' call in the west. The rest we will trust to the wind. Hail, Gahenya, Lieutenant."

"Hail, Gahenya, sir."

Fading silence, bricks against back, warm sun on face, wind … and wheels. Yes, a wagon's wheels breaking silence.

"Colonel, I think it is time to get up. The big horse is coming."

Mitterhal opened his eyes and immediately extended his scope. The chimney was right, at least on two counts. It was actually a mule, not a horse, though it was big. Extremely so, in fact. And it was definitely coming this way. Behind it rolled a hefty farm cart flanked by two horsemen. One driver on the cart held the reins, his back to a load of cordwood.

"Hmm. Right on schedule," the colonel said, retracting his scope and preparing another honey-dipped cherry.

Indeed it was. Every year at this time the three young men would deliver a winter's worth of firewood, cut and split. They never said a word, and neither did Mitterhal. It was the perfect arrangement. They would simply drop the load in the stock house behind the manor and leave. In a week or so they would be back with a load of hay for the goats. Good clean hay, free of the weed.

"Fine lads," he said aloud.

"Colonel, I was just thinking. Maybe we could invite the horselads to our picnic. There is plenty of food left."

"Don't be ridiculous, Chimney."

"I am sorry, Colonel. It was just a thought."

"Do us both a favor and keep your silly thoughts to yourself."

"As you wish."

Mitterhal munched on his honey-dipped cherry.

"Colonel?"

"What?"

"May I have your permission to inquire further about the bee?"

Mitterhal repacked his pipe—only the leaf, not the bean. "You do not need permission for that," he said, reaching in his vest for the flint box. "Speak your mind."

"If a bee dies after it stings, how will it know if the hive continues?"

"It doesn't need to know, Chim. It's got faith, to whatever degree a bee can possess such a thing."

"Faith?"

"Yes, it's what empowers the living to live with purpose and the dying to die with grace." He sparked up the flint.

"But, Colonel, that sounds like love."

Mitterhal gagged on the smoke and immediately removed his pipe to let the coughing fit run its course.

"Colonel, are you okay?"

"I'm fine. Just give me a moment."

"Colonel?"

"What!"

"You told me once that I can have love even if I am not of the living. Does that mean I can also have faith?"

The mule cart continued to amble slow and steady up the carriage road. Already Mitterhal could hear the heel chains of the great beast clinking in its harness. Soon they would be leaving the carriage road to cut across the south pasture and make for the gap in the wall by the beehives. What inspired them

71

to do this? he wondered. How many years now? Six, seven, maybe eight? Hard to tell anymore. He'd stopped counting a long time ago.

"Colonel?"

"Yes, my friend?"

"Can I have faith as well?"

"Yes, yes, you can. Where there is love there is faith."

"What if I lose the love? Will I also lose the faith?"

"That depends."

"On what, if I may ask?"

"On whether or not you accept the loss of your love."

"I do not think I could ever accept losing the purpose in my puff."

Mitterhal smiled and dipped a large silver spoon into the jar of honey. "Well, then, you better make damn sure you don't lose it. Here try a little bit of this, it will lift your spirits." He smeared a generous portion of honey on the bricks and watched the sweet treasure ooze into the nooks and crannies of the sun-baked masonry. "There, that ought to do the trick. What do you think?"

"I am afraid I cannot taste it."

Disappointed, Mitterhal closed the lid on the jar and relit his pipe. "No, I suppose not," he said with a sigh. "What a shame. Never to know the sweetness of honey."

"Will you describe it to me, Colonel?"

"Describe what?"

"Sweetness."

"Why, yes, of course. It is a … Sort of like … eh … Well, kind of … Not so easy to describe, you being a chimney. All I can say is that it serves as a reminder to those of us who can taste that there is more to life than pain and suffering. If I had to describe it as a sound, it would be the carefree laughter of a child. Or as a sight, the sun's reflection on the Haven. If it were a smell, it would be a field of gahenya in full bloom just after a rain. It pains me to think that you will never know the joy that it brings."

"But, Colonel, I know all those things. I can taste. You just didn't put the honey in my mouth."

"What in holy blazes are you talking about?"

"My mouth. The place where my smoke comes from."

As Mitterhal's gaze scaled the masonry, he calculated the height he would gain by placing his bucket on the crate and standing on it. Maybe, just maybe … No, absolutely not, he concluded. There was a fine line between bravery and foolishness. "You will be blowing smoke for a long time if you think I'm going to crawl up your bricks like a spider to stick a lick of honey down your stack."

"You could try, Colonel."

"Try?" He puffed incredulously on his pipe. "I could also try to grow a third mouth on the top of my head. That would be a lot easier."

"But, Colonel, you have only one mouth. How could you grow a third before the second?"

"Exactly my point. It won't happen. And don't get fiddly with me. What makes you so sure you would taste the honey even if I did attempt such a foolish task?"

"I can taste the tar pitch on the inside of my smoke chamber."

Mitterhal took a moment to clean out his pipe. He then cut a slice of pumpernickel and smeared it with honey. The chimney's deduction seemed sensible enough, though he still was not keen on making the climb. How could he get out of the predicament and still save face? The sun glistened off his silver soot scraper, lying on the crate. He squinted at the tool.

"Very well, Chimney. Let's use the soot in your stack as our starting point. Imagine if you will, the pitch building up to the point where your smoke has nowhere to go but back. Then think about the taste of the black sticky mass as it congeals in your chamber and oozes down your firebox."

"That would not be a pleasant taste at all, Colonel."

"No, it most certainly would not. Now imagine tasting the exact opposite. That would be sweetness."

"Ooh, that sounds wonderful."

"It is, my friend. It is indeed."

Mitterhal spent the rest of the afternoon enjoying his picnic. Eventually the draught mule passed the breach in the wall with the empty farm cart in tow. Halfway through the south field on the way back to the carriage road, one of the horsemen veered on his mount and hailed a salute. The colonel acknowledged the gesture with a raised pipe. He then went back to savoring the taste of his honey-topped bread.

15
The Colonel, the Soldier, and the Smoking Goat

The Silvermine Bridge was an engineering feat that marked the zenith of peace for the tribes of Gwyntahlynn and the Toriceans who colonized the Three Havens. The footings of the great bridge were cast at a time when the spirit of fellowship ran strong in the region and cooperation had yet to be haggled as a commodity. The Gwyntahmahoma had contributed substantially to the project both in sweat and know-how, for the crafting of stone was no mystery to the tribes. The main truss deck of the bridge spanned Wulfhaven harbor on a series of enormous block pylons, high enough to allow passage of the tallest Toricean frigates up the mouth of the Pemihawynn River. The delving of the tunnels into the jagged feet of the Awshaw Mountains was the last link necessary to culminate the joint effort that had spanned the pride of the region.

With the tunnels and the bridge complete, trains were able to circumnavigate the entire lake in both directions, thus facilitating a trade route no longer limited to ships. The Gwyntah, in particular, were awed—initially—by the powerful steam engine that chugged over the trusses and blew clouds of white smoke over the crags of their sacred coastland. So much in fact, they honored it with a name. *Tuftash* they called it, which in their tongue meant smoking goat.

Mitterhal kept his beehives near the break in the fieldstone wall, just uphill of the outbuilding on the highest verge of his south pasture. Viewed from the hay house, the hives appeared to be nothing more than a cluster of boxes. Upon closer examination, one would discover that the boxes were actually stacks of boxes comprised of wooden crates with holes drilled in their sides. An even more daring investigation would reveal the faded letters and numbers that corresponded to the munitions they once held. Indeed, the ammo crates had long been dispensed of their explosive contents. However, the live payload they now housed was no less volatile.

In the sedate light of dusk, on the leeward side of his smoke pit, Cornelius Mitterhal removed a wooden frame from the top crate of his hive to inspect its waxy surface. Seeing no brood or eggs, he carved out the contents of the frame with the sharpened edge of a dismantled bayonet. Slabs of raw honeycomb plunked into the tin bucket at his feet. He made sure to keep his motions smooth and easy, not too fast, not too slow, cautiously unrestrained. He hummed an old war hymn to steady his nerves while he worked his craft. Funny how the hymn fell in sync with the swarm. Or was it the other way around? Hard saying anymore.

He had just begun another round when he caught the change in timbre. So subtle at first, he barely noticed it. He carefully placed the frame back into the top crate and listened to the bees. They seemed agitated. Warily, he watched their restless movements on his bare arms. Yes, they were definitely on the alert. A threat of some sort, somewhere. He turned to the pasture, keeping his motion fluid.

The silhouette of a soldier stood in the breach of the wall, his musket drawn, aimed directly at a hive. What was he thinking?

"At ease, soldier. Don't be a fool. If you pull that trigger we'll both be plucking stingers for a week."

"Don't worry, sir. Musket's got a bead on every one of 'em."

Mitterhal grumbled as the realization of who it was sank in. Willis Hume, who else? Time was of the essence. The buzz mounted. He knew he had to act fast—but not too fast. He strode to the smoke pit and stoked the blaze with a dampened mix of gahenya and goat hair that he kept in a bin. A noxious yellow cloud belched forth into the twilight and engulfed the entire colony in a tranquilizing haze.

With the crisis averted, Mitterhal whipped his head around in the smoke. "You can tell that foolish gun of yours to relax now. The bees will be sacked for the night."

Willis lowered his musket. "How do you do it, sir?"

"Do what?"

"Keep from getting stung."

"Trust me, lad, I've been stung many times. The trick is keeping your nerve about you and taking the time to learn their tune. Threatening to blow their hive sky high will only cause problems for everyone. You need to lighten up with that musket."

Willis hopped over the wall and sat on a boulder near the circle of stones upwind of the smoke pit. "I know, sir. Musket can get testy at times. But its intentions are always good. That's all that really matters, don't you think?"

"Not if it causes more problems than it solves. How do you function with others?"

"To be honest, sir, I try to avoid crowds as much as possible. It keeps things simple that way. Master Schnites is ... was ... the only one who understood Musket. Besides my brothers, of course. He used to let me work his goats every winter when I returned from the pass. He was always good to Musket and never asked questions."

"Why do you speak of him in the past?" the colonel asked.

"He's changed now. He doesn't want anything to do with Musket anymore. I told him about the plans to rebuild the bridge. It turned out he already knew about it. He said it would be good for commerce in the Haven to reconnect the rail, and that new policies would prevent us from repeating old mistakes with the tribes. I told him that Musket didn't think the tribes would agree. When he asked me how Musket would know that, I told him about our meeting with the chief across the Haven. After that he told us to leave the farm and never come back."

Mitterhal stepped out of the smoke, sorry he had asked the question. Pain throbbed in his temple. His work with the bees was catching up with him. Time to change the subject. "Looks like you're growing up," he said, reaching for a slab of comb honey in the tin. "You have a mustache now. I would think a swarthy young soldier like yourself would be spending your leave chasing the lasses in Wulfhaven."

"There's no time for that, sir. The Haven is at war and nobody even knows it. My father hasn't stopped playing his pipes since I told my brothers about the bridge. Others have heard the call and gather."

"Others? What do you mean?" Mitterhal wiped a long strand of drool that stretched over his chin. He carefully folded the handkerchief and put it back in his pocket with a shaking hand.

"Troops still muster in the pass, sir. Survivors. Hundreds of them just like me who made it through the smoke. I taught them the war hymn about the bleeding rabbit. They like it. They're ready to fight, sir. They just need an order."

"Fight?" Disoriented, he looked to the west. The sunset's glow was all but gone. "Fight what? The bridge?" He teetered on the edge of collapse. "You've said nothing of an enemy."

Willis blinked and addressed his musket. "I know we have to tell him, but why does it have to be now?" He raised the gun and pointed it at the colonel's head, blinking rapidly. "Yes, but he doesn't look well. You know what happened last time."

Mitterhal's ears began to ring. He tried to focus on the soldier's mouth to better understand his words. All he saw was the black muzzle of the musket inches from his nose. The one-way debate became a jumble. Dizziness. Collapse felt imminent. The gun hammer clicked, and the colonel clutched at his handkerchief.

"We are the enemy, sir, of all who plan to wrong the wolf."

The ground came up. His crumpled handkerchief hit the grass.

"It is over, Colonel. The Torics have sounded the retreat. Wolf scouts confirm the report. The pipers await your order."

"Order? I have no order."

"Where are you going, sir?"

"To find McFadden."

"Sir, the gahenya is still smoldering. It is not safe yet."

"Let the seed smolder, Captain. The shadow can do what it will."

"But you are unarmed. There may still be hostiles."

"Look at the field, Marlin. Do you honestly believe there is anyone left in a condition to be hostile? It's over. You said it yourself. If an order is what you want, I'll give you one. See to the dead and wounded, Torics as well. Take command of what is left of the guard, and don't ever ask me for another order again. I am done with this war."

Mitterhal awoke, propped against the soldier's combat pack. Shadows danced in the field grass. A fire blazed in the smoke pit. Something soft dangled over his shoulder—a rabbit pelt. In his lap he found his handkerchief, neatly folded and on it his pipe, perfectly centered. A steady purr came from across the pit. Willis Hume lay stretched out on his back, snoring in the matted field grass. The barrel of his musket moved up and down like a seesaw on his chest.

Again, something soft, but this time wet, like a tongue.

"What in holy—"

He turned at the snort. A white form cleared the wall; one great leap, up and over.

Mitterhal picked up his bucket of honeycomb and approached the fieldstones where the phantom had vanished. He sat on a boulder near the base. "You can come out now, little fellow," he said, tapping his pipe on the bucket. "I have what you want."

Sure enough, a set of curved horns rose from behind the wall. Slowly, like two crescent moons, they moved upward, silhouetted by a set of curious ears. The eyes came next, illuminated by the fire, their black rectangular pupils locked on the bucket.

"Ah, yes, that's it," the colonel said encouragingly. "My, how you have grown. Now come on back over and we'll have ourselves a little picnic. There's plenty of sweets for all of us." He reached into the bucket and tossed a honeycomb into the grass by his feet.

The three-legged billy leaped the wall, dislodging a stone along the way. The stone rumbled down, followed by the distinct double click of a musket.

"Don't move, sir," Willis said from across the pit. "I've got a bead on the beast."

Mitterhal wrenched forward in shock. "Drop that gun, lad!" he roared. "You put a plug in that goat and I'll have that musket rapped so tight around your skull, it'll pop your mustache off."

In a flash the goat was gone, back over the wall with the honeycomb in its mouth. Willis, in reaction to the threat, swung the barrel back to the colonel and held him at gunpoint. He shook his head as if trying to shed water from his ears.

"No, Musket," he said, lowering the weapon. "Not this time. I think we better listen to him."

"You're damn right you better listen! I've had enough of your talking musket. Get a grip on yourself, lad. This nonsense has to end."

"Please, sir, you're upsetting Musket. We're sorry about scaring the goat, but we thought it was—"

"No, lad! There is no we. There is only you. You! You! You! You are sorry. You are the one holding the gun. You are the one responsible. The gun is a gun and nothing more. Look at it. What do you see? Is there anything on that cursed thing that resembles a mouth?"

Dejected, the young soldier searched the weapon in vain. "Not really, sir. But we—"

"It very well can't speak then, can it? The voice you are hearing is yours. The sooner you face that fact, the better off you and everything else you're terrorizing will be."

Willis stood stunned with gun in hand, paralyzed by the colonel's words. When at last he looked up, his eyes were swollen and red, yet somehow beyond tears. It was a broken look that caught Mitterhal off guard and sliced deep into his shielded conscience.

He looked into the traumatized face and suddenly saw a boy of twelve standing on the front line of battle, staring across a blood-drenched field at a line of cannons that stretched as far as the eye could see. Nausea crept in his gut and siphoned the rage out of his veins. How could he have been such a fool? He stared at the soldier, so pale and weak, stripped of all fight.

Bile on his tongue, Mitterhal wiped his lips with his handkerchief. What could have possessed him to undermine the one and only pillar of faith that had borne the lad through his trauma? He swallowed back the frothy acid. He had to. To leave the hopeless soldier in such a state was unacceptable.

"Listen, lad. There comes a time when we all hear voices. Some of us just get there sooner than others. I have a good friend who suffers the same condition as you."

"You have a friend?" Willis asked, appearing to liven at the notion.

The colonel straightened his posture and wiped the foam off the corners of his mustache. "Am I really that crass?" He crossed his arms at the chest. "Anyway, that's not the point. What you need to know is that the voice you are hearing is real, regardless of whatever batty place it comes from."

"But you said it yourself, sir. Musket doesn't have a mouth. It can't speak."

"That was a rash statement. I thought you were going to shoot my goat. I was not myself when I said it. The truth is, I believe your musket is doing everything it can to look out for you in the only way it knows how. Its intentions are noble, but its actions are founded in fear."

"I've never known Musket to be afraid of anything."

"Trust me, lad. It was born out of your horror and that's the only thing it knows now. You told me it spoke to you for the first time on the field of battle. Up to that point, it was just a gun. It chose that moment to commit the unreal so it could help you in a very real way. To that end it succeeded. Now it is your task to assure it that it no longer needs to fear for your safety. Once you do that, you might even teach it some good manners."

A weightless expression settled on the soldier, the same charmed look Mitterhal remembered on the lad after composing the war hymn at the hearth.

"Truth is I like you, Willis. You've got a lot of grit in your gut and you don't let the hard knocks tear you down. That's a good quality for a soldier. But you have to let up now. Otherwise you'll be fighting a battle that never ends."

Silence ensued in which both the colonel and the soldier stood staring at the sky, connecting the dots in the celestial dome. Patterns within patterns drifted westward across the infinite shadow, isolating whatever earthly worries were tearing at their wounded hearts. Eventually Willis broke the silence. "I didn't tell you everything, sir."

Mitterhal, wary of the confessional tone, lit his pipe. "About what?"

"About what I did after the battle ... when I saw the goats."

"You told me plenty, as I recall. You said you were hungry and shot one of them. A more than justified act, given your predicament. There is no shame in that."

Willis kept his sight on the stars. "The first shot didn't kill it. I lamed it in the left flank and it made for the high slopes before I could get off another shot. I followed the blood trail up until I saw ravens circling the ridge. I knew that was where it meant to die. It was a hard hike, but I got there by evening. I found it lying under an overhang with its head up. So calm, watching me approach. That's when I saw how big it really was. More like an elk than a goat. The eyes wouldn't leave me. They were so steady. I hated myself for shooting it. I didn't want to kill it but I did. Musket insisted. That was when I heard the music."

"What music?" Mitterhal asked, intrigued by the tale.

Willis kept his gaze locked on the southwestern sky. "My father's pipes. They came from above, the very tip of the peak. I knew they were his. My brothers and I know every one of his tunes by heart. He used to play them for us after Mother told her stories from the Old Tome. I wanted so badly to join him, but I was too weak. I prayed to God for the strength to climb farther. The music stopped shortly after that.

"He came to me just as the sun fell beyond the ridge. It was so good to see him again. I asked about the battle and he told me not to worry. 'Your strength comes first, my boy,' he said. We gathered some scrub and made a fire. Then had our fill of goat. We recapped all my mother's tales from the book. She loves telling stories, you know. I think you would like them. Then we ran through all the crazy pranks my brothers and I would play on each other while we worked the fields in Tufthaven. We laughed a lot about that. Not once the whole night did he mention the war. Then at dawn he told me to go back to the pass where my brothers would be waiting for me. He said he still had to man his post on the ridge.

"I didn't leave at first. I couldn't. I stayed for three more nights listening to his pipes on the peak. A storm came on the morning of the fourth day, so I buried what was left of the goat and made for the pass."

A sorrowful look came over Willis. "I haven't seen him since. Every time I think of going back to the ridge, my brothers send me on another mission to gather tidings in the Haven. One of these days I hope to make the climb again. I wonder if it will ever happen."

The colonel leaned down to pick up his honey pail. "Your father sounds like a good man, as do your brothers. Strong souls, if you believe in that sort of thing. I'm sure they give whatever army they serve a distinct advantage. If you're anything like them, I suspect you'll have your wish. Until then, you best lighten up. Here, try a bit of this." He reached into the bucket and tossed a fragment of honeycomb across the smoke pit.

Willis caught the perfect pitch. He then looked to the colonel, appearing suddenly aghast at what he saw. He raised his hand and pointed the sticky treat over the fire.

"Easy, soldier," Mitterhal said. "It's just a bit of mountain candy to cheer you up. Nothing to get rapt over."

Seeing no change in expression, Mitterhal looked over his shoulder to see what the dumbstruck lad might be pointing at. There atop the wall, like a sentient statue only three paces away, stood the herd's lead buck. Its long white beard and thick curved horns flickered in the firelight.

"Well, I'll be a nanny's nipple," the colonel said. "If it isn't Old Smoker himself stopping by to pay a visit." He looked back to Willis, who remained frozen in awe. "What's the matter, lad? You look like you've seen a ghost. I assure you this old fellow is as real as they get. He's all goat you might say. Little Three Legs must have told him about our picnic."

Mitterhal took three steps toward the wall and tapped on the tin rim of the honey pail with his pipe.

The brawny beast descended the wall with the ease of a mountain cat. Even with hooves on the ground, its omniscient eyes came shoulder-high to the colonel. Mitterhal set the bucket on top of a nearby boulder and restocked his pipe. The goat quickly made for the sweets.

"Easy there, big fellow," he said, blocking the way with a sidestep. "We aren't finished with introductions yet."

At last, Willis composed himself enough to speak. The musket hung limp in his arms, muzzle down. "That's a big goat, sir."

Mitterhal placed a firm hand on the snout of the imposing beast. "Very astute, lad. But he's not just big. He's sure-footed and intuitive as well. A good leader, for sure. You won't find a billybuck like this on that Schnites farm in Wulfhaven. No, my friend, this brute is a descendant of an old mountain variety. Wild at heart, far too self-assured to become domesticated." He reached into his pocket for the flint box and lit his pipe. The smoke wafted beyond the hives and into oblivion. "But as you will see, even Old Smoker has his vice. Watch this," he said with a sly wink. "It's one of my favorite tricks." Mitterhal removed a honeycomb from the bucket and smeared it on the stem of his pipe.

The action perked the ears of the beast. Right away, its long probing tongue lapped furiously at the pipe. Every eager slurp drew the smoke inward through its mouth until white wisps puffed out of its flaring nostrils. "There you have it, lad. And that's why we call him Old Smoker. What do you think?"

Willis rubbed his eyes. "I've never seen anything like it. Wait till my brothers hear about this."

The colonel chuckled and replenished his pipe with more honey. "If your brothers like this, they'll really get a rise out of how I convince the nannies to give up their milk." The old billy nudged the colonel with one curved horn in an attempt to attain more of the sweetened treasure. "Now, don't get greedy, you old rebel," he said with a firm swat on the flank. "I thought I taught you good manners."

The loud slap snapped Willis out of his spell and sent him reeling into a fit of laughter. Even the colonel chimed in with a hardy hoot of his own. Echoes of their amusement carried over the pasture and lightened the night.

All the while, the long white beard of Old Smoker swayed back and forth like a wind-blown kilt with every lap of wild mountain honey. The three of them carried on as such until dawn, laughing, lapping, and swapping stories around the light of the fire. The colonel, the soldier, and the smoking goat.

16
Smokeless House

The Old Mitt's stock house loomed up slope from the manor, nestled in a stand of gnarly oaks at the base of his north pasture. By all accounts it was a barn, however the chimney had suggested that the colonel not call it that, especially when in earshot of the beechwood—which for all practical purposes meant always. In actuality, the barn did house a wide variety of stock: primarily firewood, hay, and honey. The crates and barrels of munitions that were too heavy to move, Mitterhal simply covered with burlap and imagined away.

The front entry consisted of two hefty oak doors set on metal tracks that could be rolled aside with a hearty effort. Silver chimes dangled just inside the entry so that they could twinkle in harmony when the doors were opened and the wind blew. Mitterhal had discovered the collection of chimes tucked away in a cedar chest in one of the guest rooms of the manor when he first returned from the war. What possessed him that following spring to hang the melodic ornaments in the stock house remained a mystery, like so many anomalies from those early days. The wild goats loved the chimes; or rather, the treats that came with them. For it did not take long for the wily breed to figure out that twinkling chimes meant open doors, and open doors meant honey.

"Wake up, Colonel. The horselads are back."

Mitterhal opened his eyes. Sure enough, the chimney was right. Two horsemen flanked a cart while a third lad rode on the bench and steered the mule. Already they were cutting across the south pasture from the carriage road. The draught mule, an impressive beast, toted a load of hay five bales high. The lads were right on schedule. A week had passed since they had delivered the wood. Mitterhal watched them pass through the breach in the wall by the hives and make for the stock house.

"Are you awake yet, Colonel?"

"I am."

"Why do you think the horselads bring the wood and hay to the smokeless house?"

"They're good boys, that's why."

"I agree, but I cannot help but notice that one of them has red hair."

"Yes. And your point?"

"Oh, none, really. Only that the one who almost hit you with the snowball also had red hair."

"That was ages ago, Chim. Let it rest."

"I suppose you are right. Do you ever get lonely, Colonel?"

"What kind of a question is that? How could I possibly get lonely with you babbling on all day?"

"I guess what I mean to ask is, do you ever wish we had more visitors?"

"I need visitors like you need a brick massage! Now get a hold of yourself. You're being extra drippy today. It's giving me a headache."

Mitterhal gulped down a heap of honey, then placed the jar back on the crate next to the weighted stalks of gahenya by his pipe and flint box. He pressed on his temples to help the sweet medicine do its work. In time he heard the chimes in the stock house twinkle in the wind. Amazing how far the sound carried. The goats heard them too. The herd funneled out of the knolls in three single-file lines, on course for the beehives. Mitterhal extended his scope to the line nearest the base of the knolls, the pain in his head already waning.

"Well, won't you look at that, Chim. Little Three Legs is leading one of the lines. Old Smoker must have upped his rank."

"The crippled yearling is not so little anymore, is it, Colonel?"

"You're right about that, and not so crippled either. All those days chasing rabbits have finally paid off for the little bugger. Who knows? He might even have a go at the rut this year. Wouldn't that be something?"

The goats advanced beyond the knolls and the upper south field to where the stone wall crested over an easy fold in the land and a stream swelled into a shallow basin. All the while, Mitterhal tracked the march with his scope. The three lines converged into one at the swell and continued downward along the wall, led by Old Smoker. The herd stopped just prior to the beehives at the base of the north pasture, horns up in the direction of the stock house.

"They seem to like the music," said the chimney.

"That they do, Chim, but it's not the chimes they're after. It's the honey that gets their horns up. The lads better put a little pepper into their work or they're going to have a house full of scavengers to deal with."

The emptied hay cart rolled into view shortly thereafter. Both horsemen eyed the herd as they rode away. One of them, the one with the red hair, rode bareback and kept a bow at the ready as if expecting a charge. They passed the wall and entered the south field as the goats cleared the breach and ambled down to the stock house.

Mitterhal watched the cart descend the pasture, far from the matted tracks that marked its original ascent. Curious. The lads had never gone that way before. Why so close to the manor? They stopped at a cluster of boulders in the field. Mitterhal honed in with his scope. The elder of the two horsemen appeared to be scolding the red-haired one, while the driver of the cart watched on, shaking his head.

"Hmm. A little scuffle in the ranks it appears."

The red haired horseman suddenly bolted away from the others. To Mitterhal's utter shock, the lad charged straight for the manor.

"Oh, how exciting," the chimney said. "I think we may have a visitor."

"Quiet, Chimney. I don't want to hear a word from you. Do you understand?"

"I do, Colonel. Is everything okay?"

"Quiet!"

Mitterhal got up from the bucket and tucked away his scope. He considered lighting a smoke, but then thought better of it. Striding to the edge of the platform, he crossed his arms and monitored the lad's advance.

It was a fast horse, unimpeded by saddle. The lad leaned forward, as if part of the beast, his long hair flapping like a mane over his quiver of arrows. He charged the courtyard wall and cleared it in one bound, holding tight to the horse's neck on impact. Over the wall, he cantered around the hedge of laurels and stopped at the front of the manor, directly in line with the colonel's platform. There he remained without a word, rewarding his mount with an easy pat to the neck.

"Shouldn't you say something?" the chimney asked.

Mitterhal spun around. "I'm getting to it. I thought I told you to stay quiet." Another quick spin and he addressed the lad. "That's a fine steed you ride."

"It's a highland breed," the lad said, looking up steadily at Mitterhal.

Already the colonel liked him. "What is your name?"

"Donavon."

"You ride well, Donavon."

Long they stood in silence, sizing each other up. Eventually the older horseman rounded the manor from behind, having taken the breach in the wall farther up the hill. Meanwhile, the mule snorted as it stopped at the far side of the courtyard wall. The driver dismounted the cart and climbed over the wall, a satchel strapped to his shoulder.

The older lad reined his horse in front of Donavon. "When I say wait, I mean wait. Know your place, little brother!" He yanked his mount around and saluted the rooftop. "Hail, Gahenya, sir," he shouted, his right fist pressed to his heart. "I am Adman McFadden. We have been ordered by the mayor of Wulfhaven to deliver a gift from across the Haven. Gwyntahpynn Choroqua sends it with utmost regards. He says it was the wedding gift given to Hayalgaila, high priestess of Gwyntahlynn, wife of the Lord Baron Augustus Mitterhal and mother of the Mahocpynn."

Mitterhal's gaze locked on the lad's horse. McFadden? Why was that name so familiar? The horse shifted uneasily: ears forward, head high above the withers, tail twitching. "Breathe, lad," the colonel commanded.

The proud rider balked at the order. "Your pardon, sir. What did you say?"

"I said, breathe! That's a highland mount you ride, not a common ass. It is bred to mirror its rider. You've got it all bound up. You need to relax, take a deep breath."

Donavon brought his horse shoulder to shoulder with Adman's, smiling defiantly. He then hailed the third lad who lumbered on foot across the courtyard with the satchel. "Hurry up, Francis. The Old Mitt's giving our big brother a ridin' lesson. You can't miss this."

"Shut up, Donny," Adman said. "I'll drop you right here if I have to."

Francis hustled to stand next to his brothers and saluted the rooftop. "Hail, Gahenya, sir," he said, breathing heavy from the haul.

The chimney was next to speak, much to Mitterhal's irritation. "I'm so excited, Colonel. We have not had a visitor since the man in the black robe walked through the butterflies. Let's invite the horselads up for a picnic."

"That's enough out of you," the colonel said. "This is no time for a picnic."

All three brothers snapped to order, peering up at the platform in perfect silence. Mitterhal eyed them fiercely, still annoyed at the chimney's outburst. An owl hooted in the beechwood, breaking the silence. How unusual, Mitterhal thought, for the nocturnal bird to be so mouthy at this time of day. The commotion must have jarred it out of a nap. The sooner they were done with this nonsense, the better.

"Leave the gift on the stoop," he ordered. "I will get it later."

The lad with the satchel, Francis his name, stepped forward and bowed respectfully. "I am afraid we cannot do that, sir. By order of the mayor we are not to leave the premises until we know the gift is in your hands."

"Well, I'm not coming down to get it, if that is what you're suggesting."

"Not at all, sir," Adman said, pressing forward on his mount. "I will bring it up to you at once."

"You will do no such thing! I give the orders here."

Again the owl hooted, dispelling yet another standstill. Mitterhal scanned the beechwood's branches, but saw nothing.

"Colonel," the chimney whispered, "the red-haired horselad seems strong and fearless. Maybe he could put the honey in my mouth?"

Not a bad idea, thought Mitterhal. When else would such an opportunity arise? Decision made, he squared off to the boys. "Very well. The ladder is set behind the house. Send the bareback rider up with the gift."

Adman nodded to Francis and then glared at Donavon. "You better behave or you'll be mucking every stall in the village."

Francis handed his brother the satchel. "Here you go, Donny. Have at it, brother."

Mitterhal returned to his bucket while Donavon made his ascent. He wanted to be seated in case a dizzy spell struck. Eventually the lad's red hair flapped into view midway up the second ladder that hooked the ridge. At the hook Donavon stopped to tie back his hair and adjust the satchel on his shoulder. From there he walked the pointed ridge cap toward the platform. His movements were easy and fluid. Impressive.

The owl hooted cheerfully as Donavon stepped onto the planks. Mitterhal remained quiet, watching from his bucket.

"He's here," the chimney whispered.

"I can see that. I'm not blind, you fool."

Donavon eyed him guardedly. "Who's a fool?" he said, looking down at the gahenya stalks on the crate. "You're the one smoking poison on a rooftop." He tossed the leather satchel at the foot of the crate without the slightest pretense of ceremony. "There you have it, old man. Take your gift."

"I am sorry, Colonel," the chimney said. "I did not mean to make things awkward. It's just that—"

"It's too late for that, you twit. I told you to stay quiet."

Donavon shook his head and turned to leave.

"Wait!" Mitterhal shouted. "I have a task I must ask of you."

"My task is done," Donavon said. "I don't need to listen to this."

Mitterhal held out the honey jar, doing his best to keep it steady. "Take it, lad. Pour it in my chimney."

"What?"

"I said put the honey in the chimney."

"You know you're crazy, right?"

The owl hooted, not nearly as courteous as before. Donavon leered at the network of branches. "Not a chance, sister. I don't want any part of this. He's as cracked as they get."

An ear-piercing screech shot out of the leaves.

"What's going on up there?" Adman shouted from far below. "I told you to give him the satchel and get on your way."

"Shut your flapper, I'm busy!" Donavon shouted back. A wild look came over him, and he charged at the chimney. At the base he leaped straight up and managed to get a grip on the ornate brickwork near the top. He pressed himself up by the fingertips and hoisted a leg over the chimney's rim. Seconds later he was up and straddling the smoke chamber. "Give me the jar."

"Donny, you're a dead man," Adman warned.

A fire blazed in Donavon's eyes. "I said toss me the jar, you damn fool!"

Steady, Mitterhal stood up and lobbed the jar. Donavon snatched the precious treasure out of the air and raised it high to cast it down.

"Wait, lad," he commanded. "You must remove the lid first."

Donavon smacked the jar on the lip of the masonry as if cracking an egg, and flung the gooey shards down into the stack. He then jumped off the chimney, falling on the planks with an awkward twist. The impact rattled the platform. Getting up, he left a bloody handprint on the wood.

"You know everybody says you were a great man. All I see is a crazy fool. I can't believe my father followed you. No wonder he's dead." He scowled at the beechwood. "Are you happy now?"

"Who cooks for you?" the tree answered.

Red-faced, Donavon stormed off the platform and across the ridge with a noticeable gimp. Halfway down the ladder from the eave, he whistled. His horse dashed out of the courtyard and around the house.

Shortly thereafter, Mitterhal saw Donavon round the laurels at full gallop with Adman in hot pursuit. Again, Donavon cleared the wall in a single leap, leaving Adman behind as he spurred his horse toward the breach in the wall.

Francis, meanwhile, stood alone in the courtyard, shuffling his feet in awkward silence. Not until Donavon was halfway across the south pasture did he address the colonel. "Sorry about my brother, sir. He doesn't always mean what he says. Hail, Gahenya." He saluted and then ambled back across the courtyard and over the wall to the mule cart.

Long Mitterhal stewed in his thoughts, watching the mule cart wind down the carriage path to the village. Silent and still he remained, even after the plume of dust became but a puff. It was late afternoon before the chimney dared to speak.

"I must say, that was a wonderful picnic. It was so nice of the red-haired lad to give me the honey. I really liked it. It tasted just like you said it would. Maybe next time we could invite the others so we could all enjoy the sweetness together."

Mitterhal blew a smoke ring and watched it dissolve against the bricks. No sense killing the chimney's pleasure. "It has been an eventful day for sure, my friend." He tugged the brim of his goat-hyde hat over his eyes. "I feel a good nap is in order. I am glad you liked the honey."

"Colonel, before you nap, do you think we could see what is in the satchel?"

"It's just a gift, Chimney," he said, glancing at the leather bag. "A silly custom, nothing more."

"Yes, but I am afraid I will not be able to nap until I know what is inside."

"Since when do you sleep, Chim?"

"All things sleep, Colonel."

Odd comment, Mitterhal thought. "Very well." He reached for the bag. "For the sake of a good nap, let's have a look then."

Placing the satchel on his lap, he undid the buckles and lifted the flap. "Hmm … what do we have here?" He reached inside and removed a soft velvet sack. "It appears we have been given a bag within a bag. How pretty. Are you satisfied now, my friend?"

"Not quite, Colonel. What do you think could be in the second bag?"

"You don't miss a beat, do you? I suppose we should find that out too." Untying the drawstring, he reached inside and removed a smooth silver chain. At the end of the chain hung a pendant. The center stone, a deep blue sapphire the size of a musket shot, was set in delicate stalks of shimmering vines. Mitterhal gazed at the myriad of woodland etchings that adorned the pendant, spellbound by the sight.

"It is beautiful," the chimney said. "The stone is so blue, like the box you sang to on our first sunset."

"It is indeed." Mitterhal held the pendant higher for a closer look. "Made for a queen by the looks of it."

Back and forth the sapphire swung, drawing him deeper into the ripples of light that danced within its facets. The light stirred him into song as he began to hum the familiar melody from his music box.

Celebration, song and dance
See the wagon's ponies prance
Beneath my tapestry receive
Your mother's blessing.

"Colonel, the horselad said this was a wedding gift given to the Mahocpynn's mother. I wonder who the Mahocpynn is."

Mitterhal lowered the pendant and peered across the Haven to where the sheer mountain cliffs cascaded into the harbor. He spoke in barely a whisper, as if to mimic the wind. "I believe he was a music chief."

"Oh, what a perfect gift. I like music."

"So do I, Chimney. So do I."

17
The Chimney's Gift

Uryan McFadden was a Lakwynnian lieutenant who had lost his left leg from the knee down early in the war. A formidable warrior on a horse, he was the beating heart of Mitterhal's cavalry—an officer who instilled courage in the troops by the raw example of his injury. The colonel had been fond of him. When the battle at Spaulding Pass was over and McFadden had yet to return, Mitterhal set out into the smoldering field of gahenya without escort to find him. The toxic fumes of the tar-soaked bales had nearly claimed the wounded horseman's life by the time he found him, next to his fallen steed, still clutching his bloodstained saber. In his last gasping breath, McFadden asked the colonel to take care of his family. Cornelius Mitterhal gave him his word that this would be so.

"Did we do it, Colonel? Is the bear down?"

"It is down, Lieutenant. The hive is safe."

"... Look at her, sir. So beautiful, so silver."

"Who do you speak of, my friend?"

"Behind you in the smoke. Her white sails ... The men are boarding her. Do you see?"

"I do. It is your time, Uryan. The Silver Girl has come. The war has finally claimed your last talon."

"Colonel, my family ... My children ..."

"They will be fine. You have my word on that. Sail to the Haven's coast with your

brothers and be at peace. Your service in this world is over. Hail, Gahenya, Meguntoc."
   "Hail, Gahenya, Mahocpynn."

Mitterhal awoke from his afternoon nap with a violent jerk. He immediately reached for the handkerchief neatly folded in his upper vest pocket. Another war dream had invaded his peace. He sat in the cool shade of the chimney's shadow without saying a word, patting dry the beads of sweat that had pooled on his forehead.

"Colonel?"

"Yes, Chimney?"

"Where do you go when you close your eyes?"

"Nowhere. I sleep."

"You have a lot to say when you sleep."

Mitterhal stretched his arms and legs to relieve the lingering spasms in his twitching nerves. "Meaningless babble, I am sure. They are only dreams, a place for the mind to rest. Pay no attention to them."

"I do not think I would get much rest in that place. It does not seem friendly there."

"I told you to ignore the nonsense, Chimney. That is an order."

"As you wish, Colonel. If it interests you, I have something that may cheer you up."

"And what is that?"

"I cannot tell you. It is a gift. I am sworn to secrecy."

"Really? Another gift. How intriguing. Tell me, my good friend, how will your gift cheer me up if I do not know what it is? Will you at least tell me if I guess?"

The chimney hesitated. "I suppose I could do that."

"Good, how many hints do I get?"

"Hints?"

"Yes, hints, clues," said the colonel, sly. "You cannot play a guessing game without clues. What fun would that be?"

The chimney hesitated again, this time longer. "Very well, I will give you three hints, but you must ask the questions first."

Mitterhal squinted as he set the flint to his pipe. "Fair enough. We can start by assuming that this gift came from the sky—you being a chimney."

"Yes, it did. It is very light and floats on the wind."

"Perfect, then for my first hint I will ask, when exactly did you find it?"

"That would be your second hint."

The colonel cocked his head and mocked a puzzled look. "But I have only asked one question. How can that be my second hint? You must follow the rules, Chim."

Mitterhal watched the smoke rise over the rooftop, pleased that he had outwitted his friend so early in the contest. A period of silence elapsed before the chimney responded.

"Very well, Colonel. To answer your first question, I did not find the gift."

"What do you mean you did not find the gift? How can you have it if you didn't find it?"

"It was given to me by the one who did find it."

Mitterhal shot a glance at the old beechwood. A bird had chirped, diverting his attention. "Chimney, you and I are the only ones up here," he said, keeping one ear to the tree. "Unless you heaved your masonry off the footings of this house and floated off the rooftop, I do not see how such a meeting could occur. Explain yourself."

"Certainly, Colonel. The gift was given to me when your eyes were closed. I believe that answers your first question as well as the second regarding how the gift could be in my possession if I did not find it myself. I can also tell you who gave it to me, but I am afraid that would be your third hint. Perhaps it would be more effective to use your final question on the qualities of the gift itself. I wish I could be more helpful but as you say, I must follow the rules."

The lupine leaf burned hot in the colonel's pipe as he realized that he had been outsmarted by a stack of bricks. Something drew his attention back to the branches of the beechwood. Another bird chirp, though not quite. More like a squeaky giggle. He scanned the network of branches in a futile attempt to spot the source of the elusive chirp, all the while seething at being bested at his own game.

"Have you thought of your third question?" the chimney asked.

"No, Chimney, nor do I intend to. Why not just tell me so we can be done with this silly game?"

"I would, Colonel, but I cannot tell you until you are ready. I made a promise."

"Ready? Ready for what? And to whom did you make such a ridiculous promise?"

"I am sorry, but those are two questions and you have only one left. Which would you like me to answer?"

The pipe fumed; Mitterhal's patience teetered on the verge. "Now listen here, Chimney. I'm getting tired of your niggling. If you are trying to cheer me up you're doing a horrible job of it. I suggest you start producing some answers. Otherwise you can go back to blowing smoke."

A daunting silence followed as the colonel stood on the edge of his platform, toggling his attention between the chimney and the tree.

"Under the circumstances," the chimney said, "I suppose we could bend the rules. If you must know, my promise went to the whispering tree. She told me that it was important not to give you the gift until your war wound was healed."

The colonel slumped. "Ah yes, the talking leaves. Of course. I should have known. Well, at least we now know that your twiggy friend is a she. Though I wonder how a tree comes to know of war wounds, or even war for that matter."

"She does not just whisper. Sometimes she sings. But only when your eyes are closed."

Mitterhal blew a single smoke ring. "I see. How convenient."

Deep down he knew the chimney meant well, despite its delusional state, and should not be held entirely accountable for its behavior. It was, after all, just a chimney. He decided not to press the issue. Rather, he spent the remainder of the afternoon blowing smoke rings in thoughtful silence.

By early evening Mitterhal decided to leave the rooftop. He was feeling a bit melancholy and wanted to harvest a new batch of honey from his hives before dark. The chimney had been uncommonly quiet throughout the afternoon. The colonel got up, careful not to wake his snoozing comrade.

"Colonel?"

Mitterhal grimaced. "What is it, Chim?"

"You are leaving before the sun sets. That is not like you. I've been thinking about your war wound. Perhaps if you told me more about how you received it, we could come up with a remedy. Then I could give you your gift and we would not have to play the guessing game."

"No, Chimney, I've had enough. The game is over. You ask too high a price."

"But, Colonel, the whispering leaves—"

"There are no whispering leaves!" he cried, reaching for his flint. His voice carried off the rooftop and raised the horns of every goat in his pasture. "We've been through this before. You are delusional, Chim. Keep your gift."

"But she said that you knew her father. She wants you to have the gift in return for keeping your promise to him."

Mitterhal turned away to light his pipe. A tremor traveled down his arm to his shaking hand, causing him to lose his grip on the flint. Honey, fresh honey. That's what he needed. The firebox bounced once on the platform, and then wedged between a gap in the weathered planks. He knelt down to pry it out and heard a squall pick up in the south pasture. Peering out across the lupine, he spotted the three-legged billy staring at him from atop a grassy knoll. Its curved horns reflected red in the evening light.

The colonel's gaze continued downslope to the village, taking him back to the day when the yellow wagon rolled into his yard. It all came back to him in that moment: the celebration, song and dance, the captain's war medals, the goat-hyde pipes, and yes—of course, he remembered now— the little girl by the fieldstone wall who whispered to the wildflowers. And her giggles, he remembered them too. So pure and innocent.

"Colonel, do you remember the whispering girl who brought you the pastry that day when the people came to honor the other colonel?"

He looked again at the billy on the knoll. "I do, Chim. She was a feisty lass, as I recall. I liked her spirit."

"She told me a secret that day."

"And what was that?"

"She said her name was Enyalda McFadden and that she could speak with trees."

The leaves rustled in the old beechwood. Mitterhal turned to inspect the tree, and a nervous giggle came from somewhere in the canopy. Taking three steps to the rear of the platform, he studied the tree at length. His gaze locked onto the enormous branch that hovered low over the back eave of his house. The sudden urge to appear presentable came over him. He fastened the silver buttons on his vest—the effort helped steady his hands. After securing the top-most buttons, he turned his back on the ancient limb and noted the perfectly straight line of smoke that streamed out of the chimney. It was not the mountain breeze, he concluded, that rustled the leaves. Like a statue he stood, hands clasped behind his back, staring into the plume, cautiously aware.

"Colonel, are you still there?"

It was getting dark. A faint glow of crimson hung over the Haven. Mitterhal started to light his pipe, then realized his flint was still wedged between the planks of the platform. The cold pipe dangled in his mouth like a dormant twig. In that rare smokeless moment, the question struck, a question so basic, he had never thought to consider until now. Who had kept the fires stoked all these years?

A pitter-patter sounded far below, near the gnarled trunk of the beechwood. The scampering of a woodland creature. Or was it footsteps? He decided not to look, to simply let the mystery be. It was much better that way. He stepped off his platform and onto the roof ridge.

"I am tired, Chimney. I think it is time to call it a day."

"But, Colonel, what about your gift?"

"Keep it. It is too late for presents now."

"As you wish. I will keep it safe until you are ready. Good night, Colonel."

Mitterhal shuffled across the ridge and down the roof toward the eave, using what little light remained of the day.

18
Rankwall's Rabbit

There are those who believe that war is no place for mercy. That victory is the only standard by which success can be measured. That in the final analysis, the victory justifies whatever means were used to achieve it. In no other man was this philosophy more embodied than the notorious commander in chief of the Lakwynnian army, General Thurman Rankwall.

A strategist through and through, he approached war as if it were a game; a series of contests and maneuvers in which men were positioned like pieces on a chessboard to execute his designs and be sacrificed when necessary. Cold, calculating, and efficient, he possessed the uncanny ability to detach himself from sentiment of any kind, thus sparing his decisions of softhearted concerns. For Rankwall, to fight with honor was academic, tolerated only if success was not jeopardized; whereas to fight with compassion was never an issue, for he never held the capacity to comprehend it.

"Smells like compost," the colonel said after a taxing climb up the ladder. Old age was having its way with him and a good smoke was in order. He took a deep breath of the autumn air that filtered through the branches of the beechwood. An organic aroma hung over the land.

"I agree," said the chimney. "The pasture is exceptionally fragrant this morning."

Mitterhal took stock of his surroundings while he packed and lit his pipe: the mountain goats remained huddled in the cedar grove that bordered the meadow; field swallows swept low in the lupine, dipping now and then for their breakfast; the catkins on the branches of the beechwood dangled with a slight lean to the east.

"A storm is coming, Chimney. It won't be long now."

"Are you sure? There is not a cloud in the sky."

Mitterhal examined the end of his pipe. The smoke rolled over the rim of the bowl and down its sides like steam on a kettle pot. "Read the wind, Chim. You can smell it on the breath of trees."

"But, Colonel, trees do not have mouths."

"All life breathes, Chimney, regardless of the method. Even you need air to make your smoke."

"Are you suggesting I am alive?"

"Well, you are certainly not dead, I'll give you that."

"I did not realize there was a difference."

The colonel scanned the bone-dry bricks down to the flashing embedded in the masonry. Not a drop of morning dew had condensed on the lead, further validating his prediction of rain. He looked to the clear blue sky with growing concern. "Alive or not, you've got plenty of spirit." He sighed long and deep while the smoke did its work. The aches and pains of a hard life were catching up fast, and he knew his days of climbing the ladder were ending. So much of reality could be controlled by the mind, but old age was not one of them. The chimney had been his steadfast companion through it all, a true friend in every sense of the word. Soon even that would end. How could he possibly break the news?

"Colonel?"

"Yes, Chim?"

"I am scared."

"What on earth are you scared of?"

"I am afraid of the storm."

"You are a chimney, Chim. Solid as stone. There is nothing this storm can do to harm you. The wind is our friend. Remember? No matter how harsh it gets."

"I know that, Colonel, but you are not made of bricks and mortar like me. What will happen if the wind blows you away to the rabbit's peace?"

"Then I will use the wind to talk to you. That was our deal. Right? Rest easy, my friend. All is good."

"Colonel?"

"Yes, Chim?"

"How do you know so much about the wind?"

"What do you mean?"

"You read it and listen to it. Sometimes you even sing with it. Where did you learn to do all that?"

Another deep inhale and the twitching began. It started at his brow and moved down his face to his neck, past the shoulders to his fingers. The jar of honey slipped out of his hand and shattered on the planks. "No place in particular, Chim," he said, ignoring the disaster at his feet. "Just a lifetime of paying attention, I suppose. Kind of like you and your rabbits. The more you watch, the more you know. Think of all the things they've taught you."

"I don't think they taught me anything. I just like to watch them."

Mitterhal stepped away from the sticky shards. "That in itself is a lesson. The fact that you invested so much time watching the little buggers should tell you something about yourself. Think about it. Why would a chimney care about a rabbit?"

"I just like them."

"Of course you do, that much is obvious. But there has to be a reason why you like them so much."

"There does? What is it?"

More twitching. "I don't know, Chim, I'm not the chimney. You are. What do you think?"

"Well, I like the way they move."

"Okay, that makes sense, you being unable to. But a lot of things move. What makes rabbits so special?"

"They move fast."

"Ah, now we are getting somewhere. So, you like rabbits because they move fast. And when do they move fast?"

"When they run."

"Yes, yes, and when do they run?"

"When they are being chased."

"Exactly!"

"Exactly?"

"Yes, Chim, exactly."

"What do you mean by that, Colonel?"

"Exactly that. The rest is up to you. I'm not going to do all the thinking for you."

"That is fair enough. Thank you, Colonel. I think I will think about it."

Mitterhal stepped over the glass at his feet and returned to his bucket. He took out his handkerchief to wipe the spittle that had frothed around the edges of his mouth, and then pressed the damp cloth to his temple. Already the pain in his forehead throbbed and it was only morning. Of all days to drop the honey. He closed his eyes to help center his thoughts. Time was running out. The rabbit's peace he had promised his friend, and the rabbit's peace he must deliver, though he still had no idea how. What he did know was that he would not leave the rooftop until he figured it out. On that thought, he nodded off into a daydream even as a tiny dust plume crept up the carriage path from the village.

"So that is your plan, General. To drop the hammer at Spaulding Pass. And what could we offer our enemy that would entice them into this trap? The bear has become fat and predictable, but not stupid."

"You, Colonel. You will be the bleeding rabbit. You have been a thorn in their side ever since we took control of the lake. The loss of the Lyssia to the Guard was a terrible blow to the Toriceans and they will be eager to make an example of you by asserting their authority on the Three Havens. We must use this to our advantage. When they hear your pipes challenge them to open battle, they will jump at the opportunity to crush you and your Haven Guard once and for all. What they will not know is that six of my regiments from Meridia will be right behind you, ready to engage. And once you lure them into the pass, they will not be able to outflank us no matter how many cannons they bring. We will have the high-ground advantage."

"Your plan is ambitious, General. One that could succeed if all things fall into place. However, if the timing is off, then it could very well be our own trap that we are setting. High-ground advantage or not, my men will not last long against Toric artillery in the open field. If you are delayed for any reason, it will be a dead rabbit that awaits you at the pass."

"All you must do is draw them in and my forces will do the rest. We will sweep them like a storm. I will be there myself to command the assault. I assure you, the glory will be ours."

"Wake up, Colonel. There is a wagon on the way."

Mitterhal opened his eyes, the pain in his head pronounced. His chin was drenched in saliva. "What did you say, Chim?"

"A wagon has left the village and rides the carriage path to the manor."

He shook his head and peered down slope, spyglass extended. It was indeed a wagon, a rickety old black thing drawn by the village draught mule. Only it was not the lads who rode it. Grim were the two hooded figures that sat on the bench. The one on the left who held the reins was enormous and dwarfed the other. The chassis listed unnaturally to the left as it ambled up the farthest corner of the south field.

"What do you see in your glass, Colonel?"

"Hard to say just yet. We will find out soon enough."

"Colonel, I thought more about the rabbits while you were sleeping. I like the way their ears go up just before they run."

A twitch, a little different from the others. "Yes, they are certainly wary little creatures. They don't miss much. Unless of course it comes from the sky."

"If what comes from the sky?"

More twitching. "The attack, Chim."

99

"Oh, you mean like the lakehawk?"

Ringing in the ears. "Yes, something like that."

"Are you okay, Colonel?"

"I am fine, Chim."

"Colonel?"

"What?"

"I would like to give you your gift now."

He wiped the froth off his chin. "Very well, where is it?"

"It is tucked in the lead flashing below my east face."

"Hmm. I thought I looked there after our little game the other day. Let's have a peek then, shall we?"

Warily he peered around the backside of the chimney where the platform terminated, studying the flaps of lead flashing that folded over the bricks and onto the roof slate. Sure enough, something thin and white protruded out of a void where two flaps overlapped. With a bit of effort he leaned over the edge of the platform and pried up the lead. It was a feather—big as the blade of a bayonet, wide bands of white on black. Or was it black on white?

"Well, won't you look at that. A lakehawk feather. How divine. You are right, Chimney, it is very light indeed."

"Do you like your gift, Colonel?"

"I do, very much. You have outdone yourself, Chim. I am sorry to say I have nothing to give you."

"But you already have."

"What are you talking about?"

"You gave me the purpose in my puff and showed me sweetness."

Silence. Mitterhal stayed on his knees, studying the plume. So sleek and elegant, yet dreadful—the bearer of a deadly tool. He pondered the stark bands of white and black. Where was the gray? How could something so light carry such weight? Questions—they kept coming. How did it get here? Who was the giver?

"Colonel?"

"Yes, Chim?"

"I have to go now. *Su gahwynn.*"

"Chimney, where are y—"

"Hail, Gahenya, Colonel!" The voice boomed from below. "Might we have a word with you, sir?"

Mitterhal opened his eyes, his bearings shot. He was still kneeling by the chimney with the feather in hand. The wagon—that's right. How did it get here so fast? The chimney's shadow had shifted. Another lapse, apparently. Losing grip, time fading. Not yet! Must compose. Wipe foam, a terrible headache, no honey.

Before getting up, he took off his goat-hyde hat and inserted the feather into the braided band above the rim. The action settled his nerves. He cleaned his face as best he could with his handkerchief and wiped the sweat off his forehead. Then, standing up, he put on his hat and strode to the front edge of the platform, arms crossed over his chest.

The draught mule chewed on the grass in his courtyard, still hitched to the rickety cart. The hooded man on the right stood before the cart bench, a wooden voice horn in hand, while the massive one remained seated. A long braided beard extended down to his chest. Even seated he was nearly as tall as the other man.

"Forgive the intrusion, Colonel," said the man with the voice horn. "A pressing matter requires your council."

Mitterhal swayed on the edge. "Put that silly thing away. I can hear you fine. And with whom am I to have this council?"

The man handed his voice horn to the big fellow and lowered his hood. "Marlin Barleycopp, sir, Mayor of Wulfhaven. I was hoping we might discuss an issue of political importance."

The name resonated. He needed a smoke, time to scroll through his thoughts. After a long draw on the pipe, it came to him: the celebration, the parade, the yellow wagon that rode up the mountain from Wulfhaven.

"Yes, I remember you now. The peacock with the war medals. You went by a different title back then, as I recall." Mitterhal gestured to the ramshackle pony cart. "I would expect a man of your status to travel by finer means."

"It is a cover, sir, a necessary precaution." Barleycopp glanced at his hooded cohort. "This is not a meeting we wish to advertise."

"I see," said the colonel, wary. "And who is the hidden giant who drives your secret chariot?"

Barleycopp nodded. The behemoth rose. The cart creaked under the shift in weight. His hands, the size of the draught mule's hooves, drew back the hood and revealed a face ravaged with scars. His deep voice resonated as if rising from a bottomless chasm. "Jeziah McCaskel, sir. Chief cipher-at-arms of the Haven Guard."

The contraction hit hard and fast, without warning. Mitterhal pressed his shaking fingers to his temple and shut his right eye. "What makes you think I have any interest in politics?" he asked, focusing on the mayor with his left.

Barleycopp gazed across the south pasture, where a few stray swallows still swooped low over the gahenya. After the lengthy pause he returned his attention to the rooftop. "It's General Rankwall, sir. He is chancellor of the province now and aims to rebuild the bridge over the Haven. The Gwyntahmahoma will not tolerate another breach of trust."

Mitterhal reached for his handkerchief with his free hand, keeping the pressure on his temple with the other. "Why do you bother me with this nonsense?" he asked, swabbing the drool off his chin. "It means nothing to me. If this is what you have come to discuss, then save your breath and get on your way."

Again the mayor fixed his gaze on the swallows. He seemed torn over what to do. At last, he clasped both hands behind his back and spoke. "I understand, Colonel. My apologies for disturbing you. We will not bother you again. Stay dry, sir. The field swallows are feeding low today."

Barleycopp nodded to the chief cipher, who returned to his seated position and snapped the reins. The riggings in the mule harness tightened and the wagon rolled.

"Wait!" the colonel shouted.

The wheels stopped at the far end of the courtyard.

"How do you know about the swallows?"

The mayor got off the wagon and strode back to the hedge of laurels, where he had addressed the colonel from the podium nearly eight years prior. "I was not always a politician, sir. It is one of many tricks I learned from a great warrior who could read the wind."

Mitterhal swayed on the edge of his platform, fighting off the tremors. The contractions made him nauseous. "Tell me, Captain. Why was the bridge destroyed in the first place?"

"We did it, sir."

"Who is we?" Head pounding. Mouth foaming.

"The Haven Guard, sir."

"And on whose … order did this Haven … Guard act?"

Barleycopp froze, staring dumbstruck at the rooftop.

"I said, on whose order, Captain?"

No reply.

"Answer the question, Captain. That is an order!"

A low drone sounded from the far end of the courtyard. Jeziah McCaskel stood up in the wagon like a dark stone giant out of an ancient myth. His hum dropped in timbre to the depths of the earth.

"Do not do it, Jeziah," Barleycopp commanded. "He has the sickness. You will send him into seizure. Hold your chant. That is an order!"

Too late, order denied, the chief cipher-at-arms of the Haven Guard raised his mighty arms and delivered his message.

Osprey strikes down with its talons from heaven
The fountain will flow from the heart of our Haven
High on the ridge mountain goats stand awaiting
Out of the herd spirits ride concentrating
On the song, the song above us

The rabbit will run under shade of the raven

Bound by the wind to the coast of our Haven
The pipers will play from their heights in the heavens
Guarded they are by the wolves and their brethren
Hail! He booms above us!
Hail! She sings among us!

Mitterhal's tremors escalated into sharp spasms. He felt a tooth crack as he clamped down hard on the stem of his pipe. His jaw snapped open at the sting and his pipe fell to the slate. It wobbled down the roof like a wounded rabbit, over the eave and out of sight in the shrubberies below. To the south and west he saw the first wave of storm clouds looming over the distant broads. A voice whispered in the tree. "Chimney not to worry is to where your peace it went."

He spun around, teetering on the edge. "Who said that? Show yourself!"

More tremors; vision closing like tunnel.

"I said, who said that!"

There, in the leaves. Crouched on the big branch like a squirrel: young face, wide eyes, hair as red as burning bush. Where is handkerchief? Must clean face. Tunnel spinning, bucket bouncing, body fighting … falling … floating.

Run rabbit run! Deep into the raven's shadow. The yellow eyes of the wulf's weed are on you. Trust them. They will see you through the smoke. Listen to the music and surrender your cares to the lakehawk's talons. Feel the wind under its tail carry you away, over cedars, pines, and firs to pastures where the yellow-winged wagon rides on seeds of air. Fly now, my brave friend, to the peace you deserve. Your service in this world is over.

19
Song and Dance

By the war's end, Cornelius Mitterhal had lost all interest in the affairs of society. Too many good men had died under his command. Before surrendering to the wulfweed, however, he secured an arrangement with Captain Marlin Barleycopp that funneled all compensation for his war service to a fund that would aid the families of the fallen. Mitterhal also gave Barleycopp explicit instructions to spare no expense at meeting the needs of Lieutenant Uryan McFadden's children. Many of the priceless assets buried in the vault below the colonel's chimney were included in the endowment, which Barleycopp served as sole trustee.

As such the children of the late war hero were closely monitored by Barleycopp, albeit discreetly, and when the time came for the orphaned family to leave Wulfhaven, he was quick to act on the colonel's behalf and establish a home for them on a parcel of land that bordered the highland village of Cotton Crown. Mitterhal, by that stage, had succumbed utterly to the mountain flower and knew nothing of the arrangement, though at times he did lend half an ear to the songs and whispers that trickled out of his beechwood.

When Cornelius Mitterhal opened his eyes he knew something had changed. No sky, for one thing. He sat upright in his leather chair in front of a crackling fire. At last count he'd been on the rooftop; now he was in the hearth room. How did he get there?

On the mantel he saw his broken pipe, propped on the flint box next to his goat-hyde hat, the lakehawk's feather still tucked in its band. To his right was a nightstand with a bowl of water on it. Next to that, a folded washcloth—still moist it appeared. A savory aroma drew his attention across the room to the parlor. Daytime shadows flickered on the parlor wall as he detected a subtle scraping that came from the kitchen. The stir of a ladle in a stew pot, he guessed.

Indeed, something was much different. He looked to the sunlight that filtered through the leaves by his windows. Leaves? No ... Yes, definitely leaves. But not outside. They were inside, draped around the wavy glass casements. More hung from the exposed beams overhead, others stemmed out of pots that lined every sill. Was this really his house, or just another dream? A soft melody seeped from the kitchen. He felt like a child again, humming along with the tune as he lay in his crib.

Celebration, song and dance,
See the wagon's ponies prance,
Beneath my tapestry receive
Your mother's blessing.

In time a young woman appeared. Mitterhal watched and listened, ensnared by the motion of her slender form. She padded lightly out of the kitchen and across the room like a cat, unaware that he watched. To each plant she gave her undivided attention, whispering to them while she tiptoed through her chores. Her hair, unkempt and coarse, was the color of straw highlighted in red—like a burning bush over a tiny stem. The sight compelled Mitterhal to make himself known.

"What have you done to my house? It looks like a forest in here."

Caught in midwhisper, the young woman sprang like a kitten, piercing the air with her squeak. She landed flat on her feet and faced him. Her startled eyes flared like crystals, just long enough to spark his memory before she covered them with her wild locks. It seemed like a lifetime ago that he had last looked into them. Her shell had changed but not the eyes.

"Ah, yes, the little girl who climbed my ladder. My my, how you have grown."

She shaped her mouth as if to speak, but no words came out, only a strained noise through her puckered lips. After several attempts she managed to force out a single word. "Multlak," she said, her voice raspy.

"Multlak," Mitterhal repeated. "That means lakehawk. You speak Gwyntah?"

She nodded, lips firmly closed.

His eyes narrowed. "You have a pretty face, what I can see of it."

She giggled, but then cupped both hands over her mouth.

105

The old man remained stone-faced, assessing once again the plant life that adorned his hearth room. "You know, there's a little tweeter in my beechwood that chirps just like you."

The young woman shifted awkwardly under his scrutiny, unable to produce another word. The effort seemed to bring her to the brink of distress, and then, as if an internal bond had snapped, she broke into a spirited dance that raised the colonel's brows.

How beautiful, he thought. Like a sunset over the Haven. Long he watched her spin around the room, captivated by her charms. The show inspired him to reach for his pipe on the mantel. He put both hands on the arms of his chair and pushed.

Stab! Back to the cushion. The searing pain shot from his ribs, up the spine to his shoulders, and down his right arm. In an instant, the young woman was at his side, holding the moist washcloth to his forehead and rubbing his back. Her lips at his ears, she whispered some kind of charm in the language of the tribes. *"Prista su hunwynn al etsa mit hutzspa."*

The words relaxed him. "Who are you?" he asked, panting.

She put her finger to his lips and hummed a sweet note. Warm light beamed through the windows as she continued to rub his back. He felt sleepy, drawn to the leaf shadows on the plaster walls. A breeze blew out of her mouth and tickled his mustache—a crisp mountain breeze that leached the pain out of his body. Deeper and deeper he slipped into a dream, the strength in his limbs returning.

Ah ... the air so fresh, the pasture so pure. How good it feels to climb again. To taste the blue blossoms and scale the steep slopes. How I've missed the power in these legs, the earth under my fe— Hoofs? What is this? Oh, well, no matter. No time to fuss. Must go up. Up! Up! Up! That is the way. The herd is waiting. There they are on the ridge, above the blue. Here comes one now. A black one with a beard. Wait. Since when do goats wear robes? What do you want?

"I want you to rest."

Rest? Nonsense, I must climb!

"The bleeding within has stopped, but there is still a great deal of swelling and the bones need time to heal. You will not be climbing any ladders soon."

Ladders? I am not climbing a ladder. I am climbing a mountain!

"You are a tough old goat. But you really must keep hydrated and rest."

"Nonsense!" the colonel shouted. His eyes snapped open and locked onto the flames in his fireplace, which rolled over the logs like molten water. Only they poured up instead of down.

"A little prayer might not be a bad idea either," came the all-too-familiar voice of Pastor Marcus Poulakis. He leaned forward in his chair, his black robe hanging like a curtain over his knees. "Welcome back, my good friend. You had us all fooled. We did not think you were going to make it. The mayor will be very pleased to hear of your recovery. He feels horribly responsible for what happened."

"What happened?" Mitterhal asked, still dazed.

"You had a fall. A big one too. It's a miracle you are still alive." Marcus smiled. "I am sorry to say that your shrubbery was not so fortunate."

Mitterhal groaned. The young woman sailed across the hearth room from the kitchen and held a mug to his mouth. The contents smelled like a zesty mix of ginger and honey.

Marcus waited for the colonel to finish his medicine before continuing. "I did not know of your accident until evening. The storm had already struck by the time your chief cipher got word to the abbey, so I could not make it up the mountain until the next morning. That would be yesterday. Barleycopp stayed with you all night. I've never seen the mayor so unraveled." He looked to the girl and smiled. "Enyalda stayed with you too. Quite a masterful nurse, I've come to learn."

Enyalda blushed and raised her potion to Mitterhal's lips for another swallow. She wiped the dribble off his chin and curtsied before scampering back into the parlor. Shortly thereafter an enchanting melody ebbed out of the kitchen, her crystal voice pure and clear. Both men gazed into the fireplace and listened.

The coals shifted, casting the pastor out of his spell. "She has a love of life most remarkable given her fear of society. Do not let her muteness fool you. She is a very perceptive young woman. Even as a little girl her gifts were apparent to me. She has learned to compensate for her malady through song and dance."

"She is not mute," Mitterhal said. "She speaks the language of the tribes."

Marcus's bushy eyebrows went up in surprise. "That I did not know. Her only exposure to the Gwyntahmahoma would have been her mother's midwife. And she went back across the Haven a year prior to Enyalda's accident."

Mitterhal boosted himself up in his leather chair. Already the sweet concoction was taking effect. With his pain subsiding, his thoughts cleared, as did his memories—to some degree. They scrolled back to the day when the little girl had brought him the pastry. What had her elder brother said that day on the rooftop? Some sort of mishap. Yes, a kick. That was it. By a horse.

He eyed the pastor. "Might it be the horse's kick that you refer?"

"You know of it?" Marcus asked, suddenly grave.

"Somewhat."

"It was a heartbreaking tragedy. Such a promising young girl stripped of her speech. Barleycopp brought her to me right away, but there was nothing I could do. The damage was done."

Marcus slouched and stared at the coals.

Mitterhal rubbed his chin, reading the pastor's posture. There was more to the story than a horse's kick, that much was obvious. "I find it curious that the lass was taken to a pastor after the mishap, and not a physician."

The clergyman turned to him, eyes burning with conviction. Mitterhal knew the look. He had seen it before, but when? And where? Memories only went so far.

"We are leaders, Cornelius," Marcus said, regaining poise. "At the very least we have that in common. Leaders solve problems. You know that better than anyone. Sometimes it is best not to burden the final authority with details. She is in a better place now and has you to thank for that. Let us leave it at that and concentrate on your recovery."

"Save your concerns, Pastor. It's just a few broken bones."

"It's not your bones that I speak of, Cornelius. Tell me, how much do you remember?"

"About what?"

"About the war, your family, anything prior to the wulfweed?"

Mitterhal made another attempt for his pipe on the mantel. A smoke was definitely in order. Again the pain stabbed his ribs, and he collapsed back to the chair. Effort thwarted, he looked to the pastor. "Marcus, would you be so kind as to hand me my pipe?"

"I will not, my friend. Like I said, it is a miracle you are alive. Anyone else would have been long dead by now. Not even the Gwyntah would dare to poison themselves to the extent that you did. Your body has reached its threshold. No more wulfweed, Cornelius. The question still remains to what degree your mind has been compromised. The fact that you remembered the conversation about the horse kick is promising. It is the memories prior to your own trauma that will be the true test. Until then, I must insist that you refrain from the pipe, even the common smoke for now."

The conversation dropped to a crackling silence. Both men looked to the fire as if it might join in the chat. As the flames flickered, ghostly shadows scurried across the bricks and suspended the lifeless in light. All the while, Enyalda sang in the kitchen, seasoning the silent dialogue with her verse.

"I do have memories," Mitterhal said. "Fragments and shattered visions, nothing solid, nothing real."

"You are not alone in that, Cornelius. The few who returned from Spaulding Pass say the same. Many of them have no recollection at all of what happened, even to this day. Others speak of it as if recounting a disjointed dream."

"What do they say?"

"Every account is different. The music is the only thread that runs common among them. One thing is certain, Cornelius. Whatever happened at Spaulding Pass took the fight out of the Torics. It enabled

Rankwall to launch a counter offensive in the south that finally put an end to the war."

"Rankwall?" The name permeated his memory like a foul stench. Blue veins constricted around Mitterhal's arms as awareness hardened into thought. "So that explains it."

"Explains what?"

"Why Rankwall's forces failed to support us at the pass. It is clear to me now. They were never meant to. What a fool I was to trust him. He gave the enemy a rabbit to chase in the north and then struck at their empty den in the south. That's why the bloody bear came at us with everything it had. They expected Rankwall to be there as well—to defend the Haven, as any sensible general would. They never anticipated that he would sacrifice his own treasure to initiate an attack on their turf. A brilliant plan really. Except for one thing."

"What is that?"

"He never told me. We were his damned rabbit, Marcus!"

The singing in the kitchen stopped. An ember shifted in the fireplace. Smoke rolled up the flue. Mitterhal snorted like a wild goat, glaring at the coals. The pastor said not a word, but closed his eyes in prayer. The two men remained as such, processing their faiths as each saw fit, until at last Marcus opened his eyes to say his piece. His words were calm yet powerful.

"Blessed is the Haven, Cornelius. The blossoms in our fields, the rain on our rooftops, the children in our streets. The rabbit you speak of was anything but damned. You thwarted the advance of ten regiments with your one. That does not happen without help. I believe with all my heart that the general's rabbit was in good company that day."

Mitterhal settled back in his chair, exhausted by the aches and pains of his fall. He allowed his mind to relax and consider the truth in the pastor's words. It was not the first time the holy man had made sense, but the thought only made him cringe.

"My head hurts, Pastor. I can't listen to your nonsense anymore. It's time to take your preaching elsewhere."

Enyalda appeared, out of nowhere it seemed, a tray of fruit tarts in her hands. She delivered her treats with a song and a smile, though she kept her eyes veiled behind her hair.

Marcus accepted a tart. "Hmm, how lovely. Thank you, my dear." He took the pipe off the mantel and looked at the colonel. "It is a blessing to see you back to yourself again, my good friend. Barleycopp will be happy to hear the news. Let me know if you would like me to prepare a eulogy for your shrubbery." He bowed and took his leave, staff in hand.

Enyalda saw him to the parlor. At the door the pastor turned to her. "Make sure he gets plenty of water," he said quietly. "And do whatever you can to keep him still. I will be back in three days. His memory is returning rapidly. Have your brothers fire a flare if I am needed sooner. Oh, yes, and one more thing." He handed her the colonel's broken pipe. "No more wulfweed."

Enyalda curtsied then scuttled back to her chores, leaving the pastor in the wake of her spirited song and dance.

Part II
Off the Roof

1
The First Supper

Enyalda McFadden never knew her mother. She and her twin brother Donavon were tangled at birth and pushed into the world in a fever, out of which only they survived. Muma was the Gwyntah midwife who saved the children and embraced the role of surrogate mother through tragic circumstance. Growing up, Enyalda loved the soft-spoken old tribeswoman almost as much as she loved her father, though she seldom saw him. Word of the lieutenant's pending arrivals after weeks, sometimes months, of absence brought great excitement to the McFadden compound on the outskirts of Wulfhaven. So much so that the spry little girl made a habit of climbing the tallest tree at the front of their horse pasture to get a bird's eye vantage of her father's approach. Often she would mimic the calls of songbirds to pass the time while she sat in the branches and waited.

Enyalda's tireless surveillance won her the privilege of being the first of her siblings to greet their beloved father when he returned from battle. How she loved it when he scooped her up onto his warhorse and raced across the field at full gallop. She never forgot the feeling of the wind whistling through her wild locks as she nestled in the security of his powerful arms.

Those were the good days, when Lakwynnia's fight for independence was a distant rumble to a carefree six-year-old girl. It was not until the war ended and Father never came back to take Enyalda galloping in the field that the first kernels of sorrow were laid bare. Even then, the devastating news of her father's death could not break her resilient spirit. She still had Muma then, and it was through the old woman's love and grace that Enyalda learned patience, kindness, and the power to listen. Skills she never lost, even in the speechless years that followed the dreadful incident in the barn.

By the time Enyalda was eight, Muma was gone. Sent back across the Haven by the general's son, Fergus Rankwall, the appointed chief constable of Wulfhaven. After learning of the considerable funds set aside for the lieutenant's family, he commandeered the role of guardian to make sure the children of the late war hero received a proper upbringing and that their fortune—he said—was well managed. In truth, the arrangement was doomed from the start. All the McFaddens considered Muma an integral part of their family and were heartbroken when she was forced to leave. Enyalda's eldest brother, though not yet a man, had his own ideas of how the family should be raised. More often than not, Adman's strong will clashed with Rankwall's, which resulted in frequent beatings for all the boys. Fergus never beat Enyalda, however. Rather he would console her after the boys had received their discipline, and comfort her in ways that sapped the joy out of her songs.

Those days were over, thankfully. Fergus was long gone, never to subject his cruel authority over anyone again—though Enyalda never forgot the eyes that had emptied her heart of innocence. To this day, the fallout of his malice was evident in the cautious way she avoided eye contact with men of any sort. Even the colonel, whom she trusted more than anyone, received only a sideways glance at best.

It came with such a glance on a pleasant afternoon in early spring that Enyalda popped her head out of a blooming hedge of laurels to investigate the subtle snort that came out of the colonel while he napped in a wicker chair under the shade of the Great Beech. Concerned by the break in rhythm, Enyalda hurried to his side with a freshly clipped laurel branch to monitor his breathing. She kept her lips close to his ear and watched the pink petals waver in and out under his nose, ready to whisper one of Muma'a blessings should the need arise. In truth, she only half expected the tremors to occur. Five weeks had passed since his last seizure. And though the winter had been a challenge, she sensed that the colonel's withdrawal from the wulfweed was almost complete. Another snort and the old man's eyes opened, and she spun into a dance.

"Good morning, my dear," the disoriented old man said. "Or afternoon, or whatever it is. How goes your day in the gardens?"

With a sweep of her arms, Enyalda widened her dance and looked up into the network of branches that towered overhead. Her bare feet tapped over the beechwood's litter from the previous year. The colonel's recovery delighted her, yet at the same time frightened her. His question, though simple, called for an answer, and that required words. Words that she knew, when spoken, would compel her to look into his eyes. That was the dilemma. It was not that she didn't know the words. Quite the contrary, she knew the words better than most. It was delivering them without looking into his eyes that posed the greatest challenge. She swung the laurel twig over her head, giving herself time to prepare her song. Yes, singing. That was the solution. It was one of her most profound discoveries since the incident in the barn—words could be sung without looking into the eyes.

The day is bright, no longer night
For you I bring this lovely sight.

She curtsied next to the colonel's chair, holding out the laurel branch while smiling at the dead leaves by his feet. Mitterhal took the twig from her hand and brought it to his nose.

"Why thank you, pretty miss," he said after a deep sniff. "Might I hear you speak a word today?"

She said nothing, teasingly holding a finger to her lips and looking up and away with exaggerated defiance. It was a game they played ever since his fall off the roof. True to form, the colonel cleared his throat to tease her with a rhyme of his own.

You know, my dear ...
If you keep me guessing on what you mean to say,
I may jump to a conclusion you would do best to throw away.

His tone was a bit gruff, Enyalda thought, and the melody unrefined, but the colonel's attempt at song was genuine and she danced in delighted response. It gave her great joy to hear the old curmudgeon engage with her in such a way. So much so, she celebrated his impromptu verse with a giggle and even risked an extended look into his eyes while she danced. They sparkled like blue crystals set in a weatherworn hide. How strange, she thought, never to have noticed that until now. But then again, how could she? The branches of the Great Beech had brought her close to the colonel, but not that close. Only once in the very beginning, when the wise old tree told her to climb the ladder and introduce herself to the chimney, did she ever get close enough to notice his eyes. Even then the beechwood's mission had preoccupied her.

The colonel, for his part, appeared charmed by her dance. Had she considered the full extent to which his admiration might have wandered, her steps would surely have faltered, but he simply watched her performance with the same reverent gaze she had seen him use on countless sunsets.

"Tell me," he said as she opened her shawl and spread her bare arms like the wings of a carefree butterfly. "What inspires a pretty young lass like you to spend her time with an old goat like me? You should be frolicking with

115

the young bucks in Wulfhaven."

Suddenly embarrassed, she scurried out of sight behind the broad trunk of the Great Beech. There she remained and sang her response, safely shielded within the root burls of the ancient tree. Her bashful song trickled into the weightless current of an afternoon breeze.

Some things they have
That you may not,
But happiness
They bring me not,
The voice I hear
In flower and tree
Is lost when others
Smother me

The colonel was already out of his wicker chair and well underway to his stone wall by the time Enyalda dared to peek around the trunk. She was sorry their game had ended so soon, knowing he would spend the rest of the afternoon sitting by his beehives and gazing up at his chimney. So without further ado, Enyalda went back to her chores in the gardens, humming softly amidst the buzz of the colonel's pollinating bees.

Gardening was but one of Enyalda's passions. She was also a marvelous cook. Initially her talent sprouted out of necessity, though from there it blossomed into a refined art. None of her three brothers were particularly good at it themselves, and so it was only natural after Muma was sent away for Enyalda to continue the role of feeding the family. It was the ideal task, as it turned out, with which to satisfy her insatiable need to nurture.

And so with a song in heart, Enyalda left the colonel's gardens for his kitchen, where she plopped a handful of egg-sized turnips into a steaming hot copper pot, whole and unpeeled, exactly how the colonel liked them. It was an awkward twist of fate really. Not that she had anything against turnips. They had their place in this world just like anything else. It was her brothers who hated them, especially Donavon. He was the one most likely to protest. Francis, her middle brother, would politely endure the bitter bite for the sake of the common good. Whereas Adman ... Well, he would simply gobble up everything else in the stew and leave the unwanted tubers shamelessly discarded on the table while going on and on with his politics.

So be it, she thought. *"Su shakina noch ah humala,"* she whispered to the potted amaryllis on the nearby windowsill. It was one of Muma's memorable sayings: you can't please everyone. How right she was. At least by keeping the turnips large, her brothers would be able to spot them easily and elude them with minimal complaint—or so the amaryllis seemed to suggest.

Francis was the first to arrive, earlier than promised. He was always good that way. He entered the kitchen smiling, a leather satchel hanging from his shoulder and an oak keg clamped in his sturdy hands. He greeted her as he lowered the keg to the floor and set the satchel on the counter next to her cutting board.

"Let's see," he said, opening the satchel. "We've got fresh peppercorn, nutmeg, a handful of hazelnuts, mushrooms, a hunk of brisket, and half a dozen red pearl onions. I believe that completes your list. Oh, and of course, one cask of Cotton Crown's finest."

He hoisted the heavy keg and plunked it alongside the other ingredients, inadvertently crushing one of the onions. Enyalda swept her hair back to better assess the size of the brew cask.

"Don't worry," Francis said. "I know you only needed a half pint for the pot. We'll take care of the rest. Well, I best be off to find Donny. He left for the tavern this morning all puffed up about something." Francis grabbed his empty satchel and started to leave, but was stopped by a quick pinch to the arm and a peck on his scruffy cheek. "You're welcome, sister," he said, smiling. "We'll see you tonight."

After Francis left, Enyalda immediately went to the amaryllis to comfort it with a song. The flowering bulb was still grieving over the crushed onion.

Shortly thereafter, Enyalda placed the remaining ingredients into the stew broth and set them to simmer. It was time to check on the colonel. Last she knew he was still by the hives. As it turned out, she did not have to go far. She passed out of the kitchen and into the parlor, where she opened the front door and found him one step down on the outside, his hand extended for the knob.

"I am concerned about the goats," he said with a huff that echoed a snort. He stepped up and across the threshold, without the slightest care to her startled squeak. "Something's got their horns up."

Enyalda scuttled ahead to stoke the fire before he got there. She was already kneeling at the hearth, reviving the coals with a bellows, by the time he settled in his leather chair.

"The herd's been huddled down by the cedar grove in the south pasture for nearly three weeks now." He removed his hat and set it on the nightstand next to his cane. "For some reason Old Smoker's been keeping them away from the manor."

Enyalda grabbed the feather duster she kept tied at her waist and swept it every which way across the fireplace mantel. If the colonel wanted to speak she would listen, but the truth was that she was more than happy that the voracious flower munchers were keeping their distance. It gave the laurels a rare opportunity to express themselves without being oppressed. Around the room she fluttered her duster while the colonel ranted on about the habits of his goats. Nothing he said warranted a response.

The hearth room was thoroughly dusted by the time Adman burst through the front parlor. "Get your fixing kit, Enya! Donny had it out at the tavern again."

Enyalda darted to the kitchen for the kit. When she returned Donavon already sat at the long wooden table in the hearth room. Francis was at his side, pressing one of the cloth tablemats to the left side of Donavon's face.

Adman scowled at the carnage, his arms crossed like a general. "He picked a fight with Angus this time."

"I didn't pick it," Donavon said. "He had it coming."

"Maybe, but all the same you didn't have to take it out on every one of his brothers."

"They got in my way."

"And why wouldn't they? Brewmaster Garrison said you tore into Angus like a crazed ram."

Donavon snapped a glance at his sister as she approached with her fixing kit and a steaming bowl of broth. "He called her a bane of nature. You would have done the same if you w—"

Enyalda snatched the tablemat out of Francis's hand and stuffed it in Donavon's mouth. Quickly, she dipped a swab from her kit into the broth and smeared it into the raw gash under his left eye. Donavon bit down hard on the cloth and grunted.

Adman waited for Enyalda to perform the procedure that of late had become all too common. "No, brother, I would not have done the same," he said when the shock appeared to subside. "I would have made sure I had some backup before I cracked his jaw. You're lucky they didn't kill you. The McGregors are a tough lot. Besides, we all know that Enya's not a bane. Tearing up Crown Tavern didn't prove a thing."

Knowing she was the subject of discussion, Enyalda couldn't resist expressing herself on the matter. She spun away from Donavon and did her best to imitate a barred owl while she flapped her arms around the table.

Whoo! Whoo! Whoo!
Who cooks for you?
Boo hoo hoo!
Big boo boo on you!

"You're not helping, sister," Adman said, frowning.

Francis, however, laughed at Enyalda's nonsensical song. Even Donavon cracked a smile, which reopened the cut under his eye.

"Look, Donny," Francis said. "How can our sister be a bane of nature when she does such a fine job imitating it? I think big Angus is just jealous that he can't milk a pigeon."

They all laughed at that. The outburst inspired Francis to fetch the brew cask in the kitchen while Enyalda resumed dressing her twin brother's wounds. Her task became more manageable once the ale was on tap. All three of her brothers took part in the keg with hearty spirits. At last, Adman looked to the colonel who sat quietly in his chair by the hearth, seemingly oblivious to the events around the table.

"Enya! Fetch the colonel a grog. He looks thirsty."

Enyalda, who had her hands buried in Donavon's hair as she examined a wound on his scalp, glared at her bossy brother.

"All right then, I'll do it myself." He strode to the cask and filled a mug. "Someone around here's gotta show the colonel respect." The froth bubbled over the rim as he approached the hearth. "Here you go, sir," he said, holding out the mug. "Compliments of Cotton Crown tavern, the finest brew in all the highlands."

The mug hung like a judge's gavel under the Old Mitt's nose. Something between a snarl and a groan escaped his clenched jaw. "What I could use is a smoke, lad. Why don't you try pouring that out of your gob?"

Adman withdrew the mug, visibly deflated by the sharp remark. "I'll have to work on that, sir," he said, and retreated to the table.

Francis eased the awkward moment by mentioning the latest village gossip. "Hey, Adman, what do you think of Brewmaster Garrison shooting that she-wolf in his goose coop last week? I wish I could have seen his face when he realized the pesky fox nabbing his hens was really a wolf. And to think, only a few weeks after the Grange boys shot that big male in their sheep field."

Donavon chimed in while Adman gulped his ale. "That was Patsy Grange," he said, cringing at Enyalda's probing fingers. "He's been bragging every day at the pub how he dropped the beast in one shot from across the field."

Adman wiped the brew foam off his trimmed goatee. "That doesn't surprise me with that new musket he's got. It's got a riffled barrel that gives it three times the range of Father's old flintlocks. I'm trying to get one myself. Patsy won't budge an inch on where he got it. Not even his cousins know."

"He's nothing but a tickle pitcher if you ask me," Donavon said. He winced as Enyalda extracted a finger-sized shard of glass from his head. "Anyone can knock off a wolf with a gun. I'd like to see him get close enough to tag one with an arrow. That would be something to brag about."

"She was desperate!" the colonel suddenly announced, rising out of his chair.

Everyone froze. The three brothers watched in astonishment as Old Mitt hobbled toward the table with his cane. Enyalda's fingers stilled in Donavon's hair as the colonel seated himself in the wooden armchair at the head of the table. He did not say a word at first, but she could tell by the rhythm of his breathing that he had something important to say. Nervous, she continued her work on Donavon while making ready for the words.

The chair creaked. The colonel leaned forward and planted both elbows on the table. "A wolf is too cunning to get caught in a goose coop. Only a mother with young to feed would go that route. The male they shot in the sheep field must have been her mate. She was desperate."

Enyalda gasped. Her bloody hands went to her face, barely able to muffle her sob. She charged into the kitchen and made straight for the amaryllis. "Why, why, why?" she wailed as tears smeared her brother's blood on her cheeks. She wiped her eyes, and the severed onion shoots on the cutting board came into focus. "But mother wolf is not an onion," she whispered defiantly to the flower.

Another one of Muma's sayings came softly to her lips: *'Gahutah heim nahuntah.'* To live is to die. Whispering the words helped bring her back to the task at hand. Putting her sorrow on hold, she thanked the amaryllis for the encouragement and lifted the lid on the copper pot to test the turnips for their tenderness. Supper was ready.

She carried the stew in on a wide wooden tray, stopping at the colonel first. His bowl had the biggest turnip; it rose out of the savory depths like a mountainous white island in a misty sea. When all had been served, Enyalda sat in front of her own bowl and put both hands together in prayer. Francis was the first to follow suit, followed by Adman and finally Donavon, though grudgingly. The colonel, who had already started munching on his turnip, froze in midchew with fork in hand.

Adman cleared his throat in preparation of the prayer. "Dear God, thank you for the food on this table and the land that provides it. Amen."

Good, but not good enough, Enyalda thought. This was a special occasion and warranted more. It was the first night the colonel had made the effort to sit at the table with her brothers. She kept her hands together, knowing the prayer would not end until she gave the signal.

Francis got the hint, as usual. "And dear God," he added, "we also thank you for the family we share it with ... all five of us."

The colonel's fork clinked on the table. Enyalda peeked through her hair. His hands came together to a point beneath his trembling chin. Concerned that the sickness was coming back, she forgot that her brothers were still waiting for the signal to end the prayer. She rocked her head while monitoring the movement of the colonel's lower jaw.

Oddly enough, the colonel himself gave the signal to end the prayer. "Amen," he muttered after a tough swallow.

"Amen," Francis said, followed by Adman and Donavon.

Relieved, Enyalda stopped rocking and sipped her stew. This was the moment she had prayed for. The most important people in her life together at last, connected by the body's most basic need. A wave of elation swept over her that almost brought her to speak.

Donavon broke the spell. "There's turnips in this stew," he said boorishly.

"Shut up, Donny," Adman said around a mouthful of brisket. "Pass the bread, will you?"

"Get it yourself."

"Ease up, brother," Francis said to Donavon while passing the bread to Adman. "Enya worked hard on this stew. It's better than the slop you would have come up with."

"I didn't say it was bad. I just said it had turnips in it."

"We all heard what you said," Adman said, "and we all know what you meant."

"You're not fooling anyone," Donavon said. "Look, you've already got one dropped by your bowl."

On and on went the banter. The colonel, meanwhile, dug into his big turnip, unfazed by the distractions around him. Enyalda savored the precious moment, basking in the gruff love around the table.

As she'd expected, Adman eventually steered the conversation toward politics. "We've got more things to worry about than turnips," he said, wiping his mouth and returning the cloth napkin to his lap. "The Pogetsa are cracking down hard on the fountain folk in Wulfhaven. It's only a matter of time before they do the same up here in Cotton Crown."

"Why would they bother with a highland village?" Francis asked. "All they care about is keeping order in Wulfhaven. We've got nothing to do with that."

"We've got everything to do with that," Adman retorted. "The fountain folk are protesting the rebuilding of the bridge. Whether we join them or not, the Pogetsa know our ties with the Gwyntah run strong in the highlands. In many ways we're even more of a threat because they can't keep track of us so easily."

"That's right," Donavon said. "A pogie would stick out like a sore thumb up here. Three steps and I'd have him kissing the gahenya with an arrow in his ass."

"Don't be an idiot, Donny. The Pogetsa are ruthless. You take one down, they'll send ten more to set an example. And if they can't find you, they'll take it out on everyone else. The entire village would be locked up by the time you turned yourself in."

"Who says I'd turn myself in? Maybe I'd just kill every one of 'em and show the village what it means to stick up for yourself."

Adman dismissed the rash comment and looked to the colonel. "What do you think, sir? What should we do if the Pogetsa come to Cotton Crown?"

Enyalda shifted in her chair and began rocking again. Why did her brother have to be so blunt? The colonel wasn't ready for this kind of talk. She closed her eyes and listened to the colonel chew his stew. Back and forth she rocked her head while counting his chomps. In her heightened state, she heard what sounded like the snort of a horse in the front yard by the flowerbeds. Strange, she thought. Her brothers knew better than to tether their horses by the flowers.

After what seemed like an eternity, the colonel lowered his fork and looked directly at Adman. "We should invite them to dinner," he said, and resumed his assault on the large turnip.

The blunt statement strangled the conversation. Not even Francis could revive the talk at the table. The squelch was shattered by three harsh thumps on the front door. Everyone froze, except for the colonel. He switched his fork for a spoon and began slurping up the juices in his bowl.

Three more knocks jarred Enyalda out of her chair. Cautiously she approached the door in the front parlor, making sure her hair sufficiently covered her eyes before springing the latch. Slowly, she opened the door and saw two hefty leather boots on the stoop. In an instant she recognized them and dared not look up, fearing the eyes above them. Rather, she let out a nervous chirp and scuttled back to the hearth room to stoke the fire. What better way to soften her brother's punishment than with a cozy reception for the sheriff?

Adman was the first to speak when the boots stepped through the parlor and into the hearth room. "Good evening, sir," he said, nervously standing at attention. "Can we interest you in a mug?"

The boots advanced. Enyalda dared a peek from the hearth. The sheriff was solid in stature, not overly tall but wide. Everything about him was thick—his hands, his shoulders, his face. Even his earlobes seemed to be made of a substance denser than flesh. When he spoke, his voice was calm but carried a presence that demanded attention.

"No ale tonight, Adman. I'm here on business." He took off his wide-brimmed hat and faced the head of the table. "Evening, Colonel. It's been awhile. Good to see you well. You had the whole village on edge after your fall."

Enyalda placed another log on the fire before moving in for a better vantage. A slight twitch over the colonel's right eyebrow drew her in closer. His spoon teetered like a plume pen balanced on a finger. Her gaze locked on the spoon, she watched and waited for the tremors to begin.

"Sergeant Hoffman?" he said, shaking his head as if waking from a dream.

"Not anymore, sir," the burly man replied. "I keep it nice and easy now. Just a sheriff in a sleepy village." He tilted his head, causing an unsettling crackling noise in his neck. "For the most part that is." He sent a menacing glance to Donavon. "At any rate, I see you're enjoying a fine dinner, so I'll be quick. With your permission, I would like to give the young scrapper here a little look over. Make sure all his marbles are in order, if you know what I mean. It will take but a minute."

To Enyalda's shock, the colonel directed his attention to her. "Enyalda, my dear. I think the stew could use a little more fresh pepper. Would you be so kind as to grind some up in the kitchen? And perhaps another bowl for the sheriff."

She set out on her task, anxious to shed the attention. The last words she heard before entering the kitchen were the colonel's: "By all means, Jarvis, do your job."

Several minutes later, Enyalda returned with a shaker of freshly ground pepper in one hand and an extra bowl of stew for the sheriff in the other. She tiptoed into the hearth room so as not to interrupt their discussion, but what she saw dispelled any attempt at discretion. There before her, with his face pressed flat against the table, was her beloved brother. The sheriff had wrenched one of the cloth napkins tight around Donavon's neck and pinned it to the table with his dagger. She heard her brother's muffled protests and horrified, dropped the bowl.

Everyone—with the exception of Donavon—turned their heads toward her. Enyalda knelt down to pick up the fragments of the clay bowl. Within seconds, Francis was at her side, taking hold of her shaking hands.

"It's okay, Enya. Sheriff Hoffman is just getting a few things straight with Donny. Why don't you let me take care of the mess?"

She dared a glance at the table. Wiping her eyes, she saw Donavon sitting upright again and rubbing his neck. The cloth napkin was heaped on the table and the dagger gone.

Sheriff Hoffman strode past her with hat in hand. He turned around at the door for one last word to Donavon. "I almost forgot," he said, tilting his head and making the same crackling noise in his neck. "Your training begins behind the tavern at dawn. Don't be late. You'll be working with Angus. Bring an extra set of clothes." After a respectful nod to the colonel, he looked to Enyalda. "My apologies for interrupting your dinner, madam." He put on his hat and left.

The colonel immediately went back to his stew.

With the sheriff gone, Francis helped Enyalda up. "Come on, sister, relax and finish your supper. You've worked hard today."

She rose and let him escort her to the table. Adman stood behind her chair and seated her while Francis picked up her bowl of cold stew.

"Let me get you a fresh batch. I'll be right back," he said, making for the kitchen. "Anyone else up for seconds?"

Enyalda looked across the table at Donavon, who appeared unusually reserved. A flash caught her eye, directly in front of him, next to the dagger hole in the table. Intrigued, she got up and leaned forward for a better view. The silver brooch sparkled in the lamplight—three crossed stalks of the mountain flower set in a cluster of amethyst. She stretched out her arm to touch it, but Donavon grabbed it before she had the chance.

"That's Donny's new badge," Adman said. "Our little brother got himself a job working for the sheriff. He and Angus McGregor are going to be Cotton Crown's new deputies."

"Yeah, carting dung for the drunks!" Donavon snarled at Adman. "Thanks for the backup, brother."

The colonel let up on his turnip. "You'll do fine," he said after wiping his mouth with a napkin. "Your new boss knows the rules. He'll teach you some good manners. All in all, I'd say you got off easy."

"You call that easy? He almost slammed my face through the table."

"Trust me, lad, that was mild. You know, they called him the Hoof during the war."

"Why was that?" Francis asked, returning from the kitchen.

Mitterhal stabbed at the last remnant of turnip in his bowl. "Because it was what you got in the rump if you didn't do your job."

Enyalda's hands went to her mouth. It was a mystery, even to her, what made her giggle at times. Certainly, the notion of one of those hefty boots delivering a swift kick to her brother was by no means humorous. Yet there was something irresistible about the colonel's crass statement.

"You think that's funny?" Donavon said to her while she squirmed in her chair. "Maybe you'll be the first one I arrest for disturbing the peace!"

The weedy threat was all it took to send her over the edge. Unable to contain her laughter any longer, she popped off her chair in a burst of song and dance. The rapture spread to her brothers, and in no time they were back at their mugs. Even Donavon seemed to forget his grudge as he watched his sister flap her arms around the hearth room, hooting like an owl. All the while, Mitterhal lounged in the firelight, watching the shadows dance without so much as a single twitch.

The evening proceeded as such into the late hours, mixed with laughter, banter, tales, and song. By the night's end, one thing was certain. The Old Mitt's withdrawal from the wulfweed was complete.

2
Clean Up

Not a lot happened in Cotton Crown according to Donavon McFadden.
A sleepy highland village, it was nestled in a cluster of alpine pastures high
up on the mountain for which it was named. Indeed, the pace of the village
was slow and steady, as one might expect of a community that thrived on
wool. Sturdy thatched-roof shelters made of stone dotted the grassy knolls
amidst herds of highland sheep. Ancient fieldstone walls mottled with lichen
partitioned the land into a montage of terrestrial shapes and contours. To
hike the pastures was to wander a primordial past. With the exception of the
colonel's manor at the fringe of tree line, the only evidence of a more recent
authority was in the main hub of the village.

The jailhouse, oddly enough, served as the official center for village
affairs. Built of bricks imported from South Bay, the impressive two-story
structure imposed a stark elegance that was distinctly Toricean. Not that
Donavon was interested in architecture, or even history for that matter. His
familiarity with the building—especially the block of cells that led to the
sheriff's office—was purely due to circumstance.

Conveniently located across from the jailhouse and next to the weaving
mill was Crown Tavern, another of Donavon's haunts. Unlike the jailhouse,
that building was made of stones native to the mountain. To call it a tavern,
however, was not entirely accurate. While it was indeed famous for its alpine
ale brewed exclusively with local hops, the function of the age-old
establishment went far beyond that of a mere pub. It was a place where the
informal wrinkles of highland life could be smoothed out in an atmosphere
free of convention. Everything from the trading of local sheep stock to the
more cryptic dealings with the Gwyntah was discussed there. And though the

doors of the tavern were open to all, it was always best for first-time visitors to keep one wary eye on the exit.

Donavon had both eyes on the exit when the harsh reality of dawn broke the mist and struck the backside of Cotton Crown Tavern. The sun arrived late, as it always did on the southwest slope of the mountain, but not late enough for Donavon, who approached the closed doors of the tavern's basement with a splitting headache. The pains of the previous day's donnybrook had caught up with him. Had not Enyalda awoken him in the dark hours of the morning to redress his wounds, he would still be sacked on the colonel's hearth room floor, wrapped in a blanket. Next to him limped Angus McGregor, apparently in no better shape. Neither one said a word as Sheriff Jarvis Hoffman began their orientation by swinging open the basement doors and introducing them to the bowels of the brew house.

"There it is, boys. Beautiful, isn't it? Such a shame it has to go."

A waist-high heap of excrement and other unspeakable substances loomed before them. Upon the mound were more mounds, sublets of filth that created the visual effect of a desolate wasteland topped by toxic peaks. The stench was suffocating. Above the pit, Donavon saw eight holes cut in the floorboards, equally spaced and each one the size of a modest pumpkin. He had looked through the holes plenty of times, but never from this angle.

Sheriff Hoffman, for his part, seemed unaffected by the reek. He simply tightened the shoulder straps on his loaded combat pack and inhaled a long, deep whiff. "Excellent," he said, stepping toward the edge of the cesspit. "There's a morning's worth of honest work here. When you're done, make sure you line the empty pit with a cartload of ash. Then you can go upstairs and clean up the mess you made yesterday. I'll be out of contact for a day or two, depending on the weather. The tavern will be spotless when I get back. Any questions?"

It was a statement of fact more than an order. One that not even Donavon could muster the courage to challenge.

"Where are you going?" Angus asked, his words mumbled on account of his broken jaw.

Donavon cringed at the clumsy question.

Hoffman, clearly unimpressed, brought his scowling eyes to within an inch of Angus's swollen chin. Though the beefy young man was a full head taller than the sheriff, he suddenly appeared puny.

"Where I am going has nothing to do with what you are doing! If I were you, I'd keep that dribbling jaw of yours shut until you have something smart to say." He turned to Donavon, the veins in his arms bulging from the tightened shoulder straps. "And how 'bout you? Any brilliant comments you'd like to add?"

Donavon had planned to keep a low profile—to simply do as he was told without fuss so he could catch up on some much needed rest later. Had it not been for Angus's blunder, he might have done just that. But the truth was, even as a toddler, Donavon McFadden had never been one to sidestep a direct challenge. Against all better judgment, he looked the sheriff straight in the eye and gave his bloodshot reply.

"None that a hoof would understand, sir."

A myriad of expressions pulsed through the sheriff's face. What began as disbelief led to fury followed by resolve and finally topped with a hint of admiration. All the while, Donavon maintained a fierce gaze, determined not to show his fear, even when the sheriff approached him and made the unnerving crackling noise in his neck.

Hoffman's hot breath struck Donavon in the face, like the opening of an oven door. "You've got your father's guts, boy, and his sense of humor. That's good. Your timing's a bit off, though. We'll have to work on that." He hawked up whatever loose debris was in his throat and launched the sticky missile over Donavon's shoulder, hitting the highest peak in the cesspit with spot-on precision. "You can start over there."

He turned around and was off at full stride. His pack-mounted snowshoes swayed like rackets over his head with every step. "You boys better hop to it," he said as he faded into the mist. "The stench only gets worse as the day heats up. Hail, Gahenya!"

"What a stupid question," Donavon said to Angus once the sheriff was out of earshot. "How do you expect to be a deputy if you can't think for yourself?"

Angus tightened his grip on his shovel and glared. "What do you mean by that?"

"You saw the snowshoes on his pack. A stone-cold drunk could have figured out where he's going just by looking at him."

A ponderous air settled over Angus as his attention shifted to the snow-capped peak that hovered high above the morning mist. "What do you suppose he's going up there for?" he said, letting the insult slide.

"Who knows and who cares? Like he said, it's got nothing to do with us. Go grab the cart and muck buckets. Let's get this stinking job over with."

Not a lot was said from that point on. The young deputies covered their faces with scarves and got to work. Donavon consoled himself by imagining how much he was upsetting the flies. Every stab of his shovel devastated another layer of their homeland. Bucket after bucket slurped into the cart they'd positioned outside the doors. Angus was not nearly as successful at distracting his senses. His progress diminished with every heave of the shovel and Donavon noted the steady decline. Eventually, Angus dropped an empty bucket by the cart and staggered to the corner of the tavern where a giant trumpet vine climbed up the cobbles to the eave.

"What do you think you're doing?" Donavon shouted out the basement door. "We're not done yet."

Angus remained unresponsive, staring vacantly into a cluster of horn-shaped red flowers.

Donavon stormed out of the basement. "Listen here, slouch. You better get moving if you don't want my shovel in your face. There's no way I'm doing this on my own."

Getting no response, Donavon nudged him in the midsection with the blunt shovel handle. The jolt to the gut was all it took to jar loose the gates on Angus's gloom. In an instant the trumpet vine was drenched in vomit.

Donavon turned away in disgust, having caught a taste of the splash, and wiped his own mouth with his spotted sleeve. He looked back and saw Angus still convulsing. The scene was repulsive. Though pity had never been a foremost of Donavon's concerns, he laid his hand on the shoulder of the big wretch nonetheless, supporting him while he finished draining his stomach of misery.

When at last the heaving subsided, Angus spoke, though he still had a sickly pallor. "I can't do this, Donny," he said, breathing heavily and wiping the residue off his chin. "The smell ... It's sickening. Hoffman's gonna kill me."

"He's not going to kill you," Donavon said. "Come on, you big ox, get a hold of yourself."

"How do you know? He's capable of anything when he's mad."

Donavon rubbed the back of his sore neck, recalling the sheriff's recruitment tactics the night before. "Yeah, now that you mention it, I think you might be right. He had my face pinned to the Old Mitt's table last night with a cloth and dagger. I'll tell you what; I'll do the rest of the mucking if you haul the buckets. Can you at least handle that?"

"I think so." Angus took a deep breath, the color in his face returning. "Hey, Donny? I should never have said what I said about your sister. I don't know what got into me. It's just that she doesn't sing to me anymore, ever since she moved up to the manor."

"Old Mitt's got nothing to do with that and you know it. You asked her to marry you. What did you expect? You know that stuff scares her to death."

"I know, I was stupid. Do you think she'll ever sing to me again?"

"Who knows? I'll talk to her. It's the least I can do for breaking your jaw."

"Thanks. Hey, that was a crazy thing you said to the sheriff. Did you see his face when you called him a hoof? What was that all about?"

"That was his nickname in the Guard. Old Mitt told us last night."

"Really? What else did he say?"

"Not a whole lot. He went on all night about his goats. He's just as crazy as ever if you ask me."

"Do you ever wonder what our fathers saw in him?" Angus said wistfully. "Your brother says he was a great leader."

"Adman's a suck-up. What does he know? He'll say anything to get in with the big shots. As for our fathers, they're both dead. That says it all, don't you think?"

"I don't think our fathers would have followed a crazy man, Donny. They were too smart for that."

"Maybe the old coot was different during the war, but he's as cracked as they get now. You know he's been smoking the wulfweed all this time on his roof. I saw the seed pods on his crate last fall when Captain Marly had us give him that necklace from the tribes."

"The bean?" Angus asked in disbelief.

"Yeah, the bean."

"Wow. No wonder he talks to his chimney."

"You better believe it. Come on, let's get to it. We'll never finish this job if we keep on yapping."

By noontime the cesspit was empty. The two young men removed their scarves and made ready to change their clothes. Neither one was particularly hungry, so both agreed to get right back to their assignment upstairs—after an ale, of course. No sooner had Donavon removed his shirt than a posse of horses charged around the trumpet vine. Adman was at the head of the pack, followed by the McGregor boys and several other locals in the village. Francis was last to round the corner in a horse cart filled with sacks of oats.

"There's been a robbery, sir!" Adman shouted.

"What should we do, sir?" one of the McGregors asked. "There's a dozen eggs missing in Garrison's goose coop."

The mob burst into laughter. A shutter in the top window of the tavern swung open and revealed Serena Schonhauser's bare arm. "Help me! Help me! Someone call the deputy! I'm in distress!" In her hand was a cherry-red undergarment that swept the stone sill with every dainty twist of her wrist, inciting more howls of laughter.

Donavon remained straight-faced through the entire charade. He had never been fond of practical jokes, even when he wasn't the subject. That Adman appeared to be spearheading the gag made it all the worse. Looking to his left, he saw Angus gawking like a spellbound bull at the busty barmaid's garment.

"Let's go, you big oaf," he said with a hard shove to Angus's shoulder. "We still have work to do."

Seth McGregor, Angus's eldest living brother, dismounted. An ugly black shiner festered under his right eye. "Come on, Donny, ease up. We're just letting you know there's no hard feelings on our end. Our fathers fought hard together in the war. McGregors and McFaddens shouldn't be beating each other up." Seth extended his hand.

Donavon considered the gallant gesture. Truth was he had nothing against Seth McGregor. In fact, he kind of admired him. He was one of the few who didn't cater to Adman's incessant bossiness. He was tough and smart and knew how to hold his ground. Never quick to start a fight, but always quick to end one. Donavon knew he had caught Seth off guard with his left hook during the brawl. And though many of the details were lost in the dustup, he was almost certain Seth was the one who had thrown him headfirst through the tavern window.

Donavon grasped the outstretched hand. "No hard feelings, Seth. Sorry about the eye."

Cheers resounded. Serena Schonhauser came out of the tavern with her red undergarment still in hand and incited more revelry by kicking up her skirt while everybody clapped. Such was the way of Cotton Crown. Cooperation was essential to life on the mountain, as was a good time. To hold a grudge in the village was simply not practical. And while conflicts were inevitable, in the highlands, resolutions came quick.

Adman eventually raised his voice over the hoots and catcalls. "I propose that we give our hard-working deputies a break and move the excitement into the tavern. All in favor, say aye."

"Aye!" answered the mob.

Angus dragged his gaze away from the flopping skirt and raised his fist. "What do you say, Donny? We could use a breather."

Donavon glared at the ground, caught in a quandary. He hated how his brother always stole the show. The last thing he wanted was to contribute to the excitement that Adman had stirred. Yet to mop up the tavern while everyone else rejoiced was just as dismal a prospect. Overtired and fatigued, Donavon felt his own fuse running short as Adman approached.

"You're off the hook, little brother," he said, putting his hand on Donavon's shoulder. "Go get some rest. We'll take care of the mess from here."

Donavon swiped away Adman's hand. "Since when did you become sheriff?"

Francis—always the mediator—stepped in. "It's not his order, Donny. It's Enya's. She wants to make sure your wounds don't get infected." He pointed to the horse cart. "How about you take this load of oats up to the Old Mitt's stock house? We'll make sure the tavern is spotless by sunset."

"That's right, Donny," Seth McGregor added with a good-natured jab to the shoulder. "Hoffman doesn't have to know who fixed the place up.

Only that it's done. We'll keep it a secret. Next time, try to use the front door instead of the window when you leave."

Donavon responded with a hearty jab of his own, then looked to Francis. "You've got yourself a deal, brother," he said, heading to the horse cart. "The tavern better be spotless or I'll have you all looking like Seth." With a leap he was up on the cart and off with a snap of the reins.

Weariness hung heavily on Donavon as the cart rolled to a halt in front of the colonel's stock house. Slouched on the bench, he gazed at the wood grains of the hefty doors. The day had caught up with him: his head pounded, his lesions throbbed, and his body stank to the point where even he was disgusted. So much had happened in such a short time. Hard to believe it was just about this time yesterday that he socked Angus in the jaw. The grime of the morning's labors clung like tar pitch to his clothes. It took every ounce of effort just to get his aching body off the cart to unhitch the horse.

The horse whinnied when he released the hitch, snapping him out of his malaise. "Easy there, big fella," he said, holding tight on the tether. "What's got you spooked?"

He heard a scuffling in the dirt from the side of the stock house. Donavon turned around in time to see the tail end of a badger plow through the tall grass in the direction of the colonel's beehives. "There goes a fat one," he said with a pat to the horse. "You must have busted up its nap with all your fuss. Too bad I didn't have my bow ready."

The horse continued to fidget. Something still had it spooked. Another badger most likely. Whatever it was, Donavon had learned a long time ago never to dismiss the instincts of a horse. He let go of the tether to grab the metal pry bar in the front seat. In an instant the horse was off at a gallop, back to the colonel's manor, leaving Donavon alone with the cart.

"Stay out of Enya's flowers!" he shouted.

With pry bar in hand, he inspected the side of the stock house. Sure enough a substantial hole had been excavated near the rear corner. At least a month old, maybe two, by the looks of it. Pretty big for a badger, he thought. The sight of the hole rekindled his pulse. Few things excited him more than a challenging hunt. He went back around the corner to the front and gave a firm sideways tug to the track door. He sniffed at the stale, musty air inside.

At first glance he saw nothing unusual. The hay bales were exactly where he and his brothers had stacked them last fall, as was the heap of cordwood. Scanning the walls, however, he noticed that the lowest shelf had collapsed onto a stack of buckets. Jars of the colonel's honey lay scattered on the earthen floor, several of them broken and still oozing their sticky contents. Upon closer examination Donavon saw trails of dried blood leading to the broken glass. Or were they leading away? He wasn't sure. Some of the stains had crusted over while others were more recent. He followed one of the trails back to the far end of the haystack and noticed several dismantled bales hidden in the shadows. He moved in for a closer look, dropping the pry bar and grabbing a pitchfork that hung on the wall. Cautiously, he shoved aside the shredded hay with the prongs of the fork and revealed a massacre.

Tufts of gray and white fir matted with blood lay strewn throughout the nest. Old blood, Donavon noted. Blood that had long congealed into a thick, hardened mass. Tiny bones lay scattered amidst the fur, their dried strands of flesh nibbled by rodents. Poking through the grave, Donavon discovered a single paw barely larger than his thumb. He picked up the tiny paw and counted the pads—four. It was small but definitely canine.

"The Old Mitt was right after all," he said aloud. "Wait till he finds out about this."

He tallied up the evidence as best he could in the dim light. It had been a litter of three to five by the looks of it, assuming none had been dragged off. He set out to report the news to the colonel. On his way out, he picked up a piece of cordwood that had strayed from the pile and tossed it back onto the main heap. A growl came out of the wood, spurring Donavon to grab the pitchfork once again.

"Come on, you fat weasel, let's have at it!" he shouted at the pile.

Hearing no further sound, he crept forward, hands tight on the fork, ready to skewer the cornered scoundrel. He rounded the pile but found nothing. Not even a hole in the floor. Mystified, he leaned against the firewood and looked up, thinking the elusive badger might be hiding in the rafters. A log shifted against his weight, and to his shock, he heard the same growl rise up from between his legs. Donavon jumped away and roared back at the logs, his heart rate soaring.

At the base of the pile he saw a narrow cavity, small and easy to miss. Too small for a full-grown badger, he thought. He spun the fork around and stuck the handle into the opening. In an instant the tool was seized, followed by a barrage of vicious snarls. He pulled out the handle and discovered tiny teeth marks embedded in the wood, alongside streaks of fresh red blood. It was injured, whatever it was. Cautiously, he dug into the pile with the pitchfork, aware that even a squirrel in such a state was dangerous when cornered. Piece by piece he exposed the cavity until at last he caught a glimpse of the varmint's white and gray fur through the spaces in the wood. With the ferocious creature nearly exposed, he retracted the fork, ready to strike. Though what he uncovered when he kicked away the last logs froze him where he stood. There before him, with its hackles pressed to a log, was a wolf pup.

"Well, I'll be a badger's biscuit," Donavon said in surprise. "You sure are a scraggly one."

Indeed, at first glance the pup appeared to be nothing more than a tattered mass of fur and bones. It was covered from head to tail in dried blood, though the stains around its snarling jowls were moist. Amazing, Donavon thought, that the little whelp had any life left in it. A series of scabs streaked across both sides of its snout—claw marks by the looks of them. One of the gashes led to its oozing eye socket that was swollen shut.

"Looks like that fat badger's been giving you a rough run," he said, tossing away the pitchfork and kneeling. "I know the feeling. Come on, little fella, I know just the one who can fix you up. I gotta see her myself."

The pup appeared to relax at the sound of his voice, but instantly recoiled when he extended his hand.

"Don't worry. If I wanted to kill you, you'd be long dead by now."

Inch by inch Donavon brought his hand closer, concentrating on the pitch of the growl. Just when he expected, the young wolf lunged forward and snapped. With lightning precision, Donavon withdrew his right hand and snatched the pup with his left.

"Ah-ha, gotcha! You're fast, but not fast enough."

Hung by the scruff, the pup went limp, as if knowing that its long fight for survival was over. It opened its mouth and began to pant. A steady dribble of blood pattered on Donavon's forearm as he held the creature aloft. Face to face, he watched its tongue go up and down, riddled with layers upon layers of scars and lacerations.

"That's no badger that did that," he said, glancing at the honey jars on the floor. "You've been lapping broken glass, haven't you?"

The dismal revelation hit hard. Donavon had always taken pride in his resourceful approach to life, never claiming to be a victim nor offering sympathy to those who did. The world was a rough place, and there was no point polluting it with mushy sentiments. Maybe it was the lack of sleep, or perhaps it was the awakening of something deeper. Whatever it was, he knew that for the first time in his life he had a friend he could trust to the ends of the earth.

"Come on," he said, cradling the pup in his bandaged arm. "Let's get cleaned up."

3
Church and State

Pastor Marcus Poulakis never aspired to be a political man. Perhaps it was the call of the times combined with venerable wisdom that got him where it had by default. To his credit, he never allowed the stately status to distract him from his divine mission.

Marcus was well into his fifties when the Fatherland declared martial law on the province. The seeds of dissension had been sown long before, dating back to the year prior his birth, when the Haven's sixth baron was executed for succumbing to the charms of a heathen witch. The act triggered a cultural divide everpresent to Marcus. Had it not been for the good tutoring of the monks who took him under their wing at Wulfhaven abbey, he might have chosen a different platform from which to base his campaign for peace. Yet for all his tenacity before and during the war, it was his hard work after the war that cast the clearest light on his spiritual nature.

"Ah, yes, peace at last," said the exhausted old reverend, entering his private prayer chamber in the north transept of the cathedral. Like a parched sponge, Marcus absorbed the simplicity around him: no dictations, no lessons, no clergymen scrambling for mundane decisions, no sick children sneezing on his robe, no pressing issues tugging at his judgment of the moral high ground. In short, no problems. Just a small blanket mounted on a bare candlelit wall. He sighed. This was his time. The one sacred hour at the end of each day to relax his mind and recharge his faith. He knelt before the blanket in the tranquil light of the room to recite his daily prayer.

"Blessed Father, confide in me your wisdom so that I may strengthen the hearts of your children. Grant me yet one more day that I may serve this pledge with heart, body, mind, and soul."

It was a practical prayer that got right to the point. That was what Marcus liked about it. So direct and simple, yet somehow so complete. If only everything in life could be summed up so concisely. But then again, perhaps not. Truth be told, he had discovered a long time ago that it was in the shady areas of life where God's light shone most brilliantly. The prayer merely confirmed what he already knew. It had come to him in the darkest days of the war after a particularly contentious argument with Cornelius Mitterhal. The headstrong commander, for all his agnostic jargon, had made a valid point that challenged Marcus to look deeply into his faith. Not a day had passed since then that he was not driven by the intense power of the prayer—though in those days he was rarely granted the luxury of silence that he now had in the chapel sanctum.

Grateful, Marcus closed his eyes and made ready to surrender his cares to the infinite peace. A hand pressed his shoulder. It was a light touch, but for all its gentle intent, it had the same effect as a throttling jolt. Marcus opened his eyes and swallowed hard to keep his temper in check.

"Forgive me, Father," whispered the monk at his side. "There is a large man in the nave who wishes to make a confession."

Marcus glared into the blanket on the wall. The infant's coverlet never failed to relax him. He knew every stitch as if his own hand had woven it. He also knew that Brother Michael would never intrude on his chambers without just cause.

"How large?" he whispered back.

"Very. The likes of which I've only read in scripture."

Marcus nodded. "I see. Direct him to the penance chamber. I will be there shortly."

"As you wish, Father." Brother Michael bowed and left to carry out the order.

Alone again, Marcus repeated the last half of his prayer aloud. Only one man in the lake province fit the monk's description, and he was not the confessing type.

Marcus paused at the door of the penance chamber. The low droning monotone emanated from within, confirming his guess. What could possibly have compelled the Haven Guard's chief cipher-at-arms to examine his conscience? Where would he even begin? There was only one way to find out. Marcus slipped his hand up under his beard to straighten his collar. After a deep breath, he opened the door and entered.

The only vaulted window in the room silhouetted the enormous back and shoulders of Jeziah McCaskel. Marcus reflected on the irony of the hooded giant's position under the transom. Had it been daytime, the sunlight would have passed through the colored glass and highlighted an armed archangel smoting divine justice on a demon. Which would the cipher be, angel or demon? Marcus mused on the question while he waited for the warrior to end his chant.

In due course, Jeziah lowered his hood and turned his back on the window, revealing in the candlelight his war-ravaged face. A braided beard with dreads the length of a horse's tail rose up and down in measured rhythm on his broad chest. Marcus could not help marveling at the presence before him. He felt as if death itself had come to pay a visit.

"Welcome, my son," he said, sticking to protocol. "I beseech to thee under witness of our Great Father, creator of heaven and earth, that through me he may hear your plea and absolve you of your earthly sins. And to know that by his mercy you will be granted eternal life with the angels in heaven above."

No reply, only the crushing weight of the cipher's gaze. Marcus summoned his courage and advanced toward the towering form. Apparently, his protocol would have to be modified. Such was often the case when dealing with the veterans of Spaulding Pass.

"I remind you, Jeziah, that while you are in this house, you are bound by its rules. What is your sin? State it or leave."

The skin between the scars on Jeziah's forehead flushed red. "I have no confession," he replied. The statement sank like an anchor in the hallowed chamber.

Marcus furrowed his brow. "Well then, shall I consider that your confession, or would you prefer that I ask the angel in the window to escort you out the door?"

The giant grunted, appearing derailed by the option. "I deliver a message from the mayor," came the delayed response.

The pastor's eyebrows went up. "Ah, so the good mayor is behind this. And what would Barleycopp have you say that he cannot say himself?"

"He seeks a meeting with you in confidence."

"I see. And when is this meeting to take place?"

"Now."

"Now? And where, dare I ask?"

"I am not to say. Only that your safe return is guaranteed. The coach is behind the infirmary. I will wait for you there."

"Safe return from what?" Marcus asked. "You entered the house of our Great Father under the pretense of confessing your sins. Why should I acknowledge anything else you say to be true?"

A long moment lapsed while the cipher appeared to process the question. "I seek neither heaven nor hell, only to rest in the shade of the

Great Mountain. Until that day I serve the Haven, which includes your protection. You will be safe so long as I breathe."

Marcus sat alone inside the windowless coach, lurching up and down in the darkness, wondering what had possessed him to trust the grim warrior. The carriage wheels rattled like a washboard over the cobblestones. He did his best to keep a tally of the turns from the abbey. In time, the cobbles turned to gravel and the horse's pace quickened. He guessed they were somewhere between the city proper and the fairgrounds. A hard right, three slow downs, and two jarring lefts later the carriage came to a sudden stop. Marcus heard hushed voices and then what sounded like a large wooden door sliding on rollers. The carriage moved forward again, though more slowly. Marcus was greeted by the unmistakable scent of horse manure as the carriage rolled to an easy stop. He felt the springs of the chassis give and heard his escort's imposing footsteps on the soft floor. The door opened. A dim light entered the cab.

"We are here, Pastor," Jeziah announced.

Marcus stepped out of the carriage and looked around. A single lantern hung on a nearby post. They were in a building. His gaze followed the dimly lit timber into the shadowy canopy of rafters and roof purlins. Looking back down, he saw that the carriage had stopped in a wide clay aisle lined on both sides by shoulder-high stalls. He had the impression that the space around him was vast, and that the lantern's light revealed but a fraction of the structure's total interior. His eyes acclimated, and he realized where he was.

"So the Haven stables is the secret spot," he said to Jeziah, who closed the carriage door behind him.

The giant pointed to another light, trickling out from under a massive door in a partition that rose to the rafters. "This way, Pastor." Jeziah slid the heavy door aside with ease, and they entered a great wooden hall lit by more lanterns. The tack room for the Haven Guard's cavalry, it appeared. Bridle bits, halters, and stirrups dangled in neat order alongside an impressive assortment of pikes, poleaxes, and sabers. Most striking to Marcus were the rows of dust-covered saddles that hung from haunted wall mounts.

Together they walked the length of the tack room, which went on for some time, until they came to another door that bore the brass emblem of the Haven Guard. They entered the room and Marcus got a whiff of cedar. On either side were racks upon racks of uniforms and battle wear. At the far end of the armory, a man sat in a chair next to yet another door. As they approached, Marcus realized that the man, though brawny up top, had no legs. A holstered pistol strapped to a lanyard hung from the side of his chair.

"Hail, Gahenya, Father," the man said when they arrived. "It's been a while. I would kneel before you if I could. You know that, don't you?"

Marcus recognized the soldier. "There is no need for that, Duncan. I am made of flesh and blood, just like you. Save your kneeling for the church pew."

The guardman looked down at his stumps and smiled. "I might just do that, Father." He gestured to the door beside him. "Your passage is granted."

Jeziah led Marcus down a set of stone steps to a clay-tiled floor. The air was cool and damp. A line of torches lit the subterranean chamber. They followed the torches to a wide steel door mounted on thick metal hinges embedded in the masonry. There, Jeziah stopped and looked at Marcus. "We are here."

Jeziah opened the door, revealing a table surrounded by a dozen or so seated men. In an instant every man was off his chair and down on one knee, facing him. At the far end of the table, standing alone with both hands behind his decorated waistcoat, was the mayor himself, Captain Marlin Barleycopp.

"Greetings, Pastor," he said. "I am glad you could make it this evening. My apologies for the short notice. I trust Jeziah was sensitive to your traveling comfort."

"He was a fine escort," Marcus said, looking at the hard-faced men kneeling before him. He recognized several from the war. A few even attended church on rare occasion. "Rise, my sons," he said, gesturing with open hands. "You know my policy on kneeling."

The men rose to a chorus of Hail Pastors, then broke into a hymn. Marcus bowed in response to the spirited welcome.

When the hymn ended, Marlin Barleycopp addressed the group. "Well done, men. On that note we will adjourn the meeting here. You all know your assignments. We will meet again next month to follow up on operations. Any urgent matters between now and then must be brought to my attention only through the channels discussed. Remember, secrecy is of utmost importance. Not all of Rankwall's Pogetsa wear uniforms. Until then, may the light of the Haven shine on us all. Hail, Gahenya."

"Hail, Gahenya!" chimed the men in response. One by one they filed out of the room, each giving a respectful bow to the pastor on his way out. Marcus acknowledged every man with a nod while Jeziah remained silent and still, looming in the shadows like a stone monument. At the end of the procession, a young face caught Marcus by surprise.

"Adman. What brings you here, my son?"

The mayor stepped in before Adman could say a word. "Master McFadden, perhaps you could stay while we discuss matters with the pastor?"

"Of course, sir."

Barleycopp looked to the chief cipher. "Jeziah, I believe your service this evening is complete. A mission well done. You are dismissed."

Jeziah remained exactly where he was.

"You may leave, Jeziah," the mayor repeated.

An awkward moment lapsed before Jeziah replied. "I promised the pastor his safe return."

"I see. Well, that certainly presents a dilemma." Barleycopp adjusted the silver brooch on his blue braided shoulder cord. "Perhaps if the pastor were willing to transfer your promise to the eldest son of Meguntoc, we could consider your duty fulfilled?"

Jeziah's grim gaze fell on Adman and then Marcus. "That is for the pastor to decide."

"That will be fine," Marcus said, impressed by the cipher's integrity. "Bless you, my son. I relieve you of your service, though I am still open to your confession should you decide to give one. If not, I will be sure to put in a good word for you so that you may rest well in the shade of your mountain."

A slight shift in the cipher's beard hinted at a smile, though his black penetrating eyes offered no further clue. With barely a nod he ducked under the doorway and was gone.

Marcus promptly turned around and faced the mayor. "Sending the chief cipher to give a confession was an unconventional move, Marlin. If I did not know any better, I would guess you are taking orders from the colonel again."

Barleycopp's glance to Adman was enough to convince Marcus he was not far from the mark. Adman's attempt at a blank expression further confirmed his suspicion. "So how is the blessed old goat doing?" he asked the tight-lipped young man.

Adman looked to Barleycopp, who nodded. "His recovery is steady, Father. Enya stays at the manor day and night now."

"That is good. And his ribs?"

"All right, I guess. He gets around easy enough with the cane Francis carved for him, but I don't think he'll ever make it up that ladder again."

"No, I suspect not." The pastor glanced wistfully at the damp stones that lined the room. "For better or worse, the colonel's days on the rooftop are over." After a reflective pause, he looked back at the mayor. "Well then, I'm sure we have not gathered within these cheery walls to discuss the colonel's health. Shall we get to the point, Marlin?"

The mayor leaned forward with both hands on the table. "We have a problem, Marcus."

"A problem? The last time I heard you utter that word we had a dead constable on our hands. What have you decided to stretch my faith with this time?"

"That was an accident, Pastor. This matter is political."

"And the death of the general's son was not? I remind you that I am a man of God, not politics. Covering up accidents such as that are precisely why I stay out of your line of work. What do you want from me?"

139

"I need a formal statement from the church requesting a cease and desist order on the Silvermine Bridge project. Gwyntahpynn Choroqua has expressed in no uncertain terms that he will use whatever means necessary to keep the mines closed."

"Correct me if I am wrong, Marlin, but the chancellor has issued a treaty that promises no mining activity on their side of the Haven. The rail will be used strictly for transport and nothing more."

"That sounds well and good on paper," the mayor said, "but Choroqua will not buy that. And quite frankly, neither should we. What Rankwall says today has no bearing on what he will do tomorrow. We saw that in the war. He made a tactical gamble with the Three Havens that happened to pay off better than he thought. But in his sweet victory, we should not forget the deceitful methods he used to achieve it. Nor the men who died as a result."

"And why would you have the church submit this motion? Such an order falls under your jurisdiction."

"Because I have nothing to bargain with. The Haven Guard is a fraction of what it was, and Rankwall knows it. If I submit such an order, he will simply override it and continue with the project as planned. A motion by the church, however, he cannot discount so easily. Many of his constituents in Altomar still hold true to the faith. At the very least, it will delay his plans and give us more time."

"Time for what, Marlin? I have not seen you like this since the war."

Barleycopp straightened his posture, stiff and resolved. "A man of Rankwall's fiber will only bargain if he has something to lose. I need time to rebuild the Guard."

Dizziness. Marcus felt the blood thump up the sides of his neck. "By the light of the Haven, Marlin, what you insinuate is a civil war. I will not be instrumental in such madness, nor will I use the faith of our people as pawns for political maneuvering. The Haven has yet to recover from losing one generation of men, and you are already planning on how to lose the next!" Marcus loosened his collar. He felt feverish. Sweat slid down his forehead. "You asked me for a favor once, and I obliged only for the sake of Uryan's children. What you ask of me now I will not embrace. Absolutely not, Mayor."

The war medals drooped on Barleycopp's deflated chest. "Then there ends our hope for peace with the tribes. They have no tolerance for lies and even less for weakness of resolve. You of all people have earned their trust. They will see our apathy as nothing less than treachery. They will defend their sacred land, and Rankwall will respond with whatever means necessary to exterminate them. And we will have done nothing to stop it. If that is the will of the church, then perhaps we are no better off than the Torics we defeated." Barleycopp turned to Adman. "Master

McFadden, I believe we have taken up enough of the good pastor's time. See to it that Jeziah's promise is kept."

"Yes, sir," Adman said, and walked to the door.

Marcus unclipped his collar entirely. More dizziness. He felt clammy. Cold heat. He put his hand to the wall. Specks of torchlight glistened like stars on the dampened mosaic. Breathing heavily, he stared into the patterns of masonry, trying in his swoon to get a grip on something, anything, tangible. No good. Nothing. He wiped the sweat off his brow and closed his eyes. The patterns of the stones scrambled in his mind, revolving in a sea of stars. His ears rang; the vortex widened. He fell in a blur of spinning light.

Something cold touched his face. A hand squeezed his shoulder and he heard a voice. "Are you all right, Pastor?"

Marcus opened his eyes. Two upside-down faces loomed beyond a canopy of dangling war medals. It was Adman McFadden and the mayor. Together they lifted Marcus into a sitting position. Adman continued to pat his face with a moistened cloth.

"What happened?" Marcus asked, sweeping the dust off his robe.

"You fainted, Father," Adman said. "We were about to leave."

"Oh, yes, we were, weren't we? I am getting too old for this, my boy. You best help me up."

Standing again, Marcus faced Barleycopp. "Tell me, Marlin. Why would the Gwyntahmahoma trust me? I do not preach their goddess."

"No, you don't, Pastor, but you did serve as the colonel's spiritual advisor during the war. They believe he is directly blessed by their Great Mother, and that makes him the Gwyntah equivalent of a prophet. They will not question his authority or judgment. The fact that Mitterhal entrusted you with the faith of his troops carries considerable weight with the tribes, regardless of what deity you preach. And sending the lupini across the Haven during the drought only heightened their respect for you. I assure you that you have Choroqua's trust. What you do with it is your choice."

Silence stifled the chamber as Marcus considered the mayor's words. At last he walked to the doorway and turned around at the threshold. "I will not condone war, Marlin. The Three Havens have had enough of it. However, I will call for a forum open to all Haven parishes so that we may better understand the impacts of the bridge project and put the issue to a vote. If a two-thirds majority agrees to the motion, then you will have your formal statement from the church. That is the best I can do. The rest we will entrust to the good sense of our people."

Barleycopp tucked both hands behind his waistcoat and resumed his stately airs. "Then I will consider this meeting a success. By the light of the Haven, Pastor, I thank you for your time."

4

Gathering of the Guard

Enyalda wept in the kitchen amidst the cluster of clay pots she had set on the slate counter. Each pot contained a seed that she watered with care. It was her way of compensating for the loss of her trusted confidant. On the sill, above the pots, was the amaryllis—what was left of it. The wilted stem hung over the edge of the shelf as a stark reminder of the flower's recurring fate. It happened every year at this time. Enyalda had yet to summon the nerve to snip it. Such was the way of bulbs. In truth, she would get over the loss, as she had done so many times, going back to her days with Muma. *"Hein shahuna ah prista al gahut solam,"* the wise old woman would say at such times—Through shadow and light, all life returns. Just thinking the words made her smile. In tribute to the amaryllis, she sang a song of encouragement to the morning glory seeds that would soon be sprouting in the light of a new day.

Her song was ambushed by Adman's loud entry into the kitchen. "Enya, we have work to do. Visitors will be arriving tonight from the Haven. We need to get the rooms upstairs ready at once. And they will need to eat. Francis will pick up whatever you need in the village. He will also take care of the drink. Donavon is out at the stock house with the wolf splitting cordwood. He'll have all the fireplaces stoked and the lamps lit by evening. I've no doubt we can pull this off."

Enyalda wiped away her tears, not that her brother would have noticed. He was such a clueless twig when it came to sensitivity. It had always been his habit to make whatever was urgent on his mind urgent for everyone else. She also knew that *we* in his eyes meant *she*—another one of his annoying quirks. One stomp of her foot simmered him down.

He blinked and then resumed his directives at a more reasonable pace. "Sorry, sis, I'm getting ahead of myself. It's just that this is so big. The Guard is gathering now that the colonel is back. The top ranks are coming tonight to brief him on the status of things. We will need a dozen beds ready. The colonel already knows."

Enyalda went back to the amaryllis and snipped the wilted stem; the action gave her time to think. Twelve men. That meant twenty-four eyes. Everything was happening so fast. Gazing at the dormant bulb, she pined for the uncomplicated days when her foremost chore was to sit in the branches of the Great Beech and whisper blessings to the colonel through the leaves.

After a long silence, she felt Adman's firm hand on her shoulder. "I know you can do it, Enya. You have more strength than you know. You always have. Here, I picked this up in the old port on my last trip to Wulfhaven and thought you should be the one to give it to him."

Enyalda looked over her shoulder and saw a pipe in Adman's hand. She swept back her hair to examine it closely. It was a work of art. The horned head of a mountain goat was carved into the face of the bowl, behind which a silver ring sparkled at the junction where the curved stem met the burl.

"This comes with it," Adman said, reaching for a leather pouch that hung from his waistband by a rawhide lace. A goat head, similar to the carving on the pipe, was embroidered into the pouch. Above it a single word had been stitched in silver thread—*Tuftash.*

How perfect, Enyalda thought. That meant smoking goat in Muma's language. Not that the colonel was a goat. But he did like them, and he was a smoker. Or at least, was.

Adman placed the pipe and pouch in her hands. "It's greenbank smoke from the Ring in Gwyntahlynn," he said, sweeping aside her hair. "An aromatic blend, I am told. And don't worry, I've already cleared it with Pastor Marcus."

Enyalda looked up at her brother and in that moment imagined him as a noble prince of some far-off land. Such was the way with Adman. Just when his compulsive bossiness reached the brink of tolerance, he would come up with a gesture that revealed his gracious nature. It was a cycle that spread everyone's patience thin at times, but in the end, it usually worked out for the better. Enyalda set the thoughtful gifts on the counter and hugged her brother. She would do what he asked.

The manor was bustling by midafternoon. Francis returned with the requested ingredients, and Enyalda promptly recruited him to mash a bushel's worth of butternut squash in the largest copper pot she could find. It marked an unprecedented moment of delegation in the kitchen. She even entrusted him with the all-important task of stirring the gravy. There was no choice in the matter. The rooms upstairs had yet to be cleaned and the beds made ready for guests. So with Francis hastily draped in an apron and set to task, Enyalda ascended the stairs with her feather duster and a bucket full of cleaning rags.

A woozy sensation swept over her at the top of the stairwell. The space creaked with history. She had never been up there before. It had always been the barmaid's job to change the colonel's linens. She counted the unlit oil lamps mounted on the fancy woodwork that surrounded each door. Ten in all, five on each side of the hall. The doors looked like upright coffins built into the plaster. She wondered when they last had been opened.

She tried the first door on the left. The hinges creaked and sunlight poured into the hallway. The light lifted her spirits and she entered. She was relieved to find a bed, a dresser, and a desk all perfectly intact, though they were covered with a considerable amount of dust and mice droppings. Straight away she opened the weighted windows and began her work, inspired by the fresh air.

Once she was in motion, her mission seemed far less daunting. She whipped through her chore like a whirlwind, her rags spinning in frenzy. Six of the rooms, as it turned out, were furnished with beds, three of which had two. Every bedroom had a cedar chest that contained a set of extra quilts. A most fortunate discovery, since moths and mice had ravaged the bedding on all nine beds. Three more rooms appeared to be studies, lined with shelves of cob-covered books. Enyalda was relieved to see that each study had a desk, a chair, and, more importantly, a couch, which brought the total sleeping arrangements to twelve. Humming her way back to the other rooms, she absconded enough bedding out of the chests for two of the couches, but came up short for the third. She stepped over the heap of moth-eaten linens in the center of the hall and approached the last closed door. Her humming stopped. Again, she felt woozy. For whatever the reason, she had avoided this particular door all afternoon. Now with little choice she put her hand to the latch.

The first thing she saw was a loom upright in the rear of the room by the east-facing window. The square wooden frame was as tall as a grown man and equally wide. A complete tapestry was suspended in the midst of the frame by strands of crisscrossed threads. She approached the tapestry and touched it, sending an avalanche of dust down to the foot pedal on the floor.

"Ooo ..." She marveled at the sublime scene woven into the fabric.

A single green stalk of gahenya sprouted in the foreground. The stem was draped in pods, one of which was open and revealed the bright yellow seeds within. A meadow filled the middle section, stitched in the richest blue. Above the meadow loomed a mountain, and upon its silver peak stood a lone goat. Over the goat was a dark sky full of stars. Upon closer inspection, Enyalda saw that the celestial patterns in the sky revealed the open wings of a butterfly.

Her imagination soared and she felt light, as if viewing the mountain from a cloud. Floating, floating, floating. Her hands twirled in the filtered light. Wait! Something red, behind the loom, near the closet. She gasped. It was a man. Without a head! Her shrill cry echoed down the hall. Her legs failed and she fell to the floor, hands over eyes.

Francis came first, followed by Donavon. They found her on her knees, crying, her face draped in hair. "What's the matter, Enya? What happened?" Francis put a hand on her shaking shoulder.

She kept her eyes covered and pointed in the direction of the headless man.

Donavon charged the closet door, an iron poker clenched in his hand. He swung open the door, ready to strike. A horrified mouse skittered through the opening and dashed across the floor, leaving a tiny trail of dots in the dust. After a thorough search of the closet, Donavon lowered his weapon. "What's going on, Enya?"

"Easy, brother," Francis said, his hand still on her shoulder. "Give her a minute. I think the day has caught up with her. It's okay, Enya, relax."

She dared a glance at the headless man and realized it was nothing more than a uniform mounted on a rack. Relieved, she looked at Francis and giggled. How silly he looked in the gravy-stained apron.

"There, that's the sister we know," he said. "Let's get you downstairs. Donny and I will take care of everything up here."

"Hey, what's this?" Donavon asked, prodding the uniform.

Dust trickled off the gold-braided epaulettes to the tethered gators. The waistcoat, like the gators, was crimson red and fastened to the right of center by a line of gold buttons. A distinguished brass amulet hung to mid-chest beneath a white lace collar. To the left of the amulet, an assortment of brooches and medals were pinned to the velvety fabric. Below the waistcoat a pair of starched white breeches hung alongside a scabbard suspended by a black leather belt. Enyalda squeaked as Donavon grabbed the brass handle and unsheathed the saber.

"Nice sword," he said, swinging the weapon in a sweeping arc. "I could poke a pogie with this."

"I'd put that thing back if I were you," Francis said. "It's not yours and it looks expensive."

Enyalda, at ease again in the company of her brothers, resumed her investigation of the room. A portrait hung on the far wall near a child's crib. The painting depicted a man in uniform next to a woman. The same uniform, Enyalda realized, that was on the rack. Moving in for a closer look, she saw that the man's face was hard but his eyes were soft—so much like the colonel's. She put her finger on the aged cracks in the canvas and felt the love he must have harbored for the beautiful woman at his side. She wore a white gown adorned in feathers and petals. Her black braided hair cascaded to her bare shoulders from a crown of flowering vines. A blue pendant graced her elegant neck.

Donavon joined her. "Hey, that's the same necklace Captain Marly had us give the colonel last fall after the highland feast. What's she doing with that?"

Enyalda wiped the dust off a brass plate mounted on the bottom of the frame.

Francis peered at it. "What's that say? It looks Gwyntah to me."

Enyalda read the words etched in the brass. *Yan shahuna maha na geshiva kutchu.* She knew the words well. Muma had instructed her to say them whenever she awoke from a nightmare: In the shadow of the mountain, we fear no evil.

"I bet that's Old Mitt's mother," Francis said. "Remember what Captain Marly told us to say? We had to tell him it was a wedding present worn by the mother of the Mahocpynn. Why else would Gwyntahpynn Choroqua have given it to him?"

Donavon went back to the uniform and slid the sword into its scabbard. "I wonder what Mahocpynn means."

"Some kind of chief, I think."

"Old Mitt's a far cry from a Gwyntah chief."

Francis looked at Enyalda. "Who knows what he was to them. Any idea, sister?"

Enyalda suddenly felt exhausted. The words under the portrait kept repeating in her mind. Looking away from Francis, she saw a cedar chest in the opposite corner of the room and was reminded of her task. She crossed to the chest and opened it, finding an assortment of neatly folded quilts. With her last reserves of energy dwindling, she removed the blankets and brought them to Francis. He would know what to do with them.

He took the quilts. "Good thinking, Enya. Let's get you downstairs for a nap. You need to rest now. Our guests won't be showing up until later. We need you in top form tonight." He looked to his brother who was still gawking at the uniform. "Come on, Donny. You can grab that pile of bedding in the hall and get the lamps lit. I'll take care of Enya."

A solarium had been built adjacent to the kitchen on the southwest corner of the colonel's manor. The sunny room was nestled in the crease of the gable and projected out from the body of the house onto a stone terrace. The glass room was generous in size, spanning the breadth of a mule cart and extending twice the length. From the kitchen, a half-flight of stairs led to a tile floor. Interspersing the tiles were a series of sunken stone beds filled with rich black soil. A wide potting bench was set into a recessed wall near the base of the stairs. It was the only place in the room that afforded shade in the afternoon hours. A variety of herbs and flowers scented the air, providing the perfect sanctuary for Enyalda to regain her strength.

She awoke on the bench, tickled by the tendril of a flowering vine. She sat up and yawned, still wrapped in the quilts from the room with the loom. How considerate of her brother to bring her here. It was by far her favorite place in the manor, though it had never dawned on her to nap here. Safe in her space, she stretched her arms and legs and smiled at the clematis that climbed up the wall to greet her. The white petals were quick to remind her of her dream.

It had been a beautiful dream, the kind one hates to leave. She was in a forest of rich green moss and ferns, skipping in twilight on a trail of flattened stones. A raised granite ledge cropped out of the boreal carpet. She came to a set of stairs, stone stairs covered in lichen. They were old, very old. At the top of the steps she found an altar of white linen surrounded by a canopy of flowering vines, equally white. A beautiful woman rested on the altar with her back propped against the ledge of moss. The same woman from the portrait, so earthly elegant in her floral crown, yet sad. Tracks of dried tears led down her neck to the pendant that sparkled silver on the fringe of her white lace gown. Enyalda yearned to touch the sapphire in the center of the pendant, but the dream ended. Though the details of the vision were fading fast—as they so often did in the conscious world—the sad woman's parting words still resonated in her mind. "*Su gahwynn*," she had said in the language of the tribes. Thank you.

Francis suddenly appeared at the top of the steps with ladle in hand, still wearing the gravy-stained apron. "Hello, sister," he said, licking the ladle. "How was your nap?"

In a flash, she remembered her task and spun into action. She scurried up the stairs, snatching the ladle out of his hand. Into the kitchen she dashed, then stopped and retraced her steps to kiss her brother on the cheek, noting the globs of gravy and squash that were enmeshed in the black curls of his beard.

"Look's like your energy's back," he said. "Wait till Adman sees you. He thought I was crazy for laying you out on the potting bench. He's in the hearth room now receiving our guests. I took the liberty of seasoning the squash. I hope you don't mind."

In a panic she darted to the two copper pots that simmered on the wood-fired stove. Grabbing a mitt that hung on a nearby hook, she took the lid off the largest pot and stirred the mash. A dreadful moment passed while she blew on the steaming scoop in her ladle. She tasted. A bit heavy on the ale perhaps, but overall not bad. Francis had promise after all. The gravy, she discovered, had been seasoned in a similar fashion. With the immediate crisis resolved, she turned to the counter where she had left six loaves of bread to rise. All were baked and in fine shape, except for the one Francis had nibbled on.

Adman burst through the kitchen door in a hooded tunic. "Francis, they are here! Where's En— Oh, there you are." He faced his sister. "The men have gathered at the hearth, Enya. I filled all their mugs but they look hungry. Let's not keep them waiting. Is everything in order here?"

She nodded, though pensively. The notion of serving a roomful of hungry men weighed on her. It was not their stomachs she feared but their eyes.

"Good." Adman turned to his brother. "Francis, you can bring Donny his dinner. He's brooding out at the fire pit with the wolf. Why don't you go out and cheer him up? I'll let you know when the meeting adjourns. Good job in the kitchen, by the way," he said, heading back to the door.

With Adman gone, Enyalda sighed in relief. She loved her brother dearly, but his domineering presence made it impossible to think. First thing first. She went to the cutting board to slice the bread.

Francis placed a stack of plates next to her. "I guess my job in here is done, sis. Are you going to be all right?"

She stopped her slicing and stared at the bin of powdered sugar Francis had left open on the counter. His good intentions would only get in the way. There was still a lot to be done and she needed a full range of motion in the kitchen without distraction. She dipped her hand into the powdered sugar and in one quick blow encased her brother's face in a cloud of sweetened mist.

"I'll take that as a yes," he said, wiping the powder out of his eyes. Promptly he left.

With the kitchen to herself, Enyalda got to work. It would take three trips to serve all the men the main course. For the first trip she loaded the tray to capacity with five plates and the respective silverware. On each plate she placed a heaping mound of butternut squash along with a hunk of smoked mutton and a slice of buttered bread, all of which she drizzled liberally with gravy. On the colonel's plate she made sure to include one whole boiled turnip, unpeeled. When the time came to deliver the meal, she bowed to the dormant amaryllis and whispered a parting prayer.

Enyalda dared not look up when she entered the hearth room. She could feel the presence of the men clustered around the colonel by the fireplace. The low hum of their conversation halted as she swept across the lamp-lit room to the empty dining table with her serving tray. Eyes still on the floor, she was startled by a voice that came from the chair next to her. She could have sworn there were no feet there. Risking a glance upward, she realized the man who sat in the chair had no legs. Father?

"Hello, my lady," said the legless man, dispelling her guess. "So you're the one Uryan always raved about. Now I see why he called you his shining little star. I am Duncan Jacks, your father's flank man. It is a privilege to meet you at last."

Enyalda relaxed. She liked his voice. It almost made her want to respond with words. She bowed and placed the plate in front of him. Getting back to her task, she set the remaining plates on the table, making sure to put the one with the boiled turnip at the head. She had no sooner turned back to the kitchen to reload her tray, when a beastly grunt came from the shadows. The sound was deep, like a snorting bear. She gasped as she saw the hideous bearded monster in the corner of the room. Even seated, it engulfed the space around it.

"By the grace of the Great Dome," said the colonel, rising from his leather chair. "I see that Jeziah hasn't lost his charm with the ladies. Don't worry, my dear, he's as gentle as a lamb."

A round of laughter erupted that took the curse out of the room. With the men so engaged, Enyalda found the nerve to better assess the group. She recognized Sheriff Hoffman and her brother Adman. To her surprise and delight she saw Captain Marly standing next to her brother. She did not recognize him at first in his black tunic. Over the years he had made it a point to visit her family on special occasions. His visits were always followed up by good fortune, though as of late, those visits were few and far between. To see him now without his spiffy coat and fancy medals made her wonder if good fortune would follow this visit. Seeing the men make for the table, she quickly left the room to retrieve the remaining plates.

The dinner progressed in perfect pace. Enyalda performed her tasks with unwavering attention, making sure all their plates and mugs were well stocked throughout the evening. The men were not so bad, she decided, except for the bearded monster that kept to itself in the corner of the room. Bringing food to it was a terrifying experience. She felt its eyes on her, as if at any moment it might uproot itself from the chest it sat on and crush her like a chipmunk. Four times she filled its plate, the last time stacking the food so high, it nearly toppled over on the monster's lap.

When the main course was over, Enyalda cleared the table and returned to the kitchen while the men drank their ale. All that was left was dessert. She removed fruit tarts from the oven and set them on the counter to cool. She basted them with butter and then added a fine dusting of powdered sugar. Arranging the tarts on the tray, she considered how the night had gone. So far so good. The colonel's voice was strong and he showed no signs of tremors, short of the occasional twitch of his eyebrow. That had been her main concern, that a relapse would occur in all the excitement. She knew he was free of the wulfweed—physically—but traces of his war wound lingered. Being with the men in this capacity was his first real test since the withdrawal.

149

It was a great relief to see him so engaged. She lifted the tray and returned to the hearth room.

She stopped in the front parlor prior to entering the room. The general chatter had settled down. Only the colonel spoke. She peeked around the corner so as not to intrude on his words.

"Duncan, what are our numbers in Wulfhaven?" he asked, still seated at the head of the table.

"Three hundred who know the codes, sir, half of which are cavalry. Another fifty prepared to take the oath should the need arise."

"What about Multynhaven?"

"I would say two hundred or so scattered in the highlands. It will take at least a month to muster them."

"And Tufthaven?"

Enyalda saw the legless man's gaze drop to the floor. His heavy silence said it all.

The colonel turned to the man on Duncan's right. "Weydlynn, how many in Tufthaven?"

Weydlynn looked down as well. One by one, the colonel posed the question to each man at the table. The answer was always the same. Every drop of their eyes brought another twitch to his brow. Enyalda shifted the tray of fruit tarts in her hands, nervously watching the scene unfold. At length, when the silence had reached a threshold, the colonel stood up and slammed both fists on the table.

"By the Great Dome! Will somebody answer the damned question?" he roared. "I've seen more life in a heap of bricks."

At last, Sheriff Hoffman spoke. "There are none, sir."

The colonel reached for his cane to steady himself. "What?"

"There are no forces in Tufthaven."

The twitch spread from the colonel's brow to his face. The beechwood cane in his hand trembled. "Sergeant, we had seven hundred footmen from Tufthaven. They were the bloody beating heart of our infantry. Are you telling me that not one returned?"

"They were in the smoke too long, sir," Hoffman said, glancing at Captain Marly.

Even from the parlor, Enyalda could see the colonel was in trouble. The tremors were back, escalating at an alarming rate. Torn between fear and love, she wrestled over what to do. How could she deliver Muma's blessing with so many eyes to avoid? She saw him stagger; saliva began to lather and ooze down his trembling chin. Time was of the essence; his collapse was imminent. The woman in her dream suddenly came to mind. *What shall I do?* she prayed. Her prayer was answered by Captain Marly's urgent command.

"Quickly, men! He is slipping into seizure!"

At once every man rose and moved in to assist the colonel. The bustle of motion triggered Enyalda into action. Knowing there was no time for whispers or subtleties, she threw down the tray of fruit tarts and sprang from the shadows of the parlor, her hair back and arms raised.

"Yan shahuna maha na geshiva kutchu!" she shouted at the men.

The monster in the corner of the room rose to its full stature, but she paid it no heed. Nor did she acknowledge the men who stepped back in wide-eyed amazement. The colonel was her sole focus. Steadfast and sure, her burning eyes locked on his, she delivered her blessing without whisper.

"Hein shahuna ah prista al gahut solam," she repeated over and over, until the tremors subsided. Never before had she felt so empowered by Muma's words. Liberated in that moment of all earthly worries, she held her arms open like the wings of a great butterfly and absorbed the colonel's pain. All the while he remained deathly still, as if wrapped in a chrysalis.

At last the colonel blinked and looked around. Enyalda lowered her arms and became mindful of all the eyes on her. Embarrassed, she covered her face with her hair and scuttled behind the colonel to shield herself of the attention. She was relieved to hear him address Captain Marly, drawing the eyes of the men away from her.

"Tell me, Captain. What was done with the dead at Spaulding Pass?"

"They were buried, sir, in a mass grave on the field."

"And the Torics?"

"The same."

"What of the enemy's wounded?"

"By your command, sir, we tended them as best we could, then left them with what provisions we could afford. It was your last order."

"My last order? Yes, of course ..."

All remained silent while the colonel wrestled with his memories. Enyalda watched him engage with the shadows that flickered on the hearth. She could feel his strength returning—gradually. Just like the days on the rooftop when she sang to him through the leaves of the Great Beech. In due course, the colonel returned his attention to Captain Marly.

"Marlin, you told me the piper Johan Hume died on the field of battle with his five sons."

"That is correct, sir. They were laid to rest in the mass grave."

"Is there a chance their remains could have been mistaken?"

"There's always that chance, sir, with cannon fire. But not in Johan's case. I recognized the chief-piper insignia on his kilt."

"I see. Hume's pipers were deployed to the east ridge, were they not?"

"They were."

"So how is it that the body of their chief piper ended up on the front lines of battle with the infantry? He would have had to abandon his post on the ridge long before the battle started."

"I did not consider that at the time, sir. There was a lot to be done in the aftermath."

"Yes, an unenviable task, Marlin. One that I never should have left you with. But answer me this. At any point during our engagement with the Torics was the line of communication between Johan's pipers and our forces compromised?"

"No, sir. Definitely not."

"Then I have only one last question for all of you." He slammed his cane to the floor and addressed the entire assembly. "If it was not Johan leading his brigade on the east ridge, then by the light on the Haven, who was it?"

The monster stepped forward, eclipsing the hearth with its presence. Enyalda hid behind the colonel. "Huru Shakein," it droned in a voice that made her shudder. "The tribes talk of a footman-boy who walks in shadow between the Haven and the pass. They call him Huru Shakein. He will know."

"That means Talking Gun," the colonel said.

The monster nodded.

Captain Marly stepped forward. "Colonel, there is a matter pertaining to the command codes issued by the pipers during the battle that you should know. I believe it will help shed light on your question." He looked behind the colonel to Enyalda and then back to Adman. "But it is sensitive, sir. Only those who have given their oath can hear it. Master McFadden …"

"I understand, sir," Adman said, acknowledging Barleycopp's gesture to leave. "I will check on my brothers by the fire pit. Come, Enya, let's go."

She hid her face behind the colonel's back, refusing to leave.

"It's all right, my dear," the colonel said, reaching into his vest pocket and taking out the pipe and pouch she had given him earlier. "The shadow has passed. See to your brothers."

Reluctantly, she complied. Her moment of empowerment had diminished along with the crisis. The colonel's command had returned and she knew better than to defy it. She looked back only once on her way out and saw his flint already to the pipe. After a quick prayer, she turned from the swirls of greenbank and followed her brother out the door.

Halfway to the fire pit, Adman stopped and faced Enyalda. He had not said a word since they left the manor. "How did you do that, Enya? How did you make them back off like that? Every one of those men are seasoned warriors."

She peeped, startled by her brother's query and looked down on the moonlit gravel. She never liked direct questions, even when she knew the answers, which in this case she certainly did not. In fact, the entire incident in the hearth room already felt like a dream. All she knew was that she wanted her brother's eyes off her, and the best way to do that was to whisper. With her gaze still on the ground, she discerned a tiny tuft of stems in the gravel and promptly introduced herself to it. As expected, Adman marched off to the fire pit before the scraggly weed had a chance to answer. Enyalda stayed behind and politely thanked the courteous plant for its assistance, then continued to walk through the moonlight at her own pace.

Shadows danced at the fire pit. As Enyalda approached, she saw Francis sitting on one of the boulders near the wall with a content glow on his face. By his side was a cask of Cotton Crown's finest. She had expected as much. Adman had already poured himself a grog. Meanwhile Donavon wrestled with the wolf pup in the meadow grass near the beehives.

She listened to the barrage of yaps and snarls, wondering why he had to be so brutal with the poor little thing. Only a month ago it was on the edge of death. As if to confirm her concern, the bout was squelched by a piercing yelp.

"Ah-ha, gotcha!" Donavon exclaimed. "You're fast, but still not fast enough."

Adman gulped down some ale. "Hey, Donny," he shouted. "If you put as much effort into your chores as you do beating up that whelp, we'd get a lot more work done around here."

"What fun would that be?" Donavon fired back, sticking his head out of the grass. A flash of gray shot up and seized a mouthful of Donavon's long red hair. Back into the grass they tumbled. Enyalda could not help giggling at the ensuing groans.

Her chirps drew Francis out of his inebriated musings. "Swerves you right, blother!" he called over the fire, and then turned to Enyalda. "Aye, it's my savorite fister. Good timin', slith. I'bin thinkin' about da unifarse."

Enyalda giggled again and danced around the fire to her glassy-eyed brother. She snatched the mug out of his hand and cast it over the fieldstone wall, where it landed with a thud somewhere in the goat pasture. Francis barely noticed, setting his gaze back to the stars. Enyalda sat down on the boulder and hummed a tune, while she held his arm and snuggled against his side. Long she sang, knowing he would eventually sober up to his favorite verse. Absorbed in the melody, neither one noticed the wolf pup that quietly padded out of the grass and lay down near their feet.

The stars shifted in the sky as verse after verse streamed like a fountain through Enyalda's lips. All the while her three brothers went about their business around the fire in whatever manner suited them. Francis remained exactly where he was on the boulder, his gaze locked on the distant heavens. Donavon made himself comfortable in the firelight, with his head propped against a piece of cordwood. Adman, seeing no opportunity to boss anyone around, simply stoked the fire while he sorted through his own thoughts.

The night proceeded as such until at last Enyalda's song was silenced by a warning growl from the wolf pup. Donavon was the first to speak. "Looks like we've got company," he said, facing downhill toward the manor.

Sure enough, a single lantern bobbed up the carriage path toward the stock house. Enyalda shivered and held tight to Francis's arm. Two shadowy forms accompanied the light, one of them huge.

"Who do you suppose that could be at this hour?" Francis said, now sober enough to speak.

Adman walked to the edge of the firelight. "Looks like the chief cipher. Not sure who the other one is. They're coming this way. Donny, why don't you shut that whelp up?"

"Why don't you shut yourself up?" Donavon said, getting up to relieve himself in the grass. "He's just doing his job."

"Why don't you both shut up for once and give us all a break?" Francis said, unexpectedly assertive. "My head's killing me."

Enyalda watched the lantern get closer while her brothers bickered. At the stock house the bobbing light stopped and remained still for some time before continuing up the hill. Once the men were in the radius of the firelight, Enyalda was relieved to see that the shadow accompanying the monster was Captain Marly.

"Ah, yes," the mayor said, breathing heavily as he approached the pit. "Nothing like a ... good fire ... to reward a hardy ... effort." He picked up the stick Adman had used as a fire poker.

Enyalda squeezed Francis's arm tighter. She had always considered Captain Marly to be a tall man, and he was. However, seeing him so dwarfed by the scar-faced giant under the open night sky was even more chilling than in the hearth room. Peering through her hair, she saw the monster was not nearly as winded as the captain.

Adman offered to pour the captain a grog but he refused.

"That's quite all right, my boy," he said, regaining his breath. "We have had our share already. The accommodations have been more than adequate. Jeziah and I thought we would come up to complement all of you on your efforts." He fired a sharp glance at Enyalda. "Especially you, Enya."

Their eyes met before she had the chance to look away. Caught by surprise, Enyalda began to rock her hair back and forth over her face. She could feel the monster's gaze pressing down on her. To her relief, Captain Marly changed the subject.

"So this is the little one-eyed orphan we've been hearing about," he said, looking at the pup and then at Donavon. "The colonel says you've been teaching it some good manners."

Donavon shrugged. "It won't show any manners when it meets up with that badger again. An eye for an eye. Isn't that right, Cap?"

The pup, as if knowing it had become the subject of discussion, walked around the pit and plopped itself by Donavon's feet.

Barleycopp jabbed at the fire with the stick. "So the saying goes. Funny, that's exactly what your father used to say."

Adman stepped aside to avoid the sparks. "Father said a lot of things, didn't he, Captain?"

"He did indeed. But it was what he did after he said them that left the most impact. He led by example more than words. We had a saying for him— 'He could part the red tide with the crack of his whip.'"

"The red tide?" Francis repeated.

"That would be the Torics," Adman said. "That was their color on the lines."

Francis appeared puzzled. "If that's the case, I think there might be a Toricean uniform in the colonel's house. Enya found it when she was cleaning the rooms. There was a portrait, too, of a man in the same uniform next to a tribeswoman."

"That would most likely be Augustus Mitterhal," Barleycopp said. "He was the Toricean lord and baron that governed the Haven in the days of the rail. A very influential man at the time. He was deemed a defector by the Torics and executed right here at the manor, so the story goes. A fascinating man. I would be most interested to see your discovery."

"So you're saying the colonel is the son of a Toricean nobleman?" Francis asked.

"He is, though for the longest time that was only a guess. He never talked about his past. When he took up residence here at the manor late in the war, that confirmed his lineage. Up to that point, not even the Guard was sure of who he was."

"How did he become colonel then?" Adman asked.

"That is a story that could take us to dawn and still not be finished. I think a good rest should come first. We have all had a full day."

Enyalda stopped rocking. The prospect of gaining such a vital insight to the colonel's past compelled her to peek at the captain through her hair. She had to convince him to go on, and hummed a high note while she pondered the options.

It was Francis, as usual, who came to her aid. "I think you're going to have to tell us the story, sir. No one's gonna get any sleep with Enya screeching like that."

Barleycopp smiled at Enyalda and poked at the coals again. "I suppose there's no better place than around a fire. Very well, I'll give you the abridged version."

Promptly, Enyalda ceased her humming.

The captain heaved a sigh. "I'll never forget the morning he showed up. We were running training maneuvers with the troops in the fairgrounds outside the Haven stables. It was early in the war." Captain Marly looked at Adman. "Your father was as proud as a peacock as I recall, bragging to all the other officers about his first newborn son. That was when he appeared, right out of the mist like some ghost from the mountains. No uniform, no name, no credentials, no nothing. Just a pipe, his goat-hyde hat, a vest, and a worn-out pair of leather britches held up by suspenders. He walked right through the lines as if he were a general. We all just stood there dumbfounded. He came to me first and said if we wanted to beat the bear, we better listen to him. I demanded his name but he said that was not important. 'Just call me sir,' he said. I must admit that right from the start I felt compelled to listen. He's got that quality about him, you know, even to this day."

Barleycopp peered into the fire. After another poke to the coals, he continued the account. "Your father was not so easily convinced. He charged him on his mount and drew his warhorse to within a nose of his pipe. 'You expect a trained army to listen to a nameless old man that walks out of the woods and speaks in riddles?'"

"What did the Old Mitt have to say to that?" Donavon asked, obviously captivated by the story.

"He told your father to get off his high horse. That he was making the mountain goats grumpy and the sooner he learned some manners, the sooner they could get on with training the troops the right way." Barleycopp smiled. "The look on Uryan's face was priceless. The rest is history."

"So he was commissioned to colonel just like that?" Adman asked.

"Funny you would ask that. The truth is, the colonel was never commissioned to anything. As time went on we just started calling him colonel because 'sir' seemed too impersonal. He was never sworn in by Rankwall and as such was never officially recognized as an officer of any sort. He had as much authority in the Lakwynnian army as a volunteer footman. Technically speaking, of course."

Donavon spat into the fire. "Grumpy goats. I can't believe our father bought that. The Old Mitt was just as crazy then as he is now."

Adman stepped forward in the light. "Pipe down, Donny. Nobody asked for your opinion. You were too young to know anything. It's about time you started showing some respect."

"Respect what? A dribbling old coot who smoked his own men? If it weren't for him we'd still have our father."

The hackles of the wolf pup went up. The monster, which up to that point had remained deathly still behind Captain Marly, advanced on Donavon. To Enyalda's horror it extended its arm and seized her brother by the neck. Donavan pried at its wrist, to no avail, as the wolf pup gnawed at the giant's ankles. Too shocked to scream, she watched her kicking brother's feet leave the ground. The monster drew Donavon's face to within inches of its own. "Do not mock the Mahocpynn," it droned.

Donavon opened his mouth to speak, but all that came out was an airless wheeze. Unable to watch any longer, Enyalda buried her face in Francis's chest.

"That's enough, Jeziah!" Captain Marly commanded. "You've made your point. That's the son of Meguntoc in your grip."

Enyalda heard Donavon's body hit the ground and instantly went to assist her gasping brother. The wolf pup was already by his side, nuzzling his heaving chest, a bloody fragment of the monster's pants still clinging to its jowls. Jeziah loomed over them like a sentient statue.

"You have the favor of the wolf," he said before moving back to his position behind Captain Marly.

Barleycopp looked at Donavon while Enyalda rubbed his neck, waiting until the gasping subsided. "Believe what you will, Donny, but know this. The colonel loved his men like his own family. None of us knew what the smoke would do, including him. Maybe after all was said and done, he did go a little crazy. But frankly, I would be more concerned if he didn't."

Shadows flickered on the mayor's face as he tossed the poker into the fire, sending a rush of sparks into the night. "I believe that's enough storytelling for one night. Let us go, Jeziah. We must leave before dawn. Once again, I commend you all on a job well done. Your father would be proud."

Abruptly, he turned around and was off, shadowed by the chief cipher.

Enyalda continued to massage her brother's neck and shoulders while she watched the lantern bob down the hill to the colonel's manor. So much had happened in one day. It was only that morning that Adman had charged into the kitchen to inform her of the gathering Guard. Her primary concern at hearing the news had been for the colonel. Not until now under the pale light of the starry sky, did she consider the challenges that lay ahead for her brothers.

5

Pipe in the Pool

It was a sweltering summer day, a real scorcher on the mountain. Donavon stood in the entryway of the jailhouse having just returned from mucking the horse stalls in the village stables. Dripping wet with sweat, he scratched at the strands of hay that adhered to his skin, wondering what his next menial chore would be. In the narrow shade of a stone pillar, he slurped down the last drops of water from his canteen as he glared at the hot iron door embedded in the bricks. Being a deputy was far overrated. In fact, he would have tossed his badge on the sheriff's desk a long time ago had he not been convinced that Hoffman would have terminated more than just his employment.

Nearly two months had passed since he'd been coerced into service, and he had yet to see a day free of tedious tasks. The closest he had come to doing anything deputy-like had happened only last week, when Brewmaster Garrison shot one of the Grange clan's prized rams after it strayed into his hop garden. The clan was famous for their hot tempers, and Gildryn Grange was the most notorious of the lot. Hoffman had ordered his arrest as a precaution, in the interest of preserving the peace. Donavon thought the measure was unwarranted, that Garrison should have taken the heat for plugging one of their sheep, but he enjoyed executing the order nonetheless. Gildryn had put up a good fight, which was a welcome break from mucking horse stalls.

Upon entering the jailhouse, Donavon holstered the canteen next to his billy club and proceeded down the brick corridor toward the sheriff's office.

"Oh looky here." The taunt came from the third cell on the right. "If it isn't Deputy Donny boy himself gettin' back from fightin' the forces of evil."

Donavon glared through the bars. The swelling around Gildryn's right eye had subsided, but the dark bruise below it lingered. He couldn't blame the banged-up inmate for being hot and bothered, but on a day like this, he was in no mood for the jibber. "Put a bung in it, Gilly. I'll crack your other eye if you keep it up."

Gildryn's knuckles turned white as he choked the bars. "Fine by me. Why don't you take off that pretty little badge of yours so we can settle this the right way? You know I don't belong here."

Hoffman's voice echoed down the corridor before Donavon had a chance to oblige. "Donny, get your flaps in here!"

Donavon went down the hall and through the open door of Hoffman's office. Two steps in, he stopped. The sheriff's boots were propped up on his desk, his stump-sized legs crossed at the calves. Behind that his burly arms were crossed at his chest. Beyond, his wide-brimmed hat was pulled low over his eyes. If not for the blaring summons, Donavon would have figured his reclining boss sound asleep. Such was Hoffman's routine after returning from his hikes to the summit, which was an odd habit, to say the least. Whatever drew the sheriff on his monthly sojourns up the mountain was a mystery to Donavon. All he knew was that the groggy war vet would be spending the remainder of the day sacked in his office, recovering from his trip. The perfect opportunity to bust out early and check on the wolf.

"The stalls are clean and the horses watered," he said. "If there's nothing else going on, I'd like to check on Scraggs."

No reply. Donavon watched Hoffman's broad chest heave up and down in a slow, steady motion. Eventually his mouth opened and he began to growl like a bear. Donavon shrugged and turned to leave the sheriff alone with his snores. He was midway through the office door when the growling stopped.

"So you've named it?" Hoffman asked.

Donavon turned around. "Not really. He just answers to it."

"That sounds like a name to me. I wouldn't get too attached to that whelp, Donny. You're going to have to let it go once it comes of age. We can't have a grown wolf panicking the herds."

Donavon's jaw clenched. The heat, in combination with the morning's busy work, shortened his temper. "Why not? I can train it to lay off the sheep," he said, stepping forward.

"You can train it all you want. A wolf is a wolf and sheep are sheep. You can't change their nature. It's the way of things. Besides, even if you did, it would attract others. And that would only make trouble for everyone, including the wolf. I won't have trouble, Donny, not in this village."

Donavon's thoughts rolled like brew hops in a boil. Who was Hoffman to spout about the nature of things? To preach about what a wolf might think? He was just a thick-skulled relic from a bygone war trying to hold on to whatever authority he had left.

"Go to hell," he said, before setting the lid on his temper.

Hoffman's hand went to the edge of his hat. Slowly, he pushed the brim up, revealing his bloodshot eyes. "I already have, Donny. They didn't like me there. I was too hard on the demons."

Even with his blood boiling, Donavon knew it would be a bad mistake to push the matter further. Hoffman had a chilling air about him. The colonel's foreboding words suddenly came to mind—"He was known as the Hoof during the war." Donavon kept a wary eye on the sheriff's boots. To his relief, they stayed on the desk.

"I heard about your run-in with the chief cipher," the Hoof said with eerie calm. "There aren't many who have felt that grip and lived to tell about it. He likes you, you know."

"He's got a funny way of showing it," Donavon said, scratching a tuft of sweat-soaked hay off his neck.

"When you've killed as many as he, affection has a way of getting blurred. Have you thought about what he said?"

"Which grunt? The first or second?"

Hoffman sighed and tugged his hat back over his eyes. "I guess not," he said, clearly disappointed. "Go play with your pup, Donny."

Donavon looked down, unable to shake the feeling that he had failed in some profound way. He would have preferred a scolding, or better yet a beating. Something he knew how to resist. This was different; Hoffman's easy compliance unnerved him. His gaze remained fixed on the floor as shades of shame crept into his being. An honest answer was his only way out. "He told me not to mock the Mahocpynn."

In a flash the sheriff's boots were off the desk. "That's right, Donny. And do you have any idea what a mahocpynn is?"

"Sure, it's a Gwyntah war chief."

"No, not war. Music."

"A music chief?"

"Exactly!" the sheriff shouted. He stood up and strode past Donavon to slam the office door shut. "And that far surpasses the rank of any war chief that walks this earth, Gwyntah or not." Hoffman's tone cooled to a whisper, though his bloodshot eyes still burned. "Once you hear the music, you will always be drawn to it. The colonel showed us the way. All of us, your father included. To the peak of the highest mountain he brought us, where we all heard the music. Some of us came back, most of us didn't."

"Is that why you go on your hikes up the mountain?" Donavon asked, with his gaze still locked on the shimmering shadows on the floor. "To get back to the music?"

Hoffman grinned and appeared to relax. "You're a smart one, Donny. Don't ever let anyone tell you otherwise. You'll hear the music someday, I'm sure. It's carried on the wind. The higher you go, the purer the tone. Not until you've sat on the highest peaks of the Haven's coast and watched the sun set beyond her farthest shores will you taste the tune."

The afternoon sun beamed bright through the window and carved a hard line of shadow on the office floor. A sense of heightened awareness swept over Donavon as he focused on the leading edge of shade. Growing up in the village, he had experienced the same sensation on various occasions—flash moments, often when he was alone on his hunts in the upper vale, watching the sunlight reflect off a mountain stream. But never like this, never so pinpoint. As he watched the shadow advance over a crack in the floor planks, he stepped into the light and felt it radiate up his legs to the core of his spine. There was no resisting it any longer. Through the shadows of shame swelled a power that called him to rise. He looked up and met the sheriff's steadfast stare.

"I'm ready to serve, sir."

"Exellent. That's the answer I've been waiting for. I was wondering how much muck you'd have to shovel before you figured that out. Now we can finally get on to business." Hoffman stepped into the light of the window. "I have an assignment for you, Donny. I've been doing some thinking on the mountain. The dawn was red this morning, did you see?"

"I wasn't watching."

"Always watch, Donny. And listen. Especially at dawn."

The sheriff's shadow drew Donavon's attention back down to the floor planks. The silhouette of his hat hovered like a storm cloud over his feet. "I'll try, sir."

After a deep breath, Hoffman left the window and resumed his seat behind the desk. "The colonel wants to visit the fountain in Wulfhaven. I don't like the idea one bit, but he insists. The square has become a hot spot for the Pogetsa ever since the fountain folk started protesting the bridge. I want you and Angus to be his escorts. Nothing fancy, just make sure he stays out of trouble."

"I think we can do that, sir."

"No, no think. Do! And there's one more thing. The Pogetsa have banned all weapons in the city proper. You'll have to go unarmed."

"Not even my billy?"

"No billy. That will only attract attention. Which reminds me, do not mention your name to anyone. You can bet Rankwall's pogies have not forgotten what happened to their first constable."

Donavon's pulse pounded at the sheriff's reference to the general's son. The fate of Chief Constable Fergus Rankwall was rarely discussed in the McFadden household. To hear him mentioned now rekindled the childhood

161

fear and frustration spawned by the cruel man's beatings. Worse was the recollection of his speechless sister in the barn, and the fury that had seized him when he found the constable with her. The details of that day nearly a decade ago were a blur to Donavon—he had been so young—but the scar it had left on his fighting spirit was as sharp as the bloodstained pitchfork that still haunted his dreams. With the fight in Donavon's heart so aroused, an idea came to him.

"Sir, I think Gilly has spent enough time in the block. With your permission, I'd like to make him an offer. Angus and I could use some backup and he packs a solid right that might come in handy."

"Gildryn is a hothead, Donny. It's not like brawling in the tavern. The Pogetsa mean business. I want you to prevent a scene, not make one."

Donavon unclipped his badge and placed it on the sheriff's desk. "I'll make sure of that, sir. Just give me a moment with him. I'll be back for this."

Hoffman glared at the silver brooch that sparkled on his desk. A smile eventually cracked his craggy face. "You are your father's son, no doubt about that. Have at it, Donny. Close the door behind you."

Two days later, Donavon, Angus and Gildryn waited for the colonel by the horse carriage in front of his manor. They stood at the edge of his yard, watching the mountain goats in the south pasture stare at them through the early morning mist. Angus, it had been decided, would take the colonel in the carriage while Donavon and Gildryn would lead on their mounts.

"You think he'll really go through with it?" Angus asked, standing by the open carriage door.

Donavon reached into his belt pouch and gave his horse a carrot. "Sarge says he's bent on it."

"Who?" Gildryn asked.

"The sheriff. He was a sergeant, you know. A real kicker in the Guard."

Gildryn merely nodded. He looked like a raccoon with his two black eyes.

The front door of the manor swung open and smacked against the outside clapboards. Through the doorway and down the steps marched the Old Mitt, accompanied by Enyalda. She fluttered around him like a prancing pixie, showering him in pink and white petals. A sizeable feather protruded from the band in his goat-hyde hat.

The colonel swiped at the floral confetti with his cane. "Stop it! Stop this nonsense at once."

Straight-faced, Donavon shook his head as he watched them cross the yard, wondering what had possessed his sister to choose now of all times to be so irritating. The Old Mitt's protests only seemed to encourage her antics. The extravaganza came to a head when they arrived at the carriage and Enyalda broke into song.

Giddy-up, Giddy-up
Clipiddy-clop
Giddy-up, Giddy-up
No time to stop!

A tune tomorrow
A tour today
Petals on ponies
That take us away!

One by one she showered the horses in flower petals. Donavon held his tongue while he waited for her silly ritual to end. At last, she stopped in front of Gildryn's horse. To Donavon's surprise, it wasn't the horse she acknowledged, but Gilly. She looked directly into his left eye, the one most recently cracked. Gildryn flinched as she tapped the tender bruise with her finger and whispered something. She then faced Donavon, glaring with disapproval. He shrugged. His sister seemed far less skittish about eye contact these days, ever since serving supper to the Guard.

The colonel, meanwhile, went to the open carriage door and tried to board. His first attempt was unsuccessful, so Angus offered his brawny arm as a prop. The colonel's cane sliced the air and landed hard on his knuckles.

"Keep your hands where they belong, lad. I'm not dead yet. Here, take this."

He passed the cane to Angus. With both hands free, Mitterhal hoisted himself into the carriage. A stream of pink petals spilled off the rim of his goat-hyde hat. Once situated in the carriage seat, he removed his pipe from his vest pocket and dipped it into the pouch Enyalda had given him.

"All right, boys, let's get on with it."

Donavon mounted his horse and nodded to Angus, who nervously handed the cane back to the colonel. His effort to close the door was thwarted by Enyalda, who scurried up and into the carriage seat, eager to go.

"Get out of there, Enya," Donavon ordered from atop his mount. "We gotta keep a low profile. The last thing we need is your song and dance in the square."

She snuggled up to the colonel as if it might convince him to override the order, but she received no such assistance. The Old Mitt simply shook his head while he encased the chassis in a haze of greenbank. Dejected, she dismounted the carriage, but made sure to kiss Angus's bruised knuckles on the way out. Angus promptly closed the door and took up the reins on the front seat of the carriage, his face as flushed as a sunset. With a snap of the reins the crew was off, leaving Enyalda waving sadly in the dust.

Only one road that descended the mountain was wide enough for a horse-drawn carriage, and that road went directly through Cotton Crown. Mornings were typically misty in the village, but not even the sun-drenched fog could mask the curiosity and enthusiasm of the villagers who lined the main street as the wheels of the colonel's carriage crunched over the gravel.

Donavon kept his horse in the lead, with Gildryn to his right and slightly behind. Angus, to Donavon's annoyance, lagged behind in the carriage as they approached the tavern, still smitten, it appeared, by Enyalda's peck on the knuckles.

"Tighten up on those reins, Angus," Donavon shouted over his shoulder. "You're riding like a dead ass."

With the carriage back on pace, Donavon assessed the onlookers. The weavers had massed around the outside of the mill and adorned the main street with scores of makeshift flags and banners hastily fabricated out of blue cloth. Children scurried about in wide-eyed astonishment, waving discarded remnants of the weavers' fabric at the Old Mitt. Herdsmen, even some with their sheepdogs, had left their pastures to glimpse the unprecedented event. At the jailhouse, Brewmaster Garrison leaned against one of the stone pillars, scratching his hairy ears with the muzzle end of his flintlock. Next to him, in the exact center of the door stood the hard-faced sheriff, his burly arms crossed over his chest.

The tavern's delivery cart, drawn by Emit the mule, appeared from behind the tavern and fell into procession behind Angus and the colonel. Three young horsemen flanked the farmcart. Donavon turned to face the unauthorized tag-alongs. They were Angus's brothers: Seth, Corey, and Dugan on the horses, and Caleb driving the cart.

"What do you think you're doing?" Donavon asked, halting the convoy.

Seth looked across the street to the sheriff, who acknowledged him with a quick tilt of his hat. "We're picking up supplies in Wulfhaven," Seth said to Donavon. "The tavern's running low on barley."

Donavon stiffened on his mount, having caught the exchange of glances. "Since when did McGregors become errand runners for the tavern?"

Seth straightened in the saddle. "Ever since a McFadden took up muck shoveling."

Donavon grunted and fired a sharp glance at the sheriff. "I thought we were going to keep this simple, nothing fancy."

Hoffman shrugged. "The tavern needs barley, Donny. What can I say?"

The brewmaster laughed. Donavon jerked his horse back around to face the McGregors.

"All right, but I'm the boss. What I say goes. Got it?"

"We got it, sir." Seth turned around to his brothers. "Isn't that right, fellas?"

"Aye, aye, Donny!" the others shouted.

Donavon wasted no time with an acceptance speech. He proceeded on course, past the weaving mill at a hot pace. Briskly they passed through the village center, trailed by a mob of cheering children. The colonel remained silent, stoic in his feathered hat, staring forward with his cane propped on the carriage floor, both hands lapped over its top.

Once they were out of the village, Donavon eased up on the pace. The road down the mountain through the sheep pastures was wide but steep. The horses were well-bred for the terrain, but even so he thought it best to take it easy on Old Mitt, especially while the morning mist still burned off the slopes. They had to halt shortly after rounding the first switchback. A line of herdsmen blocked the road ahead. Three of them were on horseback, four on foot. Side by side they held their ground, wielding clubs.

"Looks like your cousins are up to something, Gilly," Donavon said. "You better not be playing any games with me or I'll crack your third eye."

"I got nothin' to do with this, Donny, honest," Gildryn said. "Patsy is the only one I told."

"Patsy! That explains it." Donavon looked over his shoulder at the McGregors. "Listen up. We got no time for scrapping. I'll do the talking. Got it?"

"Aye, aye, Donny," they answered in unison.

Patrick Grange, as expected, advanced first on his horse, his long hair tied back with a sheepskin tether. "Mornin', Donny. Nice day for a ride."

"Get your stiffs off the road, Patsy. We're on official business."

"So are we, as a matter of fact." He looked at Gildryn. "Your eye looks better, cousin. I've never known you to fix up so quick. Our new deputy must not be so tough after all."

Donavon glanced at Gildryn. Sure enough, the discoloration around his left eye had gone down considerably since leaving the colonel's house. It actually looked better than the right eye, which he had smacked two days prior. Curious. "There's no time for this, Patsy. Move your boys or I'll have Emit do it for you."

Patrick mocked a respectful bow to the colossal draught mule. "Sorry, Emit, this is history. We wouldn't miss this if our herd depended on it. We're going with you whether you like it or not."

Seth McGregor rode forward on his horse. "You're out of line, Patsy. This is official business. You better listen to Donny or there's going to be trouble."

"And where's your badge?" Patrick fired back at Seth.

"We've been authorized."

"Authorized?" Patrick shouted to his cousins in the road, "You hear that boys? They've been authorized. We better drop our beaters."

A roar of laughter ensued, though not a single club hit the ground. Corey and Dugan McGregor rode up to assist their brother in the scrap. Angus had just dropped the reins to do the same, when the colonel's command blasted out of the open carriage and froze them all in their tracks.

"That's enough yapping! You boys are worse than squawking hens. Get this rabble moving, Donavon, or I'll do it myself. And pick up the pace while you're at it."

The order spurred Donavon to think fast. The Grange boys were as stubborn as they were unwieldy. Their minds were made up, that much was clear, and there was no way to counter that without causing a serious delay in the mission. After weighing the options, he surprised all by responded to their ultimatum with unprecedented civility.

"All right, Patsy, but what I say goes. No scenes, no weapons, nothing to stir up the pogies. Once we're at the square, we're gonna split up. No clustering around the colonel. With a little luck, no one will recognize him. When he's done at the fountain, we're out of there. No delays. Got it?"

"We got it, Donny," Patrick said, a bit overzealously. "Come on, boys, you heard the boss. Drop your beaters, let's go."

With a hoot and a holler, the eager young herdsmen threw down their clubs and fell into procession behind the colonel. The four without horses climbed aboard the tavern's mule cart, raring to go. Donavon snapped the reins of his own steed and pushed forward at a much more vigorous pace, contributing not a word to the revelry. After years of scrapping on the mountain, he knew perfectly well that keeping the Grange clan in order was like trying to tickle the belly of a cornered weasel.

The old port district of Wulfhaven was as diverse and vibrant as its history. A huge wharf supported by a network of stone pilings and cribbing extended far out into the harbor where the lake level was deep. The wharf was furnished with an assortment of boom hoists, swiveling counterweights, and rope riggings, engineered to load and unload the large trade ships that sailed in from the broads. Closer to shore, stemming from the base of the wharf on both sides, rows of docks provided a place for the lesser vessels to berth when they came into port. The Docks, as they were known, were built on sturdy slabs of granite to better withstand the icy assaults of winter.

Where the Docks ended the Promenade began, which served as the main artery between the harbor and the city proper. Paved in cobblestones, the Promenade also served as a causeway for a plethora of merchants and street vendors, along with a fair share of beggars and fortune-tellers. From the Docks, the Promenade hugged the shoreline until it veered inward through the old port, ending at an ancient archway that marked the entrance to Wulfhaven's main square.

In the exact center of the square, within an evening shadow's length of the cathedral, was a pool that had never been known to run dry. It was believed that a spring tapped deep into the roots of the surrounding highlands and supplied the pool with its crystal clear water. In the midst of the pool was a fountain from which towered the statue of a beautiful woman—a goddess of an ancient faith. It was one of the few relics left by the ancestors of the Gwyntah that had remained unspoiled by conflict. The statue's right arm extended to the sky, upon which hand was perched a butterfly. That the artisans of old were able to shape its delicate wings out of marble was a true tribute to their trade. At the feet of the goddess sat an ever-watchful wolf, her loyal guard. The expression carved into its stone face was a fierce reminder that its divine keeper was not to be harassed.

The highland crew halted midway on the Promenade, within sight of the main square. The pivotal moment had come for Donavon. He had been dwelling on how to handle the dicey arrangement ever since they left the mountain. To enter the square with the Grange clan would be an utter disaster—that much was certain. As it was, they were already turning the heads of local vendors and market folk hustling about on the cobbles. He needed to break up the group and divert the attention.

"Seth, you and Patsy take the boys to the grainer and load up Emit. I'll take the colonel to the square with Gilly and Angus. Dugan and Corey will stay here with the carriage and horses. We'll meet back at this spot once the colonel's done at the fountain. Any questions?"

"Yeah, I got a question," Patrick said. "Why do you get to have all the fun? We didn't come all this way just to toss barley on a cart."

Donavon drew his horse to within a snort spray of Patrick. "Because this is not about fun. And even if it were, you agreed that I was the boss. Remember? Besides, whatever goes in the mule cart is yours. I'm not going to tell the McGregors to load it for you."

Seth McGregor promptly stepped in. "What are you talking about, Donny? Our load is for the tavern."

"Not anymore. It's going to the Grange clan for the ram that Garrison shot. Now let's get things moving."

A commotion suddenly broke out near the entrance of the square. A squad of Pogetsa advanced from under the arched pillars, blowing their whistles to clear the crowd. In their midst was a line of captives—a dozen or so—who limped along with their hands tied behind their backs. Several had bloody foreheads and a dazed look about them. Donavon and the boys watched in grim silence as the Pogetsa marched down the Promenade toward the detainment house, dragging their catch through the throng of leering onlookers. *If only I had my bow*, Donavon thought.

"You boys must be from the mountain," came a voice from behind the mule cart after the Pogetsa had passed. A fat man smiled slyly at them from a nearby booth. A merchant, it appeared, by the array of goods under his canopy.

Donavon maneuvered his horse under the canopy. Looming over the counter, he glared down at the bald spot on the fat man's head. "That's none of your business," he snapped. "What else did you hear?"

"Oh, nothing much really," the smug merchant replied. "Just a few things about colonels and taverns and rams and such."

Gildryn dismounted and strode under the booth. He grabbed the merchant by the collar, much to Donavon's chagrin. "You better keep that fat flapper of yours shut if you know what's good for you."

The surprised man raised his hands in compliance; his fleshy neck jiggled like a sheep's bladder. "Oh, my, let's not get hasty here. I just happen to have a great deal on barrel staves today. Great for taverns, in fact. Solid oak. Two for one if you ask nicely."

"Let him go, Gilly," Donavon said, adding a sharp kick to Gilly's shoulder. "You're not helping."

Patsy Grange walked up to the booth and grabbed a coil of thick rope that hung from a hook on one of the several gold-painted wooden poles that supported the merchant's canopy. "How much for this?" he asked, sneering at the fat man. "I heard it's great for stringin' up loose-lipped hawkers by their tongues."

Donavon leaped off his horse, intent on defusing the scuffle. With his feet on the ground, he looked out toward the colonel's carriage and realized to his utter shock that it was empty.

"He's over there," Angus said, pointing to the archway that led to the main square.

Sure enough, Donavon got a glimpse of the colonel's feathered hat bobbing up and down on the Promenade like a buoy in a river current. Furious for letting the mission slip, he shoved past Patrick and headed for the square at top speed, shouting his orders on the way.

"Angus, Gilly, let's go! The rest of you know the plan, so get to it. Corey and Dugan, stay here. Make sure Fatty keeps his mouth shut!"

The square was a swarm of activity when Donavon finally caught up with the colonel. Good, he thought. The crowd might miss Mitterhal in all the commotion. Gildryn was next through the archway, followed by Angus, whose bullish momentum sent the herdsman careening into Donavon like a billiard ball.

"Watch what you're doing, you blind ox," Donavon shouted to Angus.

A round of applause broke out for a group of street performers in a sectioned-off area near the stone pillars. Two strapping men dressed as gladiators juggled wooden scimitars. A pretty young woman stood precariously balanced, one foot on each of the gladiators' shoulders, receiving their spinning props with flawless agility. Relieved that the cheer was not directed at the colonel, Donavon allowed himself a moment to admire her captivating show.

A boy sneaked out of the crowd and tugged on the colonel's vest. "I like that feather on your hat, mister. Is it real?"

Gildryn, who was closest to the colonel, sprang into action. "Get gone, you nervy little rat," he said, gearing up for a swift kick.

The boy scuttled behind the colonel and sneered at Gildryn. "I'm not a rat!"

"You'll be feeding a whole lot of 'em soon if you don't buzz off."

"Ease up, Gilly," Angus said. "He's just a boy."

"That's right, I'm just a boy," said the boy. "Pick on someone your own size."

The colonel raised his cane to get a better glimpse at the youngster clinging to his vest. "What's your name, lad?" he asked, appearing amused by the youth's feistiness.

"I'm Barusta. I like your feather. It's big. Can I have it?"

The Old Mitt, for all his cantankerous ways, remained surprisingly good-humored with the lad. "I suppose it is," he said, removing his hat and acting as if the feather had just landed there. "It's quite big indeed, now that you mention it. Looks like the tail feather of a lakehawk to me."

"A lakehawk!" said the boy, wide-eyed. "How'd you get that?"

"It was a gift from a friend."

"That must be some friend you got. If I had that feather I would never give it away. Not even to my best of friends."

"Is that so? What would you do with it then?"

"I'd keep it someplace safe where nobody could take it, then I'd charge people lots of money to see it."

"I see." The colonel placed the hat back on his head. "Well, I'm afraid you'll have to come up with another scheme to make your fortune. This feather won't serve that purpose. Good day, lad. It has been a pleasure." He nodded to the boy and continued toward the center of the square.

"The money wouldn't be for me, mister," the boy shouted, just as

Donavon took a step to follow. "I would give it all to Madam Hume so she could build the school she always talks about."

The colonel stopped, as if suddenly struck by a dizzy spell. Slowly, he turned around to face the boy. "What did you say?"

Donavon stepped in. "That's enough chatter, kid. Time to get a move on."

"Wait," the colonel said, shaking off the spell. "Where might we find this Madam Hume?"

"Why, she's at the fountain," the boy answered. "She's the Fountain Lady. Where else would she be? Who are you, mister? You're not from around here, are you?"

Donavon upped his order. "You heard me, kid. You better shove off or you'll be getting that kick after all."

The colonel tapped his cane to the cobbles. "I am Cornelius. Come with me, lad. I want you to introduce me to your fountain lady."

The boy bowed and then darted off through the crowd in the direction of the fountain. "Follow me, mister!" he shouted before vanishing into the forest of legs.

At the fountain they found Barusta talking to an old woman dressed entirely in black and seated at the edge of the pool. A group of children sat clustered around her. Barusta stepped forward, eager to make the introduction. Again, he bowed. "Madam, this is Mister Cornelius. Mister Cornelius, Madam Hume."

The old lady smiled. She had a pleasant nature, despite her gloomy attire. "It is a pleasure to meet you, Mister Cornelius, but please pardon Barusta's manners. I see there are others in your company deserving of an introduction as well."

"We are family," Donavon said.

Angus and Gildryn looked at each other and shrugged.

"Family? I see," the madam said, sizing up the group. "Then allow me to introduce you to our family. Children, say hello to Mister Cornelius and his charming relations."

"Hello, Mister Cornelius," the group of children chimed.

Donavon sighed, sensing their cover at risk. He scanned the area around the fountain. The children's outburst appeared to pass unnoticed, short of a few curious glances. Still, he was anxious to shed the attention. It was only a matter of time before someone made the connection.

The colonel revealed no such concern and responded to the fountain lady's refined etiquette with like flair. "The pleasure is all mine, Madam. Your family is most gracious. Might we join you?"

"By all means. Your timing is perfect. It is story time for the children and today's tale comes with a special message from the Old Tome. Please join us."

The colonel carefully made his way through the cluster of children toward the fountain. Donavon stood motionless, derailed by the move, wondering what to do. An elderly man sitting with a pleasant old lady around a horde of children by a fountain was one thing. Adding three gruff highlanders to the mix would only compromise the mission.

"Come on, guys," he said, pointing to an empty stone bench tucked away by a nearby flowerbed. "Let's have a seat over there."

Donavon monitored the activities in the square while he, Angus, and Gildryn sat under the leaves of a dogwood. A good portion of the crowd lingered beyond the entrance of the square, though many wandered around the flowerbeds that surrounded the fountain. At the pool, opposite to where the Old Mitt and the fountain lady sat, a group of musicians played their flutes, lutes, and reeds amidst a circle of drummers. Their music floated over the fountain like a mist, drenching the square in a constant stream of sound. Donavon especially liked the drums. Still alert in the shade of the dogwood, he kept a careful tally on all who came within a stone's throw of the colonel; and in so doing, became aware of the shifting patterns among the fountain folk. For every one who came to the fountain, another would leave for the archway where the gladiators performed their stunts. The organized beat of their comings and goings shed light on a question that had been gnawing at him ever since they arrived. How could the crowd be so bent on entertainment after the Pogetsa had just swept the square?

"The Old Mitt's putting on a good show for the little squeaks," Angus said, breaking the silence. "Look, I think he's gonna give that Barusta kid his feather."

Sure enough, Barusta stood up straight and proud while the colonel, who had just removed the feather from his hat, stuck it through a buttonhole on the youth's vest. An enormous cheer erupted from the children. The colonel sealed the occasion with a sortie of smoke rings. Scores of little hands went up as the children tried to stick their fingers through the ethereal wisps.

Gildryn slapped both hands to his knees. "I betch'ya the Old Mitt's chimney taught him that move."

Angus laughed while Donavon told Gilly to shut up.

"Come on, Donny, I'm just lightenin' things up," Gildryn said. "Don't you think you're gett'n a bit testy with this deputy stuff?"

"Yeah, Donny," Angus said, still chuckling. "What's happening to you? Used to be you were the first to fire off a crack at the colonel's expense. You're not starting to respect the Old Mitt, are you?"

Donavon glared at Angus. "I'm just doing my job, you big oaf."

"Sure you are."

Donavon changed the subject. "Looks like there's more to this gathering than meets the eye. I wouldn't be surprised if everybody in the square is in on it. Look at those musicians on the other side of the fountain. That girl playing the flute was just at the archway with the juggling gladiators. I bet they're running shifts to keep the pogies guessing."

The three watched and listened for some time. Angus kept his gaze locked on the group of pretty young women who danced in the middle of the drum circle. Donavon watched the fair-haired flutist in her tight-fitting skirt, though for the sake of the mission he made sure to keep one eye on the colonel. It was Gildryn who pointed out the young man who charged through the archway and into the square. Straight for the musicians he went, waving his arms emphatically. The music stopped. One of the musicians laid down his reed and ran toward the cathedral. The flutist darted around the pool toward the children, the lower half of her skirt flapping like a wind-swept curtain with every urgent stride. Donavon caught a whiff of her earthy fragrance as she passed the bench. Had the circumstances been different, he might have introduced himself.

"Quickly, Madam!" she said, sliding to a stop in front of the colonel. "Weirmen have landed at the Docks and are making down the Promenade. We need to get the children to safety at once."

Madam Hume remained calm but wasted no time with her response. "Of course, my dear. All right, children," she said, smiling. "Follow Flarynn to church. Go now and remember your prayers. There will be plenty of story time tomorrow."

Barusta was the first to get up, the feather still tucked through the buttonhole on his vest. "We're not leaving without you, Madam."

"I will be fine, Barusta. You must go. There is no time for discussion. Hurry on now."

Angus looked at Donavon. "Weirmen? Did you hear that, Donny? How'd they get past the pogies at the Docks?"

"I don't know, Angus. Something's not adding up. You better get your brothers. Follow the children to the cathedral and then leave the square out the back."

"Right away, Donny."

In a flash Angus was up and running, taking only five great strides to get to the group of children. Like a loading boom on the wharf, he scooped up two of the youngest with his brawny arms and placed one on each shoulder. "Come on, you little whelps. Let's have a race. First one to church gets a free ride on a mule cart!"

There was a port in the northwest quadrant of Lake Lakwynn that catered to no other authority than its own. Massive harbor locks stood as sentinels around an enormous weir that had been built during the age of the rail to control the water's level. The Weirs, as the port was called, was inhabited by exiles who would not conform to the laws of the province. They had no formal government, though a loose code within the anarchy gave structure to a brutal pecking order. Since the Weirs was considered part of the province, an unwritten arrangement existed between it and other more civilized societies that allowed for a certain degree of unruliness so long as the lake's water level was properly managed. And while the weirmen were certainly not immune to every law of the land, authorities tended to turn a blind eye to the raucous revelry that came with their visits. Needless to say, it was not an arrangement embraced by the church. However, the stability it provided for the lake's economy muffled the cries of the righteous.

Like a wolf, Donavon sniffed at the apprehension in the air. His keen sight fell on the steady stream of water trickling out of the fountain. There was nothing to do but wait and watch. Sunlight reflected on the water, shimmering around the paws of the fountain guardian, and sent his thoughts back to his wolf pup. Would Enyalda know what to do if he didn't return? What if the badger came back? The mere notion made him growl.

"What's up with the growling, Donny?" Gildryn asked, snapping him out of his trance. "Looks like they've made it to the arches."

Indeed, the crowd at the entrance began to spread. Through the widening gap Donavon saw the first of the marauders appear. Gruff men for sure, shoving anyone aside who got in their way as they strode through the square.

"My God," Gildryn said. "There's a whole boat of 'em. We should have bailed while we had the chance. They're comin' this way."

"Just stay put, Gilly. We're gonna ride this out. And whatever you do, hold your temper."

The chief weirman was a hulking thug covered in tattoos and stinking of fish and whiskey. Donavon caught a whiff as he passed the bench, a long-handled fishing gaff swinging in one hand. Directly to the edge of the pool he went, only paces away from the colonel and the fountain lady. He set the gaff down and removed his tattered shirt, exposing scar-laden skin over hard muscles. Stepping into the pool, he plunged his reeking shirt into the water and leered into the serene face of the fountain goddess.

"A good day for a swim, my lady!" he bawled at the towering monument.

A reed player from across the fountain stepped out of the circle. "There is no bathing in the pool," he said so all could hear.

The chief weirman turned around slowly and eyed the musician. He nodded to several swarthy men who stood nearby. They stripped the man of his reed and dragged him forward.

"I take it you're the one to enforce this rule?" the weirman said, stepping out of the pool.

"The water is sacred," the man said with trembling courage.

The weirman snatched his gaff and brought the sharp spur to within an inch of the musician's chin. "Would you really deprive me of a swim on such a hot day?"

The reed player gawked at the sight of the blade. "There are no weapons allowed here," he said, though in obvious fear of his life. "You are breaking the law."

"Weapons? What weapons?" the weirman asked in mockery. "Oh, you mean this?"

In one swift motion he spun the gaff around and jammed the end of the pole into the reed player's gut, doubling him over at the waist. He then drove his waterlogged boot into the musician's face, sending him back to the cobbles in a violent burst of mist. The crowd gasped at the outrage.

"Don't worry, mate, it's not really a weapon, just a tool of the trade. Anyone else have a policy they'd like to share?"

The challenge went unanswered, though several drummers stepped forward to tend to their unconscious comrade. The boatman went back to rinsing himself of the day's plunder. The rest of the crew swaggered around the fountain, stirring up whatever mischief they could muster.

Donavon remained on the bench. It was his duty to watch, and watch he did, unnoticed, overlooked for the moment, mastering his own fears as best he could. He counted the weirmen. Forty or so in all, maybe fifty. The colonel remained calm and cool, smoking his pipe as if it were just another day in the park. And as the tension mounted, it seemed to Donavon in the heat of his vigil that the Old Mitt grew in majesty before his very eyes. That he might not be a madman after all, and in truth never really was, and that his father had not been a fool for following him, and that should the time come to act on his behalf, he would do exactly that— just as his father had.

The chief weirman stepped out of the pool and shook himself like a dog. Tying back his hair, he noticed the fountain lady glaring at him. "Look, mates, the old fountain hag has finally made a catch." He smirked at the colonel. "And who might this lucky old goat be?"

The colonel said not a word, drawing deep on his pipe. He appeared oblivious to the boorish weirman.

Donavon leaned forward on the bench. "This doesn't make sense," he said quietly to Gildryn. "These guys are pirates and opportunists. They've got nothing to gain and all to lose by doing this. Why would they risk a run-in with the pogies just to harass a bunch of activists? Unless …"

"Unless what, Donny?"

The realization struck like a bolt. "Unless they got nothing to lose and all to gain by doing it. We gotta get the colonel out of here, Gilly. The pogies are in on it."

"It's a little too late for that, don't you think?" Gildryn said, just as the weirman snatched the pipe out of the colonel's mouth.

"What's the matter, old buzzard. Has the pipe scorched your tongue? Speak up, you old fool. Tell us who you are."

"You are a monster," the fountain lady said.

"Shut up, hag. Let your boyfriend speak for himself."

The colonel leaned forward, both hands on the top of his cane. "Your manners have failed you, weirman. You are in need of a sunset."

For an instant, the eyes of the weirman chief betrayed him, and Donavon saw the time to act. He took a deep breath, feeling the strain in his own will. He then removed the silver brooch pinned to his chest and handed it to Gildryn. "Take this, Gilly, and give it to Enya. Tell her to take care of the wolf. I will get their attention. Once they're on me, get the colonel out of here. Strap him to your back if you have to."

"Don't be crazy, Donny. These guys'll kill you."

"Just do it."

Donavon stared at the fountain statue as he rose from the bench. How beautiful the goddess appeared in that moment, how alert the wolf, how weightless the butterfly. How strange, he thought, to even notice. A calm came over him—an otherworldliness that took him away and showered him in peace, even if only for a moment. Just enough to wash away his fear and allow the command to stream through his mouth.

"Give him back his pipe." The words flowed, cool and clear.

The world changed in that moment, grim though it seemed. The gang of weirmen closed in around Donavon, yet his will hardened all the more. Alert and steady, he walked toward the pool.

As if sensing an unseen threat, the chief tossed the colonel's pipe into the pool and grabbed his gaff. "Another policy maker, how exciting," he said, inflating his chest to its full breadth. "And do you have any last words before I gut you alive?"

Donavon stopped within a gaff swing of the burly thug. "I do. I am Donavon McFadden, deputy of Cotton Crown. You are under arrest."

Laughter burst out around the pool.

As he'd hoped, the leader took the bait and joined in the amusement with his ruffian crew. "We got a live one here, mates!"

Donavon jumped on the lapse, knowing that his first shot had to be a good one. He led with his left, giving it everything he had. It was a direct strike to the jaw that would have sent any scrapper to the floor, but the burly boatman only staggered. It was just enough for Donavon to strike again and send his gaff splashing into the pool. That was all he could make of the opportunity, however, before the rest of the pack closed in and dragged him down. They kicked and beat him before lifting his limp body to face their infuriated chief. But even as they did, Donavon heard a voice, distant at first, coming from the archway, approaching rapidly.

"Make way! Make way!"

Into the crowd and through the square charged Emit the mule, dragging the tavern cart filled with herdsmen flinging armloads of barrel staves into the masses, inciting bystanders to take up arms. As the cart neared the pool, Angus leaped off the back with one end of the merchant's rope looped around his forearm and the other secured to the rear hitch of the cart. He plowed ahead in line with Emit, heaving the rope tight and cutting down a score of weirman along the way. The Grange boys jumped from the cart at the pool, armed with half sacks of barley and grain. Chaos ensued, like a pillow fight gone berserk. Then, from the direction of the cathedral came a cry that split the crowd. Six horsemen charged through the square on highland steeds, their lances lowered and shining bright—gold as the merchant's canopy poles.

Donavon's elation at the sight of his comrades was short-lived. Two of the thugs still had hold of him, and the chief delivered a roundhouse punch that sent his field of vision spinning. The jarring blow toyed with Donavon's already rattled senses, and in his delirium he flinched as an enraged gladiator charged him, a wooden scimitar held high. He closed his eyes and braced for the decapitating blow—but then was suddenly freed of his captors' clutches. His eyes rolled open, just enough for him to stagger to the fountain pool. There he remained with hands on the cobbles, fighting for consciousness.

A violent tug on his shoulder brought him back to his senses. The weirman chief held him tight by the scruff, though the big man now reeked of fear. How long had it been? Blood seeped out of the boatman's hair and madness was in his eye.

"You and I have a score to settle," he snarled. "You're going down, mate."

Donavon struggled, but the weirman's powerful hands held like clamps and drove his head into the water. He tried to get up but the clamps kept him under. A burning sensation stirred in his chest, along with a pressing need for air. Pulled up at last, he gasped for breath, still in the weirman's clutch.

"How's that, mate? Ready for another?"

Back into the water; he barely closed his mouth in time. The cycle repeated, and with each dunk Donavon's lungs buckled more under the strain. At last, when his last gasp was spent, he heard music. It was a soothing melody, similar to the one the musicians had been playing at the fountain.

So this is how it ends. It's not so bad really. His lungs filled with water and his body went limp. A woman's voice rose over the music. So soft and pure, yet firm in purpose.

"Open your eyes," she commanded.

He did—for to deny the voice was not an option—and in so doing saw the Old Mitt's pipe lying at the bottom of the pool. With the vision came strength, and he reached out to grab it, drawn to the carved horns on the burl. But it was not the pipe he found in his hand. Rather, it was the weirman's fishing gaff. His grip around the gaff tightened, and with every ounce of energy, he thrust the handle of the gaff out of the pool, instantly freeing himself of the clutch in his watery tomb.

Rising out of the pool, he saw the weirman chief on his knees, gargling blood and holding his cracked windpipe. Apparently the handle had found its mark. Horror spawned in the boatman's eyes as Donavon spun the gaff, ready to cut him down with the working end of the tool. He would have done just that, yet his hand was stayed by a command that thundered over the square.

"Stop!" the colonel ordered.

Donavon wavered, his borrowed energy fading fast. He stood breathless with rage, holding the blade to the gasping weirman's neck. He glanced to the wolf at the feet of the goddess and his grip on the gaff tightened.

"I said stop, Donavon! Drop the gaff. He is a countryman in need of a lesson in manners, which you have delivered. Now you must leave him with the wits to reflect on it."

The world closed in on Donavon. He made an effort to speak, to deny the Old Mitt his order, but all that came out was a lung full of water. Gasping and weak, he threw the gaff back into the pool and collapsed. But not before leaving a six-inch slice in the weirman's cheek as a reminder of his lesson.

6
Keepers of Peace

Pogeya was a Gwyntah word, which literally translated meant to keep. The root word *etsa* meant peace. When the war ended, it only made sense to General Thurman Rankwall that combining the two words would mean keeper of peace. Had he done his research, however, he would have discovered that in the dialect of the tribes, *keep* was synonymous with *possess*. Had he ventured further into their philosophy, he would have learned that true peace, according to the Gwyntah, was a natural state forever in flux; and to suggest that one might possess it was not only irrational, but an insult to their goddess. It turned out to be a vital error in judgment that forever plagued his ambitions in the Haven. And though few would argue his brilliance as a military general, the vernacular blunder not only emphasized his ineptitude as a linguist, but as a statesman.

Rankwall's Pogetsa was deployed to the Three Havens within months of his inauguration as Lakwynnia's first chancellor. Essentially a security force, its prime directive was to enforce provincial law in the Haven and to serve as a deterrent against opportunists, who after the war would have plundered the vulnerable region. Comprised exclusively of transplanted soldiers who had fought under Rankwall, the organization was run with strict military efficiency. The chief constable of the Pogetsa was also appointed by Rankwall and answered directly to him. Out of principle, the mayor of Wulfhaven was included in the hierarchy, but his role amounted to little more than a formality.

The first chief constable proved to be an utter failure. His personal failings led him astray from his duties and inevitably resulted in his death, though the incident was never officially confirmed to be anything other than a tragic accident. Had the dead constable been anyone other than Thurman Rankwall's son, the rumors surrounding the incident might have been buried along with the charred remains of his body. Since it was Fergus Rankwall, it took the Haven's most esteemed reverend to put the case to rest. Though not even the sworn testimony of Marcus Poulakis could diffuse the dark cloud of suspicion that hovered over the sons of the late Lieutenant Uryan McFadden.

Chief Constable Heinrick von Krutzwig stood in his office at Pogetsa headquarters, brooding at the damage report rolled out on his desk. "Demolish?" he said to the chief engineer standing on the other side of the desk. "Why can't you just repair what was damaged and build on it?"

Barbarus Haunch leaned forward, his fleshy finger hovering over the five red circles on the bridge sketch. "That is the case for two of the five damaged piers. The stress cracks on these three, however, are too extensive. They will not support the compression from the train. Their blocks will have to be dismantled and recast at the footings. It's as if he knew precisely where to direct the ordnance. Impressive, really. Mitterhal certainly knew his masonry."

"Spare me the commentary, Barbarus, and just stick to the facts. How long will it take to complete the demolition phase?"

"That depends on how many men we have. As it stands now, it could take a year just to clean up the wreckage and get the piers ready for the masons. The water level of the lake will have to be dropped. Had the bombardment been concentrated on the trusses or the main deck, the repair would be a straightforward matter of replacing the timbers. Labor intensive for sure, but not nearly as tricky on logistics."

Krutzwig slammed his fist on the desk and then strode to the window at the back of his office. He scowled at the harbor view without saying a word. How he hated the Haven. The land stank of savages and mix-breeds. Everything about the region vexed him: the people, the culture, the climate. Even the looming mountains reminded him every godforsaken day of his mortal insignificance. He was there for one reason and one reason only—to get rich. The chancellor had promised him a sizeable share of the tariffs once the Silvermine Bridge was reinstated; it was an impossible offer to refuse. He snarled at a trade ship leaving the harbor. Here he was six years later and still nothing. The thought enraged him, and he jerked away from the window.

"That is time we can no longer afford, Barbarus!"

He strode to the decanter on the wall shelf and poured two double shots of gin. "Where there is a will, there is a way," he said, handing one of the glasses to the engineer. "The chancellor has made it his top priority to reinstate the rail around the lake. If it is strictly a matter of men, then I can have a barge load of grunts brought in from South Bay." He downed the gin straight in one gulp.

"That will be expensive," Barbarus said, still holding his glass.

"What did I say about commentary? You are an engineer, Barbarus. I suggest you stick with that and leave the financing to me. It pains me to see you so distracted. Have your drink."

"Constable, on the subject of financing, I would raise another point, if I may?"

"And what is that?"

"The politics surrounding the project are likely to pose a significant threat to the workmen. I suggest we double their pay to offset the risk of a Gwyntah attack."

A grave air fell over the constable. He smacked his shot glass down on the desk, catapulting drops of spirits onto the damage report. "Leave that to me, Barbarus. The Pogetsa will be their incentive. Now I urge you to have your drink and get your mind where it belongs."

Someone knocked pensively on the closed office door just as the chief engineer forced down his gin. Krutzwig heaved a sigh. "What is it?"

The door opened slowly and a plain-faced middle-aged woman entered. It was Harriet Simpleton, the office clerk. Her timid posture all but squelched her womanly form. "Captain Rueger needs to speak with you at once, sir. He says it is an urgent matter that requires your immediate attention."

Pouring another glass of gin, Krutzwig told her to send him in. Then he dismissed Barbarus, ordering him to have a materials list and a timetable on his desk in two days.

Momentarily alone, Krutzwig downed his second drink, wondering what the illustrious war captain had in store. It had to be big. Rueger never broke up a meeting without good cause. He was the epitome of a military officer. In fact, it often puzzled Krutzwig why he and not Rueger had been appointed chief constable. Without question, Rueger had the credentials—perhaps it was just that. Krutzwig went back to his desk and mused on the gin-splattered damage report.

The captain entered the office, announcing that there had been an incident in the main square involving the weirmen.

Krutzwig kept his eye on the plans. "What have they done this time? I thought we bought their allegiance."

"We did. By your order they were told to intimidate the protestors at the fountain."

The red circles on the bridge plan swelled out of focus. "Let me guess," Krutzwig said, rubbing his eyes. "Our charming friends from the Weirs got a little carried away with their assignment."

"In a manner of speaking, yes. Certainly their chief boatman did. He was crippled by a youth who claims to be the deputy of Cotton Crown."

Krutzwig looked up from the plan and sneered. "Cotton Crown? Does this youth have a name?"

"He is alleged to be the youngest son of Uryan McFadden, Colonel Mitterhal's first lieutenant during the war."

Krutzwig slammed his fist on the desk. "I am perfectly aware of who Uryan McFadden was, you idiot! I don't need a history lesson. I would like to know how a highland boy was able to prevent a boatload of thugs from carrying out a simple order. We paid a pretty penny for their cooperation."

"He had support, sir. Several comrades from his village as well as the protestors at the fountain."

"Did he now? Another McFadden to stir up the dregs. How wonderful."

"There is something else you should know, sir. Colonel Mitterhal was in the square when the incident occurred."

Again Krutzwig struck the desk, jostling a vial of black ink to the floor. The bottle shattered. "I thought he went insane! What the hell was he doing there?"

"Witnesses say he was sitting with the orphans at the fountain."

"Arrest him!"

"The colonel?"

"No! The boy, you idiot!"

"On what charge?"

"I don't care. Disturbing the peace. Inciting a riot. Possession of a deadly weapon in the city proper. Surely he had a weapon, Captain?"

"Actually, sir, according to reports, he used the chief weirman's own fishing tool against him."

Krutzwig lurched back to the window, eyeing the swollen sails of the trade ship now bound for the broads. He waited for his gin rage to settle. "An example must be made, Hans. The chancellor will be here in a month expecting results. We are past the point of delays, and I won't have these highland half-breeds gumming it up. We're going to have enough problems with the savages once the project begins. We must send a clear message that severe consequences will fall on all who impede the process. I want you to take a company of your best men up the mountain and arrest this McFadden boy. Make sure Glockstoff goes with you. In fact, have him report to me at once."

"Yes, sir."

Hans Rueger left and Krutzwig immediately went back to the decanter on the shelf. After pouring his drink, he shrugged in disgust at the trail of black footprints that followed him from the desk.

Chadwick Glockstoff entered the office. His probing, rat-like eyes noted the ink trail from the desk to the shelf, and then to the couch where Krutzwig was slouched. "You wanted to see me, sir."

Krutzwig lurched up from the cushions. "What took you so long?"

"I was in the middle of an interrogation."

"How nice. I'm sending Rueger and his men up to Cotton Crown to arrest that rebble-rouser McFadden. I want you with them. Make sure those highland stiffs know we mean business."

"By your command, sir."

"Do not come back without him."

"Absolutely, sir."

"Who were you interrogating?"

"An inciter in the square. He claims he saw our patrols transporting surveyors to the mines."

"What evidence does he have?"

"We don't know yet. He refuses to speak until we give him back his musket."

"His musket! What is he thinking? He must be mad."

"Actually, sir, I believe he is. He just sits in his cell and sings."

"What do you know about him?"

"Only that he served in the infantry for the Haven Guard. Over the years he's been given quarter at the Schnites compound."

"What in the world was Sebastian Schnites doing with a lunatic?"

"Apparently Poulakis set up the arrangement after the war. Schnites agreed to shelter the soldier over the cold months in return for labor on his compound."

"So that explains why Schnites withdrew his investment in the restoration project last week. Whatever that loony boy said must have turned him. This is messy, Chadwick. I don't like it. Not a bit. A shell-shocked soldier spouting off our plans is one thing, but Schnites has influence. We need to clean this up before it gets worse."

"Same as before?"

"No, this one will require more planning. In the meantime, I want that musketman kept in solitary. Not even a roach gets into his cell. Understand?"

"Understood, sir."

7
Tough Talk in the Garden

Enyalda knew her flowers. To suggest otherwise was an insult to the obvious, like saying a baker did not know her bread, or a brewer his beer. Or worse yet, a mother her children. For like a mother Enyalda loved her flowers, all of them, whatever their color or quality. And in the waning weeks of summer, when their splendor had been all but spent, she cherished them all the more and went to great lengths to remind them of their importance in the world. Indeed, it was confidence they needed at this time more than anything—short of water, of course. To be admired even when their beauty had wilted and the sun's power no longer fed their fragile esteem.

And so it happened in the final days of August, Enyalda roamed outside the colonel's manor for hours on end, whispering encouragement to every perennial she could find—a considerable task, but one she embraced with delight. It had been a wonderful year getting to know them. Growing up, she had always been aware of their presence on the premises, but seldom had the opportunity to chat with them for fear of being spotted by the colonel from his rooftop. Most of the wild strains she already knew by name thanks to Muma's tutorage. Others—the cultivated ones not native to the Haven—she was less familiar with and felt compelled to name them herself. To address them in the same manner as a nameless weed would have been discourteous, if not downright rude.

There was a buzz in the gardens while she made her rounds, as if the honeybees knew it was their last chance to stock up on nectar. The casual pace of summer was winding down and the time to gather was fast approaching. Enyalda sighed at the thought, but such was the way of things. Her musings passed over the colonel's hives and out into the goat pasture, where every blade of grass seemed bent on making a point. She knew it was their nature to be chatty, especially when the wind blew, but as of late the grasses had been more impulsive than ever. Ever since the colonel's trip to the fountain, in fact. If only they would restrain themselves and wait their turns to speak, she might then know what they were trying to say. But that would be a far cry from reality. More likely that the colonel's goats would decide to slide down the slopes on their horns, or the mountain itself rise out of the earth on two skinny legs and tiptoe across the Haven. She chuckled at the absurdity.

"You are all giggles this morning, my dear," said a gruff old voice from behind her.

Enyalda popped out of the perennials like a snapdragon seed. She loved the colonel dearly but hated how he sneaked up on her. It was one of his most unnerving habits. She made a quick curtsy and smiled back the words that knocked on her lips.

The colonel leaned forward on his cane. "No breakfast this morning?"

She gasped, hands flying to her cheeks. How could she have forgotten something so basic? The perennials had been extra needy of late, and yes, she had spent the better part of the last three nights mending her brother's wounds after the brawl in Wulfhaven, but even so there was no excuse. The colonel still had to eat. She lowered her eyes and covered her face with her hair.

"Don't worry," he said, lighting his pipe. "I was merely making conversation. I survived the trauma just fine."

Not sure how to reply, Enyalda went back to her task in the garden, already planning how to make up for her blunder with a tasty lunch.

"You've been spending a great deal of time in the gardens," he went on. "What do the flowers say when you whisper?"

She made no response, not even in song. The answer was complicated and would take some time to arrange in verse. Besides, the direct question made her nervous. The truth was, it was not what the flowers said, but what they wanted to say that made her whisper. It had always been that way, even as a little girl. Flowers did not have mouths, so the responsibility fell on her to provide one for them. It was the same for all plants, grasses and trees alike. Even the Great Beech with all its ancient wisdom needed her mouth to voice its words; words that filtered through its leaves and into her lips as whispers.

With a painstaking effort, the colonel got down on one knee and examined a flower stalk that had long gone to seed. "What is the name of this plant?" he asked. "I like the arrangement of the leaves."

Still wary of the colonel's intentions, Enyalda swept away her hair to examine the flower. An intriguing choice, she thought. How appropriate for him to notice. Indeed, it was one of the southern Toricean strains that she had named herself. The compound leaves climbed the waist-high stalk to a condensed mass of ruddy husks at the top. Each leaf segmented into a pinnate series of smaller leaflets that created the visual effect of rungs on a ladder. Had it been spring, the rungs would have ascended to a dreamy cluster of heavenly blue blossoms at the highest point on the stalk. "Jahacco balhalad," she whispered in the colonel's ear.

The old man's bushy eyebrows went up as he ran the translation. "Now that's an interesting name. And what does dream ladder have to say today?"

Enyalda, realizing she had been tricked into speech, scowled and made a sweeping gesture toward the stalk, indicating that the colonel could ask it himself.

"I am sorry, my dear," he said, a sharp gleam in his eye. "It is not my policy to speak with plants."

The callous comment infuriated her. How dare he belittle her beloved flowers? What did he expect of her? She never asked him what his chimney said. And certainly if she did, she would never have snubbed it off so boorishly in its own presence. Real words came dangerously close to escaping her lips. Sensing her tongue at the brink, she stormed off toward the pasture, leaving the old man to fend for himself in the perennials.

At the fringe of the pasture, Enyalda seethed. The mountain goats had scavenged nearly all of the wildflowers along the wall. She watched them meander in the field without the slightest care to how much of a menace they were to the world. Stubborn bullheaded beasts, she thought. Just like the colonel. She sat and stewed, arms wrapped around her bent knees until her anger ran its course. As her thoughts cooled, they rolled back to childhood and the countless hours she'd spent in the branches of the Great Beech listening to the colonel lend his mouth to the chimney. The wind picked up and the grasses screamed for attention. Frustrated, tired, and overworked, she covered her ears with her hands and wept. When her tears ran dry, she wept yet again, realizing she had turned her back on the one man who had single-handedly taught her how to express her faith in a broken world.

It was nearly lunchtime when she heard the firm, steady thump of his beechwood cane coming toward the wall. Paralyzed on the rock, she wondered how she could ever face him again after her disgraceful behavior in the garden. The thumps got louder and eventually stopped directly behind her.

"Do you think dream ladder could forgive an old fool for not seeing past the end of his pipe?"

She acknowledged the question with a sniffle and a nod.

"That is a relief," the colonel said. "I went too far trying to get you to speak. You give so much of your voice to others but leave none for yourself. So delicate you are, like your flowers. I thought I would spark things up a bit

185

and draw it out of you, an old trick I used on the troops when the warring got to them. I was a fool to use the same tactic on you. Forgive me, my dear."

She remained quiet while the sentiment settled. Every passing second chiseled at her fear to be heard. Chip by chip her defenses crumbled. All the while, the colonel stood by her side, humbly holding his hat in hand. When her courage peaked, she looked him straight in the eye, for what she had to say required his undivided attention. And so for the first time since her trauma in the barn, Enyalda McFadden spoke the common tongue at a volume meant for the common ear, though her words were mixed and the phrasing measured.

Dream the Lady in her you I saw
on wall her portrait beauty
Sad the days she counts them all
her tears they fall for you

Blue her neck on pendant sparkles
light the shines on loom
A tapestry she wove for you
near window in the room

The dream a crown she wears in
white, the blossoms grace her hair
Dare to bloom the vines in
shade, your mother's nest they share

Long she lay on moss and stone
no dance, no song, no motion
Sleepless rest in empty nest
her shadow shields your home

Pass the time in portrait frame
with love she lost in war
Stay I will till know you are
her child lost no more

When she was done, Enyalda turned around on the rock and covered her eyes with her hair, embarrassed by her outburst. Both stood silent while the wind whistled through the gahenya. In time the colonel spoke, though his voice was distant and removed.

"There is so little I remember from the first days on this mountain. So much is lost. A mix of voices ... and visions. That is all. The room you speak of, the one with the loom, it's what drew me back to this house after the war. So long it had been. When I opened the door I knew it all. The tapestry, the uniform, the portrait. And the crib where she sang along to my little blue box ... the greatest of love. I went to the rooftop after that, never the room. So much death and loss. When you screamed that day, I knew what you saw. And when your brother brought you down the stairs, I knew she was with you. That she always was, right there to comfort you with her whispers ... just like in the leaves of the beechwood. I know that now. I remembered her song. Not even the wulfweed could strip me of that."

Enyalda sat still on the boulder, her head bowed, connecting the colonel's words with her own. There was so much more to say, to ask, to explore. What blue box? Yet for all her yearnings, she would say no more, feeling stuck like the wise old lichen on the rock beneath her, frozen in a timeless state of revelation. She remained as such until the colonel spoke again and snapped her out of her muse.

"Strange, the goats have their horns up," he said with an air of urgency. "Would you be so kind as to fetch my scope? It is on the mantel in the hearth room."

She looked up and saw the weather-worn wrinkles around the colonel's eyes flex as he squinted down slope. A plume of dust rose in the distance, just outside the village. Like a jackrabbit she jumped on the order, relieved to rid her body of its idleness. She darted back to the house and into the hearth room. The scope was exactly where the colonel had said it was. She snatched it off the mantel and dashed back to the door. On the way she heard the clink of metal on slate, coming from the kitchen. She veered at the parlor to investigate, putting the colonel's order on hold.

Donavon had returned from his first hunt since the brawl in Wulfhaven, and had decided to use the kitchen counter as a butcher block. Less than amused, Enyalda gasped at her twin's mess. The skin of the unlucky varmint was folded fur side out and draped over the dish rack where the salted pink liquid drained into the sink. A badger by the looks of it.

"There'll be plenty of meat for the stew tonight, sis," Donavon said, proudly holding the severed head aloft.

Revolted, Enyalda charged forward and met her brother eye to eye. "This mess on counter not I want in kitchen chop your badger not!"

"What did you say?" Donavon asked in wide-eyed surprise.

Enyalda covered her mouth with her hands, equally stunned.

"Enya, you're speaking." He dropped his hunting knife to the floor. "When did you start that? And what are you doing with the colonel's war scope? I don't think he'd want you running around with it."

Feeling the cold brass pressed against her face jolted her back to task. "Out at once and no more wait his seeing glass investigates!" With those words she rushed out the door, leaving Donavon to sort through his own thoughts in the carnage of the kitchen.

The plume of dust was sweeping quickly through the south pasture by the time Enyalda returned. The colonel snatched the scope out of her hand without the slightest attempt at a thank you. In the blink of an eye he extended the tool and aimed the lens at the advancing cloud.

"They are riding in formation," he said. "Two, three, one followed by three rows of four abreast—Rankwall's lads." He retracted the scope and tucked it inside his inner vest pocket. "Come, there is little time. Back to the house."

Halfway down the hill and into the gardens, Enyalda realized they were not going to make it at their hampered pace. The same thought must have crossed the colonel's mind, for he simply stopped.

"Go to the stock house, my dear. If your brother is not there, then I want you to release the wolf and hide yourself in the hay."

No! Not the hay, anything but the hay. She shook her head in defiance, her thoughts racing, and grabbed the colonel's hand. "Faster our way we make," she whimpered, tugging.

He pulled back his cane as if ready to strike. "I said go!" A terrible fire burned in his eyes.

Enyalda, horrified by the command, darted behind the nearby hedge of laurels. But it was not to the stock house she went. Rather she arced around the laurels and made straight for the stone terrace at the bend in the manor, desperate not to stumble in the blur of her own tears. At the terrace she charged the glass door of the solarium. In she went and up the stairs to the kitchen, ignoring the cries of her loved ones.

It was quiet when she got there. No brother in kitchen. Just the badger ... or parts of it. Where was he? Dizzy. Probably at the stock house with the wolf. Feeding it. Dizzy still. Yes, most likely, with the hay ... The blood, kitchen spinning, knife on floor, heavy stinking breath, big hands— No! Not knife ... Pitchfork, straw screaming, fear, no voice, hay in face, more dizzy, more hands, more shadows, just like barn—blackness.

Enyalda never went to Crown Tavern. Never. Though she was not in the least bit oblivious to what went on there. Her brothers were regulars, and at suppertime when they talked around the table, she would listen and learn. Thus it was not entirely by chance that after regaining consciousness on the kitchen floor next to Donavon's hunting knife, she envisioned the brazen gold seal of the Pogetsa posted over the stove and riddled with darts.

The vision dissolved as she shot up to counter height, inadvertently laying her hand on the badger's dismantled backbone. Disgusted, she jerked her hand away. How long had it been? No time to wonder.

Movement in the window drew her attention outside. Men—lots of them—in the center pane beyond the dormant amaryllis bulb on the sill. Men in uniform with guns, towering around the colonel on their horses, exactly where she had left him by the laurels.

If only the amaryllis were in bloom. What would it tell her to do? What would Muma do if she were still here? Nothing in all her experience had prepared her for this. She was on her own with no one to confide in but herself. Where were her brothers? She thought to pray. Perhaps the Great Mother had an answer. Or would the Father be more likely to respond in this case? Another movement caught her attention in the lowest corner of the window.

It was Donavon crouched like a wolf, obscured in the wavy glass, slinking around the backside of the laurels with drawn bow in hand. The men with the guns were on the other side of the hedge, unaware of his approach. As the danger mounted, she remembered the colonel's words to Adman when he'd asked what to do if the Pogetsa ever came to the mountain—Invite them to dinner. Enyalda turned around and looked at the salt cabinet Donavon had left wide open. Suddenly she was struck with the irrepressible urge to bake fruit tarts. The mere thought calmed her. That she could do, she was certain of it. She smiled at the sleeping bulb in the window. "Nowhere else but noted is the way that you speak," she whispered.

And so, without a motion wasted, Enyalda cleared the counter of badger parts and moved to her task, knowing exactly what had to be done.

8

The Ninth Rule

The Pogetsa rarely bothered with the highlands. When they did, it was usually some hapless recruit ordered by Krutzwig to post his monthly decrees on the front door of the jailhouse. The parchments with their official seals were given special observance by the regulars at Crown Tavern. In fact, an entire interior wall had been dedicated to their display, complete with dart holes and lager stains.

On the opposite wall was a tablet of tavern rules, centered between the raised ceiling and the fireplace mantel. Unlike the stained documents across the room, special care had been given to the slate's preservation, for long it had hung from the black wrought-iron spike imbedded in the central support timber. Though the letters had been smudged by smoke over the years, few left the tavern ignorant of the rules.

Donavon knew every rule by heart. He didn't always heed them, though he did try. Some of the statutes were self-evident and made perfect sense, such as, "Put not off your clothes in the presence of others," or "Being set to ale scratch not, neither spit cough nor blow your nose, except in absolute necessity." Others were more open to interpretation. Rules such as "Speak not with too great a cause before wiping your lips, for it is uncivil." Many an eve after a long day on the hunt, Donavon found himself sitting at the hearth with mug in hand, trying to decipher the meaning behind the cryptic words.

So it happened that as Donavon peeked through the laurel leaves to better tally the squad of mounted soldiers that surrounded the colonel, the ninth rule in the tavern code came to mind. "Spit not in the fire, nor stoop low before it, neither put your hands into the flames, nor set your feet upon them, lest you be the meat that is cooked." Long had he dreamed of hunting pogies, but never like this. He always imagined them on the run, dodging for cover under the barrage of his arrows. Now he was not so sure. Seventeen, he counted—how odd, that was his age—thirty, maybe forty paces away. All armed with riffled muskets and sidearms. He counted the arrows in his quiver. Fifteen. That would leave two standing, assuming that every shot was perfect. Every shot of his, that is. He felt for his hunting knife, the last-ditch backup, but it was not in its sheath. Idiot!

"Permission denied, Captain." The colonel's words fired through the leaves.

"This is not about permission," came the pogie leader's curt response. "By order of Krutzwig, we will search your premises if you do not comply."

"Is this what it comes to, Captain? That you arrest a lad for doing a job that you should have done yourself? He should be commended for opposing the weirmen, not punished. You boys are worse than the Torics. At least they had dignity."

There was a pause, ever so subtle, but a break in flow nonetheless, just like in the square when the colonel had told the weirman chief he was in need of a sunset. Donavon sniffed at the wind that filtered through the leaves. Weakness, yes, that was it. He could smell it in the air. The scent was encouraging. Still he remained in the laurels, biding his time for the right moment to strike, and then it dawned on him. They were after him, not the colonel. He relaxed his bow. If they wanted to take him, they would have to find him. No sense making it easy.

"He incited a riot in the square," the captain of the Pogetsa said. "Many were injured. Justice must be served. He will be given the opportunity to plead his case in trial."

"I know all about Krutzwig's trials," Mitterhal said. "And what of the weirmen? Will they be held to the same justice?"

"They have been banned from the square indefinitely."

"Banned? Captain, do not insult yourself by expecting me to fall for this nonsense. We all know your boss's agenda, and he's using whatever means to fulfill it."

Again a pause, a little longer this time. Another whiff passed through the leaves. Good, Donavon thought. The colonel was chiseling at the pogie cap's resolve.

"I am sorry, sir, but there is no compromise in this matter."

Donavon grinned. An apology—good. Better yet, he called him sir. It was working. The Old Mitt was actually getting it done.

Another pogie nudged his horse forward, a slender man with beady eyes. "You heard the order, men," he said, addressing the group. "You six in the house, the rest of you sweep the premises." His voice was raspy, almost rat-like, if a rat could talk.

Donavon reloaded his bow. He thought to step out and pin the rat man right between the eyes, to shut him up for good so the colonel could do his work, but his bow was stayed by the approach of a horse galloping through the gahenya. He could not see the rider from his vantage in the hedge, but noticed several pogies check the lock on their muskets. Eventually the horse leaped over the wall and rounded the laurels at a controlled canter. On the steed, to Donavon's great relief, was Sheriff Hoffman.

He halted alongside the colonel, whom he acknowledged with a calm tilt of his wide-brimmed hat. "Good day, sir." The colonel nodded in reply and dug into his vest pocket for his pipe and flint box. Hoffman looked to the lead pogie. "Captain Rueger, what a pleasure. Welcome to the highlands. What brings you up this way?"

Rueger glanced at the rat man before answering. "We are here on Krutzwig's order to arrest Donavon McFadden for inciting a riot in Wulfhaven Square. We have reason to believe he is quartered in the colonel's manor."

"I see." A long pause followed. "Well, if that's the case, then I suggest you fellas pack it up. Whether he's here or not is irrelevant."

"What are you saying, Sheriff?"

"What I am saying is that you will all be dead men before you take my deputy."

At once every musket was up, followed by a chorus of metallic clicks. Rueger drew out his pistol and advanced on Hoffman, horse to horse. "You will produce the fugitive," he said, drawing back the trigger and bringing the barrel to within an inch of Hoffman's ear.

Flinchless, Hoffman glared at the captain. "Put your peashooter down, Rueger. You're in the highlands now. It won't do you any good up here." He looked to the others who held him at gunpoint. "That goes for all of you. I'm your only lifeline out of here."

Donavon held his breath. What was Hoffman doing? This was suicide. He hadn't even brought a gun. Where was his gun? At a complete loss, Donavon shifted his aim to the rat man. The sheriff was close enough to dispatch the lead pogie by hand once the arrows started flying. As for the others ... Well, no sense planning too far ahead. He drew back the arrow.

In that shadowy moment between action and decision the sheriff made an unexpected move. He took off his hat and tossed it high. Like a spinning bowl of leather it swished through the air. A shot was fired in the distance, somewhere in the south field by the sound of it. Not quite a musket, more like a flare. A barely discernible flash of red appeared in the sky through the leaves of the laurels. Another shot was fired. The same hollow thud, though even more distant, probably from the village.

All the pogies looked down slope except for the lead captain. His eyes remained fixed on Hoffman along with his gun. "What exactly was that about, Sheriff?"

"I've just informed the boys in the village that the terms have been delivered. Unless they see two more flares fired from those knolls in the south field, you and your men will not pass through the village alive."

The beady-eyed rat man cantered forward. "You think we're going to buckle up to your band of shepherds just like that? We are not unarmed weirmen."

"No, you're not. But neither are the men waiting on those flares herdsmen. You see, I happened to be enjoying a fine ale at the tavern with some friends from the Guard when your little party passed through. Most of those boys still hold a grudge over Rankwall's no-show at Spaulding Pass. They wouldn't think twice about dropping every one of you. In fact, that's exactly what they aim to do if they don't see two flares fired out of that field. Those are the terms I've arranged for you. Take it or leave it."

"He's bluffing!" shouted the rat man. "Our orders hold."

"Am I?" Hoffman looked at Rueger, who seemed less convinced. "Are you ready to make that call, Captain? Did you ever wonder how we did it? How we stood up to the bear? I assure you that if you attempt to leave this mountain with the son of the Guard's first lieutenant in your custody, you will find out quick."

Another scent passed through the laurels, similar to fear but not quite. A combination of some sort, almost sweet. Captain Rueger lowered his pistol. Somehow Donavon knew he would. It was the sweet smell of defeat in the air. And … fruit tarts. Enyalda was baking fruit tarts.

"How do we know they will hold to the terms?" the pogie captain asked.

"You don't," Hoffman said. "You best keep that in mind the next time you set out for the highlands. As for now, listen up. When you get to the end of the south field stop, reverse your hats, and wait for two flares to be fired from the knolls. Do not proceed until you see two more flares answer out of the village. You can keep your weapons, but be sure the hats of every one of your men stay reversed. That's important, Captain. If the hats are not backward when you enter the village, they will assume a breach of terms. Once you are through, do not look back and under any circumstance do not change the position of your hats."

A long thoughtful moment passed. The sweet aroma wafted from the manor over the gardens, catching the attention of several soldiers.

"This is ludicrous," the rat pogie said.

"Shut up!" Rueger shouted. "Fall back in formation and make ready to ride. We will adhere to the terms." He looked hard at Hoffman. "You realize, Sheriff, that this move will not go unanswered. Threatening Lakwynnian officers is a serious crime."

"Just get your boys off the mountain, Captain, and keep your hats on backward. We can debate policy later."

Rueger snapped his bridle and made for the carriage road at a hot trot. Behind him the Pogetsa followed in tight formation.

Donavon barely contained his elation at seeing the pogies turn tail. He stayed put in the laurels nonetheless while the two war veterans spoke quietly together as they watched the dusty cloud move down the pasture. Not until the signal flares were fired over the village did Donavon shed his cover. "You did it, Sarge! You stuck it to the pogies!"

Both Hoffman and the colonel turned around in surprise. "Well, there you are," Hoffman said. "Quite a fuss you've created, Donny. Your little scrap in Wulfhaven has got everybody up in arms." He pointed to the bow in Donavon's hand. "What do you think you were going to do with that?"

"It's all I had time to grab. My gun was back at the stock house."

"You know, Donny, there's a fine line between bravery and foolishness. 'Never spit in the fire, nor stoop—'"

"'—low before it,'" Donavon said, cutting off the sheriff. "'Neither put your hands into the flames, nor set your feet upon them, lest you be the meat that is cooked.' I know, sir. The exact thought came to mind when I had that rat pogie lined up for a shot. Just tell me one thing, Sarge. How did you do it? How did you get the men ready so quick?"

"If you really want to know the truth, I didn't. That was Seth and Angus up on the knoll. I got the Brewmaster to fire the flares from the top of the jailhouse."

"So you were bluffing."

"Some might call it that. I prefer to think of it as creating an illusion. It's what you do when you know you're cooked. Isn't that right, Colonel?"

"You did well, Jarvis. Very convincing," the colonel said, enjoying his smoke.

"With all due respect, sir," Donavon said to his boss, "you walked straight into a hot spot unarmed. That pogie captain could have dropped you right then and there. You might brush up on the ninth rule yourself."

"You're a wise guy, Donny, just like your father. I made a calculated risk. There's a difference. But I'll admit it was a stroke of luck that Krutzwig sent his top dog to do his dirty work. Rueger is a military man through and through. He saw combat in the South Bay and knows it was our stand at the Pass that gave them the cakewalk at Altomar. He also knows that by every conceivable model, we should not have won that battle. Playing on that was just enough to tweak him."

"What was all that about backward hats?"

The question drew a rare smile out of the sheriff. "Oh, that." He looked up to the high peak. "That was just a little something to give our brothers who caught a cannon ball at the pass a good laugh, just in case they were watching. You've got to keep your sense of humor, Donny, more so than ever when the flames are on you. It's what keeps the glue in the illusion."

"That's enough sweet talk, Jarvis," the colonel said with a wink. "You're giving away all my secrets. We got our work cut out for us. This Krutzwig fellow seems hasty. He took his mitts off sooner than I expected. The uprising in the square must have rattled him, so we'll have to use that to our advantage. In the meantime get word of this to Barleycopp at once, tonight if possible. Send him the message that our time frame has been compressed and the plan must be revised."

"What about Donny, sir? The Pogetsa will be back for sure, and they won't be played so easily the next time."

"You're right, but they won't be back right away. Thanks to your ploy, Krutzwig believes the Guard is stationed here on the mountain. Marcus's parish vote on the bridge project is in two weeks and Krutzwig will not risk swaying the sentiment by mounting an unpopular campaign against the Haven's honored. We must use this time wisely. Perception is everything. As for Donavon, he will have to leave the mountain."

"What?"

"Don't worry, lad. I know just the place for you, but it will take some briefing."

A medley of bird songs passed through the leaves, followed by a long pure note taken to its limit. Enyalda rounded the hedge with a wicker basket draped in blue fabric. She went directly to the sheriff and curtsied, hiding her eyes behind her hair.

"Spare not your belly a just reward," she said, holding out the basket.

"Don't mind if I do." He reached under the fabric and extracted a handful of fruit tarts.

Enyalda handed him a napkin and skipped to the colonel to repeat the routine. Moving on to Donavon, she did not curtsy but kissed him twice on the cheek.

He looked at the mound of tarts that still remained. "What were you planning to do, sis, feed the pogies?"

She giggled and set the basket on the grass next to his feet. Her hands free, she spun into a dance and swept the yard, dodging the brown piles left by the Pogetsa's horses. "Friend or foe it makes no matter, the pits will sink when mixed in batter."

Sheriff Hoffman picked up his hat. "I best be off to get the rundown from Garrison. Your sister makes a fine tart, Donny," he said, mounting his horse. "I never heard her talk before. That last little ditty belongs over the tavern mantel." He looked to the colonel. "Good day, sir. I'll have word sent to Barleycopp at once." A quick tilt of the hat and he was off to the village.

195

9

Child's Play

Pastor Marcus Poulakis made it a point never to use the word orphan; it was such a stifling term. He simply referred to them as the children, for that was exactly what they were—children. When Lakwynnia's struggle for independence finally ended, he ordered the bells of every parish church in the Haven to ring for three days from dawn till dusk. Not for victory, not for freedom, not even for peace. It was strictly for the children that they rang, so that the cries of the fatherless would not go unaccompanied.

Marcus cherished the children, and their innocence. Yet for all their delicate virtue, he found them to be remarkably resilient. Pliant as mortar yet solid as stone, they were the source of his inspiration as much as he was theirs. And when it came time to rebuild the pillars of faith that had crumbled in the aftermath of war, it was to them that he looked to lay the foundation.

Marcus dropped the quill and buried his face in his hands. Writing a sermon was like raising children. There were rules, important rules one must adhere to without exception. Yet, just like a child, a sermon needed freedom to grow and explore the many facets of the world—to develop in stature and context via insight and experience. At times this meant bending the rules. Not the essential ones, but the "fillers," as Marcus secretly referred to them. Conventions that gave structure to society yet were not necessarily mandated by the Almighty. It was a tremendous responsibility that usually came naturally to him. Which was why he sat in his chambers seething at the useless doodles in his sermon book.

The service was only two days away and he had yet to come up with anything beyond the expected protocol. It was not for lack of things to say, quite the contrary. The political climate in the Three Havens was charged. Perhaps it was just that. There was too much to say, too many paths on which to veer and wander without direction. It would be his last sermon before every parish from Wulfhaven to the north highland districts of Multynhaven cast their votes on the bridge project. He felt pressure from all sides, squeezing him like a vice, tightening on his resolve to be neutral. He could see their eyes now, the parishioners in the pews, looking to him for an answer. Just like the liberation when all turned to him, as if by divine magic he would cast a spell that would simply plop them on the path to salvation.

If only he had that power, God forgive him, he would certainly use it now. How ironic that a bridge, or the lack of one, could have such a profound impact on peace. What message did it give to the next generation to say that the only way to live in harmony with the Gwyntahmahoma was to keep the physical link between them severed? Marcus sighed. Was peace really that fragile? Who knew? What he did know was that he was getting nowhere with his sermon. Furious at his clammy surroundings, he strode to the entry of his chambers and swung the oak door open, intent on a fresh perspective. Brother Michael balked in the doorway, his hand raised as if to knock. Both retracted in surprise.

"What is it, Michael?"

"Forgive me, Father, is it a bad time?"

Marcus strode past the monk and down the corridor. "When is it not?" he shouted over his shoulder. "Come, I am in a hurry."

"The Gwyntahmahoma have responded to our inquiry," said Brother Michael in hot pursuit. "Gwyntahpynn Choroqua says that he does not regret the death of Sebastian Schnites, but swears under witness of their Goddess that the attack was not issued on his order, and that in the interest of peace he will personally see to the beheading of any Gwyntah who may have acted independently."

"How reassuring," Marcus said, continuing his brisk pace. It suddenly dawned on him that he had no idea where he was going.

"Shall I inform the Pogetsa of the Gwyntahpynn's statement?"

"No, they will only twist it to their cause. We shall go to the mayor with this. Barleycopp can decide what to do with it."

"What do you think, Father? Do you think the Gwyntah did it?"

Marcus stopped at the entrance of the high, vaulted rectory hall. Choroqua's long reign in Gwyntahlynn was checkered with brutality, and his methods seldom fell in sync with the church. Still, he was not a liar. "Contrary to popular belief, my good brother, I would say no. The evidence trail is too perfect. Something about it feels staged." He loosened his collar while he processed what he had said. "Michael, I want you to forward the

Gwyntahpynn's statement to Barleycopp in person. To nobody else, not even his aide. Is that clear?"

As Brother Michael bowed and left him, another clergyman charged through the hall. It was Brother Liam, the chorus conductor.

"There you are, Father," he said with labored breath. "I have an urgent matter regarding the choir."

Marcus dashed for the south exit of the rectory. He was midway through the chamber when Brother Liam caught up with him. "Father, our lead tenor has come down with the chills. He was to do the aria during the service offertory."

The south exit was only strides away, though it seemed like miles. How he craved the fresh air, the sunlight, the openness. He felt his internal temperature rising. Peace, that was all he wanted, a chorus of silence to center his thoughts. Brother Liam, for all his musical talent, was not providing that.

"Father, I was wondering if—"

Marcus stopped three steps from the exit. "What, brother? What were you wondering? That I might do the aria myself from the pulpit?"

"No, not at all. I was just thinking—"

"What! What were you thinking? That I would call on the Great Father to drop a lead tenor from the sky?"

"Forgive me, Your Grace. I can see that—"

"What! What can you see? That I have other things to worry about than an ailing singer? That in two days I am to give a sermon in which I have no idea what to say? Or perhaps once, just once, somebody might approach me with a solution rather than a problem? What exactly do you see, my good brother? I beg of you to let me know!"

Brother Liam trembled like a lone mouse in the great hall. "I might be able to rewrite the aria for an alto," he said meekly. "I'll get to it right away, Your Grace." He bowed and disappeared into the shadows of the rectory.

Alone at last, Marcus opened the door to the south exit. He felt dizzy, but the fresh air relaxed him. Already he regretted his harsh treatment of Brother Liam. He looked up and made a mental note to be extra pleasant at the next choir meeting.

The midmorning sun struck the mosaic above him at an angle, adding tantalizing dimension to the stone. He took in the splendor of the premises, modeled after Toricean abbeys of old. Every building had its place, every space had its purpose, every statue had its spot. The dining hall, the library, the chapter house chambers, all came together in a sensible layout of predictability.

Where to go? he thought, feeling refreshed already. West perhaps, around the dining hall to the main cloister. Then again, maybe not. The monks would soon be gathering there for second prayer. East, he decided, around the backside of the cathedral toward the infirmary. On his way he marched past the spot where Jeziah McCaskel had met him that fateful night with the closed carriage and brought him to the Haven stables—the very place where all this madness began. What if he had not harkened to the cipher's summons that night? Was it really wise to test the status quo of a land that had yet to recover from a generation of men lost in war? Could the Haven sustain another blow?

Yelling children broke up his thoughts. He looked to the lesser cloister between the infirmary and the dormitory. It sounded like a fight. Appalled, Marcus charged the cloister, preparing to deliver the wrath of God. When he rounded the corner of the dorm, what he saw was a far cry from a brawl.

The children had gathered in the center cloister around the statue of a crowned saint. They all faced a boy who stood on the bench in front of the statue, a large feather pinned to his cap. Marcus recognized him at once. How could he not? It was Barusta. Quickly he concealed himself behind a nearby pillar, curious to see what the little rascal was up to this time.

"All right, listen up!" the boy told his entourage. "Overall not bad, but you gotta tone down the rage. Weirmen are pirates, not barbarians. You gotta be rough and tough, but not out of control. Think of yourselves as bandits pulling off an easy heist."

"I don't want to be a weirman," squeaked a voice out of the group. "I want to be Deputy Angus."

"Look at the size of you, Uli," Barusta said. "How do you expect to pass as Deputy Angus?"

"You could stuff me with rags."

"Forget about it. You can be one of the herdsmen if you want. As for the rest of you, try to spread out. You're too clustered. Deputy McFadden needs to be able to walk through you when he orders the arrest. All right, let's try it again. Everybody in position."

Another run-through began. One of the larger boys in the group stepped forward and confronted a boy in leather britches who sat on a bench, holding a cane and had a makeshift pipe in his mouth. "And who is this old goat?" the ruffian boy shouted.

"You are a monster!" said a girl in a black shawl who sat next to the boy in the britches.

"Be quiet!" the ruffian snapped. "Let your boyfriend speak."

On cue, britches stood up and shook his cane. "You've got bad manners, weirman. You gotta see this sunset."

"No! No! No!" Barusta shouted, charging at the boy in britches with his script in hand. "You have to stay seated, Crista. The colonel doesn't get up until the end when Deputy McFadden rises out of the pool. Also, it's 'You are in need of a sunset,' not 'You gotta see this sunset.'"

"But that doesn't make sense," Crista said.

"That doesn't matter. You can't just make up lines that were never said. We'll lose our credibility."

"What's that?"

"Don't worry about it. Just stick to the script." Barusta returned to his position in front of the statue. "All right, let's try it again. Everybody ready? Crista, what are you doing?"

"I still don't get the whole sunset thing," Crista said, leaning on his cane. "Why would you need a sunset just because you have bad manners?"

Barusta shrugged. "How should I know? It's probably a metaphor."

"What's that?"

"It's when you describe something by calling it something else. The fountain lady uses them all the time in her stories."

"So seeing a sunset would be like getting a good hard wooping?"

"I suppose you could think of it that way if it gets you to remember your lines."

The girl in the black shawl stood up. "I don't think it's a metaphor. I think the colonel really meant a sunset. Pastor Marcus has always told us that you can see the light of God in a sunset or a sunrise."

"I agree with Carynna," one of the weirmen said, stepping out of the pack. "I bet seeing the light of the Great Father would fix anyone's manners."

"What about the Great Mother?" the girl said. "It could be her light too. The fountain lady says she is just as real as the Father."

"Don't let Pastor Marcus hear that," Crista said. "He calls all that stuff a myth."

Barusta stepped in. "He just says that because it's his job. Do you really think Big Robes would let us listen to the fountain lady if he thought her stories were steering us wrong? Now come on, we're losing time. Madam Annie will be calling us in for lessons any minute."

The rehearsal resumed. Marcus watched and listened. Joy mounted in his heart with every successive take, in spite of Barusta's reference to "Big Robes." To see the children so engaged in a common project by their own accord brought tears to his eyes. He imagined them on stage, performing their skit in Wulfhaven's opera house. What a treasure it would be for all to see. He heard a woman's voice behind him just as his vision went blurry.

"Here you are, Father. Such a precious sight, isn't it?"

Marcus turned around and accepted the tissue that Miss Annabelle Rafferty, the children's house madam, held out to him. "Miss Rafferty, what a lovely surprise," he said, wiping his eyes.

"The surprise is all mine, Father. What brings you out here to the dormitory in the middle of the morning? I thought you would be with the monks for second prayer."

"I was feeling a bit cramped in the cathedral and decided a walk of the abbey would do me good. I could not help but hear the children's rehearsal."

"Yes, hard to miss, isn't it? They've been working on the reenactment all week. They want to perform it in the square to raise money for the fountain. So wonderful to see."

"The fountain, not the church?" After a thoughtful pause, Marcus nodded. "A cause is a cause, I suppose. I take it Barusta is in charge?"

"Yes. He's actually written a script based on the accounts of eyewitnesses. He's been such a perfect little boy lately. Not once have I had to send him to chambers. I think he may have found his calling."

"Well, well, that is inspiring indeed. Perhaps the Great Father has decided to spare us all of the blessed boy's mischief. I will be sure to give thanks at prayer time."

"You may wish to thank another as well," Miss Rafferty said, smiling. "Do you see what Barusta has on his hat? He calls it his director's feather. Colonel Mitterhal gave it to him just prior to the incident at the fountain. All the children are tickled by it. It has given Barusta tremendous confidence."

"Confidence has never been the boy's problem, Miss Rafferty. But if that feather is all it takes to keep him out of trouble, then by all means, it is a miracle worthy of praise. Let us be sure to include the good colonel in our prayers tonight."

"Absolutely, Father. I am sure the children will be more than willing to oblige. Will you be joining us for dinner then?"

Marcus looked at the young actors busy at work beneath the sculpted eyes of the kingly saint. Barusta's feather swayed back and forth before the statue's scepter. The effect was hypnotic. A light breeze wrapped the abbey and further swept away the pastor's thoughts. Suddenly there were no problems, just a crisp fragrance in an early autumn day.

"Father?"

"Yes?"

"Will you be joining us for dinner?"

"Yes, yes, of course. A wonderful idea. Good day, Miss Rafferty. I believe I have a sermon to write."

War was a mystery to Marcus. The Great Exception, he called it. Thou shall not kill except ... Except when? When the only alternative was to be killed? Perhaps, but even that was subject to judgment. How many times in his lifetime alone had that same principle been used to justify the most contemptible of acts? At what point did the survival of one justify the suffering of another? And when did it stop becoming an issue of survival entirely? In the case of war, who made that call?

Cornelius Mitterhal was also a mystery to Marcus. Eccentric yet brilliant in his approach to war, he was a true master of perception. A charismatic tactician whose contagious view of the world delved so far into the realm of myth, one could get lost simply listening to him. Which was why it was all the more a mystery to Marcus that the agnostic war commander had insisted that his men receive the blessings of an ordained pastor before every major military operation.

Marcus sat in his chamber over his sermon book, remembering the solemn day nearly a decade ago when the first Gwyntah scouts arrived from Spaulding Pass with word of victory. It had been raining all day.

"A Mahunamaha Montayega geh hunwynn solam," they said. To the Great Mountain Montayega their noble spirits have returned.

The words brought little comfort to the mothers, wives, and children of the Three Havens who waited anxiously in the shadow of invasion. Two days later the Guard returned, what was left of it. To this day, Marcus could still feel the shock wave of grief that shook the land. Even he, in all his spiritual fortitude, had been struck dumb by the tidings and had fallen to his knees. Most of the dead he knew.

A rap on the oak door snapped him to the present. "Enter, Michael," he said, recognizing the cadence of the knock.

Brother Michael took one step into the room and bowed. "Good evening, Father. You look much more relaxed. Have you had success with your sermon?"

"Thank you, Michael. It is still in the making, but at least I know where it is going. Rest assured, the Haven will be spared a babbling fool."

"That is a relief," said the good-natured monk.

"I will be dining with the children this evening," Marcus added, walking to the wall where his black travel robe hung on a hook. "You are to lead the brethren in my stead."

Brother Michael removed the robe from the hook and held it open while Marcus slipped his arms through the loose, pleated sleeves. It was a routine tuned to precision over the years. Marcus tilted his head back and held his beard aloft while Michael tied the tethers at the collar. "The brethren will be disappointed, Father. They have many questions regarding procedures in the upcoming days."

"All the more reason for me to dine with the children." Marcus let his beard fall back into place. "Tell them to trust their instincts. Short of a cataclysm, I do not want to be interrupted this evening. Is that clear?"

"As always, Father."

Miss Rafferty met Marcus at the entrance to the children's dining hall. Her ever-pleasant presence took the chill out of the evening. How did she do it? Marcus wondered. Shine with such genuine radiance in all she did?

Her eyes were always smiling even when her mouth was not. Firmly settled in her middle years and having never given birth to a child of her own, she was now foster mother to scores, catering to the daily needs of the Haven's parentless. A selfless woman, to say the least, whose endless well of energy was a wonderful asset to the abbey.

"Welcome, Father," she said. "This is so exciting. The children have been anticipating your arrival all afternoon. I was going to keep it a surprise, but some of them overheard me talking to the cooks in the kitchen."

"So the walls have ears," Marcus said, looking to the door. "That is good to know. Shall we proceed, Miss Rafferty?"

Through the door they went. A bell rang as they entered the dining chambers. The children were already seated at the eight great tables that spanned the length of the hall. They rose at once, except for the youngest, who remained strapped in their seats. The aroma of the kitchen cauldrons wafted like a pleasant mist amidst their smiling faces.

Miss Rafferty clapped her hands twice. "Good evening, children." Her voice echoed off the masonry in the hall. "Let us give a warm welcome to our honored guest."

"Good evening, Pastor Marcus," they chimed in unison.

Suddenly, out of the orderly rows came a flurry of small children, all giggling as they flapped their arms in a sweeping motion around the pastor. An older girl approached, holding a bouquet of flowers that she presented with a bow. It was the girl from Barusta's play. Carynna, Marcus remembered.

"Welcome, Your Eminence," she said with well-rehearsed formality. "Please accept this gift and be sure to give your sorrows to the butterflies so they can take them away."

Amused, Marcus received the flowers and looked at the children fluttering around him. "Can these delicate creatures really bear the weight?" he asked, smiling at the girl. "I would not want to burden them with such a heavy load."

Carynna smiled as well. "Vahegan butterflies are immune to sorrow, Father. It is no burden to them." She gestured back to the tables. "Please allow the wolves to escort you to your seat."

A pack of little boys approached, stern faced and growling, led by Uli, the little weirman in the cloister who had wanted to be Deputy Angus. Marcus feigned a shudder. "What kind of an escort is this? I feel like I should run for my life."

"Don't worry, Father. They are your protectors and will make sure you arrive safely to your seat."

Marcus nodded and followed the pack to the head of the center table. Miss Rafferty trailed close behind, giggling with the butterflies.

Once he was seated, another bell rang and the proceedings began. Ranks of adolescents filed out of the kitchen carrying steaming pots and stacks of empty bowls that they set at the farthest end of the room. One by one, the bowls were filled and passed down the tables, while other older children set out plates of sliced bread and pitchers of goat's milk. The younger children sat with hands in laps, politely waiting for all to be served. Marcus was impressed. He looked at Miss Rafferty, seated at his side. "The children are exceptionally well mannered, all to your credit I am sure."

The housemother smiled wistfully. "If only it were always the case. I think your presence has all to do with it."

When all were served, Miss Rafferty rose to address her brood. "I know you are all excited this evening. Let us rise while Pastor Marcus gives the blessing."

Blessing? Yes, blessing of course. Who else would give it? Out of instinct Marcus grabbed his beard, as if the tug on his jaw would help spur his words. He dropped his napkin to buy more time. Miss Rafferty, to his dismay, quickly picked it up. "Thank you," he said to the well-meaning woman.

Thank you. Yes, that was it. A perfect start—so concise and to the point. He swept a wrinkle out of his robe before addressing his attentive audience. "Thank you all," he said, scanning the hall. "Looking around I see smiling faces, the light of the Great Father in every one of you. Yes, first and foremost let us give thanks to that—to the great light that nourishes our souls just as this food nourishes our bodies. Let us also give thanks to this land, our home, and all who serve it, old and young, with whatever talents the Great Father, in all his mystery, has bestowed on them. For without that, his light would have no place to shine. Amen."

"Amen," the children echoed.

No sooner had all been seated than a commotion erupted at the back end of the farthest table to the right. "Oh dear," Miss Rafferty said. "And he has been so good of late."

Barusta stood on the table with his feathered cap. As he stepped forward, his hands aloft, he inadvertently kicked a bowl of stew off the table. "Ladies and gentlemen," he announced at the splattering on the floor, "I present to you the table-eight choir!"

On cue, one of the boys nearest him began to sing, promptly accompanied by another. A bit sketchy at first, the tune revealed itself to Marcus as more joined in at the table.

"Forgive me, Father," Miss Rafferty said, red faced with embarrassment. "I will put an end to this nonsense at once."

"Wait." Marcus placed his hand on her shoulder. "They are singing the tenth hymn from the Book of Jahocwynn. Where did they learn this?"

"I believe it is one of the songs they sing to Madam Hume at the fountain in exchange for her stories."

Marcus closed his eyes to better assess the texture of sound. "Perhaps we should hear it out, Miss Rafferty."

Seeing that the children at table eight had escaped punishment, others in the hall stood up and began to sing. The hymn grew in stature with every verse, sculpted in melody by their bright voices. Even the crackling tones of the adolescents brought a timeless joy to the piece.

Marcus listened intently. And though he was by no means a singer, he could not help humming along with the refrain.

Father, bless my homeland,
Your light on crimson shores
Mother bless my homeland,
Your Haven we adore
Flowers, trees, pipes, and reeds,
granite walls and peaks
We scale the highest mountain,
your blended song we seek

All sat when the hymn ended. Just like that, the meal began, a hall full of hungry mouths slurping at their stew. The evening progressed. Marcus stole a scoop from his own bowl whenever he could while responding to the pleasantries of various children who approached him throughout the meal. Miss Rafferty kept check on the more long-winded of the youngsters. Mealtime stretched on, however, in spite of her best efforts, and it was not until late in the evening that Marcus finally finished his stew, cold though it was.

Seeing him done at last, Miss Rafferty gestured toward the kitchen and a bell was rung. "All right, children," she announced. "It is long past the time to dine. To the kitchen at once with your bowls and make ready for prayer. It has been a wonderful evening. What do we say to Pastor Marcus for joining us?"

"Thank you!" came the unanimous cry.

Marcus waved graciously and watched the children funnel into the kitchen. Table eight was the last to leave. He had hoped to speak to Barusta during mealtime and commend him on the performance, but the opportunity never presented itself. So he asked Miss Rafferty to summon him.

The dining hall had emptied by the time Barusta cautiously surfaced out of the kitchen.

"That was quite a dance you did on the table, Barusta," Marcus said, attempting to lighten the mood.

The boy squirmed. "I don't know what got into me, Your Eminence. We were going to wait until afterwards, but I just—"

Marcus raised his hand. "Please, Barusta, spare me the weasel talk. You are not in trouble. In fact, for once I am happy to say, quite the contrary. I've always known you to be gifted, even as an infant, and it is a relief to see your talents finally put to good use. I would like to know more about that feather you wear on your cap. I've been told that the colonel gave it to you at the fountain."

"He did, Father. Without me even asking. Well, actually ... At first I did, but after that I didn't. He told me it is the tail feather of a lakehawk and holds the power of command."

"The power of command? That comes with tremendous responsibility."

"I know, Father. That's just what Colonel Cornelius said."

"Did he? And what else did he have to say about responsibility?"

"He said I should talk to you about it. That you would do a much better job explaining it."

Marcus smiled, reminded of the days of war. How many times had the crusty old goat given that same directive to his troops? It was part of his mystique, his modis operandi: Empower the men with hocus-pocus imagery, only to seesaw them back to reality with a chat with their pastor.

"It is touching he would say that, but I think in this case your actions will speak louder than any explanation I could give. I have a job in mind for you and your feather, if you agree to abide by the rules. You would be doing a great service for the church."

A wily look came over the boy. Marcus had seen it before in the penance chamber—his devious little mind at work, sifting through the quagmire between right and wrong. At ten years old, the streetwise boy had already learned how to guard his thoughts. "What are the rules?" he asked.

Interesting, Marcus noted, that Barusta would ask for the rules before the task. He scowled, wondering how could he get through to the boy without hammering him with a list of dos and don'ts. It had to be simple. Yes, that was it, simple.

"Actually, there is only one rule you must follow, my son, though I admit one could argue that it consists of many. You must do your job to the best of your ability with heart, body, mind, and soul."

Barusta stared at him with the look of someone who had just been told the obvious. As if he'd been reminded that the sky was blue or mountains large. "How else would I do it, Your Eminence?"

The boy's question rang like a great bell. A lifetime in the ministry had attuned Marcus to the unexpected. It was his job, after all, to hear people out and guide them to clarity. Only a handful of times had the roles been reversed. That a troublesome ten-year-old could do it with a single question astounded him. At last, when the ensuing silence had been purged of all its worth, Marcus rose and wiped the evening's breadcrumbs off his robe.

"That will be all for tonight, Barusta. Get a good night's sleep.

Tomorrow we will discuss the details of your job after first prayer."

Barusta bowed. "Good night, Your Eminence." In a flash he was off, darting to the door.

"Barusta!"

The boy stopped just prior to the exit and turned around.

"Just between you and me," Marcus said, "I think 'Big Robes' is so much more fitting, don't you?"

Barusta smiled and disappeared.

10
Music Chief

Gwyntah lore was rooted in a longstanding oral tradition. Basic teachings were passed on through a compilation of mantras. Concepts of a more profound nature were preserved in verses. The highest principles—those of spirituality and ethics—were set to music. For music, according to the Gwyntah, was the language of the spirit and could not be corrupted by the limitations of a phrase. As such the legacy of the Gwyntahmahoma, along with all their mystic subtleties, were hallowed in chants, hymns, and melodies. To chant the verses was to know the tribes, and to hear the music was divine.

The settlers of the Three Havens were intrigued by this fusion of music and lore. Many saw it as an opportunity to expand their own spiritual horizons, a freedom sorely missed in the Fatherland. The first attempt to put these enigmatic conventions into writing were in the scrolls of Jahocwynn, or dream spirit. Gwyntah shamans were invited to chant on the sacred grounds of the monastery that later became Wulfhaven abbey. Monks kept meticulous record of the stories, psalms, and hymns that were created from these visits. The translations were compiled into a tome and called the Book of Jahocwynn. Haven folk adopted the book and in a curious twist of reasoning, christened it the Old Tome, despite the fact that there was nothing old about it.

A waft of incense stirred Cornelius Mitterhal from his nap. The floral fragrance eased the shift in consciousness. He had been a goat grazing in a meadow of luscious flowers. It was a good dream and he was annoyed to leave it. Silent and still, he remained in his chair while his eyes adjusted to the light in the hearth room.

A distant whisper drew his attention to the picture window. Enyalda stood on a pile of books propped on a chair, her arm stretched to the transom above the window. So still, so locked in concentration. Only her mouth moved. What in holy blazes was she up to now?

Something moved inches away from her extended hand—a flap of yellow in the sunlight, too small for a bird, too big for a bug. Another flutter and it landed on her finger. Mitterhal marveled at the sight of his caregiver. So divine, just like the goddess in Wulfhaven Square, whispering to the butterfly. He waited until she was safely on the floor before speaking.

"Looks like you made a friend."

She stopped whispering and the butterfly left her finger. It fluttered whimsically about the hearth room and eventually out the window. Enyalda waved good-bye and lowered the sash.

"Easy come, easy go," the colonel said.

She peeked through her hair and spoke. *"Mynwah yan vahegan a baha yan Havynn."*

Mitterhal straightened in his chair. The words were a bit out of order but he got the idea: *We fly on the wagon to the Haven on a wing.* How interesting that she would say such a thing, especially in Gwyntah. Still, he thought it best not to let on that he knew what she had said. It might stifle her way. Rather, he asked her to fetch his pipe and flint box off the mantel.

She did; he thanked her and fired up his pipe. When he felt enough time had passed, he returned to the subject. "You know, my mother used to sing a song about a flying wagon. It had a catchy melody."

He paused to taste the greenbank as it entered his lungs. Such a smooth smoke, nothing like the wulfweed.

Enyalda broke the silence. *"Gelbynn Vahegan?"*

The colonel exhaled. "Yes, the Yellow Wagon. Only she sang it in Toricean." He cleared his throat to better carry the tune. "'On Yellow Wagon, you and I, to the Haven we will ride.'"

Enyalda spun into dance, spurred by his verse. She arced her arms like a ballerina and continued to sing where he had left off.

Upon arrival at lake shore,
We will open wagon's door.
By the fountain we will be
Blessed in love eternally.

"You know the song," Mitterhal said. "Very nice. You do it justice, my dear. Much better than I could ever do." He closed his eyes and hummed the melody, letting the music seep into his memory.

Enyalda accompanied him in verse, sending him further into a trance. As

209

he slipped away, he saw himself as a boy sitting in the baron's chariot with the blue box on his lap, his mother by his side. His father sat across the cab in his black boots and crimson suit. His gold buttons glistened in the light that filtered through the wagon's windows.

> *"Sing me the song about the yellow-winged wagon, Mother."*
> *"I will, Cornelius. With your father's permission."*
> *"Of course, my dear. Our little music chief should not be denied his order."*
> *"Very well. Open your box, Cornelius, and relax. It is a long ride down the mountain to Wulfhaven. 'On Yellow Wagon you and I, to the Haven we will ride …'"*

Mitterhal was still locked in tune when he opened his eyes. How long had it been? Enyalda fluttered about the hearth room, humming the hymn in harmony. She appeared as weightless as the flowery braids in her hair. Up and down, this way and that, her feet barely touching the floor. How beautiful, he thought. Like a butterfly with wings of petals.

Eventually he stopped humming and so did she. She blinked as if returning from a trance. "How was your little trip?" Mitterhal asked. "If I didn't know any better, I would have believed you were a butterfly on your way to the stars. I'm glad you came back."

After gathering herself, she made a sweeping curtsy in front of the fireplace. "Easy come, easy go. On the yellow-winged wagon both we go."

Mitterhal, hearing her put his own words into rhyme, relit his pipe to prepare for their game. It had been a while since they'd played it. He never considered himself a poet, but for the sake of Enyalda, he tried. "Easy is as easy does, fly away and hear the buzz."

She giggled, excited by the challenge. "No buzz there was on a butterfly's wings, lest it be a creature that bites and stings."

He grunted and took a toke from his pipe, buying time to answer her rhyme. She jumped on the lapse and sang another line.

"A bee you be, I'm happy to see, flower to flower you hop in a tree."

He exhaled and cast his challenger in a cloud of greenbank. "Yes, hop, hop, hop. I hop in your tree. Buzz, buzz, buzz. Look at me I'm a bee." He puckered his lips and jiggled his jaw, making his mustache flap like wings in the smoke.

Enyalda chirped in delight. Both hands went to her mouth to hold back her laughter. She remained as such, unable to respond.

Mitterhal taunted her with a raised brow. "What's this, no rhyme? Now that was a quick victory."

She hid her eyes behind her hair, appearing embarrassed by her outburst. "Laugh you make me," she finally said, still covering her mouth.

"Nothing wrong with that. No need to hide your pretty face."

Still, she kept herself shielded behind her braids.

"Come, now. Don't get all locked up on me. There's no better medicine than a good laugh." He leaned over in his chair to poke the coals in the fire. "Your father had a real knack for it, you know. He could get the men laughing in a swarm of hornets. Just enough to keep their heads in the game. A rare talent. He happened to be a good singer as well. Just like you. It must run in the family."

Enyalda swept aside her hair at the mention of her father. How powerful she looked when focused. It was not just Uryan's voice she had inherited, but his eyes. Like gateways to another world set solidly in their sockets. What a shame to keep them hidden.

"That's more like it," he said, as an idea came to him. "Enyalda, would you be so kind as to fetch me the blue box on the shelf above the mantel?"

She scaled the stack of cordwood next to the hearth and reached for the middle shelf, but then she stopped when her hand came to within inches of the box.

"Don't worry, it won't bite," the colonel said.

She took it and descended the logs.

"That's it. Now open the lid."

After another hesitation she did.

A beautiful melody seeped into the room as the tiny brass gears awoke from their slumber. Mitterhal absorbed the sound. How enchanting to hear the precious tune released from its timeless vault. More enchanting was Enyalda's expression when she saw what was inside.

"Go ahead," he said. "Take it out. I want you to have it."

She set the music box on the nightstand and removed the silver necklace within. Awestruck, she stared at the blue sapphire mounted in the woodland etchings. She didn't make a sound, not even a peep, as if hypnotized by the swaying gem.

"Ah, yes, so lovely, isn't it? It was my mother's. A wedding gift, I've been told. You have the perfect face for it."

Still shocked, she knelt before the colonel, as if to pray.

The sight incited Mitterhal to reach for his cane and rise. "Now that's enough of that, lass. I've had more than my share of kneeling and saluting for this lifetime. That's a necklace made for a queen. Get off your knees and just promise me you won't hide your face when you wear it."

Enyalda rose. A change had come over her, as if she were, in truth, a queen, crowned in her flowery braids. She remained as such while the fire crackled beside her. Mitterhal left the manor to let her be. No song, no dance, no word. Just a beautiful woman, secure in the light of the hearth.

11

Word from the Mountain

The Gwyntahmahoma had a name for the greatest mountain: Montayega. It embodied their faith and traditions. Many of the poems and hymns in the Old Tome centered on this symbol, and so inspired Haven folk to incorporate the mountain's lore into their own faith. Some claimed it was blasphemous to do so, while others saw it simply as an exploration into another way of thinking. And even the most pious of critics could not ignore the faint pulse of truth that gave life to the lore.

Marcus placed his sermon book next to the Old Tome on the pulpit. It was early morning, the day of the service; dawn's light dimly lit the empty pews. He embraced the cavernous space, the holy silence, the soft fragrant air that hinted of myrrh. How he loved this time, the miraculous inception of a new day. The page markers in the leather-bound tome were in place. For better or worse, he was ready. Soon he would read from the Book of Jahocwynn and prayed the Great Father would understand.

Brother Michael entered through the south transept with a brass oil lamp to light the candles. Marcus was happy to see his good-natured confidant.

"Good morning, Michael. Today is a fine day to preach."

Michael walked up the sanctuary stairs and bowed. "It is indeed, Father. I take it you are satisfied with your sermon then?"

"We shall see, my good brother. At the very least it will wake up the sleepers in the back pews."

Michael smiled. "I don't think there will be any sleepers today, Father. Already they have gathered in the square to hear you speak. Many have come from as far as Multynhaven and spent the night in the square. I think we may have to keep the doors open today."

Marcus looked at his closed sermon book. So small it appeared next to the Old Tome, its pages wide open like chapel doors. Only a handful of times had the spacious cathedral ever been stretched beyond capacity. The most memorable was when the entire Haven Guard had gathered in the square with their families to hear his service just prior to their stand at Spaulding Pass. So great was the host that day, he had moved the pulpit to the top of the stone steps outside the cathedral. It was an event forever etched in his memory. The square had been a sea of tear-drenched eyes. Stone-faced Gwyntah warriors had gathered around the fountain to honor the service at a respectful distance. And the pipes, yes, the colonel's pipers had lined the stone stairs of the cathedral and backed the choir during the introit. He clearly remembered the reverberation when all joined in to sing the tenth hymn.

"If that is the case," he said, "then so be it. Regardless, I want you to leave the right side of the nave reserved for children."

"The entire right side?"

"Yes."

"Father, that is half the capacity of the cathedral. There will be many left standing outside."

"Then you are right, Michael, there will certainly be no sleepers. Which reminds me. I want all to remain outside while the children are escorted to their seats. I will signal when the gathering bells are to stop."

"Who will escort the children, Father?"

"The children of the abbey will do the escorting, led by Barusta."

"Barusta?"

"Yes, he has sworn to behave. I want an area sectioned off near the base of the steps for parents to bring their young ones. Have the brethren space themselves around the perimeter to insure the children's safety. From there they will be escorted up the steps and into the nave by the abbey's children, child for child. Once they are seated you may open the doors to all. Brother Liam will lead the introit when the bells are silenced, after which we will move to announcements."

"The introit before announcements?"

"Yes. A change of procedure might do us all a bit of good. And one more thing, Michael. The children will be singing the offertory today, hymn number ten from the Book of Jahocwynn. I want every monk in the abbey to back them in chant."

"The Book of ..." Michael paused. "As you wish, Father."

"Good. By the grace of our Great Father, that is all."

The monk bowed and proceeded to light the candles of the sanctuary in silence.

When the candles were lit, other monks began to file through the south transept. One by one they bowed in front of the high altar before seating themselves in the first three rows of pews. A low deep hum permeated the sacred space as Marcus waited at the pulpit for the last of the holy men to be seated. He then descended the carpeted steps and raised his staff, silencing the chant.

Marcus took a deep breath. "Good morning, my good brothers. Procedures will be different today. Brother Michael will inform you of the arrangements. Whatever questions you may have, I leave to his discretion. The rest I entrust to yours. Bless you all."

He tapped his staff twice on the tile floor and then set out for his private prayer chamber in the north transept.

When does a breeze become wind? Where does light turn to shade? What makes a cause worth sharing? Who takes the time to care? Questions. Marcus loved them, he always had, even when he struggled for the answers. He had never known his parents; the abbey was the only home he knew. Fishermen from the Weirs, he had been told, had found him in an oar-less dory, bobbing outside the harbor, almost as far out as the broads. Nothing else, just a blanket, a baby, and a boat—and questions. The monks named him Poulakis, after the fishing vessel that brought him to the abbey. It meant lake savior in the language of the tribes. He chose "Marcus" during his self-conscious adolescent years, to shed the stigma of his pagan name. In the end he kept both.

The candles in the sanctuary flickered in the breeze when the gathering bells sounded and the carved oak doors of the cathedral were opened. Alone at the pulpit, Marcus squinted in the light that poured through the narthex and fused into the shadows of the nave. Silhouetted in the exact center of the entry, against the backdrop of the square, stood Barusta. Like a solemn little golem he peered out at the masses with his arms crossed over his chest and the feather in his hat. Impressive, Marcus thought, so poised at his post. The boy looked back, and Marcus raised his staff to signal the start of the proceedings. At once, Barusta gestured down the steps and the children began to file in.

They came in pairs down the center aisle. At the first pew on the right, Barusta stopped and directed them to their seats. Row by row he repeated the procedure, sending some of the escorts back to receive more children while others he kept seated to accompany the youngest. The pews on the right side were nearly filled to capacity when Barusta turned back to address the pulpit.

"All the children are seated, Your Eminence."

Marcus acknowledged the report and raised his staff to Brother Michael, who stood in the narthex by the chapel doors. The brethren entered, followed by a flood of parishioners. Twelve monks followed Brother Liam to the choir box while others stood in the perimeter aisles to direct the people to their seats. Marcus remained still, watching the wave of worshipers swell into the left side of the cathedral. When at last the holy chapel was filled to the brink, he signaled Brother Michael for the bells to be silenced. They stopped on cue, and in that instant he became aware of the hordes of people still congregated outside. "So it begins," he said quietly to himself as the choir monks began their chant. He raised his staff high, signaling all to rise. When the introit ended, he made his opening statement.

"May the words spoken today be accepted by our Great Father. Amen."

"Amen," answered the people.

Marcus lowered his staff. All who had seats sat. The rest stood in a crowd at the rear of the nave that overflowed through the narthex and out the open doors into the square.

"Good morning, children," he said, looking to the right. "Today is a good day. Would anyone care to venture a guess why?"

A petite girl in the third pew chirped her response. "It's sunny."

Marcus left the pulpit, tugging gently on his beard. He descended the steps to the sanctuary and walked to the third pew. "Sunny," he said, smiling at the girl. "Yes, that is true. The light of the Great Father is shining brightly on our land today." He looked to the others. "And who here can tell me how he does that?"

Silence followed.

"Anybody? Don't be bashful. This is your day to be heard."

"The sun!" a young boy shouted.

"The moon!" said another.

"The stars!" came yet another.

Marcus smiled and scratched his coarse gray beard. "The sun, the moon, and the stars. All very good guesses, and logical, I might add. But the light that shines on the Haven is everlasting and comes from within. It does not set with the sun, nor wane with the moon, nor hide behind clouds on starry nights. It is a special light that requires special lamps. Do you know why these lamps are so special?" He paused so that their imaginations had a chance to wander. "It is because they live and breathe and have voices of their own. They play in our streets and shine on our mountains and cast light on our foggy shorelines. Sometimes they laugh, sometimes they cry." He peered up into the eastern light that filtered across the high vaulted ceiling. "But at all times they shine." He looked back to the children. "Does anybody here know where these lamps may be found?"

Another girl stood up, midway to the back. "We are the lamps," she called. Her response brought smiles from the left side of the chapel.

"That is absolutely correct," Marcus said, raising his staff in encouragement. "And that is a tremendous responsibility. To keep our land aglow no matter what darkness may come. Is that a task you can handle?" He presented his challenge to all the children with both arms held high.

Silence again.

Barusta stood up in the front row. "Pastor Marcus has asked us a question!" he shouted over the pews. "What's our answer, Crista?"

"Yes, we can," Crista answered, standing up in the sixth pew.

"Carynna, what's our answer?"

"Yes, we can!" she shouted from near a stone pillar.

"Uli?"

"Yes, we can." His voice squeaked from somewhere indefinable.

"Table eight, what's our answer?"

"Yes, we can!"

"Everybody, what's our answer?"

"Yes, we can!" came the resounding cry from all the children.

Marcus stood still, until the walls of the cathedral had absorbed the last echoes. "Good," he said. "That is why today is a good day. By the grace of our Great Father, may your light shine extra bright on the days ahead." He made a sign of blessing and then ascended the steps back to his pulpit.

At the pulpit his demeanor changed, becoming all business. He put on his round spectacles and sorted through a collection of notes. After a quick scan he looked to the left. "Before we get on with today's sermon, I believe Miss Annabelle Rafferty has some announcements for us."

Miss Rafferty rose from her pew and made for the lectern on the lower left side of the chancel. Her quick steps echoed on the tile. "Bless you, Pastor. And bless you all. First off, as chairlady of the weaver's guild, I would like to thank all who participated in choosing this year's tapestry theme. Their fine work will be put on display in a tent on the Promenade near the Docks and can be viewed there. Donations gladly accepted. Secondly, as most are aware, an open forum meeting is scheduled in the chapter house chambers immediately following today's service. The objective will be to further understand the impacts of a yea or nay vote on the Silvermine Bridge project and how we as a community of faith might prepare for Chancellor Rankwall's scheduled visit to the Haven next month. And finally, the family of Sebastian Schnites thanks all of you for your prayers and support during their time of challenge. They have graciously donated one month's supply of goat's milk to the orphanage for all that has been done. Thank you and bless you all."

Marcus nodded as she returned to her pew. "As always, Miss Rafferty, we thank you for the updates. With regards to the post-service meeting, I cannot emphasize enough the importance of everyone's participation. I ask that all of you search deep into your faith with open minds and hearts so that the challenges inherent to this issue will guide us to consensus rather than discord. Whatever is decided, it is imperative that in the end we speak with one voice." He scanned the pews over the top of his spectacles. "Are there any other announcements?"

"I have an announcement," said a well-tailored man, rising to speak.

Marcus recognized him at once. The bank chairman Melvyn Nevills, an avid proponent of the bridge. "What is your announcement, Master Nevills?"

"In light of the recent tragic death to Sebastian Schnites, the harbor watch is asking for volunteers to help patrol the shoreline at night. Proficiency at arms is advised but not required. The Pogetsa will be holding training sessions in the commons for all who are interested in serving their community."

Marcus removed his glasses. "Master Nevills, I believe your announcement would have been more appropriate in the meeting following this service. However, now that the issue has been raised, I will add that while caution is advised, it is important that we keep our fears in perspective. Regarding the conjecture over Sebastian Schnites's death, we should refrain from judgment until all the facts are known." Warily he peered out into the pews. "Are there any other announcements?"

Seeing no other requests, he put his spectacles back on and made a sign of blessing over the open tome on the pulpit. The time had come. "Today's sermon begins with a reading from the Book of—"

A disturbance came from the left: Miss Rafferty, clearing her throat. She pointed to the narthex. Marcus squinted. At the rear of the center aisle stood a young man with his hand up. It was Adman McFadden, of all people, from Cotton Crown. How had he missed him?

"Master McFadden, forgive me. What is your announcement?"

"I bring word from the mountain, Your Eminence. Colonel Mitterhal has a gift for the church and humbly requests that his emissaries be permitted to present it on his behalf."

Marcus wavered. The colonel humble? Never. He was up to something. He looked to the children, to Barusta who sat proudly with his feather in the front pew. A gift Mitterhal had given the boy, and now a gift for the church. Yes, he was definitely scheming. What could it possibly be this time? A goat horn perhaps, or a wolf pelt? Some other pagan artifact to incite a whirlwind of controversy? How far would he go to push his myth? Whatever the gift, there was no refuting it now. Anticipation permeated the chapel like embers in a smokehouse. To deny the people their prize would be like stealing candy from a child. Once again, the conniving old goat had his back to the wall.

"A word with a gift," Marcus said to Adman. "It is not normally the policy of the church to accept surprises during worship. However, in this case an exception may be warranted. I grant you the colonel's request, but be quick. We are in service."

Adman looked back and signaled beyond the chapel doors. The masses shifted as all strained to see who might enter. A communal gasp further sucked the air out of the nave as two men in formal guard attire strode the center aisle toward the pulpit. Between them they carried the legless war hero, Duncan Jacks. When they were halfway down the aisle, Marcus recognized the escorts. Weydlynn Roth, the horseman, held fast to Duncan's right and the piper Terrance Calhygan had the left. They stopped at the first step of the sanctuary where the carpet began.

Duncan held a loosely rolled fabric that draped to either side of his well-defined arms. "It is an honor, Your Eminence, to be humbled once again in your presence. In the spirit of this gift, the colonel has asked that I clear the air regarding a conversation you had with him prior to our stand at the Pass."

"I am not aware of any such air that needs to be cleared," Marcus said cautiously, "but let us not deny the colonel his say."

"With respect, Your Grace. You told him the Great Father does not meddle in our politics. That even war, like a fire gone wild, will run its course, and that all who remain true to his purpose will know his mercy. The colonel wants you to know that he took stock in your words and understands them now. But he would also add that many a great forest have been set ablaze by small fires. Fires easily quelled had they been addressed with prudence. He hopes that this gift will serve as a reminder of the peace we once shared with the Gwyntah and the fire we still might smother before it spreads to war. It is very dear to him, woven by his mother Hayalgaila, high priestess of Gwyntalynn, and beloved wife of the Toricean lord baron Augustus Mitterhal."

Another gasp escaped the nave. So the rumor was true. The colonel's mother a priestess. Marcus had suspected as much even during the war when the colonel's lineage lay wrapped in riddles. How perfect that the old goat chose now, on the cusp of a broken union with the tribes, to confirm the gossip. For though it was generally known that the baron's wife had been Gwyntah, there had been no written record of who she was or what had become of her. Some said she returned to Gwyntahlynn after her husband was executed on the mountain. Others believed it was the abduction of her only child by the Torics that led her, grief-stricken, to the Silvermine Bridge, where she severed her connection with the Haven.

Marcus signaled to the choir box. Two monks came forward to receive the gift. Each took one end of the woolen cloth and at nod from Marcus, they unrolled it. They held it shoulder high with their backs to the pulpit for all to see. Marcus could see only that it was a tapestry and that it must be beautiful, judging by the reaction of the people. Slowly the monks turned around to face him.

It was Marcus's turn to gasp. The goat, the mountain, the stars, the lupine in the foreground, the ethereal wings of the butterfly—it all struck him like a ram. He knew every stitch as if spun out of the fabric of his own soul. The scene was identical to that on the blanket that hung on the wall of his private prayer chamber—the very same blanket that the crew of the *Poulakis* had given to the monks a lifetime ago when they brought him to the abbey.

The light in the upper nave dimmed, as if a great cloud had passed over the cathedral. Marcus swooned, feeling the need for air. He put his hand on his face to subdue the intense twitch over his right brow. But then, as if the revelation of the blanket was not enough, he was aware of a commotion outside. Brother Michael broke through the cluster at the narthex and strode up the center aisle. Something terrible was happening. The disciplined monk never broke protocol during service.

Michael stopped at the tapestry. "Forgive the interruption, Your Grace. The Pogetsa have surrounded the cathedral. Terrance Calhygan, Duncan Jacks, and Weydlynn Roth are under arrest for threatening the lives of provincial officers on Cotton Crown Mountain. Out of respect for the church, they will not enter on condition that the accused give themselves up immediately and without incident."

"Respect?" Marcus said. "What respect is this?" He looked at Duncan, suspended in the arms of the guardsmen. "Duncan, is this true?"

"It is not, Your Eminence. We swear by the land for which we fought that we were not on the mountain when the incident occurred. Yet we will not have this house defiled by arms. We will abide by their terms." He made his best attempt to bow while suspended.

Speechless, Marcus watched as Duncan and his escorts turned to depart. Feeling powerless, he searched for words, anything to shed light on the outrage. His pulse pounded. His neutrality was at risk. He needed air. What word could possibly describe this sin? The men were halfway down the aisle when it came to him.

"Shame," he said, loosening the collar around his neck.

The twelve monks in the choir box shifted nervously in their seats, a new concern in their eyes.

"Shame," he repeated louder, knuckles turning white around his holy staff.

The standees in the narthex parted to let the men through.

"Shame!" he shouted from the pulpit, his need for air becoming critical.

A breeze suddenly passed through the open chapel doors and fanned the tempest within. "Shame on the Pogetsa! Shame on the corrupt. Shame on these men who tarnish our honored. How dare they defile the house of our Great Father? How dare they claim to respect our home? How dare they call themselves peacekeepers? Brother Liam, begin the offertory!"

Brother Liam stood up in the choir box and made a sign of blessing. The chant began. Madness burned as Marcus raised his staff over the drone of the monks. "Sound the bells!"

He turned to the right; the children's wide eyes tempered his wrath. His breath wheezed in and out, short and choppy. Balance teetered on edge. More air, dizziness—must inhale. He focused on the first pew: a feather, Barusta, solid as stone, waiting for the word.

"Barusta," Marcus said, trembling and spent. "Lead your choir."

Outside the cathedral, the colonel's emissaries descended the stone steps to face their accusers. Yet even as the chained cuffs snapped tight around their wrists, the bells high up in the steeple sounded and the children's voices poured out the open chapel doors, backed by the drone of the monks. Many both inside and outside of the cathedral remembered the words and joined in, just as they had done on the eve of the Guard's stand at Spaulding Pass. So it happened that as the tenth hymn of the Old Tome swelled in the square, some thought they heard the distant requiem of goat-hyde pipers. Others said the music was taken up by the wind and carried clear across the harbor to the shores of Gwyntahlynn.

12
Voices and Visions

The imagination, according to the Gwyntahmahoma, was a blend of mind and spirit. All had it, some more than others. *Jahacco huru* they called it, dream talk. It ran naturally in children, though was by no means limited to child's play. The shamans in Gwyntahlynn considered it powerful medicine for the sick and traumatized, regardless of age. At its best, *jahacco huru* fed the faith; at worse, madness. When induced by smoke, the altered state fell somewhere in between.

Enyalda hated barns, all barns. Barns with horses, barns with sheep, barns with oxen, goats, or chickens. They were built to confine. Like jailhouses, designed by men to spread their dominion on the world. She even hated the empty ones—morgues of dead grass. She avoided them at all cost, just as she avoided men. Except for her brothers, of course, and the colonel, and perhaps a few others like Captain Marly, Pastor Marcus, and that charming legless one who'd come to dinner, and maybe the sheriff if she really thought about it, and Angus in spite of his gawky habits, and possibly a few of the herdsmen, rough though they were around the edges. Her list of exceptions, she had to admit, was expanding. Regardless, she still hated barns.

Her speech had improved dramatically since her spat with the colonel, though out of habit she still phrased her thoughts in verse. The effect was a hybrid stream of poetic prose that ebbed and flowed with her fancies. Her flowers didn't like it, not one bit. They preferred her whispers, as did the trees and shrubberies. The grasses in the pasture were too busy squabbling amongst themselves in the autumn winds to notice the difference. Her brothers certainly did, especially Francis, who had been extra helpful in the kitchen. Even Adman made it a point to set aside time in his busy schedule to hear what she had to say.

Donavon, strangely enough, seemed the least enamored by the change. He had been distant of late. At first Enyalda attributed it to his near fatal experience at the fountain. His body had been sorely treated by the weirmen, and mending it required almost every healing blessing Muma had taught her—an exhausting effort to say the least. Yet even after his cuts and abrasions had scabbed, the impact on his spirit remained raw. She saw it in his far-off gaze across the Haven; it betrayed his every glance. Something had happened at the fountain that he was not disclosing. So concerned, she dared a visit one day to the colonel's hay-laden stock house with a basket full of gingerwhip cookies, hoping to lighten her brother's mood. She warily approached the open track doors. The smell of dead grass frightened her.

Donavon was there with the wolf. The creature, lying under the shelf of honey jars, growled upon her entry, though immediately stopped when it caught whiff of her scent. Her brother stood only paces away, stoic with bow drawn, aiming at the shadows in the rear of the stock house. A stuffed burlap sack hung from a collar tie in the rafters and swayed ever so subtly against the backdrop of hay bales. It looked like a giant pincushion riddled with needles. Donavon fired his shot.

Thwap! The arrow pierced the right side of the sack and sent it spinning left. Enyalda squeaked at the impact.

"What brings you here, sister?" Donavon asked, still facing the sack and reloading his bow.

"For you, my brother, I've made this trip. I've brought your favorite gingerwhip."

Thwap! Another arrow struck the sack, dead center. Donavon turned around. "Thank you, Enya," he said, though his face remained stern.

Something warm and moist lapped across her bare foot. The wolf had snuck up behind her and lay submissively beside her. The sensation of its rough tongue on her skin made her giggle. Looking down, she marveled how much it had grown since the spring. Peering into its one working eye, she saw it was still a puppy at heart, but not for long. Soon it would be ready to go about its business doing whatever grown wolves do.

"Looks like Scraggs wants in on the goodies," Donavon said, taking a gingerwhip from the basket. "He's got a ravenous sweet tooth, you know." He flicked the cookie with his thumb. Like a spinning gold coin it bounced squarely off the wolf's head and landed on the floor. Its snout went down, but not for the cookie. Rather, it rested atop Enyalda's foot.

Donavon frowned. Enyalda giggled again, amused to see her brother so mystified. It inspired her into verse. She bowed to the wolf and picked up the cookie, only inches from its jowls.

Sweet is your tooth and good are your manners
To deny your body its treat
But spare not your belly a just reward
Even a wolf has to eat.

She tossed the cookie up and in a blink it was gone; snatched in midair by the wolf.

"You have a good way with him, Enya." Donavon reached in the basket for another cookie. "You always have, with all things alive. Not even old Fergus could take that away from you."

She shivered at the mention of Fergus. Her brother never brought up that name. Why now? The wolf licked her trembling fingers. Donavon had a fell look in his eye.

"I swore after that day in the barn, Enya, that I would never let anything happen to you again. Ever. He had it coming. You know that, don't you? Even the pastor saw that. If Adman or Francis were there, they would have done the same. The pure should never suffer, not by the likes of him. I live that moment every day."

Enyalda swallowed hard. Why was he saying this? His lost gaze was back, combined with something terrible and fierce—an old wound he bore from childhood, not of the body but the mind. Then it dawned on her. She had to set him free, relieve him of his watch over her. What happened in the barn those many years ago had been just as bad for him as for her, if not worse in another way. The pitchfork, the fierce hatred, the taking of a life by his own hand. A child should never be driven to such violence. The wolf's tongue on her fingers soothed her fears. She had to be strong for Donavon's sake. Strong, yes, and convincing. No song, no dance, no riddles, just straight speech. She summoned her most persuasive smile and caressed her brother's locked jaw with her finger. "Fine I am and fine I will be. What was done is done."

He closed his eyes, appearing to savor the words. She was thankful he did not see the tears that welled in her own eyes. Long he stood engrossed in his thoughts.

"I heard her voice, Enya," he said, snapping out of his trance. "The fountain statue spoke to me, as clearly as your words are to me now. And her music. It's in the woods, wherever I go. The trails I hunt, the streams I fish … At night when I try to sleep, I hear her song in the owl's call. She is calling me, but for what I don't know. It's driving me mad. And now I am to go to Gwyntahlynn … by order of the colonel. For my own good, he says, but what about yours?"

Tears pressed yet again, though she fought them back. Must be strong. "You hear her song in birds and trees but still you do not hear me." She slapped his face, instantly perking the ears of the wolf. "Wake up, my brother. Listen and trust. I said I am fine, you must go where you must."

The wolf snatched the unguarded cookie in Donavon's hand.

"Hey, watch it, Scraggs! That's my hand you almost took."

The paws went up. Big paws, Enyalda noted, as they thumped her brother's chest. The wolf lapped vigorously at his face, smearing it with soggy chunks of gingerwhip cookie. Who would have thought a wolf could provide such friendship? Then again, why not? Her flowers had done the same for her. And what about the chimney, far and away the most bizarre friend of all? Look what it had done for the colonel.

Seeing her brother in good spirits at last, Enyalda scurried to the shelf of honey jars. She placed the basket there and stole away a jar of gold. Outside, she reveled in the sunlight and skipped back to the manor, her mission complete.

Two days later Enyalda was in the kitchen when Adman burst through the front door blaring the news.

"It's in! It's in! The results are in!"

She set her ladle in the pot and hurried to check on the colonel. He had been napping peacefully in his leather chair next to the fireplace. Surely not anymore, thanks to her oblivious brother. Why did he have to be such a thug?

She rounded the corner of the parlor just as Francis sprinted through the wide open door, apparently in the same frenzy as Adman, though not quite as obnoxious.

"There you are, sister. The news is in! Poulakis says no to the bridge!" He hugged her, spinning her around with feet off the floor.

She peeled herself away, unconvinced that the news justified jarring the colonel out of his slumber. Adman was already with him, ranting on and on about politics. The colonel, still waking, appeared more interested in the glowing embers of the fire than her brother's stream of gossip. She ran to his side, seeing his blanket on the floor.

"Don't worry, my dear," he said as she stooped to pick it up. "The fire's good and warm. One of those gingerwhips of yours and some goat's milk would do fine about now."

Thankfully Adman let up on the colonel and looked to Francis, his thoughts still racing. "Come on, Fran. Let's find Donny. He's probably with the wolf." As suddenly as they appeared, they were gone, the door slamming the clapboards as they left.

Two more days passed and not a whole lot happened at the manor, short of a few late-night visits by the sheriff and his friends. Seth McGregor and his brothers also paid a visit, asking permission to launch fireworks from the knolls in the colonel's goat pasture. Enyalda kept to her chores and stayed clear of the commotion. She did enjoy the fireworks from afar, especially when they were answered in like fashion by the other mountains in the surrounding highlands. They reminded her of sparkling fireflies.

The colonel spent more time napping than anything else, though on occasion he would wake up and jump to task. At such a time, in the latter half of a morning, while he was tending his hives, Enyalda spotted a lone dark figure moving up the pasture toward the manor. It was a man for sure, with a staff and a beard, bushy and gray. He parted the meadow grasses in his long black robe. Pastor Marcus! Thrilled, she charged through the field, eager to show off her new words.

"Hello, Enyalda. What a pleasure it is to see you," the holy man said, breathing heavily from his hike.

She suppressed the urge to sing and prepared to dazzle him with straight talk, but the wind picked up and the meadow made a terrible fuss. Of all times, with of all people! Why did the grasses choose now to be so distracting? Defeated, she let her hair fall over her eyes. "Hello," she muttered, staring dejectedly at her sandals in the gibbering sedges.

"Hello, indeed," he said encouragingly. "Very nice to hear you speak. And where might I find the good colonel this lovely morning?"

Enyalda swept the hair out of her eyes. She liked his voice, always had. So much like the colonel's, only softer. The meadow finally relaxed and suggested that she present her words the old way, wrapped in song and dance.

The bees, the bees, that's where he will be
Near the pit by the hives, if you look you will see
The smoke on the rise, the grass in the breeze
The colonel's awake
Follow me if you please!

They found the colonel at the hives, puffing up a storm on his pipe. Enyalda stopped at the smoldering fire pit, daring to go no farther. Pastor Marcus did the same, catching his breath. They waited long unacknowledged. Enyalda felt the tension mount. At last, the colonel placed a frame of honeycomb back into the open box in front of him.

"It was foolish for you to travel without guard, Marcus."

"How I travel is my own business, Cornelius. But if it lightens your mood, I'll have you know that Barleycopp has seen to my safety. Your chief cipher escorted me up the mountain and awaits my return at the tavern."

The colonel dragged deep on his pipe and then exhaled into the top hive, appearing satisfied with the information. "That is good," he said, spreading the smoke with an easy wave of his hand.

A light breeze blew the smoke toward the pit. Enyalda gasped as Pastor Marcus strode undaunted toward the open hive. She raced up and over the fieldstone wall for safety.

"That's not the wulfweed in your pipe again, is it?" he asked, swatting at several bees that landed on his beard.

"What I put in my pipe is my own business, Pastor. But if it lightens your mood, I'll have you know that it's goat hair mixed with common smoke. It keeps the bees honest. Speaking of which, don't swipe at the clingers. It only makes them edgy."

"Goat hair?"

The colonel merely grunted and shrugged off the comment. "So what's your business here?" he asked, pulling out another rack of honeycomb to inspect.

More bees enmeshed in the pastor's beard; others began to march across his bald scalp. "You have created a storm in the Haven, Cornelius," he said, growing chary at the mounting buzz. "Sending your men to church was a bold move."

"Not as bold as yours from what I've heard. The tenth hymn … led by children. Not even I could have dreamed that one up. This storm you speak of is all yours."

The pastor's body jerked. Enyalda winced at the holy man's ungodly twist. She watched him pinch at his robe down by his legs, appearing to curtsy to the colonel in a fever.

The colonel quickly put the lid on the hive. "I thought I told you to leave the bees alone! Once you get them going, there's no stopping them."

"Then you might start blowing some of that goat hair my way!" cried the pastor.

The colonel grabbed his honey buckets and strode to the heaping pile of goat hair at the edge of the smoke pit. "You're a fool, Marcus!" He set down the buckets and tossed an armful of hair into the flame. The pungent cloud wrapped the hives.

Enyalda sighed in relief as Pastor Marcus eased up on his bee-swatting dance and flicked the sedated creatures out of his beard. Still she watched from behind the wall, not entirely convinced the crisis was over.

"Your little honey makers have an attitude," the pastor said.

"What do you expect?" the colonel answered. "You threatened their queen."

"I did no such thing. You're the one poking at their hive."

Mitterhal's scowl could have wilted a flower. "It's your distrust that they smell. It might as well have been a threat."

"I beg their pardon then. It was not my intention to offend them."

"Save your begging, Pastor. They'll be sacked for the rest of the day."

Enyalda saw the colonel wince and grab his left hip. The excitement must have tweaked his injury. Only a year had passed since his fall off the roof, and though his mind and spirit had recovered nicely, parts of his body were still knocked out of place. Immediately she hopped the wall and retrieved his cane, which he'd left leaning against a hive.

"Thank you, my dear," he said, taking it from her. "Perhaps you could whip up some more of those cookies for us, and some ointment for the pastor's stings. We will see you at the hearth."

Enyalda hurried to task. At the colonel's hampered pace, she had just enough time to mix the batter and get the cookies in the oven. Like a leaf in the wind, she flew down the slope toward the manor, waving to the hedge of laurels as she passed.

In the kitchen she was mortified. Something had ravaged her cupboards! The basket of eggs she had placed on the counter earlier was now on the floor. Most of the cracked shells were licked dry of their contents. Miraculously, two eggs had survived—just enough for the cookies. What could have done this and how did it get in? She looked to the draped fronds of the amaryllis. Sound asleep on the sill—no help there.

At last, scanning the carnage, she found her answer by the flour bin that had fallen on the floor. Paw prints, distinctly white and large, and canine. She traced the powder trail along the cabinets. To her horror they led directly to the open door of her solarium. Not the flowers! A surge of maternal rage pumped through her veins. She lunged for the cast-iron pan that hung on the wall and charged down the stairs, ready to pummel the life out of the omnivorous beast.

At the base of the stairs, all was intact. The incriminating prints led directly to the terrace door that swayed back and forth in the breeze. Moving to the door, she discovered the latch strike jiggling loosely in the cracked jamb. She could hear the rumblings of the colonel and the pastor, still engaged in debate by the sound of it. They approached the manor from somewhere behind the hedge of laurels. She dropped the pan and sped back to her task, relieved her loved ones had been spared the pillage. On the way through the solarium, she stopped at the herb bed and plucked a stem from the aloe plant, being sure to thank it for its generosity.

In the kitchen, she assaulted the mess like a whirlwind, traveling backward in time, barely conscious of her actions. Thankfully, Francis was not there. His good intentions would have only impeded her flow. And so the kitchen was restored to order in minutes—nothing short of magic by her brother's standards.

She whipped up the batter in the same manner. The eggs, the flour, the ginger, the milk, and the most important ingredient of all—wild mountain honey. She paused only once to ponder the colonel's honey jar left curiously untouched on the edge of the counter. Not even a lick or a paw print.

The front door slammed open. Enyalda hugged the counter. The colonel and the pastor were still in dispute; she could hear their muffled discourse through the walls. The conflict made her nervous. Pastor Marcus was usually so pleasant. Perhaps it was the stings that made him snippy. She squeezed the juice of the aloe plant into a porcelain mortise, along with a dab of honey and some other medicinal seasonings. After mashing the ointment into a workable paste, she recited a quick blessing and made straight for the hearth room. In the parlor she heard her brother's name mentioned and something about the fountain. She stopped so as not to interrupt the discussion.

"You told me yourself, Cornelius, he was deprived of air, on the verge of death. It is not uncommon for the mind to play tricks in such a state."

"Yet he still had the strength while submerged to crack the weirman's larynx with a gaff handle. That's a powerful delusion, Marcus, wouldn't you say? Open your eyes, she told him. Why can't you do the same?"

"Do not try to draw me into your myths, Colonel. The power of the mind over the body is a mystery for sure, but to say it came from an ancient pagan queen is pushing it."

"And what if the command came from one of your statue saints in the abbey? What then? Would you be so quick to pass it off as a delusion? The lad's got a strong mind, Marcus. Not easily swayed by nonsense, just like his father. What difference does it make if the voice came from a statue? Or a living flower, for that matter? Or a bush? Or the working end of a loaded musket! The voice is the voice whatever the vision."

"Yes, Cornelius, the voice is the voice, I'll give you that. But there is only one voice in this world that defies death. The one we all must answer at some point or another."

"Fine, but that is not to say that the voice of your God did not pipe through the Goddess. Even by your thickheaded principle, that is possible. Something got the lad's rattled skull out of the pool. To call the voice a delusion is a denial of the evidence."

Pastor Marcus appeared to soften. Enyalda saw his posture change, his guard drop, just like a year ago when the colonel first awoke from his tumble off the roof. "You are right at least in one regard, Cornelius. Young Donavon has a strong will. I saw it even as a child. The death of Fergus only confirmed it. Never had I seen such resolve in a boy. Such a brutal act for one so young. I prayed that day for his soul and his sister's. And mine."

"Yours?"

"Yes, mine. Imagine that? The Lake Savior himself. Does that surprise you, Cornelius? It shouldn't. It was your own captain who spearheaded the cover-up. Barleycopp had members of the Guard burn Uryan's barn, horses and all, to make it look like an accident. All that was left were the constable's charred remains. Uryan's children were brought up here to the mountain for their safety. Rankwall was furious at the death of his son and convinced that one of the elder McFadden brothers did it. They would have felt his justice too, had not Barleycopp come to me. He needed an alibi for the children, one that not even the Pogetsa would dare to contest. I met with the boys first, then Enyalda. It was she who convinced me to give Barleycopp what he wanted. She never said a word, so torn and broken. Only nine years old, clinging to a potted flower as if it were the only thing shielding her of the horror. I lied that day under oath in the name of the Great Father. Not a day has passed since then that I don't ask for his forgiveness."

Enyalda's vision blurred. They burned the horses! The barn yes, but why the horses? Mortified, she leaned against the parlor wall. Though she wept for the horses, she kept an ear to the conversation at the hearth.

"It wasn't just her voice at the fountain," the colonel said. "The lad said he heard music. Melodies from the Old Tome. Just like my men at the pass. They heard it too, all of them, in the pipes that blew on the east ridge."

"Were they not your pipers on the ridge?"

"So I thought for all these years, until Barleycopp told me otherwise. Johan Hume was assigned to lead the company, yet his body was found on the field of battle with his sons. Not one of his pipers confirms ever being on the east ridge."

"And you are certain the music came from this ridge, that it was not an echo from another position?"

"Nobody is sure of anything. The wulfweed settled thick in the field. All that is certain is that the command codes were heard and followed by all the men on the lines, and that for the life of them, Marcus, they were not dispatched by me."

The colonel's declaration snapped Enyalda out of her woe. She could feel the weight in his words. He needed a cookie, but they were still in the oven. Perhaps a dance and a song would do. She wiped her eyes and waltzed into the hearth room with the ointment, doing her best to mimic a swan. She took the long way, slow and steady, wading through the room until she was certain their eyes were on her. Then she sang a verse that was sure to relax the colonel, for many times he had sung it himself on his rooftop.

Celebration song and dance
See the wagon's ponies prance
Beneath my tapestry receive
Your mother's blessing.

She stopped at the hearth. To her delight, even Pastor Marcus was swayed by the words—the perfect time to address his stings. She took his hand and led him to the colonel's leather chair, where she directed him to sit. She placed the bee balm on the floor and knelt before him. Then, ever so carefully, she lifted his black robe over the knees and up to his thighs. The sight of the stings made her coo like a pigeon. How pretty they looked, like blooming red roses on blue branching veins.

Over by the mantel the colonel grunted, not sharing the same sentiment. "Now that right there is the ugliest pair of whites I've ever seen. You need to get out in the sun more, Pastor."

One by one, Enyalda dabbed the welts with the ointment. Pastor Marcus stared stoically into the fire, obviously not pleased with his compromised position. Then she saw it—the twitch. She wasn't sure at first, but it happened again, over his right brow, just like the colonel's. A coincidence perhaps, but what were the odds? Could it really be? No, the colonel's skin was dark and leathery. But the eyes, they were exactly the same, so deep and blue and penetrating. It would explain so much. Not just the eyes, but the mind and temperament. But that would …

The door in the front parlor swung open. Someone charged through the parlor and into the kitchen. "Enya, where are you?" It was Donavon, frantic. Seconds later he rounded the stairwell into the hearth room. "Enya! Something's wrong with—" He stopped dead at the sight of the partially naked pastor in the colonel's chair. "What's going on here?"

The colonel slammed his cane to the floor. "Mind your manners, lad! The pastor had a run-in at the hives. What is it with you boys and knocking anyway? What do you need? Speak up."

Donavon looked to Enyalda still kneeling on the floor. "Something's wrong with Scraggs, Enya. He's got an ill look about him."

I'm sure he does, she thought. Calmly, she stood up and handed Pastor Marcus the ointment and cloth. Some of the stings went high above his thighs, and she thought it best that he tend to their treatment himself. She then hurried past Donavon to check on the cookies, gesturing her brother to wait.

In the kitchen she was delighted to find the amaryllis awake. After removing the cookies from the oven and setting them on the counter to cool, she whispered her question to the long green fronds of the groggy bulb. *"A nahala Muma wulf ach nahock prunus?"* How would Muma feed a wolf prunes?

13
Across the Haven

Peace between Gwyntahlynn and Lakwynnia panned down to one raw element—trust. The Silvermine Bridge embodied it. Within its tangled ruins were the fragments of a shattered trust that many in the Haven believed could still be salvaged. Indeed, the tribes had contributed substantially to the railway effort in the beginning, not only in word but deed. The train passage that bore through their sacred coastland was initially embraced as a grand temple in honor of their earth goddess. Not until more tunnels were dug and carloads of ore stripped from the pillars of their Great Mother's stores did the sentiment change. Even then, the lapse in judgment might have been excused had there been the slightest attempt at a thank you.

The wolf was red. Donavon stepped out of the colonel's stock house and tightened the hip belt on Hoffman's combat pack. Everything around him was aglow, even Scraggs by his side. He looked to the source of the hue. The rim of the high peak shimmered in the red dawn. Directly in front of him, in the pasture by the cedar grove, ethereal horned forms waxed and waned in pockets of crimson fog. How he loved it when the morning mist hugged the slopes and made the colonel's mountain goats look like grim soldiers awaiting their call.

"That's a hefty pack you got," said the old man from behind him.

Donavon spun. How did he do that? Just appear like a ghost? Not even Scraggs had picked up on his scent. The Old Mitt hobbled to within a cane swing and fired up his pipe. Smoke hovered over the carved goat head on the burl. The sight flashed him back to his vision in the fountain pool.

"Sheriff Hoffman gave it to me," Donavon said, adjusting the quiver of arrows on his shoulder strap. "He told me to bring it back without a scratch."

"That would be the Hoof for you." Mitterhal stacked both hands atop his cane. "Better make sure you do what he says. In the meantime, I want to brief you on the Gwyntah. They will have questions. How you answer is critical. We'll start easy. What is your name?"

Pipe smoke twisted in the mist. Donavon squinted. "My name?"

The cane sprang up and nipped Donavon in the cheek. The wolf growled. "Wrong answer, lad. Try again. State your name?"

"I am Donavon," he said, rubbing his face.

"Better. But be sure to state it in full. McFadden is the name they will recognize. What is your business in Gwyntahlynn?"

"My what?"

Again the cane struck, this time smarting the right side of Donavon's temple. "Wrong answer. Don't ever answer their questions with a question. You'll be dead before you hit the ground. Now try again. State your name and business."

"I am Donavon McFadden. I seek council with the Gwyntahpynn."

"Not bad. Now say it with conviction."

Donavon repeated his response, still wincing at the blow.

The colonel's cane sideswiped him just above the left ear.

"What was that for?" Donavon exclaimed, the wolf snarling louder.

"I said conviction, not prediction. You look like you're about to get smacked in the head."

"Maybe 'cause I am."

"That's irrelevant. You'll have only one chance to make an impression. Do not give them a reason to doubt your heritage, especially the Gwyntahpynn. He will challenge your claim, and when he does it is imperative that you not flinch. If for any reason he suspects you false, you will be executed on the spot. Again! Your name. Your business."

"I am Donavon McFadden. I seek—"

Another sweeping blow, more snarls from the wolf. "Look me in the eye when you speak."

"I am!"

A direct shot to the head. "There is madness in your eyes. Do not ever present your terms in anger."

"I'm not!"

Another strike. "You are."

"You're the madman!"

Smack. "Irrelevant. Stay to the point."

"I ... I am—"

"Who are you, lad? Do not hesitate. Answer the question!"

The cane sliced through the air. Donavon caught it in mid-swing. "I am Donavon McFadden, son of the One Talon," he said, holding the cursed stick firmly in place. "And I am done with this briefing. If you strike me again I will feed your old bones to the wolf."

The colonel nodded. "Good. Very good. Remember these lumps on your skull when you talk to the Gwyntahpynn. You'll do just fine. Now get your paws off my cane and listen up. Arrangements have been made for your transport tonight across the harbor. Jeziah will meet you at the abandoned rail depot by the east gate of the bridge. You must trust in whatever he says."

Donavon recalled his encounter with the giant last spring at the colonel's smoke pit. "I will listen," he said, rubbing one of the welts on his head.

"That you will. When you leave the mountain, do not take the main road. Use your hunting trails. Once you are down, stay out of the city. Wait until dusk to go to the depot. The Pogetsa have upped their patrols along the shore. Jeziah will brief you from there."

"And what do I say to the Gwyntahpynn once I find him?"

"You will not find him. He will find you. Just answer his questions, stay on point, and do not hesitate. Remember, there's not a question he will ask to which he does not already know the answer. It is not what you say but how you say it that will interest him. Look him in the eye when you speak, never away or down, but do not, under any circumstance, challenge his authority with a direct stare."

"That kind of limits my options, doesn't it?"

"Yes, very much. That is why he is the Gwyntahpynn. But there is a trick, so long as you are subtle and have the strength of mind to use it. You must look through him when you speak."

"Through him?"

"Yes. Imagine an object directly behind him. It doesn't matter what it is, so long as you are familiar with it and can sustain the vision in your mind. Look through his eyes and focus on it. It is an effective technique that will earn his respect if used correctly. However, if you try too hard you will come across as nothing more than a cross-eyed fool."

The wolf made a high-pitched moan, something between a yap and a bay. Remnants of its puppiness lingered. Donavon tightened his shoulder straps and looked into the sunken socket where the wolf's left eye would have been. "Come on, Scraggs, let's go. We gotta long walk ahead of us. Any other pearls of wisdom, Colonel?"

"As a matter of fact, there is." He reached into his vest pocket. "It might get cold where you're going. Make sure you keep your head warm." He pulled out a garment and tossed it to Donavon. "I never thanked you for the wake up."

Donavon caught it and recognized it at once. It was the hand-knit hat Muma had made for him when he was a boy. Enya had one just like it. Feeling the prickly wool brought him back to that wintry day when he and Angus were getting their thrills pelting the Grange's sheep with snowballs. He remembered his sister, twelve years old, charging through the frozen pasture, hysterical in tears. How she yanked and pulled at his jacket until he and Angus finally agreed to let up on the sheep and to check on the Old Mitt on his rooftop. A good thing they did, as it turned out. They found him sound asleep in a snowdrift next to his chimney without a jacket, so far gone that Donavon had to climb up the ladder to shake him out of his snow nap. He never forgot the insane rant that followed; how the old fool spouted on and on about happiness, and how his chimney had no reason to get up because it couldn't. The incident had left Donavon wondering what his dead father had seen in the madman, and whether he should have just let the crazy old coot freeze to death for his own sake.

"Thanks for giving it back," he said, at a loss for anything better.

With that he set out for the north pasture, eager to get a move on. The wolf bounded ahead, as if knowing that Donavon would head for the elk trail that skirted the high peak and meandered down the northwest side of the mountain. The red mist was lifting and the day promised to be good for travel. Even over the rough terrain, Donavon saw no problem making the rendezvous by nightfall.

The depot was a barren place, a breeding ground of rust. Railcars rotted at the station's loading ramps, wheels fused to tracks. The treasure they'd once held had long been plundered, Donavon was sure. Yet he climbed one nonetheless for a peek inside. Scraggs, unable to follow, whined most unwolf-like from the tracks below. Peering into the car, Donavon grimaced at the stench. A decade's worth of stagnant rainwater festered inside, along with whatever hapless creatures may have ventured in for a swim.

From atop the car Donavon scanned the yard in what little light remained of the day. The wolf growled, prompting him to turn around. A massive shadow stepped out from behind the station house.

"Easy does it, Scraggs," Donavon whispered. "I believe our tour guide is here."

Jeziah McCaskel wasted no time with niceties. "Follow me and keep the wolf quiet."

They rounded the corner of the station and made straight for the shoreline, where the ramparts of the bridge ascended the banks. Jeziah moved with uncanny stealth for a mammoth, pausing at various times to assess the twilight. There was something surreal about him. Not just his size, though that in itself was a marvel. More his general presence, troll-like, as if he had been recruited out of one of Muma's fairy tales to parley with the real world. They stopped at the base of the bridge buttress where the embankment got steep. A barred owl called from a distant tree, reminding Donavon of his sister.

"Who cooks for you?" he whispered nostalgically into the cold black water.

"Quiet," Jeziah said. "We wait here."

They waited in silence until not a trace of daylight remained in the west. Donavon heard the owl again. Another answered from afar, somewhere on the bridge, and then another—very near. The giant, who had gone into a trancelike hiatus, stirred into action and told Donavon to follow. They sidestepped the embankment to a patch of alders. Jeziah inserted his arm into the foliage and heaved on something large. A boat slid on the gravel and rustled the crispy leaves. To Donavon's amazement, Jeziah lifted the wooden vessel and walked effortlessly into the water as if he were wielding a great shield. Without a sound, he lowered the dinghy and held it still in the waist-deep current.

"Get in the boat," he instructed. "Stay close to the bridge when you cross. We have muskets over every pylon up to the wreckage. You will be on your own after that. Be quick. Do not linger on the shoreline. Follow the trestle to the mines. Above the tunnel is a trail that the tribes use to guard the entrance. Follow it upward and into the mountains. Stay to the south slopes when you ascend."

Donavon stood frozen. He wanted to ask, *That's it?* and then thought better of it. No sense making the grim cipher any grimmer. Resolved to his task, Donavon rocked the boat with one foot on the stern and the other on the shore. "In you go, boy," he said, tossing in the pack. The wolf leaped in. Donavon was about to do the same when he felt Jeziah's crushing grip on his shoulder.

"State your name and purpose for crossing the Haven."

Donavon glared at the troll. "I am Donavon McFadden, son of the One Talon. I seek council with the Gwyntahpynn."

The grip relaxed. Donavon exhaled. Apparently, he'd passed the test. Then, as if some other force had seized him, he added a little flair of his own, surprising even himself. "I'll let you come along if you promise not to sink the dinghy."

The grip tightened again, though with less menace, maybe even a hint of affection. Without further word, Jeziah let go and disappeared into the night. Shortly thereafter, the barred owls resumed their calls.

The trip across the harbor was thankfully uneventful. Donavon wondered how much of that was due to chance. He rowed at a steady pace, aware of the silent eyes that watched him. He stopped only once to survey the collapsed pylons in the moonlight. Five had been hit, three mangled beyond any hope of use. Metal, wood, and masonry twisted together like lath work in crumbled plaster. To see the carnage at such an intimate level was chilling.

His thoughts drifted to the tavern and the yarns that had spun out from that historic night when the Old Mitt sacked the bridge. What a sight it must have been when the *Lyssia* opened fire. Donavon imagined Captain Marly high up on her upper deck, conducting his pipers while the cannons blasted to the music. And his father, he imagined him too on his warhorse, chanting with the ciphers from the shoreline. Many versions of the tale had been told in the pub, but one testament always rang true. A statement was made that night, and a promise to the tribes. Donavon pondered that promise all the way to Gwyntahlynn. When at last the dinghy's hull scraped on the far shores, he peered up into the harsh crags and wondered what part of that pledge he now served.

They camped that night, man and wolf, only an hour or so before dawn, high above the tunnel of the silver mines where the cliffs tapered to an alpine dell. The craggy terrain had been a challenge, especially for Scraggs. Several harrowing moments had occurred, when Donavon had to hoist the wolf up with a rope. The loaded combat pack did not help. By the end, both were exhausted. They slept late into the morning, heedless of the passing day. At noon, Donavon got up to make breakfast. Enyalda had packed a fine assortment of jams and bread; and of course, her irresistible gingerwhip cookies.

"I don't know about this stuff," Donavon said to Scraggs. "It's good, but you can't climb mountains with it. We need meat. What do you say we go on a hunt?"

The wolf licked its jowls at the mention of hunt.

They came upon a herd of wild goats by midafternoon. Donavon removed his pack and crouched behind a boulder while Scraggs slinked downwind and out of sight. Both knew the routine. Donavon kept his eye on a first-year billy, arrow ready, waiting for it to catch the scent. It felt good to have his pack off.

The breeze shifted, as did the horns of every goat in the herd. As predicted, they bolted at the scent of the wolf. Directly toward Donavon they charged, oblivious of his presence. Donavon stepped out from behind the boulder and released his shot. The young billy took the hit in the shoulder and kept on running. It veered downslope with the arrow bobbing from its side. Scraggs bounded out of the scrub in pursuit of the injured prey. Donavon watched them disappear beyond a knoll. The goat's death cry came shortly thereafter. Around the knoll he found them in a field of gahenya, the goat silent and still next to the panting wolf.

"You've come a long way since scrapping with badgers, my friend," Donavon said, unsheathing his knife. "Congratulations, you're in the big game now." He laid his hand over the heart of the goat and closed his eyes. "*Su gahwynn,*" he whispered. It was one of the few sayings he remembered from his days with Muma—thank you. He then removed the heart with practiced precision and gave it to Scraggs.

They camped that night at the spot of the kill, in a field of gahenya gone to seed. Donavon gathered tinder in a nearby grove of stunted cedars, while Scraggs gnawed on a raw quarter flank. The sunset was striking, as were the stars that followed. The meat sizzled long into the night.

Donavon reclined against his propped pack and took it all in. How could it get any better? Fresh game on the fire, the crescent moon clear in the east, a good friend by his side, and the stars. Endless stars, more than he could possibly count in a lifetime. If only his sister were here to sing her songs. Yes, that would top it all. He smiled at the wolf, thoroughly stuffed.

"What do you think, Scraggs? You think we could make a go of it here? You won't get shot by any herdsmen on this side of the Haven."

The wolf answered with a lazy sweep of the tail and a yawn.

"Not a bad idea. Get your rest, you've earned it. We got some climbing tomorrow."

Donavon ate the cooked goat, lean and tender, as Scraggs slept, paws twitching in a dream. He munched on one of Enyalda's gingerwhips for dessert, watching the smoke sail through the moonlight in ghostly forms. In time the wind shifted. Scraggs snarled, still locked in a dream, or a nightmare, by the sound of it. The legs jerked out of control.

"Easy there, big fella. That's what happens when you eat too fast."

Another snarl, teeth bared. "All right, that's enough of that," Donavon said, nudging the sleeping wolf with his boot.

In a blink Scraggs was up, snout to the cedars, his tightened shackles twitching in the light of the fire.

"What's got into you, boy? Snap out of it, you big yellow belly."

The wolf slinked backward, tail tucked tight between its legs. Donavon had never seen him so spooked. Even as a badger-ravaged pup clinging to life, he had shown more fight than this. Nightmare or not, the sight was downright unnatural. To make the moment all the more bizarre, Scraggs yelped and bolted off into the night.

Donavon's first thought was a bear. What else would terrify a wolf? Another wolf perhaps, or a mountain cat? Cautiously, he unholstered the flintlock pistol that Hoffman had given him. He aimed the barrel upwind into the cedars and pulled the lock two clicks back.

"All right, little kitty. Come and get your treat."

Something stirred in the grove. A shadowy figure strode into the light, tall as a bear but not as wide. It was human. A man covered in pelts with a pack. He walked directly toward the remains of the goat.

"Drop that gun!" Donavon ordered. "Or I'll drop it for you."

The musketman turned to face Donavon, his eyes cold and black in the firelight. "I don't think Musket would like that."

"What?"

"My gun. It does not like to be dropped."

"Hold it right there, funny man. You got three seconds to make it happen if you want to live."

The stranger's eyes blinked in rapid succession. Then, he lowered the musket and began to sing.

There's a rabbit in the Pass
Yes there is, yes there is
Bleeding in the grass
Yes it is, yes it is

A wolf is in the wood
Yes it—

"That's it!" Donavon yelled, cutting him off at the verse. "I said I'm gonna drop you, and I mean it."

"My apologies," the musketman said. "I can't help it when there's a gun pointed at me."

"That's the craziest thing I've ever heard. You better start talking straight or you're a dead man. What are you doing here?"

"I'm patrolling the mountain. I saw your fire."

Donavon looked him up and down. He was a young man with a mustache, about Adman's age. He wore a combat pack, similar to Hoffman's from what he could make of it under the pelts. Something sparkled in the firelight over the visor of his cap—three crossed stalks of the mountain flower.

"You fight for the Guard?" Donavon asked.

"I do. My brothers await my return at the pass."

"What pass?"

"Spaulding."

"Nobody goes there. What are you doing here in Gwyntahlynn?"

"I told you, I'm patrolling the mountain. I'm hungry. May I have some of that treat you promised?"

The question caught Donavon off guard, prompting questions of his own. Who was this man? What were his intentions? Why hadn't he simply sniped him and Scraggs from the cedars? It would have been an easy kill. There was plenty of goat, he decided, so feeding him seemed fair enough.

"Fine, but the gun stays on my side of the fire."

The soldier handed over his musket, stock first. "If that is your wish."

"Have at it," he said, pointing to the kill and moving back to his spot by the fire. From there he watched the soldier shed his pelt-covered pack and go about his task. He was good with a knife, obviously a man well-practiced at life in the wild. Donavon holstered his pistol and held the musket in both hands. It was sturdy and light, Toricean made by the look and feel of it. He sat down, resting it on his lap. A name was engraved in the polished brass stock—Gen Simon Harthmocker.

"Fancy gun," he said as the musketman approached the fire with strips of raw goat on a stick. "How'd you get it?"

"It was given to me."

"Let me guess. Simon Harthmocker?"

"No, that was the first owner. Colonel Mitterhal was the second."

"Mitterhal? When did he give it to you?"

"At the pass."

Donavon eyed him suspiciously. "That was ten years ago. You would have been just a kid."

"I was a herald bearer for the infantry. This goat was young. The meat cuts easy. The last time I had wild goat was—"

"Why did he give you his musket?" Donavon asked.

"I don't know, he just did. I insisted on holding the first line with my brothers. I think that had something to do with it. It's not easy to track a wild goat on the mountain. How many shots did it take?"

Donavon ignored the soldier's digression. "The same brothers who await you at the pass?"

"Yes. I bring them tidings every year, keep them informed on what goes on in the Haven. They are very concerned about the plans to rebuild the bridge. I shot my first goat on the east ridge after the battle. I didn't kill it in the first shot."

"How long have they been there?"

"Since the battle. I don't like killing them. They are wise to our ways. I stick to rabbits now."

"No, not the goats, your brothers."

"They never left."

"The war is over," Donavon said. "Why would they stay?"

"They sing war hymns for the army."

"What army?"

"The army that comes every spring and fall."

From across the fire the soldier stared with a washed-out gaze at his musket in Donavon's hands. "You're right, I almost forgot," he said, appearing to address the gun. He propped the spit of meat over the coals and disappeared into the flickering meadow grass. Minutes later he returned with an armful of lupine stalks, which he promptly scattered on the fire. A pungent cloud encased the meat and blew toward Donavon.

"What do you think you're doing?" Donavon said in alarm. "It's fall. The wulfweed has gone to seed!"

"No worries, comrade," the soldier said. "I cook with it all the time at the pass, even in the fall. It's a great way to flavor the meat. My brothers love it. It gets them singing. Sometimes the entire army will join us in song. Very uplifting."

The breeze shifted, and Donavon held his breath. There was something profoundly insane about the man, yet at the same time genuine. Similar to the colonel, at least in that respect. No surprise he spent his days cooking with gahenya in the wild. Another shift; the smoke cleared. Donavon stole a breath of semifresh air.

"You think I'm crazy," the soldier said, taking hold of the spit. "That there is no army." He held the meat where the smoke was thickest. The aroma was captivating.

Donavon considered speaking his mind. To let the war-torn soldier know it was more than his imaginary army that made him seem crazy. But the smoke shifted yet again, and he took in half a lung of it before he could get out a word.

The soldier removed a strip of goat from the stick and took a bite. "It takes a lot to kill you, you know," he said between chews. "The smoke, that is. A passing whiff will do no harm. In fact, it will help you focus on the music."

"What music?" Donavon asked, risking another breath.

"The command codes. It's what keeps us fighting as a unit. Without it, we'd be lost in the smoke."

Donavon swayed, smitten by a heady sensation—similar to drowning in the fountain in the clutches of the weirman. He rubbed his eyes. Something strange was happening. His fingers and toes tingled. He thought he smelled tar.

"Easy does it, comrade. Don't fight it."

The soldier's voice was different, higher in pitch. Donavon looked up. The smoke took shape. The great horned goat on the colonel's pipe suddenly came into being, like a giant apparition suspended over the fire. Then the wolf. It was Scraggs, only as a tiny pup, blood dripping from its lacerated tongue.

"That's it, you're doing fine," the soldier said.

Above the smoke Donavon saw the tablet of tavern rules hanging from the crescent moon. Beyond that, the sheriff's hat spun like a saucer through the stars. "What's going on?"

"You've got the sight."

"What sight? All I see is—"

Pipes sounded from high up on the ridge. He recognized the melody at once. It was the same tune the attractive young flutist had played at the fountain before the weirmen showed up. Donavon looked at the soldier, and to his utter astonishment saw that he had lost his mustache.

"Can I have my gun back?" the soldier boy asked. "My father is calling.

I need to get back with my brothers right away."

"What's going on here? You're just a kid. Where did these bales come from? They stink."

"They've been saturated in tar. I really have to go. The bear is coming. I need my gun. We have to draw them into the smoke."

The apparition of the goat disappeared. Donavon tossed the musket over the fire, compelled by the boy's urgency. Catching it, the soldier loaded it with uncanny efficiency. The slug, the powder, the ramrod; it all happened in seconds. He then mounted a bayonet to the end of the barrel, spinning it tight to the threads as he sped off into the field.

"Thank you for the treat, comrade." he shouted out of the pungent mist. "Hail, Gahenya!"

The music stopped. Long Donavon stood by the fire, alone, staring at the moon. The sky above was clear but a low-lying fog masked the land about him. No, not fog. Smoke, lots of it. Bales of gahenya smoldered on all sides. Where was he? His bearings were shot. It felt like a dream, only dreadfully real. Then he heard it, approaching from the west. Hooves.

Through the smoke, the mist, the darkness they came. Fell men on horses, great in stature, their expressions dire and keen. Like rolling thunder they shook the scorched earth over which they galloped. Donavon braced for impact as they bore down with lowered spears. Yet the kill strike never came. They checked their steeds in the last instant and formed a circle around him—a ring of grim horsemen in a haze of spears. Steam blew out of the horses' nostrils, flaring in and out by the light of the blaze. Amazed to be alive, Donavon assessed the riders that glared at him. Soft hearts they certainly were not, but why had they spared him? Then he saw it, etched in silver on the crowns of their cavalry helms. Three crossed stalks of the mountain flower—horsemen of the Guard.

The ring parted, and through the opening came a lone rider without shield or spear. A brass-handled saber hung from his hip. He bore a whip in his hand, like a serpent's tail, and a corselet of bronze wrapped his torso. On his head was an officer's hat, distinct from the other war helms. His fierce gaze burned under its brim. He looked at the carcass of the goat, then the fire, then back to Donavon. He cracked the whip. "State your name!"

"I am Donavon McFadden, son of the One Talon."

"That is a bold claim. Prove it."

The colonel's cane lesson came to mind. "No," he said without hesitation.

The horseman's eyes narrowed. "What did you say?"

"I prove nothing to no one." He looked straight into the burning eyes. "If you were going to kill me, I would already be dead."

The eyes cooled. The horseman's hearty laugh split the night as he looked up at the moon. "Thank you, Great Father," he said, coiling his whip and hooking it to his saddle. He addressed the rider to his right. "I told you he'd have a good sense of humor. Spear!"

The man tossed him the spear, which the officer caught halfway through his dismount. As he reached the ground, Donavon realized the officer had only one complete leg. The left ended at the knee. He loped to the fire using the spear as a crutch and stopped directly in front of Donavon. Then to Donavon's astonishment, the warrior threw down his spear and hugged him.

Donavon was seven years old when the war ended. There was not much he remembered of his father, only vague impressions left by short visits between battles. The missing leg he did remember, along with the red stubble on his chin, and perhaps the voice, if he really thought about it. But far and away the clearest memory was the power he felt in his father's embrace when he returned from his battles on his warhorse.

"Look at you," the horseman said, still clutching Donavon by the shoulders. Pride welled in his eyes. "Look at what you've become. How is your sister?"

"Enya is fine, Father."

"And your brothers?"

"The same."

"Good. He kept his promise then."

"Who kept his promise?"

A single pipe sounded in the darkness from somewhere high and distant. The drone snapped the horseman out of his muse. "Our time is limited, son. The wulfweed burns. We must be quick."

"Father, where are we? This feels like a dream."

"It is, my boy. You are on the Mountain."

"So it's only a dream?"

"If that's what you think."

"I don't know what I think."

"Listen to me, Donavon. Know that I am proud of you, dream or not. Priests and shamans, dreamers and thinkers. They'll all have you spinning circles around yourself if you let them. Trust in who you are. That is real. Believe what you see and you will see what you believe."

Another pipe sounded and then another in eerie harmony. Uryan picked up his spear and tossed it to the other soldier. Back in the saddle, he turned his fierce gaze on the horsemen. "The smoke has settled," he shouted. "The pipers call from the east. Prepare to ride!"

"Father, when will I see you again?"

"Look to the mountain goats, Donny. They will guide the way." He unhooked his whip and cracked it high. "To the Haven's coast, men. Sing your song. Hail, Gahenya!"

242

"*Maha Gaila!*" they shouted in return, spurred by the whip.

The one-legged horseman flipped around his officer's hat and set it backward on his head. "One more thing, Donny," he said before speeding off at a gallop. "Next time you see the Hoof, tell him we said thanks for the laugh. *Egrahc!*"

Black smoke rolled in and shut out the sky.

"*Har geshank al guntoc!*"

Donavon turned over with a splitting headache. Something jabbed him in the gut. It felt like a stick. He opened his eyes and focused on the sharp end of a spear, only inches from his face. "*Har geshank al guntoc!*" he heard again. The sun was up; he rubbed his eyes. Was it still a dream? His forehead pounded. That was real. More spears, all pointing at him. Behind each spear was a painted face, fierce and foreboding. Whatever they were trying to convey, it was not good morning.

One of the men held up a rabbit pelt he'd found by the cold ashes of last night's fire. Another rummaged through the combat pack.

"Leave that alone!" Donavon said.

The spears came closer. A young face with black stripes loomed over him. "*Har geshank al guntoc!*" he repeated, and kicked Donavon hard in the leg.

Donavon got up. Seven Gwyntah he counted, all armed. An impossible fight. He looked beyond them. No sign of Scraggs anywhere. The one who delivered the kick eyed him viciously. "*Sach a yam!*"

Those words he knew. "I am Donavon McFadden. I seek council with the Gwyntahpynn," he said, eye to eye.

An older man stepped forward. His face had no paint, but was half riddled with burns. Scar tissue extended from the right side of his head, down his neck to his arm, as if he had been dipped in a caldron of boiling oil. His right hand was nothing but a melted, fingerless stump. He raised the stump and the young stripe-faced warrior backed off. He then interrogated Donavon with his eyes. After a lengthy scan, he voiced a command to the warrior who had been rummaging through the combat pack. The warrior stepped forward with Donavon's canteen.

Donavon grabbed it. His throat was parched, and the water felt good going down. The scarred warrior then nodded to the striped-face one, who tethered Donavon's hands and shoved him forward. Apparently, that was to be the extent of their compassion. No further words were exchanged, though Donavon got the distinct impression he was in for a long walk.

14

Into the Ring

Of all the natural splendors of Lakwynnia, none surpassed the majesty of the Awshaw Mountains in Gwyntahlynn. The Great Ring it was called. The dormant volcanic range was indeed great, as it was circular. Perfectly so, in fact. The heavenly perimeter was ever crowned in white and fed myriads of streams that emptied into a vast, pristine plain of forests and pastures. The diameter between any two points of the Ring's perimeter stretched for leagues and could be crossed by foot in four days, but only by the swiftest Gwyntah scouts with knowledge of the trails. Few Toriceans ever set foot within the realm, for the mountains were sheer and, in spite of their beauty, offered no easy way in. Likewise, there was no easy way out, even for those who had been granted the rare privilege of a visit by the tribes. And so the Great Ring remained the home of the Gwyntahmahoma: pristine in isolation, pure in splendor, unconquered by the pioneer spirit.

Donavon's captors stopped at the base of a steep spur. They had been hiking all morning, breaking only for water. Donavon looked beyond the bluff to the high peaks where he guessed the warriors were taking him. The long slog had played on his thoughts. The Old Mitt was right. No doubt it was going to get cold where he was going. He had never hiked the Awshaws before, though not a day had passed since the big dustup at the fountain pool in Wulfhaven that his eyes were not drawn to the ashen slopes that loomed over the harbor's west bank. Growing up in the highlands, he had often wondered what mysteries lay beyond the mountains. Now, by point of spear he would find out.

A spring bubbled from a crevice in the rocks near the spot where they had stopped. Donavon was unfettered and allowed to rest by the clear pool. Exhausted, he filled his canteen. The bite of the cold mountain water on his face sharpened his senses. The wind shifted. He caught a whiff from above and looked up. Upwind on a boulder only an arrow shot away stood Scraggs, ears up, still as stone.

"*Wulf!*" one of the warriors called.

The stripe-faced Gwyntah drew back his bow and took aim.

"No!" Donavon shouted, hurling his canteen at the bowman. The spray of water was just enough to send his shot off mark. The arrow bounced off the bluff and Scraggs disappeared.

The warrior threw down his bow and lunged at Donavon. The attack came quickly but Donavon countered by driving his shoulder into the warrior's midsection. They grappled in the gravel by the edge of the stream until the older Gwyntah with the scars broke it up.

"*Nish hayem!*" he commanded, threatening both with a curved blade mounted on his wrist. He added harsh words to the striped Gwyntah, who released his death hold on Donavon's neck and walked away in shame.

The scar chief, not at all pleased, shouted another command and the party quickly made ready to leave. Donavon's combat pack was returned to him, minus the weapons, and he was pushed forward once again, though his hands were left unbound. A good thing, as it turned out. The hike became steep and precarious as they headed straight for the snowfields.

The afternoon slogged on without event. The snowfields were deceptively far. Donavon passed the time by coming up with names for his captors. Scarchief he christened for obvious reasons; Stripes, Blue, and Nosebleed for the patterns of war paint on their faces. The one who scouted ahead he named Tiptoe, and Pickpack was the warrior who had rummaged through his combat pack. Lastly, there was Notalk. He never said a word, though his watchful eye never strayed.

They reached a circular stone structure early in the evening, tucked away in a dell of highland scrub at the fringe of the snowfields. Windowless, the yurt sprouted out of the mountain like a mushroom. The lichen-covered door faced east and a sweeping view of the harbor. One by one the warriors entered, except for Notalk who remained outside with Donavon. Smoke soon rose from a flue in the top of the dome. Donavon removed his pack. He could see the sun glistening off the cathedral in Wulfhaven, the steeple burning like a tiny candle flame. How odd to see it from this side of the Haven.

The door to the yurt opened. Notalk gestured for Donavon to enter. Inside, he leaned his pack against the stone interior. The entire party sat cross-legged around a small crackling fire in the center. Animal hides lined the floor and walls. A cozy night, Donavon thought as he assessed the primitive arrangement. Space would be limited for sure.

Scarchief grunted something and pointed to a tight spot between Blue and Nosebleed. Donavon got the hint and squeezed in by the fire. They passed him a small portion of bread and a clay cup filled with water.

"This is what you guys eat?" he asked, taking a bite. "How do you climb mountains with this?" He looked about. All eyes were on him, steady and still. Nobody said a word. He shrugged at the one-way dialogue. "Some of that goat meat would sure do good about now."

"*Tuft*," the chief said.

"Yeah, that's right, goat," Donavon said. "It would be good right now."

"*Gnish tuft*," Pickpack added from across the ring.

Donavon took a swig from the cup to wash down the bread. "Yeah, good goat," he repeated. That was the extent of the conversation.

A bowl was passed around with a thick pasty substance in it. Each man took a big scoop and smeared it on their bread. Donavon sniffed the bitter mass. It was lupini made from the processed bean of the gahenya plant. The scent took him back to the great drought, when crops had failed in the Haven and everybody in the village was forced to eat the stuff. Fortunately, even as a child Enyalda had figured out a way to spice it up. The memory of his sister made him sigh.

The warriors sat long in silence, chewing on lupini and bread, when at last Pickpack emptied the contents of the small wooden box in front of him. Three carved figurines fell out, two goats and one wolf. The goats were half white and half black, the wolf all black.

"Hey, that's mine," Donavon said, recognizing them at once. They were the bone figurines Muma had given him as a child. He and Enyalda had made up a game with them to pass the time on cold winter nights. "My weapons are one thing," he said, holding out his hand, "but those have sentiment. Hand it over."

Pickpack looked to Scarchief, who nodded consent. The figurines were passed around the ring and returned to Donavon. Grateful to have them back, he obliged the chief in his own language, remembering the words Muma had taught him long ago. "*Su gahwynn*," he said, putting the figurines back into the box.

The warriors continued chewing slowly on their bread. Donavon was impressed at how still they remained. Great hunters they would make, for sure. Yet one thing they all seemed to lack was a sense of humor. Having nothing better to do, he decided to test it. He opened the lid of his box and removed the three figurines. Like dice he shook them in his hands and cast them back into the box. Both goats landed on their sides, white side up, untouched by the wolf. "Two white goats. That's a drink for me, tavern rules," he said, bringing the cup of water to his lips. "Who else is in?"

Nothing but blank stares.

"Come on. You scrappers seem like the adventurous type. Who's next?"

Nothing.

He shrugged and rolled again. One goat landed on its feet, the other white side down and touching the wolf. "Too bad. That would have been an ale for all of us if the wolf wasn't touching the goat. I guess it's just me." He took another swig from the cup.

The warrior to his right with the red paint under his nose did the same.

"Hold it right there, Nosebleed. That's a foul. You'd be buying everybody at the table drinks for that. I'll let it go this time since you're new to the game. Here, take this." Donavon handed over the figurines and placed the box in front of him. "Give it a shot."

The puzzled warrior looked to his chief, who made an ever so subtle nod of consent.

Nosebleed dropped the dice into the box. One goat stood on its feet touching the backside of the downed wolf.

"Well, I'll be a herdsman's bride," Donavon said, raising his mug high. "That right there we call a holy hump. Beginner's luck. We all drink to that!"

Nobody moved.

"Come on." Donavon looked to Scarchief. "You don't have to play, but you can still drink. What else we gonna do besides sit around and stare at each other?"

Shadows flickered on the charred side of the war chief's face, his guarded eyes locked on Donavon's. Slowly he raised his mug and brought it to his unsmiling lips. The other warriors did the same.

"Now we've got ourselves a party," Donavon said, slapping his knees. "All right, Nosebleed, pass the box to Notalk."

The game went on long into the night. The warriors caught on quickly in spite of the language gap. Donavon was surprised at how many Gwyntah words he actually knew when put to it. Scarchief refused to roll the bones, but partook in the drinking when prompted. The highlight of the night came when Tiptoe rolled a Happy Haven. All three figurines landed on their feet, and Donavon had every one of his captors exchange cups with each other to commemorate the rare event.

When at last the game ended, the Gwyntah settled in for the night. All the warriors left the yurt to empty their bladders under the stars. Donavon was last to leave. Before going back in he reached under his shirt and removed a loaf of bread he had swiped from Pickpack's satchel. He tossed the bread near the area where he had relieved himself. Back in the yurt he stretched out on a goatskin and wrapped himself in pelts. Sleep came fast as his last thoughts drifted to Scraggs.

The Gwyntah were far less pushy in the morning. They went about their business, hardly glancing at Donavon. When it came time to leave, Pickpack handed Donavon his hunting knife along with his bow and quiver of arrows, though the flintlock pistol was not returned. Before leaving, Donavon scanned the ground where he had tossed the bread. The loaf was gone—not a crumb.

They left the scrub and ascended the snowfield on a footpath well worn by traffic. Donavon was thankful for the boots Adman had given him prior to leaving the village. As bullheaded as his brother could be, he never slacked on practical details. Donavon almost missed him. Sort of.

They climbed through the morning and into the afternoon, drenched in sun. Donavon kept his eyes on his black boots to help fight the glare. They stopped at a sheer cliff that towered over the snowfield. A great crack split the face as if a giant blade had fallen from the sky and cleaved the mountain peak in two. The trail led directly into the chasm. Before entering, Tiptoe hailed the attention of the others from an outcrop of ledge and pointed downslope. Donavon squinted, allowing time for his vision to adjust in the glare. Far below, a tiny gray dot prowled upward through the white. He turned around, sensing a challenge. Sure enough, the fierce eyes of Stripes were on him. Then for reasons he didn't entirely understand, Donavon growled.

"*Nosh hayem!*" Scarchief shouted at Stripes. He then gestured all to enter the chasm.

In they went, Stripes first, followed by Blue. Icy silver glistened on sheer walls, deep into the gulch on jagged rock. Prisms of splintered light spilled in from high above and filtered through the ice. They hiked down and into the void where the crevice widened. The cavern sparkled like something out of a dream. Donavon marveled. The space was vast, as wide as a barn was long, and extended farther than the eye could see. A web of subterranean springs seeped out of the strata and trickled down the heights. The water fed a stream at the base of the chasm that flowed gradually downward into the depths.

They followed the stream for some time until it cascaded over a shelf of rock and into the shadows. Another stone yurt cropped out of ledge on the near side of the falls. Across the stream on a higher shelf, carved into the cavern wall, was a shrine of some sort. The outstretched wings of a great bird delineated the sides of the sanctum. Centered in the concave space stood life-sized statues of a king and queen, an infant cradled in their arms. Stripes leaped over the stream while the others made ready to camp at the yurt.

Donavon was content to call it a day. He took off his boots and rubbed the hot spots on his ankles. Doing so, he noticed Stripes on his knees at the base of the shrine, chanting by the talons of the great bird.

No bones were rolled that evening. The warriors said not a word amongst themselves. They spoke only in prayer, kneeling reverently before the king and queen across the stream. One by one they paid their respects, always alone. Donavon leaned against the outside of the yurt and listened to them chant their prayers while he sliced at his badger pelt with his hunting knife. As light from above dimmed, he gazed up into the chasm. Somewhere beyond the ice, the sun was setting. Night closed in and he fell asleep where he sat, next to the yurt in utter blackness.

Donavon awoke to the sound of Nosebleed slurping at the stream. It was dawn in the chasm, or so he guessed. The dim light had an icy blue tint. A thick blanket of felt had been draped over him at some point in the night. Notalk stood above him, assessing the shredded badger skin at his feet. Donavon got up quickly, ashamed at being caught off guard. Notalk handed him a slice of lupini-smeared bread and took the blanket back into the yurt. He ate the bread before cleaning out his belt pouch and packing it tight with the strips of badger fur.

The warriors were soon ready to leave. All except Tiptoe, who was nowhere to be found. He had been absent all morning, in fact. They hiked in single file, Stripes in the lead holding a torch, followed by Blue, Nosebleed, Scarchief, and Pickpack. Donavon was next, trailed by Notalk, who also carried a torch. At the base of the waterfall they entered a lightless passage that diverged from the stream and twisted down a sharp decent. They hiked for what seemed like hours, the air getting warmer the farther down they went. At times the passage widened into a vast cavern etched in veins of silver. Other times it became so narrow, Donavon could touch both sides with his hands. Every so often they came to a chamber where several passageways joined and the damp stale air stirred. Donavon put extra care into marking these junctions with the strips of badger fur he had packed in his belt pouch.

Eventually the passage leveled off into a vast hall with many recesses cut into the rock. Within each recess was a stone-carved rendering of a wild creature, from the common shrew right up to the mighty ibex. The air was fresh, like an autumn wind. Torches flickered along the walls. At the far end of the hall, Donavon detected the faint glow of sunlight.

They made straight for the light. Halfway across the hall, Pickpack stopped and turned around to nudge Donavon in the shoulder with the blunt end of his spear. "Goot gohht," he said pointing to the horned head of a mountain goat in the wall.

"Yeah, good goat," Donavon replied, amused at Pickpack's attempt at Toricean. That was the extent of the exchange, though for the first time since joining the group, he thought he detected a smile.

From there they proceeded to a towering archway through which streamed the sun. They stepped out onto a wide granite ledge. Speechless, Donavon stopped and squinted into a vast green vale encircled by mountains that touched the clouds. He shielded his eyes with his hands to better scan the wonder of the Awshaws. Woodland glades of every shape and size mingled with cloud-shadowed pastures of the greenest green. The land was etched in a web of ponds and streams fed by the high glens of the surrounding range. *Here at last*, Donavon thought. Inside the Great Ring of the Awshaw Mountains.

They did not linger on the ledge. Another archway, strikingly similar to the one in Wulfhaven Square, abutted the sheer rock to the left of the shelf. It marked the terminus of a long set of precipitous steps hewn into the face of the mountain. Long the treads had been there, by the look of their weather-worn edges. The steps descended several hundred feet into a dark forest of old-growth hemlocks. At the bottom, the party walked a trail of flattened stones set in a boreal carpet of moss. Donavon saw smoke through the trees.

They led him to an open glade, where a great host of warriors had gathered around a ring of monolithic stones. Through the center of the ring ran two lines of wooden poles set upright in the ground. Each pole was as wide as a tree and two horse lengths high. Many faces, some human, some not, had been carved into the poles. He walked the aisle of totems escorted by his captors. At the far end of the aisle, where the poles ended, sat an elderly man in a throne surrounded by banners of animal skins. The throne was carved out of an enormous root burl with the antlers of a bull elk mounted on the top. Scarchief stopped, and all in the party knelt before the throne. Pickpack nudged Donavon in the back with his spear, prodding him to do the same.

So this was the famed Choroqua, Donavon surmised, kneeling before the throne. He was old indeed, just like the tales told. To the right of the high chief stood Tiptoe, stiff as a totem, spear in hand. To the left were two masked Gwyntah draped in fur. The old man remained seated on his throne and raised his staff. He waited for all to rise before he spoke. Donavon did not understand a word he said, but Scarchief approached the throne with what appeared to be a rabbit pelt in his hand. More tribe-talk transpired, and Notalk suddenly turned to face Donavon.

"Gwyntahpynn Choroqua now speak with you," said the expressionless warrior. "I serve as your translator."

"Notalk!" Donavon said, stunned. "You never told me you spoke Toricean."

"You never ask."

Donavon turned to the Gwyntahpynn, thinking to get right to business. "I am Donavon McFadden. I seek—"

Choroqua raised his staff and spoke harshly. Notalk ran the translation. "Gwyntahpynn knows who you are and why you are here. Do not speak unless spoken to."

Not a good start, Donavon thought. Scarchief handed Choroqua the pelt. More tribe talk followed. Notalk listened closely, then turned to Donavon. "This skin found at your camp over mines. It is fresh and taken from rabbit. Yet it is a spring pelt and now it is late autumn. Gwyntahpynn demands an explanation."

"It is not my pelt," Donavon said, seeing it for the first time.

"If not your pelt, then why you have it?"

"I don't know."

More tribe talk ensued.

"Gwyntahpynn say you do know and if you not tell, he will order your head severed from body."

"I told you, I don't know," Donavon said, spurred by the threat. "I saw a soldier in a dream, covered with pelts. Maybe it's his. Let me take a nap and I'll ask him."

Notalk nodded and conveyed Donavon's answer, albeit somewhat abridged.

The Gwyntahpynn turned to Scarchief, who nodded in acknowledgment. "Huru Shakein," he stated.

"What does that mean?" Donavon asked Notalk.

"It mean Talking Gun. Gwyntahpynn ask if soldier you meet in dream is boy or man."

Donavon looked directly into the eyes of the high chief. "Both," he said without hesitation.

The eyes widened. Donavon looked into them and could feel the mind of Choroqua at work. The colonel's briefing came to mind. He needed an image, something on which to focus his sight. Nothing came.

Notalk spoke again. "Gwyntahpynn ask to know more about one-eyed wolf that follow you here."

Donavon's jaw clenched. How did he know Scraggs had only one eye? Blood pulsed hard through his veins. "I don't know what he's talking about."

"Then you no mind if scouts claim wolf power in temple?"

Donavon glared at Notalk. "What does that mean?"

"The pelt of wolf give great protection and power to lead. It is sacred prize among warriors."

A snarl escaped his lips. "How do I say do not kill the wolf?"

"Nobody tells Gwyntahpynn what to do."

"Just tell me!"

"*Ni wulf nahun*," Notalk whispered.

Again Donavon looked into the eyes of Choroqua. Like portals to another world they widened, and as Donavon looked through them he imagined a horned goat on the other side, fierce and unyielding, ready to charge. Below it, a one-eyed wolf pup. Music sounded in the distance; the same tune that rallied the horsemen in his dream. "*Ni wulf nahun*," he said, cold and steady.

The music got louder and drowned out the tribe talk. The Gwyntahpynn's words melted into muffled echoes. The black rhombus pupils of the goat vision sharpened. "*Ni wulf nahun,*" Donavon repeated.

More words, more muffles, more music.

"*Ni wulf nahun!*"

Silence. The goat vanished along with the wolf. Lots of tribe talk, then hands on his arms. The portals closed. The high chief of the Gwyntah stood up from his throne and announced his sentence. "*Nahuntah guntoc.*"

Donavon tried to yank his arms free, but the two masked Gwyntah held fast. He looked to Notalk, who stood somber by his side. "What's going on? What did he say?"

"You are to be executed for your insolence. Death by talon."

The masked Gwyntah stripped Donavon of his pack and weapons, and then dragged him to a platform between two totems. There they tethered his hands to ropes that were looped around two adjacent poles. The ropes were pulled tight in their loops and his arms went up, straight out to either side.

Donavon snarled at Notalk like a caged beast. "Tell your great chief that I piss on his justice. He is just as mad as the man who sent me here!"

"You should not have made challenge, son of McFadden. Gwyntahpynn Choraqua grants you a warrior's death, quick and painless." Notalk bowed low and stepped aside. "It has been my honor to serve you."

Drums boomed from somewhere behind. Scarchief stepped onto the platform, his expression grim and fierce. He held up both arms to Donavon's neck. Mounted on each wrist was a blade that curved over his knuckles. The beat thumped in synch with Donavon's heart. The tempo quickened. At last, when it seemed the pace could race no more, Pickpack cried out like a howling wolf and knelt before the throne. The drums stopped instantly. Deathly silence fell over the circle.

"What's going on?" Donavon asked Notalk.

"Shuhocra, the one you call Pickpack, ask Gwyntahpynn to reconsider judgment. He offer himself as substitute."

Blue then came forward and knelt next to Pickpack. Nosebleed did the same. Tiptoe stepped down from the high platform to join the group. Notalk turned to Donavon, his expression somber yet resolved.

"I must leave you now," he said with a respectful bow. He approached the throne and knelt next to Tiptoe.

Long Choraqua stood, his knife-sharp gaze slashing at the silent warriors. All the while, Donavon kept his eyes fixed on Scarchief, who still held the wrist blades to his throat. When at last Choraqua spoke, Scarchief's eyes softened, and he sliced at the binds with his blades. Donavon's arms collapsed.

Choroqua raised his staff and addressed the five warriors who knelt before him. They rose, and Notalk immediately returned to Donavon, a joy in his eyes.

"Gwyntahpynn grants you welcome to our land and hopes you join us at feast in your honor."

Donavon, removing the slipknots from his wrist, sighed in relief. "So I passed his test after all?"

"You did," Notalk said. "But this not your test. Yours was at sacred fountain when you fight for Great Mother. Gwyntahpynn never doubt your heart. It is we who he test."

"We? Who is we?"

"We are your pack. All who come forward will stand with you to death, and so he trust us now to run with you. We are bound until lake and sky become one."

"But I am not a Gwyntah warrior. I know nothing of your ways."

"You are wolf spirit sent by Mahocpynn. That is good enough. The rest we teach. In return you lead us to music."

All knelt as the Gwyntahpynn made ready to leave. He addressed Donavon from the throne before disappearing behind the banners of skins.

"What did he say?" Donavon asked Notalk after the high chief left.

Notalk got up from his knees. "He say your one-eyed friend also invited."

15

The Tale of Two Words

As told by the fountain lady to the children of Wulfhaven abbey:

In the beginning there were two words. They were nice words. Words that when put together carried tremendous weight, yet at the same time could be as light as a single flower petal in a mother's garden, or as subtle as a father's whisper on the wind. The words did a wonderful job at summarizing an age-old sentiment.

As time went on, however, it became evident that the two words, in all their delicate majesty, needed help and, on occasion, protection. To this purpose a school was founded in which more words were fashioned—words like Love, Honor, Reverence, Devotion. Out of these words came more words, and so on and so forth until an entire language was born and the school flourished.

Those who learned the language prospered, and through it many things were said. Those who stayed true to the school's founding principles were blessed with good manners. In this way the first two words remained intact and to this day still appear in their unspoiled form. Su gahwynn—Thank you.

Chief Constable Heinrick von Krutzwig stood rigid on the wharf. To his right, Captain Hans Rueger; to his left the mayor, Captain Marlin Barleycopp. Behind the three stood the ranks of Pogetsa, ten rows of twenty. Behind them, the marching band. Ropes draped with ribbons had been set along the Promenade to keep the crowds at bay. A needless precaution, as it turned out. Only a scattering of curious bystanders lined the ropes. Most had congregated around the weavers' exhibit to watch the ladies work their looms.

A chill autumn wind flapped the flags high up on the masts of the

Lyssia. Krutzwig perspired nonetheless, spooked by the omniscient eyes of the silver girl mounted on the warship's prow. Dreadful she appeared to him. From the base of the ramp that attached wharf to ship, he scanned the rows of cannon turrets on her starboard side—an awesome display of firepower. Clammy sweat drenched his formal attire. General Rankwall's visit did not bode well; recent events had seen to that. The question still remained to what extent the chancellor would express his displeasure—and who would be the first to feel it. The thought was sobering.

The gin Krutzwig had gulped just prior to leaving his office had lost its punch. How could things have gone so wrong? The parish vote was a terrible blow. Compounded to that were the cries of outrage that pummeled his office at the arrest of Duncan Jacks and the other two inbred war cronies. Even proponents of the bridge were appalled. Why had he not been informed that the lead suspect had no legs?

A horn sounded off the galleon's uppermost deck, and the chancellor stepped onto the ramp surrounded by his entourage of armed guards. Krutzwig snapped both of his legs together at the ankles and held a salute, more conscious than ever of the sweat under his arms. The ranks of Pogetsa followed suit, led by Captain Rueger.

After an awkward delay, the marching band began. One of the tubas lumped clumsily out of tune and the snare drums rapped a half beat off. Krutzwig glanced at Barleycopp in his sparkling war regalia, holding his hollow salute and suspiciously unfazed by the mediocrity of the music. Captain of the goat-hyde pipers, they called him. Where were his famous pipers now?

They stood at attention until Rankwall stepped off the ramp. Barleycopp was the first to receive him. "On behalf of the good people of Wulfhaven," the mayor said, stepping forward, "I bid you welcome, Chancellor. And trust your stay in the Haven will be a fruitful one."

Krutzwig held his tongue, barely able to conceal his disgust. Fruitful? The mayor's pretentious show of civility was nothing short of contempt. Did he really think his forced formality would go unnoticed? For so long Barleycopp had managed to mask his loyalty. It was only a matter of time before he slipped. And when he did, Krutzwig vowed to be there, to strip the war hero of his medals and toss his haughty epaulettes off the gallows. Until that day, he would bide his time and play the game.

Rankwall peered down the Promenade at the lukewarm reception. "A fruitful stay indeed, Mayor," he said, teeth tightly clenched behind a stiff smile. "Such a splendid time of year to enjoy the Haven. I look forward to seeing what it has to offer." He looked to Barleycopp's left. "Captain Rueger, excellent to see you again. I trust you've been keeping the men in order."

"As always, sir."

"Good." He turned last to Krutzwig. "Constable, I have been looking

255

forward to our conversation. Perhaps you and Captain Rueger would join me at Pogetsa headquarters after the festivities to discuss a few small matters of policy."

"Of course, sir," Krutzwig said, not at all thrilled at the prospect. The band stumbled on, and Krutzwig resisted the sudden urge to arrest the tuba player.

Pogetsa headquarters bustled with salutes as Thurman Rankwall marched through the main lobby, flanked by Krutzwig and Captain Rueger. Together they went up the stairs and made straight for the chief constable's private office.

The door slammed shut along with the chancellor's smile. "Let us get right to point, Krutzwig. Beside the fact that you have single-handedly undermined our relations in the Haven, are there any other blatant demonstrations of your incompetence that I need to be made aware?"

"None, sir. Only that I assure you we are doing everything necessary to counter these untimely setbacks. In fact, I have already—"

"Said too much," the chancellor interjected. "Your position is threadbare, Constable. I am not interested in your petty damage control. For the sake of your career, I suggest you stick to answering my questions."

"Of course, sir."

"First off, am I to understand that you have a legless war hero from the Haven Guard in your custody?"

"Yes, sir."

"And that it was during Poulakis's church service that you made the arrest?"

"Yes, sir, but you see we—"

"Shut up!" Rankwall looked to Rueger. "Explain, Captain."

Captain Rueger stepped forward. "We were threatened by insurgents of the Guard, sir, while making an arrest in the highlands. We received a tip that the ringleaders were planning to make a political statement at the church service. They are very elusive. It was a rare opportunity to apprehend them."

"Ringleaders? And at what point did you realize that one of these elusive ringleaders had no legs?"

"We never actually saw him, sir. The informant told us Duncan Jacks had fired the signal flares."

"I see, and who was the informant?"

"The tip was anonymous, sir."

"Anonymous. Yes, of course." Rankwall turned sharply to Krutzwig. "Allow me to give you a tip of my own, Constable. There is nothing that Mitterhal does that is not deliberate. These men were arrested by his design, plain and simple. And I will tell you something else. Madman or not, if you continue to underestimate him, he will have the entire Haven pecking at your authority like crows on carrion."

Krutzwig flinched at the metaphor. The break in eye contact drew his attention to the decanter of gin on the shelf. How he craved a slug.

Rankwall moved to the pegboard along the back wall where the engineer's damage report was posted. He stared at the five red circles on the sketch. "We have a serious problem, Constable. Thanks to your stupidity, many of our most influential constituents have withdrawn their support of the bridge effort until tensions have settled. We must get them back on board; convince them that the repair of the rail will bring stability to the province, not mayhem. First and foremost we must deal with the prisoners. Captain Rueger, you will have to take the fall."

"Sir?" Rueger said, incredulous.

"It is the only way. Tomorrow the prisoners will be released and you will make a formal statement that you acted independent of higher command and that Krutzwig had no prior knowledge of your intention to make the arrest. As such you will be demoted in rank and receive a public reprimand. Strictly semantic, of course."

"I was following orders, sir."

"I know that, Hans. But this is politics, not war. You are a good officer. You have the respect of the men and your authority will still be recognized within the ranks. However, I want you out of the public eye until further notice. Is that clear?"

Darkness hung heavy on Rueger. "It is clear, sir."

Rankwall turned back to Krutzwig. "Second, we must ease the worries of the people. I want Mitterhal invited to sit with us in the veranda as an honored guest at the opera. Grant him full military escort to and from the show."

"And if he does not accept, sir?" Krutzwig asked.

"He will. It is a challenge and he knows it. Oh yes, and one more thing. No more controversial arrests. Is that clear?"

"Most assuredly, sir."

"It better be. You've cost me a good captain. Any more mistakes and the next fall is yours."

The opera house was the pride and joy of Wulfhaven, a classic blend of Toricean ingenuity and art that exemplified the glory of the Haven's rich heritage. Magnificent in scope as well as design, it was built during the heyday of the rail, when expense had no limits, and droves of enthusiasts chugged in by the trainloads to applaud the grand productions. The auditorium was vast, providing enough seating for a small army. Tiers of balconies lined the perimeter, their ornate balustrades laced in silver. High above the imposing mezzanine loomed a veranda fit for an emperor. A heavenly terrace suspended in space, it had its own staircase and entrance and enough seating for six. Traditionally, the seats were reserved for the most esteemed patrons, though it was not uncommon—once Barleycopp became mayor—for well-mannered orphans to be granted the thrill.

Heinrick von Krutzwig had absolutely no interest in the arts. Nor did he have patience for the endless expenditures that went into sustaining them. Attending the opera was purely routine, like changing dirty socks. Normally his flask of gin made the ordeal in the veranda tolerable, though even he had the sense to refrain when in the presence of the chancellor. Thus, he stood outside the lobby of the opera house, surrounded by his armed staff, waiting for the arrival of the colonel, the mayor, and the chancellor, stone cold sober.

Barleycopp's famed Yellow Wagon was first to arrive, the team of plumed ponies driven by none other than Terrence Calhygan, the pipe-blowing scrunge that only days ago had been a prisoner. Krutzwig sneered at the chancellor's political pick. A squad of Pogetsa on horseback followed. The wagon rolled to a stop at the foot of the wide granite steps that led to the main entrance.

Calhygan dismounted and opened the golden door. Out stepped Thurman Rankwall, followed by the mayor. A polite clap seeped out of the sectioned area behind the ropes. Both the mayor and the chancellor ascended the steps while waving at the onlookers.

Krutzwig met them at the top of the steps, putting on his best airs. "Welcome, Chancellor. All is in order. The guards will escort us to the veranda."

Rankwall scanned the entry while still waving to the crowd. "Has Mitterhal arrived yet?"

"No, sir. He accepted our invitation but refused a military escort. We are not sure where he is at the moment."

A sudden shift in the crowd behind the ropes put an end to the mystery. A procession funneled out of a side street across the Promenade, led by a line of herdsmen, though they looked more like a band of thugs in their long hair and highland garb. Their demeanor alone was enough to part the masses that had gathered in the street. Behind them an enormous draught mule pulled a carriage, flanked on either side by more highlanders, mounted on stocky steeds. In the carriage sat the colonel himself with a pretty young woman. Her red bushy hair bobbed up and down as they bounced over the cobbles.

So this is the famous colonel whose going to peck at my authority, Krutzwig thought as they closed in on the opera house. He was old indeed, though not quite what he had expected. Maybe it was the alluring redhead who clung to his arm. Not bad for a crazy old buzzard.

The lowbrow herdsmen cast down the ropes and the crowd cleared. The draught mule snorted to a stop alongside the Yellow Wagon's team of plumed ponies. The driver of the carriage, a sizable young fellow, stepped down and opened the cab door. He offered his arm to assist, but quickly retracted when the old man's cane went up. The other highlanders dismounted and formed a line of escorts up the steps. When it seemed the charade could become no more audacious, the colonel's companion showered him with flower petals.

Standing beside the chancellor at the top of the steps, Krutzwig detected the uneasy shift in Rankwall. His jaw was tight and a vein on his forehead pronounced. Strange to see the chancellor so affected. The girl continued to toss her petals while the colonel labored upward, one step at a time with his cane.

Rankwall spoke first when Mitterhal and the girl got to the top. He made sure his voice carried into the crowd. "At last, Colonel, we meet at peacetime! Long overdue, I must say. What better way to enjoy the fruits of our victory than at an opera?"

Mitterhal barely acknowledged the chancellor before turning to Barleycopp. "Fruit, indeed," he said, still catching his breath from the climb.

The mayor stepped forward and held a rigid salute. "On behalf of the good people of Wulfhaven, I bid you welcome, Colonel. Shall we proceed?"

The charade became even stranger in the lobby as they walked toward the staircase that led to the veranda. The redhead suddenly sprang into a dance, as if she were a ballerina practicing for the show. She swept around the spacious chamber, stopping only once at an oil painting of the baron, Augustus Mitterhal, mounted on the wall.

Krutzwig found her dazzling to look at, odd though she was. So slender and fluid and … Abruptly her dance ended in front of him. She flipped back her hair and pierced him with her ferret-like eyes. It was the last thing he expected. He stepped back, suddenly craving a drink. Vicious.

Again it was Barleycopp who defused the awkward moment. "To the veranda then, shall we? I've heard wonderful reviews of the play. A marvelous cast."

They proceeded to the stairwell entrance, accompanied by several highlanders who muscled their way alongside the Pogetsa. The colonel, too, paused at the grand portrait of his father. The chancellor began the long climb, followed by Krutzwig, then the mayor. Mitterhal took one step, stopped, and faltered for the next. His beefy chauffer moved in to assist. A ghastly thud echoed in the stairwell as the colonel's cane came down hard on the big highlander's head.

"I thought I told you to keep your hands to yourself! I won't be carried like a cripple. Get out of my way. We'll take the low seats."

Just like that the colonel was gone, the Pogetsa stepping aside to avoid his swinging cane. His escorts trailed behind him at a safe distance, back through the lobby to the auditorium.

Barleycopp shrugged and turned to Rankwall. "He's a stubborn one, sir. Shall we join him in the common seats or let him be?"

Obviously displeased at the turn of events, Rankwall closed his hand tight around the banister and proceeded upward to the veranda.

The first half of the play turned out to be a torturous bore. More so than usual, according to Krutzwig. First the marching band at the wharf and now this. He peered over the edge of the veranda, down to the front stalls where the sheep men had gathered. The colonel sat amid his crude company and watched the performance alongside his vicious little plaything. Finally the curtains closed and the audience politely applauded. Krutzwig fidgeted in his seat next to the chancellor, craving his gin.

Miss Annabelle Rafferty, an active member of the weaver's guild as well as housemother at the abbey orphanage, took the stage while the applause simmered. "Good evening, ladies and gentlemen, Mayor Barleycopp, Chancellor Rankwall, Constable Krutzwig." She gestured downward to the common seating. "And of course, Colonel Mitterhal. It is with sincere privilege that I present to you Wulfhaven's promising young talent. The children of the abbey have put together a wonderful skit to entertain us during intermission. They call it 'A Tale of Two Words.' Please sit back and enjoy."

She left the stage and the curtains opened, revealing a backdrop of a full moon illuminated by a table of dimly lit oil lamps. An adolescent boy entered the stage from the right and walked to the center, holding a staff, adorned as a king. From the left came a girl in a white gown and a crown of flowering vines. They met in the middle by the table of lamps.

"Who are you and what is your purpose?" the king asked the queen.

"I am the first word, but I do not know my purpose," she said.

The king leaned on his staff. "I thought I was the first word, but no matter. I too do not know my purpose."

"This is a beautiful place," said the queen. "Perhaps we should call it the Haven and learn our purpose together."

"An excellent idea," said the king, raising his staff.

The king and the queen lay down to sleep, and a baby's crib was rolled to center stage by a group of children dressed as sprites and pixies. They took the moon away and replaced it with a golden sun. More pixies appeared from under the table and turned up the lamps. When all was still, the king and queen awoke.

"What is this?" the king asked, looking to the crib.

"It is our child," the queen said. "Let us call it Love."

The king raised his staff. "An excellent idea."

Another girl appeared from the left side of stage. She walked to the crib and bowed before it.

"Who are you and what is your purpose?" the king asked.

"I have no name or purpose," the girl said, "but I love this child and I would do anything to watch it grow."

"Good," the queen said. "Then you may stay with us, for you already know our child's name. We shall call you Reverence."

The king's staff went up again. "An excellent idea."

The girl bowed low. "Thank you."

A boy appeared from the right side of stage, dressed as a knight in armor. Again, the king asked who he was and what was his purpose.

The knight knelt before the queen, saying he had no name or purpose, but sought to serve the just with love and reverence.

"Then seek no more," said the queen, "for your home is now in the Haven. We shall call you Honor."

Up went the staff. "An excellent idea."

"Thank you," said the knight.

A girl in a wedding gown appeared. She danced her way to the knight and embraced him. "I have no name or purpose either," she said to the king. "But I love this knight and I would do anything to see his honor served."

"Stay then," said the queen. "For his home is yours. We shall call you Devotion.

Devotion curtsied. "Thank you."

Next came two boys dressed as footmen and armed with muskets. The king ordered them to state their names and purpose.

"We are nameless brothers and know not our purpose, but would protect all who live with love, reverence, honor, and devotion."

"Then stay you may for you have good manners," said the queen. "We shall call you Courage and Conviction and pray you are never called to task."

"Thank you," said both soldiers, saluting.

A boy in a black robe and a bushy beard appeared, no doubt meant to be Poulakis. He walked over to the crib and lifted a swaddled bundle from inside.

The king raised his staff extra high, as if to strike. "How dare you approach our child!"

"Forgive me, Your Highness," the robed boy said to the king. "Like the others I have no name or purpose, only to tell you that the time is nigh for your child to rise. A school will be needed to teach her words."

The queen stepped in front of the king and put her hand on his staff. "Then to that you are trusted," she said, "for you alone have challenged our way. We will call you Wisdom."

The robed boy returned the bundle to the crib and bowed. "Thank you."

The pixies came out from under the table again and dimmed the lamps. A black hooded figure appeared from behind the curtain.

"Who are you and what is your purpose?" the king asked.

"I have many names," the shadow said, "none of which you would like. My purpose is to bring darkness into your garden."

All cowered except for the queen. "Then stay if you dare, for even light needs darkness to shine through. But expect not a warm welcome in the Haven, for you have bad manners."

Again the pixies surfaced and reduced the lamps to their lowest settings. A black cloth was draped over the sun. The king dropped his staff and left the stage with the queen. All cried in despair, except the two boys with the muskets who took aim on the shadow.

An adolescent girl suddenly rose out of the crib. "Stay your weapons!" she cried.

"Look!" Reverence shouted. "Love rises!"

The pixies turned up the lamps and took away the cloth, restoring the sun to its full splendor. The shadow cowered and retreated behind the curtain.

"The darkness is gone," Honor said, "but where are the first two words?"

"How will we ever find them again?" cried Devotion by his side.

"Speak the names of my parents and they will come," Love answered.

"But we do not know their names," said Courage and Conviction.

"That is not true," Wisdom said, picking up the staff that the king had dropped. "You have said it all along, each and every one of you."

The boy behind the curtain stepped out and pushed back his black hood. He put on an alpine hat with a large feather in its band and walked to front and center. The king and queen entered from either side of the stage and stood next to him, each carrying a sign they kept concealed from the audience. The rest of the young actors and actresses, including the sprites and pixies, joined hands in a line behind them that spanned the full length of the stage. The king and the queen then held up their signs as all in the line bowed to the audience. The two signs together read Thank You.

A wave of applause soaked the auditorium. As the clapping waned, the smaller of the two musket boys charged forward, pushing past the king and queen.

"Uli, what do you think you are doing?" the boy with the feather shouted.

The little musket boy stopped at the edge of the stage and saluted the common stalls. "Thank you, Colonel Cornelius, for protecting our home." His squeaky voice echoed in the silent hall.

High up on the veranda, Krutzwig heard Barleycopp take in a deep breath. A man stood up far below in the common seating. "Thank you, Colonel, for protecting our home," he said, saluting. Another stood up ten rows back and did the same. A well-dressed couple in the balcony across the auditorium followed suit. "Thank you, Colonel Mitterhal, for protecting our home." Next, a cello player in the pit stood up, followed by a clarinetist, then the entire orchestra. Throughout the auditorium people rose and repeated the musket boy's sentiment, until the entire audience was on its feet in a sustained round of applause. Never before had the walls of the opera house trembled with such praise. All the while Rankwall seethed in his seat until even he had no choice but to stand and join the ovation.

Barleycopp rose with the chancellor—a little too eagerly for Krutzwig's liking. That was when he saw it glistening in the lamplight. A single incriminating tear slipped down the mayor's cheek and slid into his handlebar mustache. Krutzwig grinned. At last, the mayor's loyalty exposed. The game was over.

The next morning fell hard on Heinrick von Krutzwig. He had hit the gin with extra vigor after the previous night's debacle at the opera. He paced his office to help tide the waves of nausea. Chadwick Glockstoff stood idly by his desk, waiting.

"Do not speak unless spoken to. Is that understood?" Krutzwig said.

"Yes, sir."

"Straight answers but no specifics. Got it?"

"Yes, sir."

"Fix your collar, it's bent."

"Yes, sir."

"Where the hell is he?"

"I don't know, sir."

"Shut up, I was not asking you."

"Yes, sir."

An hour later Thurman Rankwall entered the office alone, without knocking. The dark rings under his eyes suggested a rough night for him as well, though Krutwig suspected it was more from thinking than drinking.

"Who is this?" Rankwall asked, indicating Glockstoff.

"Corporal Chadwick Glockstoff, sir," Krutzwig said. "Rueger's replacement, as requested."

"I've never heard of you," Rankwall said, frowning at the officer. "What division did you serve in the south?"

"I—"

"He gets things done, sir," Krutzwig interjected. "Neatly and without questions."

Rankwall walked over to the pegboard and glared at the engineer's damage report. "So be it," he said after a pause. "We have come to a crossroad, Constable. Mitterhal is more entrenched than I thought. Our only recourse now is force. This winter we drop the lake. Come spring we deploy the work barge, along with reinforcements. Arms will be sent on the *Lyssia*. In the meantime, I will order the Weir Port to open the gates."

"And what of the tribes, sir? They have sworn to thwart any attempt at rebuilding the bridge."

The chancellor's fist smashed the office desk like a gavel. "We will crush them!"

The impact snapped Krutzwig out of his hungover state. "Of course, sir."

"There is another matter we must address, Constable." The vein on Rankwall's forehead pulsed over his blackened eyes.

"What is that, sir?"

"Poulakis."

"Poulakis?"

"Yes. His influence extends even further than Mitterhal's. Killing wild heathens is one thing, going against the will of the church is another. We must not allow his clout to compromise our support in the south. I want you to discredit him."

"That will not be easy, sir. The Haven loves him."

"I'm not talking about the Haven. We've already lost that battle. It is the rest of the lake province we must convince. He has a track record of sympathizing with the tribes and tolerating their pagan traditions. I want you to prey on that. Expose him for the heretic that he is."

"That may require unconventional methods, sir," Krutzwig said, glancing toward Glockstoff.

"I don't care what methods are required so long as they are not traced back to the source. Understood?"

"Very much, sir."

Rankwall strode to the door. "Good. I leave tomorrow." He turned. "And, Krutzwig ..."

"Yes, sir."

"Tell the mayor not to bother with the marching band."

The door slammed shut, and Krutzwig looked to Glockstoff. "A stellar performance, my friend. Congratulations on your promotion, Captain Glockstoff. Now the real work begins. Are the channels still open with that nutty soldier we used to set up Schnites?"

"We will have to find him," Glockstoff said. "It may take time."

"Do so."

"The chancellor said discredit, sir."

"And your point?"

"If we—"

"That is not a question I detect in your tone, is it, Captain?"

"No, sir, absolutely not."

"I didn't think so. Now I suggest you get to work."

"Right away, sir."

16
Teatime at the Tavern

The first snowfall came early on the mountain. Less than a month had passed since Rankwall had left the Haven in a snit. Mitterhal sat in the rear seat of the sleigh, hands atop his cane, unfazed by the fluffy white flakes that accumulated on his mustache and eyebrows. The mule muscled through the snow, bound for the village, mushed by Angus McGregor. The colonel had ordered the sleigh readied after Adman charged into the manor and announced the arrival in Cotton Crown of Duncan Jacks, Terrence Calhygan, and Weydlynn Roth. That had been dinnertime, nearly two hours ago. The merriment at the tavern would be long underway by now. What better way to acknowledge the fine job of his men than with an unannounced visit?

"Whoa there, Emit," Angus said to the mule with a firm tug on the reins. The great beast snorted to a stop in front of the tavern. Angus jumped out of the sleigh. "Here we are, sir. Looks like a full house. I can't wait to see their faces."

Mitterhal prepared to exit the sleigh, mindful not to twist his hip. One careless move could send a jolt of pain to his ribs that would make for a most humiliating descent. He reached for the side rail, but Angus promptly seized his arm. Caught off guard, the colonel sent his cane crashing on the big deputy's head.

"I've told you time and time again, I am not a cripple. How many times do I have to crack your skull?"

By the third strike Angus let go, but only after both of Mitterhal's feet were securely planted in the snow. "I'm sorry, sir. I thought you were falling," he said, rubbing the welts on his forehead.

Together they walked to the front door, which Angus pushed open. The hinges howled and Mitterhal stepped across the threshold into the music, smoke, and mirth.

"Move aside, everyone," Angus announced to the crowd. "Make way for the colonel!"

So much for subtlety, Mitterhal thought, as the merriment petered to a snore. All those in the front room stood dumbstruck with their frothy steins in hand. A group of young men shoved through the stunned crowd, Gildryn Grange among them. He delivered a swift kick to a lush who had passed out in a chair beneath the tablet of tavern rules. The snoring stopped and the pub fell into deeper silence yet.

Mitterhal advanced toward the hearth. After all these years, the rules were exactly where he remembered them. He scanned the tablet for his favorite. Number seven: *Rejoice not in the places reserved for savvy thought.* Apparently an amendment had been added in the right-hand margin. He squinted. The white letters were small yet stark against the black slate, no doubt intended to abolish any chance of ambiguity: *(And absolutely no song and dance in the conference chamber.)*

"Interesting," Mitterhal muttered, not entirely convinced of the edit.

Scowling, he looked down to the sacked lad in the chair. Francis McFadden, of all people. What would his father think? He then turned around to size up the crowd. The Grange boys stood front and center, along with the sons of McGregor. All of them at attention, ready to jump to task in a moment's notice. Good, he thought. The unruly clan had come a long way since their trip to the opera house. Amazing what a few swift swings of the beechwood could do.

Myrtle Hornpout, the burly tavern keeper, shoved through the crowd to the hearth. She wielded a rolling pin and wore an apron covered in flour. "Welcome, Colonel," she said, making a low bow that exposed the naughty regions of her barrel chest. "Such a wonderful treat to see you. It has certainly been a while."

"Indeed it has, Madam." Mitterhal sniffed at the savory blend of aromas that had trailed her from the kitchen. The scent jostled his memory, as did her size. She had an imposing presence—the female equivalent of Jeziah. Many a meal she had concocted for the Haven Guard. "The pleasure is mine," he said. "Good to see you still taking care of the boys."

"Some duties never end," she said with a broad smile. "Shall I prepare you a turnip?"

"No, thank you. I dined at the manor. Where might I find your honored guests?"

"Ah, yes. They are in chambers with the good sheriff."

Mitterhal nodded and then struck his cane on the wide wooden floor planks. "Out of my way, lads," he said, making straight for the conference chamber at the rear of the tavern.

The Grange clan parted, leaving a swath of space the width of a cane swing. He paused thoughtfully at the arched door. The entrance code would surely have changed by now, but so be it. Funny how the wulfweed left certain memories intact. He rapped on the door with the outdated cadence and then entered.

All at the meeting table jumped to attention. All that could, that is. The legless Jacks remained seated, holding a salute. Next to him stood Weydlynn Roth and Terrence Calhygan. Sheriff Hoffman was at the head of the table, flanked by Adman McFadden and Seth McGregor. Several other members of the Guard stood rigid as fence posts around the table. Away by the hearth, Brewmaster Garrison heaved on his pipe like a knobby old goblin encased in a bank of smoke.

"At ease, lads," Mitterhal said as he approached the table. "This is a tavern, not a church service." He went directly to Duncan Jacks. "I couldn't miss the chance for a chat with the Haven's most wanted."

A hearty round of laughter followed, and Duncan raised his mug. "Aye, Colonel. It is teatime at the tavern for sure. A finer guest could not be had. To the colonel!"

All the mugs went up, the toast repeated in unison. Brewmaster Garrison stepped out of his fog bank and poured a draft from one of several kegs propped in a built-in recess by the wall.

"Here ye, Colonel," he said, delivering the mug. "A sip of the finest to wet your whistle. And perhaps a pinch of the mountain flower to spice up your pipe?"

"I'll pass on the pipe, Brewmaster, though I'll take you up on the mug. It's only the common smoke for me now. Pastor's orders."

"Aye, a sacrilege order if you ask me. It's been me most potent crop to date."

"I'm sure it has." Mitterhal sampled the draft. "And no doubt my bees would agree. But all the same, orders are orders. We don't want the higher-ups getting locked in a twist." He set his mug on the table and looked at Hoffman. "So what have our eyes seen at the Docks?"

Hoffman deferred the question to Seth McGregor with a nod.

"My mother says the wharf's been quiet since the *Lyssia* left, sir," Seth answered. "Only the regulars running their beats. Though the harbor hasn't been this low since the drought. One of our weavers at the exhibit overheard a pogie patrolman talking about the drop to his comrades. Something about making ready for the barge."

"Yes, that would be the work barge for the bridge." Mitterhal directed his comment to Hoffman. "Rankwall must have ordered the gates opened at the Weirs. I'm sure he aims to muscle on with the project come spring. That gives us the winter to plan. The bad news is he will be much less accommodating after the thaw. Along with the work barge, we can expect a battalion of his southies. The Silver Girl will be locked and loaded for sure. Once the barge is set in place, Choroqua will most likely declare war on Rankwall. We'll have to make sure our guns are in order by then. What is the tally of our fighters from Multynhaven, Sergeant?"

Hoffman was about to answer, but Adman stepped forward and blurted his report, blatantly out of order. "A hundred and forty standbys have reported for duty, sir. They trickle in from the highlands, a dozen or so at a time. We brief them at the stables and then move them out quick so the pogies don't get nosy. More are promised."

Mitterhal's knuckles tightened around his cane. The pushy lad clearly needed a lesson in protocol. What a shame to crush his passion. "And when were you made sergeant?" he asked, preparing to administer the blow.

"I'm sorry, sir." Adman glanced at the cane. "Seth and I haven't slept since we left for Wulfhaven yesterday morning. My manners may have slipped a bit."

Impressive, Mitterhal thought, peering into the eyes of Uryan's eldest son. They were indeed bloodshot, as one would expect of a soldier without rest. Yet they were also steady and sharp, gleaming with devotion, ready to accept the sting of the swing if need be. Just like his father. How interesting. He relaxed his grip on the cane and returned his attention to Hoffman.

"Tell me, Sergeant, have these two lads been made official?"

"Not yet, sir. They're still learning the chants."

"What's the holdup?" Mitterhal addressed both Adman and Seth. "The codes are the codes. You either know them or you don't."

"We do, sir," Adman said. He looked to Seth, who nodded in agreement. "We just need to study up on the appendices in the Old Tome."

"So what you're telling me is if I get Terrence here to blow his pipes, you could answer every one of his tunes in chant?"

Both nodded. "Absolutely, sir," Adman said.

Mitterhal struck his cane to the floor. "Let's have it then. Garrison, prepare the rite. Terrence, tune up your pipes."

Hoffman shifted uneasily and then stepped forward. "Here, sir, in chambers?"

"Are you suggesting the snow, Jarvis?"

"No, sir, not at all. It's just the chanting."

"What about it?"

"Tavern rules, sir."

"Ah, yes, of course. Good point." Mitterhal fired a sharp glance at the brewmaster. "Garrison, tell Hornpout I want her to amend the amendment on rule seven. Have her provide an allowance for chants."

"Right away, sir." In an instant the gnarly old scrunge was out the door.

Terrence Calhygan retrieved his pipes, which hung from a hook amidst the wall of muskets and powder horns. The veteran piper strapped the instrument over his shoulder and began inflating the goatskin bag through his blowpipe. One by one he tuned up the chanters and drones mounted to the bag.

The eerie hum struck a chord and drew Mitterhal to the crackling fire. He stood propped by his cane, staring into the flames: listening, humming, and remembering. The tones fused in harmony. His customary scowl relaxed and his mind began to wander, far, far away to a place veiled in smoke. Woozy, he took a seat near the hearth and looked up to the mantel, as if the patterns in the masonry might show him the way.

"There is doubt in your eyes, Uryan. Speak your mind."

"What purpose does it serve, sir, to offer terms to an enemy that is sure to reject them?"

"You are right, Lieutenant. The bear will most certainly snub our parley. But in so doing, they will hear your warning. And yes, they will pass it off as myth, nothing more than a desperate heathen trick. And they will laugh among themselves, and they will mock, and they will send you back with the answer we already know they will give. Not until the heat of battle, when the bear is wrapped in the Raven's shadow, will your suggestion manifest in their minds. That is when they will hear your charge and feel the wrath of Montayega's great herd descend upon them."

"What about our men, sir? How will they handle the delusion?"

"Better than they will ten regiments of Toric artillery. Coherency will be maintained through the codes. The parley will buy us time for the wolves to get the pipers in position."

"By your command, sir, I will deliver the terms."

"Do not just deliver them, Uryan. You must believe in them."

Mitterhal opened his eyes. Calhygan's pipes had stopped and a spicy aroma filled the air. He felt a hand on his shoulder. It was Sergeant Hoffman. Behind him stood Brewmaster Garrison with a smoking urn in hand. Behind the urn he saw Adman and Seth on their knees, surrounded by the circle of guardsmen.

"The rite is over, sir," Hoffman said. "The boys know the codes."

Slowly Mitterhal packed his pipe while he gathered his wits. How did he miss it? So be it. If anyone knew the codes, it was Hoffman. He rose and strode to the center of the circle, where the kneeling lads awaited their acceptance. He lingered only for a moment, preparing to hear the words he had spent nearly a decade trying to forget.

"Adman McFadden and Seth McGregor, under witness of your brothers at arms you have demonstrated proficiency in the codes. All that is left is your oath. What say you?"

The two young men recited their pledge in perfect unison:

To my soul I say speak, I will listen
To my mind I say listen, I will trust
To my heart I say beat, I will fight
To my body I say give, I will die

Mitterhal tapped the floor with his cane. "Very good. Then to both of you I say rise and fear no challenge. For you are now fighters of the Haven Guard. Welcome aboard, lads."

A cheer erupted as the men closed in to assault the recruits with a barrage of hearty slaps. Mitterhal watched through the haze of greenbank, like a proud father beaming over his boys. In time the merriment settled and the colonel took his leave.

Outside the conference chamber, the activity ground to a halt as the colonel strode back through the wide-eyed gathering. Angus met him on the way, ordering everyone to step aside. Halfway through the common room, Mitterhal stopped to inspect the tablet over the hearth. The change had already been made to rule seven—though his eyes nearly burned a hole in the slate when he read the last word of the amendment. *Absolutely no song and dance in the conference chamber—however special consideration will be given to chance.*

"Everything all right, Colonel?" Angus asked.

Mitterhal growled at the spelling error. Should he call on Hornpout to correct the correction? By rights, yes, but was it worth undermining the illusion? The rules were the rules, not to be changed on a whim, especially under witness of a packed house. He looked to rule eight: *When seasoning your stew be wise in the spices you choose, but not so wise as to insult the cook.* How ironic.

He spun away from the hearth, making straight for the door. "Let's go, Angus. Back to the manor. It is what it is."

17
Hard Lessons

Hoof—paw, hoof—paw
Forest splintered sun
Hoof—paw, hoof—paw
Catch the scent and run

Hoof—paw, hoof—paw
Hunting in the green
Hoof—paw, hoof—paw
Bounding over stream

Hoof—paw, hoof—paw
Rhythm of the drum
Hoof—paw, hoof—paw
Rabbit on the run

Hoof—paw, hoof—paw
Shadows set in pace
Hoof—paw, hoof—paw
A tie to end the race

Donavon raced through the forest glen, his target in plain sight, strung high on a wooden pole. He closed in fast, very fast. Almost in range and the mantra faded like a distant pulse. *Hoof—paw, hoof—paw* ... He stopped at the sheer trunk of a hemlock and aimed at the pelt. Nobody but him and the breath of the bark ... and ... Something else. A scent. Yes, definitely a scent ... from behind the tree— Warning! He shot the arrow and feinted right. The attack came from the left, fast but not fast enough. Donavon struck in a blink. Two quick jabs into the face of his assailer.

"Surprise, surprise! Nice try, Nosebleed."

The warrior was taken aback, yet he recovered quickly and resumed the assault with his guntocs. Donavon dodged the first two swipes, but the third came down hard on his neck. A shrill cry came from somewhere in the woods. Nosebleed backed off. Fortunately, his wrist blades were only the blunted goat horns used for training purposes. Still, not to be outdone, Donavon clenched his fists and fired two more jabs. Sure shots, he thought, but neither came close. Nosebleed countered with more talon strikes, shifting in and out of the boreal light like a ghost. Bewildered, Donavon did his best to pinpoint the mirage, but every attempt proved futile. Again he felt the mock slice of the goat horns on his neck. Another loud cry from the trees.

The bout continued. Seven times Donavon was struck on the neck; seven times the cry was sounded. Nosebleed stopped and bowed every time. At last, when Donavon's endurance had reached its limit, he conceded the fight. The others came forward, stepping out of their hiding places in the woods.

"Your speed through forest is unmatched," Notalk said. "Not even Tiptoe keep up with you. But you still clumsy at kill. Something blocks your flow."

"How does he do that?" Donavon asked, still catching his breath. "I had him dead to rights at least five times. How does he disappear like that?"

"He does not disappear. It is your eye that deceive you. Attacker's motion only suggest where you think he be. Illusion, I believe it called in your tongue. We call it *vishwaw-myah*."

Blue hailed the group and pointed to the rabbit skin mounted on the top of the pole. Donavon's arrow had found its mark, centered between the two limp ears of the pelt. All the warriors bowed their heads in admiration. Even Donavon was surprised he had made the long shot.

"Your skill already advanced," Notalk said. "It just need be refined. You must learn to think like stream. Once you master *vishwaw-myah*, real kill come easy."

"Kill?" Donavon said. "Why just the kill? This little trick will do wonders in a scrap."

Notalk tilted his head curiously. "With respect, why use discipline if not to kill? It is not wise to make enemy suffer. Great Mother not approve."

"That's exactly why the tribes get such a bad rap in the Haven," Donavon said. "It's all about the kill for you guys. There's no middle ground. We've been through this before with those pogies in the harbor. Sometimes a good stiff crack to the jaw is all it takes." He stepped toward Nosebleed. "You see this?" he said, pointing to his clenched hand. "It's called a fist. If you use it right, you won't need your blade. Your foe will remember this, but he won't remember that." He tapped the goat horn on Nosebleed's wrist.

Nosebleed scowled at Notalk and spoke.

Notalk translated. "Bruhynn wants to know what you mean by 'crack to jaw.'"

Donavon eyed the swelling around the red warrior's upper lip. "It's what you got when you jumped me from behind the tree, before you went blinking on me like that. Here, give me your arm." He grabbed Nosebleed's open hand and clenched it into a fist. "Not too tight or you'll lose power in the swing. That's it. Now hit my hand and turn your wrist slightly inward on impact. Like this. Good, now harder. Excellent! Now retract and do the same with the other. That's it. Keep in mind the guy you crack is going to be thinking the same thing, so you'll want to use your free hand as a blocker. Unless of course you're fast enough not to bother."

After several practice jabs, Nosebleed stared at his fists as if they had become separate from his arms. He held them out rigidly and mumbled something in Gwyntah.

Notalk nodded and turned to Donavon. "Bruhynn say your combat technique inefficient, but will master discipline if that your wish."

"Hah!" Donavon drove a hard jab into Nosebleed's shoulder, sending him back a step. "You've got yourself a deal. But you better stay on your toes. I'm not as sloppy as you think."

A flash of gray bolted through the undergrowth. Over the winter Scraggs had become much less skittish of the warriors, as if sensing that they were now members of the same pack. He stayed clear of their touch, though, tolerating only Donavon's hand on his scruff. Cautiously the wolf slinked through the pack and cowered before Donavon.

"What've we got here?" Donavon asked the downtrodden beast. "Looks like you've been making trouble in the woods." He reached out and latched onto one of several porcupine quills imbedded in the wolf's jowls. "That'll teach you to think before you bite," he said, and gave a hard yank.

Scraggs yelped, then growled.

"Easy does it, boy. There's no way around it. You got yourself into this mess, now let me get you out." He grabbed another quill. "All in all, it could've been a lot worse. Here's to good hard lessons." Yank. One by one Donavon plucked out the quills. Scraggs yelped every time. No more growls.

The warriors watched in silence. It was Blue, upon the last yank, who pointed out that the wolf cried seven times. "*Yam kahar heim wynn ahla wulf,*" he said to Notalk.

"*Cha,*" Notalk said to the others, who nodded their agreement. He turned to Donavon. "Just as you name us in your tongue, we name you in ours. Wulfwynn, we call you now."

"Spirit of Wolf," Donavon said, scratching his good friend behind the ears. "What do you think, Scraggs?"

Scraggs flapped his jowls, happy to be free of the quills, and let out an unabashed bay of agreement.

Nothing excited Donavon more than running with the wolf, especially when the moon was full. Scraggs had introduced him to it late last fall, a month after their arrival to the Ring. The wolf had pawed incessantly at the frosty front door of Donavon's yurt until he finally gave in. It became a monthly event thereafter.

Indeed, the thrill was impossible for Donavon to ignore, even in the winter when the biting cold numbed all but his most primal senses. Weaving in and out of the glistening balsams on snow-packed deer trails that reeked of musk, Donavon equated the feeling to a dream in which all bounds were lifted. He felt like a phantom gliding effortlessly through the forest, Scraggs always close by his side.

The coming of spring brought another thrill. Donavon's thoughts often drifted to the young woman in Wulfhaven who played the flute in the square. He remembered her skirt, snug at the waist, long hair flapping like a horsetail as she ran by the bench to warn the fountain lady of the impending weirmen. And her scent, her sweet earthy fragrance. He remembered that too, as if she were right there in front of him. And so while running with the wolf one cloudless night in early spring, Donavon, feeling extra vigorous, scaled a bluff to its highest point and let out a cry that roused the forest.

They cried together, man and wolf, howling at the moon. Eventually they dove back into the old growth at top speed. Donavon's mantra fused with every breath, *Hoof—paw, hoof—paw.* In and out of the great hemlocks they dashed, power in pace, guided by the lunar light that flickered across the ferns on forest floor. He became a wolf, striding in stealth; then a goat, leaping over logs, never once caring where his hooves might land. They moved as one, hoof and paw, until at last he and Scraggs came to rest by a trail of flattened stones.

Long the wolf sniffed the slabs; some great, some small, all firmly imbedded in the moss. There was something familiar about them. Donavon had been there before, he was sure of it. But how? And when? Where had he smelled that scent? He followed Scraggs along the trail to a ledge that cropped out of the forest. A set of stone stairs wound upward to a terrace. At the top of the steps he stopped. The space was old and bled of power. He saw an altar, wide as a bed, covered in vines that cascaded over its edge and across the terrace. Again the déjà vu struck. He sat down, suddenly weary, and leaned back on the altar. The starlight trickled through the trees. He looked up into the sparkling sea of dots, as if their ancient light might offer an explanation as to why he was there. Transfixed by the patterns, he closed his eyes and fell asleep.

Donavon was nine years old when he moved to the mountain. He did not have a lot to say about it, Enyalda even less. It all happened so fast. He remembered Captain Marly, only hours after the incident in the barn, giving explicit instructions to Adman on what to do and say. And the guardsmen, he remembered them too. Men who fought with his father in the war, so grim and resolved as they entered the family barn to execute the horses. They used sabers instead of bullets so the Pogetsa would not find holes in their cindered skulls. Most of the kills were clean and quick, but one horse fought hard to the end. Donavon listened from outside and wondered if it was his favorite.

Other images stuck: the torches that were thrown in the barn after the horses were silenced, the flames, the billowing black smoke, the men charging across the field and vanishing in the woods. Captain Marly's hand on his shoulder and his words: You must be strong, Donavon. More men will come to ask questions. Do not tell them what you did. Let Adman do the talking. Donavon remembered holding back tears. *Where is my sister?*

The pogies came the next morning, just as Captain Marly had said. They rummaged through the ash, picking through the bones. Adman answered their questions and they left. By evening the bearded giant arrived, riding a windowless wagon. He told the boys to get in. That was the last Donavon ever saw of their home in the rolling green fields on the outskirts of Wulfhaven. Up and up they went to the highland village on Cotton Crown Mountain.

Enyalda was already there, but something was terribly wrong. She was bedridden—living, breathing, and eating, but dead, her trampled spirit void of life. For weeks she remained as such, veiled in vacant shadow. Donavon held fierce vigil, leaving her side only to pick flowers for her in the alpine meadows by the spooky old manor where the crazy man sat on his rooftop. Then one day she awoke from a nap, giggling at a bouquet of gahenya he had put on the night stand next to her bed. Just like that, the shadow was gone. Enya was back with more energy than ever before. And her voice. That was back too, but only in song and whispers. How he loved it when she sang, especially about her dreams and visions. So many times he had closed his eyes and let her verses carry him away to far-off lands and mythical places.

In the first light of the new day, Donavon opened his eyes and found himself in Gwyntahlynn once again, cushioned by the mossy stones of a woodland shrine. And as the tiny white flowers in the vines came into focus, he heard his sister's song trickle through their tendrils and realized in that thin moment why the sacred space felt so familiar to him. The song faded. He stretched out his arms and yawned, making a tune of his own. The restful note was cut short by the wolf's sloppy tongue on his face.

"That's enough of that," Donavon said, wiping the slobber off his chin.

He stood up to assess his surroundings. The terrace and the altar were old, no question about that—dating back to some untold time. The curved stones leading up to the terrace, however, were different. The stairway had been there long enough for the moss and vines to creep over the treads, yet something in the stonework seemed new, or at least not nearly as ancient. The smooth curves in the risers married cleanly into the rough vertical ridges of the ledge. Strict attention had been given to the placement of every tread stone, similar in style to the tavern hearth on Cotton Crown. He suddenly craved a bowl of Madam Hornpout's stew. The thought gnawed at his stomach.

"Come on, Scraggs. Let's go."

They left the holy place and by late morning were back to the yurt. Donavon was ravenous. He sat outside and devoured his lupini bread while Scraggs scavenged for meadow voles in the gahenya. Notalk showed up, alone, just as the sun topped the sky and the shadows in the valley shrank to nothing. It had been two days since the warriors' last visit. But where were the others? Something in Notalk's stride suggested this was not a lesson.

"The lake water recedes," the warior said. "Warship bring more peace stealers to harbor. Gwyntahpynn say more will follow. He call war council with elders and request your attendance at Mother Temple."

Donavon swallowed his bread. "I am not an elder. What do I know about war?"

"You are Wulfwynn. Temple is two-day run with pack. We tutor you on way."

18
Family Matters

It was early spring, dinnertime at the manor. The winter had been a challenge for Enyalda; she missed her twin brother. As she set the table, she wondered what dinner was like in Gwyntahlynn. She shaped the colonel's cloth napkin into a cone and placed it on his plate. It loomed like a solitary mountain over a vast terrestrial plane. In truth, she did it more for her sake than his. Anything to create excitement at the manor. Adman and Francis would not be making it this night. It happened more often than not of late. She knew better than to ask. Three candles flickered on the table, one for each brother. How quiet life had become since Donavon left the mountain last fall.

The colonel grunted his way to the table. The pain in his hip was acting up, as it always did when it rained. Indeed, the sky had wept all day, the same as the day before. No shortage of tears for her perennials. She took his cane and offered her hand as a prop. Grudgingly he accepted before plunking into his chair.

Enyalda bowed, honored to serve. It was not typical for the willful old man to accept help from others, especially when it drew attention to his ailments. In fact, he had made it painfully clear to her brothers that she was the only one authorized to cater to such needs. The sting of his beechwood cane had seen to that. She leaned the frightful weapon against the adjacent chair.

The napkin was next. She swept the mountain off the plate and tucked it neatly in the collar under his chin, just the way he liked it. Next came the blessing, followed by a song, then a dance, then a ridiculous rhyme to tease his appetite. How she loved it when he tried not to smile. At last, she closed with a prayer for her brothers before dishing out his favorite meal—one large boiled turnip with a half-palm of salt and a pinch of parsley.

No sooner had the prongs of his fork jabbed the tuber than a loud rap sounded at the door. She hurried to the front parlor and snatched an oil lamp off the hook on the wall. Excited at the prospect of company, she swept back her hair and released the deadbolt. The door creaked open, revealing Sheriff Hoffman and some poor fellow in handcuffs, held tight on either side by Angus McGregor and Gildryn Grange. Water streamed off their hats like fountains in the lamplight. Enyalda stood dumbfounded at the sight.

"You gonna let us in, Enya?" Angus asked. "It's a bit nasty out here."

The sheriff entered first. He removed his soaked hat and nodded cordially to Enyalda. "'Evening, madam. Might we have a word with the colonel?"

Enyalda raised the lamp for a better view of the man in cuffs. His eyes were blue, set deep in their sockets under a prominent brow. Just like Pastor Marcus, she thought, only younger. Much younger. The rest of his face was sadly bruised and glistened with diluted blood. The sight did not warrant a song, so she answered with words—"This way"—and showed them to the hearth room.

The men sloshed to the table where the colonel sat chewing his turnip. Hoffman got right to the point. "This man was found with six others in the Granges' sheep field, sir. All armed. He claims to be their leader but won't say who they are or why they're here." Hoffman tossed the man's crimson war hat on the table. "Toric spies by the looks of it."

Mitterhal swallowed. "Toricean indeed," he said, prodding the canvas cap with his fork. "Though I've never known a spy to advertise his colors. Unless, of course, that is the intent. In either case, I believe a peace treaty was signed with the Torics ten years ago, was it not? This man has been sorely treated, Jarvis. Have you lost your manners?"

Sheriff Hoffman sent a severe look to Gildryn. The herdsman cleared his throat before addressing the colonel. "Sir, my cousins and I thought they were pogies, so we let 'em have it. When we found out they were Torics, we let 'em have it again."

"I see." The colonel turned back to his turnip. "Where are the others, Sergeant?"

"They're locked up in the jailhouse."

"You best bring them here so Enyalda can fix them up."

"Sir, with all due respect, we don't know their intent."

"All the more reason to get them out of those cells. My guess is that it was not by accident that they didn't use their guns on the Grange boys."

Hoffman nodded to Angus, who in turn nodded to Gildryn. The two young men immediately made for the door. "Angus," the sheriff said sharply before they left. "Keep them cuffed and make sure you get your brothers to back you up."

Angus nodded to Hoffman and then to Gildryn, who nodded back at

Angus. The big deputy then nodded respectfully to the colonel before ducking through the parlor and out the door.

With Angus and Gildryn gone, more nods were exchanged between the sheriff and the colonel. Hoffman removed a key from his belt and unshackled the prisoner, to whom he sent a dour nod and pointed to a chair directly across from the colonel. The prisoner nodded back and promptly sat in the appointed chair. The sheriff nodded yet again to the colonel and strode across the room to the fireplace where he reclined into a chair and appeared to nod off.

Enyalda did her best to keep track of the nods, but got dizzy with the effort. What was it with men and their bobbing heads? They could be so stingy with words at times, yet somehow still managed to make their point. It was a baffling art she had yet to master.

"So, what brings you to the mountain, soldier?" the colonel asked, finally using his words.

The prisoner straightened in his seat. "We heard there is trouble in the Haven, that you've taken a stand against Rankwall. My comrades and I have come to offer our service."

"All seven of you?"

"No, all five hundred. Maybe more. The others await your word at Spaulding Pass."

"What? Who are you?"

"We are survivors, sir. The ones you sent back home to Toricia with provisions after the battle. We have not forgotten your mercy. Twice a year we make our pilgrimage to the pass. Once in the spring when the gahenya blooms, then again in the fall when it goes to seed. At first it was to honor the dead, but now it's more. A great mystery calls us back to the pass every year."

"What mystery is that?"

"Music, sir. We hear the pipes on the ridge, just like the day of the battle. Those who were in the smoke swear by it. The others only hear wind on the mountains."

"And under whose banner do you make this pilgrimage?"

"None but our own, sir. We are no longer bound by the high command, not after what we reported at Spaulding Pass. They called us insane, victims of the smoke, and so discharged of duty to do with our lives what we will. For many of us, the pilgrimage is all that is left."

A peculiar air came over the colonel; he was still in command yet oddly passive. Enyalda, not sure what to make of the shift, grabbed the pitcher of water on the table and turned to nourish her plants on the nearby sill.

"And what do you do when you are not pilgriming, soldier?" the colonel asked. "You are still young by the looks of it. Do you have a family?"

"I have taken no wife, sir. Not sure if little ones are a good idea. I'm a mason by trade, as was my father and his. I was not yet twenty at the battle. My father was a corporal, well decorated, though he never lost his love for the trowel. He often told me how my grandfather shared the same passion, but the callings of a general always pulled him away. I regret never having met him. He served the high command in the south wars. A great leader of men, I've been told. When the campaign moved north, he disappeared without a trace. Most say it was the heathens that got him. Yet my father insisted that he just lost interest in warring and wanted to get back to his masonry."

Enyalda moved closer with the pitcher of water. Watching, listening, she assessed the colonel's every move. He remained still for the most part, his only motion in his lower jaw, chewing slowly on his turnip. And … Yes. She had missed it at first, but there was a slight tremble in the fork. She refilled his glass. Something had tweaked him for sure, but she had heard nothing in the soldier's story to cause his malaise. She hummed a sweet verse while she sprinkled his turnip with salt.

The colonel blinked and looked to her. "Thank you, my dear. I believe this young man could use your attention. Perhaps your fixing kit is near?"

It was indeed. She kept it in the cabinet under the stairs by the parlor, easily accessible for occasions such as these, though it was for her brothers that she had made the precaution.

"Sir," the soldier said, "I have come for another reason. A family matter, if you will."

The colonel nodded for him to go on.

"There is a soldier who fought for you who remains very much a mystery to us. He would have been only a boy in your infantry. We found him that first spring, living alone in the wild, clearly taken by combat. He spoke of his dead brothers like they were right there in front of him. And his musket … He spoke to that too, as if it were a living, breathing thing. We tried to help him, but he would have nothing of it. He said it was his duty to gather tidings in the Haven and report back to his brothers. The boy seemed adept at survival, so we let him be. The Little Pilgrim, we called him. He took well to the name and eventually grew to trust us. Every year we found him there singing in the pass, burning his wulfweed. Eventually he invited us to sing war hymns at his camp near the foot of the east ridge. That's when we heard the pipes."

"An intriguing story for sure. Yet I fail to see how this qualifies as a family matter."

"The Little Pilgrim had a gun, sir. One that he claims you gave him just prior to the battle. My grandfather's name is engraved in its stock."

The twitch struck hard and fast, as if a feisty gnat had lodged in the colonel's eye socket. Not since the gathering of the Guard last spring had

Enyalda seen it so pronounced. She circled the table with her fixing kit, prowling the floor like a cat ready to pounce.

"What is your name, soldier?" he asked.

"I am Nicolas, sir. Nicolas Harthmocker. Son of Christopher and grandson of Simon."

The colonel stood up and put both hands to the table, prompting Enyalda to move in. "No!" he shouted, warding her off with the wave of his hand. He stabilized himself and faced the soldier. "What has become of your father?"

"He died honorably, sir, in battle at the pass."

The colonel reached for his pipe, but it slipped out of his hand and showered his turnip with powdery ash. Enyalda gasped in alarm. Again she moved in to administer her blessing; again his hand went up to ward her off. He stood, hovering over his plate, his red eyes welling under twitching brow. "Let me be, my dear," he said, reaching for his cane against the chair. "Just let me be."

Her effort denied, Enyalda felt tears fill her eyes. Through the blur she spied his wound and knew it went far beyond her arts to heal. A deep, penetrating sorrow seized her, as if a fireball had landed outside the manor and incinerated every flower on the mountain, roots and all. Yet the colonel remained upright, somber though he was. He even managed to walk to the hearth where his silent presence stirred the sheriff out of his nap, if a nap it had been.

"Are you all right, sir?" Hoffman asked, getting up from the chair.

The colonel simply leaned on his cane and stared at the masonry. The sight reminded Enyalda of his years on the rooftop, alone at his isolated post, studying every joint in the chimney's bricks.

Seeing him shaken yet stable, she addressed her own sorrow. Why was his happiness so important to her? What had drawn her up the beechwood's branches all those years? What loss had he suffered that seemed so familiar? Loss? Yes, that was it. Not just his, but hers—loss of mother, loss of father, loss of loved ones, loss of innocence. Her trembling hands went to her mouth. She needed to leave. But where? The amaryllis in the kitchen? No. She already knew what it would say. The perennials in the gardens? No. It was spring; their lush young stems would snap at the weight. What about the grasses? Yes, that was it! They were pliable, especially when wet. And so, like a strand of hay in a windswept barn, she flew out of the colonel's manor and into the rain, making straight for the knolls in the south pasture.

Several weeks passed. The Toricean soldiers turned out to be quite charming. Enyalda liked them all. For the life of her she could not fathom why anyone would want to kill them. War was such a mystery. She had a special fancy for Nicolas. He had cleaned up nicely after the unfortunate mix-up with the Grange clan. The colonel, out of principle, invited all the Torics to stay as guests at the manor while Enyalda worked her craft. Their recovery took longer than expected, though no one really seemed to mind.

Not all the healing, as it turned out, took place at the manor. A good portion occurred at the tavern, dingy and dark though it was. Initially Enyalda resisted the notion, but eventually she came to terms with the alternative treatment. It seemed that rest and relaxation only went so far with soldier types. She stayed true to her task, however, and even went to the extreme of going to the tavern herself to make sure Nicolas and his men received their proper dosage of blessings with beer.

It did not take long for the break in normalcy to be noticed by the villagers. The highland community was spurred on two counts. One, Toricean soldiers were actually commingling with the tavern's regulars; and two, the daughter of Uryan McFadden had dared to grace the seedy establishment with her spirited song and dance. Word of the spectacle spread like gahenya on the mountain, drawing in village folk of all walks.

Once their initial shock subsided, many brought their lutes, reeds, and woodwinds, along with whatever other instruments might have gathered dust since the war's end. Those who did not play listened, or stomped their feet, or clapped their hands, or jigged through a reel of their own choosing when the spirit took them. And in so doing, the sleepy alpine village of Cotton Crown awoke from the cold winter; and the trumpet vine on the tavern walls bloomed once again to the lively hum that piped through the age-old cobbles.

Enyalda's heart thumped like a highland drum. She stopped to catch her breath, sweat streaming down her neck to her tethered corset. Even she had her limits. She had been dancing all afternoon and had forgotten to drink water. The music in the tavern's common room played on while several fresh-footed newcomers kicked to the rhythm of a quick-paced reel. A glass of water suddenly appeared in front of her. It was Nicolas. How did he do that? Emerge out of nowhere—just like the colonel. She politely accepted his offer.

"Your steps were beginning to drag," he said, piercing eyes locked on hers. "I was hoping you would rest."

Enyalda drank, and the cold water filtered through her body, as if the life-giving liquid had bypassed her stomach entirely and went straight to the places that needed it most. All the while, she kept her eyes fixed on his. What was it that made him so easy to look at?

She had no time to ponder, for the front door of the tavern swung open and Adman marched in with more purpose than usual, if that were possible. Seth McGregor stayed tight to his side. They cut through the dance floor in the common room, heading for the private chamber in the rear where Sheriff Hoffman and the others had gathered for ale.

Nicolas took the empty glass from Enyalda and handed her his handkerchief. "Looks like your brother has important news. I best get back to the meeting. Thank you for the lovely break." He followed after Adman and Seth, leaving the empty glass on the fireplace mantel.

She stared long at the glass. How odd it felt to be served. Yet at the same time, how nice. Her focus shifted upward to the support timber imbedded in the old stones high above the mantel from which hung the smoke-stained tablet of tavern rules. The fourth rule caught her attention—*If you soak your bread in sauce let it be no more than what you put in your mouth, and blow not your broth at table but stay till it cools of itself.* On that thought, Enyalda patted the beads of sweat on her neck and hurried off to offer her service in the kitchen.

The tavern kitchen was a steamy place, full of brew pots and ladles hanging from the walls on wrought-iron hooks. Great bins of wheat, barley, and rye lined the black slate counters amidst an assortment of cookware. Some of the oddments appeared specific to the brew craft, while others served a more general purpose and were easily recognized by Enyalda.

The blend of aromas was captivating—thick, moist, and natural, almost earthy, like rich black soil. She instantly fell in love with the place. It was tidy in its own organic way, like a well-tended garden free of columns and rows. In fact, she did find a garden, nestled in the atrium window, a cozy little bed of mushrooms and herbs. She clapped her hands like a young girl, excited at the prospect of getting to know them. The kitchen was not the best place to cool down, but no matter. All the windows were open, just enough to stir the air, but not so much as to stress the herbs.

"Good heavens," said the robust middle-aged woman coming out of the pantry. "You are soaking wet, my dear. There's a rack of dishrags by the sink. Take the third one from the right."

Enyalda accepted Madam Hornpout's suggestion, though in truth she thought Nicolas's handkerchief more than sufficed. She patted her face with the towel and then flapped her skirt to cool the lowers. The moving air made her giggle.

"Oh, what has that boorish mule done with my measuring cup now?" the madam said, suddenly irate. Her cutter fell like a guillotine on the chop block, cleaving a hapless onion in two. "How many times do I have to tell him? He's got enough wax in those hairy ears to make a dozen candlesticks."

Enyalda marveled at Myrtle Hornpout's arms as she hacked at the onion. They were mannish indeed, just as Donavon had said. No doubt due to a lifetime of chopping vegetables and mixing batter, among other less ladylike tasks. She kept her hair loosely bound in a bun with a broad pin that dreadfully resembled a dagger. Her bosom was vast, as if a cask of ale had been strapped sideways under her apron—a crude comparison that Enyalda had never given much credence to until now. Her brothers, after all, were notorious for stretching the truth on such matters.

A quick scan of the room revealed the elusive measuring cup lying on its side by the barley bin. Enyalda sprung to task, excited to assist. She snatched up the cup and discovered a large bowl of dried flower petals on the counter. The intriguing aroma compelled her to dip her hand into the bowl.

Myrtle stopped her chopping. "You better stay out of there, my dear," she warned. "Brewmaster Garrison doesn't take kindly to folk tampering with his hops. Heaven knows he's already a tetchy old troll as it is. In fact, if I were y— Oh, what a darling. You found my measuring cup."

Enyalda darted forward with her find. At the chopping block she spun around twice with both arms arced overhead before bowing ceremoniously to present her gift. "For you, Madam, I bring this cup and offer what I can for sup."

Myrtle eyed her warily. "So the rumors are true. You are more than just a dancer after all. Hmm, I usually work alone … Not sure if there's time to train you … You know how it is. Nothing personal, my dear."

Enyalda seized the chopper next and proceeded to dice the remaining onions at a knife-blurring pace. Within seconds the task was complete, four tidy piles ready for the sauté pan.

"But then again," the madam resumed, "things have picked up a bit. Perhaps I could make an exception in your case, at least while these Torics are here. Very well. Grab yourself an apron over there in the mop closet. We'll start with the boys in the conference chamber. Grab some bowls out of the cupboard, a dozen or so to start. The chowder in the third pot on the first stove should be just about ready. And make sure you slip a healthy pinch of black horehound in the sheriff's serving. He has such an awful time staying awake. And one more thing. Absolutely no dancing or singing in the chamber when the boys are in session."

The door to the conference chamber was thick and heavy, secured by four beastly black hinges. Enyalda stared at them with her tray full of steaming bowls, waiting for her courage to catch up. She heard Adman inside going on and on about politics. Not even the dense oak door could muffle her brother's rant. More bridge talk by the sound of it. Something about a barge … and warships … and workmen en route from the south. At last, she heard a break in conversation and knew it was time. Swallowing hard, she opened the door and entered.

All gaped in disbelief as she stepped in. The attention was stifling. If only she were permitted to dance or sing. *What a pickle*, she thought. Looking about, she spotted Nicolas at the far end of the table next to the McGregor brothers, Corey, Dugan, and Seth. Angus was seated on the opposite side, next to Adman. Next to him sat the sheriff, reclined in a chair with both boots propped on the table, apparently sound asleep. The other Toriceans were scattered throughout the room, smoking their pipes amidst more local faces, though none of the Grange boys were present except for Gildryn. Three kegs of Cotton Crown's finest were set on stands along the back wall from which hung a plethora of arms: muskets, pistols, and powder horns.

The serving tray was getting heavy and so, for better or worse, Enyalda set out to do her job. The frozen pickle, she figured, could get no worse. Her task became much easier once set to action. In fact, she barely repressed a giggle at seeing Adman so speechless. How fun it would have been to goad him in that moment with a ridiculous rhyme. She served the dozen bowls while the men watched in stunned silence. She then returned to the kitchen to fetch another tray.

The pickle had thawed by the time she returned. The men were much more talkative. Apparently her presence had been accepted. She wondered how many nods it had taken for them to reach that conclusion. Voracious appetites they all had, along with marginal manners. It was all she could do to dodge their wandering eyes. Though Nicolas, to her delight, was exquisitely well trained with a napkin. She was just getting ready to deliver seconds when a frenzied cadence struck the door and Francis charged into the room. He had been absent all day, and Enyalda was relieved to see him.

"Sir! There's been a Gwy— Enya? What are you doing here?"

Sheriff Hoffman snorted out of his nap. "Don't worry about it. She's been authorized. What do you got?"

"There's been a Gwyntah attack, sir. On a pogie harbor patrol. Our sources at the weaver exhibit saw the victims arrive at the Docks this morning. I would have got here sooner but I had to get the word to Jeziah at the stables."

"Victims?"

"Yes."

"Alive?"

"Yes."

The sheriff guzzled his draft. "Since when do the Gwyntah leave live victims? How many were killed?"

"None, sir."

"None?"

"None."

Hoffman's boots came off the table. "That doesn't sound like a Gwyntah raid to me. What makes the ladies so sure the attack came from across the Haven?"

"The weavers offered prayer shawls to the injured pogies and got themselves positioned to overhear the volunteer trainees on the wharf while they recounted the attack. Apparently four Gwyntah rappelled on board with ropes when the patrol passed under the bridge. The pogies never knew what hit them by the sound of it. Not a single shot fired. Two more Gwyntah in a long boat came out of the wreckage and took the attackers away. The three enlisted officers who led the mission were cuffed to the bow of their patrol boat, each one with a broken nose and a slice in the face. The trainees on board were spared the treatment and told to take the pogies back to the Docks." Francis paused. "Sir, they said the leader of the raid spoke fluent Toricean. You don't suppose it could have—"

"I don't suppose anything, Master McFadden!" the sheriff interjected. "And I suggest you do the same. Some of the surest battles have been choked to death by supposers." He scanned all the faces in the chamber. "Besides, there's nothing to gain by stating the obvious. I for one think it best we keep the glue in the illusion on this matter, even among ourselves."

A long silence ensued. At last, Angus slammed his forearms on the conference table. Enyalda jumped. It felt as if an earthquake had rattled the chamber. Tankards tipped and ale cascaded over the sides of the table, forming dark frothy puddles on the floor. Angus sat still, lower lip trembling, heedless of the draft that streamed into his lap.

"I miss Donny," he said. "The mountain's not the same without him."

Seth walked over to Angus and put a hand on his shoulder. "That's enough ale for you, little brother. We all miss Donny. Making a sap out of yourself won't bring him back."

Enyalda peeked around Seth for a closer examination. Thankfully, it was not an emergency. The big love simply missed his friend and needed a song to cheer him up—a relatively easy fix. She was acutely aware how much Angus loved her songs. At times his passion for her singing had become overwhelming, and it was all she could do to keep him away from her. Yet even in his gawkiest moments, Angus had remained a good soul throughout, and a loyal friend to Donavon as well, in spite of their countless fisticuffs.

She even remembered the game they had played together as children in which they all held hands and spun around in circles while chanting rhymes. Most of the rhymes she had made up herself, though Donavon had tweaked a few to his own liking. She still recalled some of his favorites and thought it would serve Angus well to hear them again. For in them rang the hope, heart, and spirit of all the fatherless children on Cotton Crown Mountain. And so with every ounce of kindness she could muster, she lifted Angus's beer-drenched hands off the table and looked deep into his eyes.

Around and around in a circle we go
Crazy old colonel let us know

287

Are we happy?
Are we not?
Do we have what your chimney's got?

Crazy old colonel let us know
Where oh where did your rabbit go?
High in the sky
Or deep in a hole
Which way do we run when your smoke rings blow?

Crazy old colonel what will we see
When we climb up your ladder to the old chimney?
Will the land in your view
Be the same that we see?
Will the song that we hear
Sound the same in your tree?

By the second verse, Corey and Dugan McGregor had joined in, as had Francis, for they too were young enough to remember the childhood rhymes. Angus came in on the third verse, along with some of the other locals smoking pipes by the hearth. At last, when the rhymes ended, the black hinges on the chamber door screeched open. Myrtle Hornpout engulfed the entry. Her glare fell directly on Enyalda.

"Daughter of Uryan or not," she said. "I told you no song and dance in the conference chamber. The rules are the rules!"

It was Jarvis Hoffman who rose to the occasion. "Perhaps you could bend them in this case, Murtie? The boys needed a little pickup. From now on we'll be sure to keep the singing where it belongs."

The smoke hung heavy in the room as all held their breath. To Enyalda's great relief, Madam Hornpout relaxed her manly arms and became once again the pleasant cook she had met in the kitchen.

"I suppose I could pass it off as chance this once. But any more slipups and you'll all be feeling my rolling pin. That goes for you too, Jarvy boy," she said with a disturbingly sultry smile to the sheriff. "It's good to see you so alert. Perhaps a little dance later, for old times sake. As you were, gentlemen."

Madam Hornpout departed and the entire chamber erupted in laughter. Even Hoffman had to grab his gut as if to keep it from exploding, his face flushed as red as a bell pepper. Enyalda, seeing the good spirits back, saw no reason to linger and slipped away to resume her chores in the kitchen.

The days passed, and Enyalda adapted nicely to her new job. The colonel insisted she stick with it, saying that her service to the effort was more important than her service to him. She did not know what he meant at first, but it became evident when shifts of weavers began funneling into the tavern for breakfast, lunch, and dinner. Apparently the mill was to remain in operation from dawn till dusk while new uniforms were tailored for the Guard.

Myrtle Hornpout turned out to be a wonderful lady to work for, so long as she did not have to repeat herself. Brewmaster Garrison was another matter. He was very much the cantankerous old troll that Madam Hornpout had claimed him to be. He had a crude sense of humor combined with a raspy laugh that sounded more like a dying goat. The interplay between him and Madam Hornpout was bizarre. They spent most of their time in the kitchen casting insults at each other while they worked their craft. Garrison saved his most lecherous comments for the untimely moments when Madam Hornpout had to concentrate on a recipe. Likewise, the madam would harp incessantly about his hygiene habits in the midst of a brew boil. It went on and on all day, and Enyalda found that the best way to avoid getting caught in the middle was to stay busy.

The one issue that Madam Hornpout and Brewmaster Garrison agreed on was the rules of the tavern. Without exception, they had to be followed. It was what kept the establishment respectable. The consequence for deliberately defying a rule was severe. Fortunately, a fair amount of wiggle room existed within each one, so that only the most deplorable drunkards ever really got the boot for good. Enyalda was thankful for the rules, cryptic though they were. They helped keep the men from getting sloppy.

The entire Grange clan showed up one day when the men were in session. The duties of sheepherding had kept them away, or so they said. They brought three dead lambs as a peace offering to the Torics. Watching Patrick Grange make an apology was like twisting a hangnail off a toe. It was Nicolas Harthmocker, oddly enough, who put an end to the anguish.

"Worry not, brother," he said. "Had we been in your shoes, we might have done the same. I'm only glad we are on the same side now. If you are anything like your fathers, it is no wonder we lost the war."

A great feast ensued which the entire village attended. The three lambs were roasted over open fires set in the street outside the tavern. The sky was brilliant blue and the clouds crispy white—a perfect day for festivity. A holiday was declared in the weaving mill, and the looms were silenced for the first time in weeks. Women, children, and men danced in the gravel in front of the jailhouse where a band of musicians had gathered on the steps. Even a few stray goats and dogs wandered about looking for scraps. Someone's adventurous pig did the same and ended its sojourn on a spit.

Enyalda, in spite of every effort to the contrary, became the spectacle of the day. She just couldn't help herself when it came to song and dance. Her hair blew like the leaves of a willow, tantalizing the crowd as she spun. So many eyes, so many men, yet not once did she feel threatened. In fact, she felt quite safe.

Nicolas made a sterling speech that won the crowd. The rumor was out that he was related to the Old Mitt in some way, though many likened him in appearance to Marcus Poulakis. Even his words were woven together with the same power and grace as the venerable pastor's. By the end of his speech, a new set of rumors had begun to circulate on the mountain.

A surprise visit by the notorious guardsmen, Terrence Calhygan and Weydlynn Roth, further heightened the event. The Torics were exceptionally taken when Calhygan played his pipes. Later that evening Nicolas announced that it was time for him and his men to leave the mountain. Enyalda wept the whole way back to the colonel's manor. The following day Nicolas found her in the knolls of the south field.

"How do I look?" he asked, holding his arms out.
"Like a bird about to fly," she said.
"No, I mean the uniform. What do you think?"
"Blue wool, silver buttons."
"And?"
"A dandelion seed on your collar."
"What else do you see?"
"Three crossed stalks of the mountain flower."
"May I hold you?"
"Yes."
"What's the matter? Where are we going?"
"To the stock house we go."
"Why?"
"The grasses are listening."
"Okay."

19

The Raven's Shadow

Mahoma meant mother in Toricean; *gwyn* meant child. The story of creation for the Gwyntahmahoma dated back to the earliest days, when the heavenly peaks of Montayega were still rooted to the earth. According to tribal legend, all things with wings, legs, branches, or fins stemmed from the womb of the Great Mother Mountain, out of which they entered the world through a vast web of subterranean tunnels and springs. Plants arrived first as seeds, and then came animals. Enormous goats were first of the beasts to scale the mountain and feed on the gahenya that carpeted the slopes. The primal herds kept watch on the sacred places where forest and fauna emerged. And so the world took shape until at last the guarded portals were sealed and the offspring of Montayega were blessed with a home.

Yet all was not in order, so the legend said, for the last of the mountain's children had yet to be born and the sacred channels had already been closed. Profound was the Great Mother's grief, for in her womb was trapped her greatest love. Streams and rivers sprouted from her chasms and flooded the land in tears, until at last a lake was made so large that its horizon touched the sky. When her grief had reached its limit and all but one spring ran dry, she called upon the Sky Father to bless the trapped inside. Then with all her might she pushed until her veins turned red and burst, and she sent her soaring peaks to where the heavens met the earth. Thus the womb of the Great Mother Mountain was drenched in Sky Father's light. When the cataclysm settled, a noble king and queen stepped out of the ash and found themselves in the Awshaws, blessed by a sunset.

"So what was in it for Sky Father?" Donavon asked, blowing on the strip of sizzling venison on his stick. "They weren't his children."

Pickpack jabbed at the coals in the fire, sending a plume of sparks to the stars. "Sky Father love Mother."

Donavon squinted at the sullen warrior. Pickpack's Toricean had improved considerably over the winter. All of them, in fact, had made it a priority to grasp the basics of the language. Donavon appreciated the effort and, in turn, did what he could to work out the nuances of their language. Communication was essential to a healthy pack.

"So he did it for the Mother, not the children?"

"Sky Father very busy," Pickpack replied.

"What does that have to do with anything?"

Notalk stepped in to clarify. "What he mean to say is Sky Father work with spirit and Mother Mountain work with body. Together they make life."

"So you're saying that the Gwyntahmahoma were really Sky Father's children all along?"

"Yes."

"But we are the children of the Mother," Donavon said incredulous. "I'll vouch for that. I heard her myself at the fountain."

"That we are, Wulfwynn, and to her we pledge. But all life starts with mother and father. There can't be one without the other. It is in the patterns of all things that breathe and swim."

"*Ni mah sahun huru!*" Tiptoe said, firing his seasoning pouch from across the pit. The supple missile struck Notalk square in the forehead. All the warriors laughed. Donavon translated silently: No more soft talk.

Nosebleed, who was sitting to Donavon's right, surprised him with a hard left jab to the shoulder. "You right, Wulfwynn," he said, fist still clenched. "We children of Mother. Notalk head in clouds. He need crack to jaw." The others laughed again. Notalk merely shrugged and went back to chewing on his venison.

The warriors broke camp the next morning before the sun had cleared the hazy rim of the Ring. By midday they reached the eastern edge of a line of knolls. The hills formed a rolling ridge that here and there fell to shadowy clefts. Within the clefts, Donavon spied old works of stone. They made straight for a pass that wound upward alongside a cascading stream. At the top of the pass the land opened into a wide, flat plain mottled with fields and orchards. Modest circular houses of earth and straw dotted the tilth, through which a network of streams and rills funneled inward like spokes on a vast terrestrial wheel. Miles away, a lone mount rose like a hub in the center of the plain. A mountain within the mountains, thought Donavon.

From their vantage in the cleft, he sighted other warriors walking inward along the spokes toward the hub, their spears pointing to the sky like tiny pins. So this was it, he mused as they descended a narrow trail in the cleft and made for the fields. The holy land of the Gwyntah—the legendary belly button of the Ring.

They trekked down and onward across the fertile plain, on a well-worn footpath adjacent to a stream. Little was said on the way as they closed in on the lone mountain. Donavon savored the sweet aroma of the orchard in bloom. Another scent came from the white blossoms that shrouded the trees directly to the left. Scraggs also caught the whiff.

"Easy does it," Donavon whispered to the wolf as he continued to scan the orchard without turning his head. He spied little eyes in the blossoms and tossed an arrow from his quiver toward the trees. A dozen children suddenly dropped out of the branches to seize the prize. The other warriors continued on as if the outburst never happened, though Donavon could not help notice the hint of a smile on Pickpack's straight face.

By late afternoon they made it to the mountain, though it had appeared much larger from a distance. It rose a thousand feet or so from the plain. A large gathering of warriors mingled at the base. Tiptoe led their procession directly through the host, many of whom Donavon recognized from his first day in the Ring at the Aisle of Totems. Others were less familiar, bearing the garb of other tribes. Many bowed, enamored it seemed by Scraggs, who stayed close to Donavon's side.

Through the gathering they plodded until they came to a great arch supported by a pair of grand pillars. Two women in white stepped out from under the arch to receive them, their complexions especially dark in contrast to their light-colored gowns. Their scent was captivating. Donavon stared at the rocky outcrops overhead to break free of their alluring spell.

"The ladies in waiting will see us through," Notalk said. "The rest will make camp on the flats."

"Why us and not them?" Donavon asked.

"Council only open to elders and war chiefs."

"We are neither."

"You are Wulfwynn. I am your translator. The wolf must stay with others."

"What?"

"It is the way."

After a moment of consideration, Donavon knelt to give his order to Scraggs. "Stay here, boy, and keep your nose on the pack. We'll be running again before you know it." A quick pat, a short whine from Scraggs, and he was up again. "All right, let's go." He strode through the archway and never looked back.

They climbed up sheer steps that hugged the outcrops. The two white-gowned women remained at the arch, and Donavon was sorry to leave them. Something about them reminded him of his sister. His woe subsided when the same lovely scent drifted down from above. Shortly thereafter they came to a small shrine on a lofty tier where two more young women handed them bowls of sweetened water.

"How do the elders make this climb?" he asked Notalk after downing his draft.

Notalk handed his empty vessel back to the women and bowed. "*Su gahwynn*," he said to them before answering Donavon. "This is path of the kaharpynn, the war chiefs. Elders do not come this way."

They continued upward, stopping to drink the sweet water at several prayer shrines along the way, each manned by ladies in waiting, as Notalk called them. All of them were young, at the peak of their beauty, and wore scented white gowns. Donavon could not help wondering what the ladies in waiting were waiting for.

In time they reached a point where the trail rounded off near the top of the mountain and Donavon got his first look at Mother Temple, her smooth circular dome mounted high upon the summit. To either side of her main body were lesser towers, shaped like upside-down beehives mounted atop connected halls. The hint of the sunset was just gracing the mighty pillars that supported her delicate arches below the dome—an awe-inspiring sight.

They continued on, reaching a stream that appeared to originate from the temple. A curious warm draft eddied off the water as they crossed an ancient footbridge. Getting closer to the peak, Donavon realized that the surface of the dome was not smooth at all, but rather a vast series of stone pavilions stacked in layers of ever shrinking rings. Onward they plodded, making straight for the vaulted chamber that arched outward from the front of the temple, a sizeable work in itself. Two more women met them at the top of the long flight of steps, although they were gowned in black. Priestesses, Donavon guessed. Notalk bowed and Donavon did the same. After receiving their blessings, they passed through the atrium and entered the main body of the temple.

The air in the sanctum was humid and laced with incense. The light was dim. A ring of arches circumvented the towering walls, high up where the dome began. The light of the setting sun filtered through the portholes, and a crimson hue colored the inner arc of the dome. Silence saturated the chamber. The Great Mother statue stood in the center of the open space, colossal in her serene beauty; just like at the fountain in Wulfhaven, only without the wolf at her feet or the butterfly on her outstretched arm. She stood instead on a monument of mountain goats, all intricately sculpted with their horns facing outward in a protective ring. The muscular legs of the great beasts descended into a steaming moat, out of which the heated spring water flowed into a narrow canal that crossed the chamber and disappeared into a tunnel.

Scanning the sanctum, Donavon saw grim men in tribal war paint lying on benches against the wall in various stages of meditation. The men were foreboding even in prayer, and he quickly surmised that his best course of action was not to act at all. Though it was all he could do not to blurt out his surprise at seeing Scarchief flat in a trance only eight benches away. He had not seen the venerable warrior since his guntocs were at his throat last fall at the Temple of Totems.

Notalk nudged his shoulder and indicated they should move to the central altar at the fringe of the moat. A variety of herbs and twigs were scattered on the wide stone slab amidst tufts of dried gahenya. Smoke, both pungent and sweet, rose out of basins carved into the marble surface. Donavon watched the wisps rise past the horned heads of the goats and beyond the Great Mother into the ethereal hue above. His nose tingled as he inhaled the scent. He felt light and heady, like he could walk on a fragrance. *Why not?* he thought, taking a step toward the misty moat.

He felt a firm tap on his shoulder and turned in confusion. "Notalk?"

A woman in black stood there. "This way, Wulfwynn."

"You're not Notalk. Who are you? I like the white gowns better."

"You must rest now." She had an old voice. "Take my hand."

"Where are we going?"

A wrinkled hand, and rough. "Have no worries."

"What's going on?"

A gentle touch on his face. "Lie down on the bench."

"But I—"

"She will show you."

Swish! Donavon opened his eyes and found himself in a field of blue. Another swish and a shadow. Two great wings overhead. A butterfly perched on a boulder, larger than any bird he had ever seen, filtering the sunshine through translucent yellow wings.

"What is this place?" he asked, stepping out of the creature's shade and into the hot sun. He scratched an itch on the back of his neck. His claws dug deep into the fur. How good it felt. Abruptly, he stopped. Claws? Fur? A quick tilt of the head and he was back at it, attacking the itch with a vengeance.

A scent wafted out of the gahenya, a living breathing scent. Ears up in the grass. *Flesh!* In a flash he was up. The rabbit flushed, no time for questions. Power in pace, the hunt was on. The hare was quick, but so was he. Quicker than ever, in fact, and stronger. Every bound brought him closer to his prey. Up they darted through fields and blossoms; higher and higher they climbed. The thrill of the chase drove him on, like running with Scraggs in the glades. *Snap!* A miss, just barely, the taste of blood so near.

The hunt continued up the glen and through the pastures to a steep ravine that lined rapids. The rabbit kept just a fang length away, always dodging his jowls at the last. And it seemed to Donavon as they closed in upon the rushing water, that he had entered a place where no man had ever been and the passage of time was but a dream. So powerful was the impression, he gave up on the chase and stopped at a cleft that fell sheer to the rapids. He sniffed at the edge. A strong musky scent. Deep hoof prints in the earth. And big. The same scent passed over the tip of his tail, fresh.

He turned around and saw them. Goats, only much larger. More like a herd of horned draught mules. Yet unlike mules, there was nothing docile about them. The hair on his hackles went up as they closed in. He searched the ravine for an escape route. The bank cut steep on both sides of the rapids—no help there. It suddenly occurred to him that the rabbit had led him into a trap. Something between a growl and a whine escaped his jowls. His options were limited. Either charge the line of horns or swim the rapids. Neither choice appealed to him. Damn the rabbit!

He faced the goats and prepared for the dash, then looked at his feet in dismay—for feet they were. Then to his hands, complete with all five fingers. Of all times to be a man! At a loss, he kept his back to the drop while the goats formed a semicircle around him. The lead buck let out a foreboding snort that could have whipped a bull. The others did the same. Time was up. He made ready to leap into the rapids, and then heard a woman's voice echo in the gorge. The same voice from the fountain.

"Open your eyes," she commanded.

Donavon obeyed.

"That's it, very good," said the aged woman in her black veil. Her old voice rang with power. "Now drink this. It will help your headache." She held a clay vessel in her wrinkled hands.

For whatever reason, he felt compelled to listen, not out of fear, but something else. Humility perhaps. She tipped the vessel and he sipped. It was sweet with a tinge of honey, like Enyalda's gingerwhip cookies. He did, in fact, have a headache, so he took another sip, then more until the vessel was empty. His focus wavered on the stone goat heads that hovered over the moat. The sight made him growl.

The old woman put her hand to his forehead. "Be at ease, Spirit of Wolf." Her rough finger slid down his face, stroking his cheek. The sensation relaxed him, as if he were a child again.

"Come now, Wulfwynn. Rise and follow me. We have work to do."

Together they left the bench and circumvented the Mother statue. Donavon kept a wary eye on the goats. From the moat they followed the canal across the chamber and under an archway into the wall. They walked a long, narrow passage to a point where the water vanished into ledge. A set of steps descended to yet another chamber of a more earthen nature. The walls were rough hewn, if hewn at all. Eons of calcium coated the once molten rock. Torches were set here and there, and prisms of light reflected off crystals set in walls. He felt like a tiny bee inside one of his sister's wild orchids. They approached the far end of the chamber, where a cluster of candles flickered on a narrow fold in the ledge. The veiled woman moved like a lynx in spite of her age. Donavon trailed behind, still gathering his wits, though his headache was gone.

The priestess turned when they reached the candles. "Come, let me have a closer look at you."

He walked closer and again she touched his face. The sensation of her finger was impossible to resist and he gazed into her veiled eyes, submitting utterly to her touch.

"It is good to see you alive and well, Donavon. I must admit there were times when I had my doubts. You were such a brazen little boy. It took vials of my best esters to keep you out of trouble."

Shocked, Donavon nearly wrenched his neck at the old woman's words. "Muma! Is it really you?" He threw his arms around her.

"It is, my good pup, but please, I am ten years older now and you are ten years stronger. Be nice to my old bones."

"I can't believe it!" he said, letting go. "I thought I would never see you again. Wait till Enya hears about this."

"Ah, Enyalda." Muma lifted the veil and revealed her crannied face. "How is my precious little seedling? Did she fare well on the mountain?"

The recollection of his sister's last visit to the colonel's stock house tempered his excitement. "She is fine, Muma," he said, looking solemnly into the old woman's black eyes. Like obsidian spear points, they penetrated his mind.

"Do not be guarded, Donavon," she said. "I know what you did and what happened to your sister. All the elders do. We were called to council as soon as word of the constable's death crossed the Haven. I pleaded with Choroqua to issue his wolves. To bring you all back to the Awshaws where we could insure that our promise to your father would be kept. Yet he refused, saying that none of you were of Gwyntah blood and so should remain with your own. I was relieved to hear that the Mahocpynn's cipher brought you to the mountain."

"What promise?" Donavon asked, still stunned by Muma's presence.

Muma smiled. Her leathery wrinkles had a warm, internal radiance. Donavon knew the glow, like an infant knows its mother's voice. To see the glow now in a candlelit cavern beneath some temple in a distant land made it all the more potent.

"Uryan loved all of you so very much," she said. "Yet the war kept him away. When your mother became pregnant, he knew he would not be there for the delivery, and so he appealed to Choroqua for a priestess well versed in the arts to see your mother through the term. Many a life debt your father had earned for his brave deeds in battle, and so the request was granted. It was obligation that brought me to your home but love that kept me there. The birth of you and Enyalda was something I had never witnessed before or since. The effort consumed your mother. I knew in that instant that my place was with you and your sister, to see you both to adulthood. When Fergus sent me away, it was all I could do not to call the shadow upon him. Such an evil man." Muma turned her head, and the light on her wrinkles faded so that she appeared dark and menacing in the stretching shadows.

Donavon, out of instinct perhaps, changed the subject. "I saw Father in a dream, Muma, on my first night in Gwyntahlynn. He rode with his men. At least, I think he did. It seemed so real. He told me they were riding to battle on the Mountain."

"I know," Muma said. "Choroqua informed me."

"But I never told him about my father. Only the soldier with the rabbit pelts."

"Yes, he told me of that too. His totem is the hawk, just like your father. Very little escapes him. He showed me the pelt that was left at your camp."

"I still don't get what that pelt was about. I almost got beheaded over it."

"You crossed over, Donavon, to the Mountain and back. It is a very ancient and dangerous practice that only the wise dare attempt. Even then, it is the wiser yet who refrain. The fact that you did it without guidance and survived is a puzzle to us all. Even Choroqua is mystified."

"But I was not alone. The soldier with the musket was there too. He's the one who put the wulfweed on the fire."

"Yes, but you see, that only compounds the mystery. The soldier you speak of is Huru Shakein. He is a *nahun-gahtta*."

"What in the world is that?"

"A trapped soul. Huru Shakein is unique among them in that his body still grows like any other, in spite of being void of spirit. That he revealed himself as a young boy in your dream is significant. Somehow you have bridged the gap between body and spirit. Normally a feat only achieved through the dark arts."

"I don't get it. How can something be living and dead?"

"The spirit on its own knows no bounds, Donavon, yet the body by its nature is forever confined to the limits of the world. The mind links the two and sustains the balance. Life is the relationship of the three. When a body is wounded, it is easy to recognize the damage: a broken bone, a ruptured vessel, a severed nerve. Not so the case with the spirit.

If the trauma to a soul is severe, it may choose to abandon its body and forsake the life it was meant to serve. Once this happens, death to the body is sure to follow. In some cases, if the will to survive is strong enough, the mind will create voices and visions in a last attempt to trick the spirit into staying. Of course, this puts a terrible strain on the mind, and more often than not will lead to madness if not grounded in faith."

"Faith in the Great Mother?" asked Donavon.

"If that is your faith, yes. But not all who live recognize the divine love of the Mother."

"The Great Father then?"

"Yes again, if that is your faith. But he too may have limits for some."

"What if you don't have a faith?"

"That is rarer than you think, Donavon. A mind that is clever enough to create an illusion in the first place will most likely craft its own faith in order to save itself."

"Is that what the soldier did?"

"No, it is what the Mahocpynn did."

"The colonel?"

"Yes. War can shatter a mind that is not firmly grounded in faith. He used the legend of the Mountain to foster confidence in his fighters. It is what gave them the strength to do what they did, regardless of the deity to which they were pledged. That and the hymns in the Book of Jahocwynn. He incorporated the sacred melodies into his command codes to further empower their spirits. And though I dare say his tactics were clever, they would never have succeeded if not for the mercy and love that backed his will."

"So the musketman bought the colonel's yarn on faith," Donavon said. "That still doesn't explain how he could be living and dead at the same time."

Muma's eyes sharpened. "Oh, you are a cunning little Wulfwynn, aren't you?" she said, pinching his cheek. "Far more attentive than I remember. Impressive. Perhaps my esters paid off after all."

Her fingers slid across his face to just above his ear, where they yanked out a sizeable tuft of his long red hair by the roots. Donavon yelped and watched her float like a shadow to the far end of the candlelit shelf. There she removed the lid from an urn and poured its crystalline contents into a flat bowl. Holding a candle in one hand, she placed his hair in the bowl and whispered something in Gwyntah while she lowered the flame. A blinding blue light blazed in the bowl. Muma quickly turned around to face Donavon, her black eyes penetrating.

"Very well, Wulfwynn. You asked, so I will tell you. The mind is the link between spirit and body. In the case of Huru Shakein, his trauma came in battle under the Raven's shadow. He was noble, yes, yet still a child at heart, easily subject to fear and impressions. Whatever the mystery, the link between his body and spirit was stretched rather than severed, and so his soul now lingers as an object external to itself. Close enough that the body still lives, but far enough that it is spared the trauma. Under the circumstance, it is not surprising that the boy's horrified spirit chose to manifest itself in a gun."

The flame subsided, leaving a pungent tang in the air. Muma turned around and poured the liquefied contents of the bowl into a slate mold, which she promptly compressed with another. Raising both arms, she spoke again in Gwyntah, though this time her voice rang with command. At last she lowered her arms and held out her shaking hands, appearing suddenly tired and drawn.

"Are you all right, Muma?" Donavon asked, hurrying to take hold of her hands. "What did you do?"

"Just a little precaution, that is all. Come, my pup, help me back up to the temple so we can catch up under the stars. Our work in here is done."

Together they climbed up the stairs to a high veranda on one of the beehive towers. Long they talked into the night under stars clear and crisp. Far below at the base of the holy hill, a scattering of torches dotted the plain. How distant they seemed, as if reflections of the stars. Donavon felt like a child again, going on and on about his dreams, visions, and schemes, as if only a day had passed since he'd last snuggled with the old woman by the hearth. How wonderful it felt to have an open ear again.

Muma said just enough to maintain the flow, but not so much to flood it. The dour subjects raised earlier in the cavern were never brought to mention. Rather to the simple themes she veered the stream to keep their hearts at ease. Such as Donavon's favorite hunting trails in the Ring, his newfound love of the run, and his refreshing sleep under the stars at the woodland shrine. He was fascinated to discover that the shrine had been the haunt of the Old Mitt's mother, herself a high priestess. More intriguing yet, the colonel was actually a Toricean general who had defected and who happened to be a skilled mason of all things, and had spent three years in the Ring making the stairs to his mother's shrine. What a tale that would make at the tavern.

And so it continued high atop the Mother Temple, where they poured their thoughts over the plain. And though many words were said, many more were left unsaid. Not until the stars had shifted and the dawn was only hours away did they leave the balcony. Muma showed him to his chamber in the tower and sang him to sleep with a long lost lullaby.

Donavon awoke to a tray full of fruit, nuts, and bread next to his bed. No meat, but no matter. It was all good when mixed with lupini. He felt surprisingly refreshed after his breakfast. Morning light shone through a portal high in the chamber. A young woman in white entered with a bowl of sweet water. After Donavon drank it, she directed him to a large silver tub filled with steaming water and gestured for him to get in. At a loss, he stood in the chamber like a beaver in a barren desert. The woman calmly removed his garments, clearly well versed in the routine. When he was in the water, she proceeded to scrub his back with a coarse woolen cloth. The sensation rippled across his sinews.

After his bath, two more ladies in white gowns came in—one carrying a war tunic, the other a satchel and a tray full of paint. After assisting him into his new garb, they had him sit. They dreadlocked his hair, shaved his face, and applied the paint. One woman removed two guntocs from the satchel and fitted them to his forearms, their leather straps cinched snug. He released the holster triggers and snapped his arms forward and down. The blades sprang out over each wrist and locked into place. He studied the ancient weapon. The blades were sleek as talons, curving over his knuckles; so intricate, yet simple. A blue crystal encased in silver was riveted to the wrist mount on the left guntoc. Around that, the face of a one-eyed wolf had been etched into the rigid leather.

The ladies led him out of the chamber and down a long flight of stairs to a room where the tribal war chiefs had gathered. A warrior approached him; the black and white war paint on his face vaguely resembled an owl. Upon closer examination Donavon realized it was Notalk

"You changed your face," Donavon said.

Notalk simply bowed and remained silent by his side. Shortly thereafter the kaharpynn began to funnel out of the room. Donavon noticed Scarchief among them. Not until the room had cleared did Notalk speak, instructing Donavon that it was time for them to enter the council.

The council chamber was lined with elaborate carvings of every animal imaginable. It reminded Donavon of the cavern in the mountain set high above the Aisle of Totems. The sound of cascading water came from somewhere behind the walls. Four rows of stone tiers, each the width of a bench, rimmed the semicircular chamber. The highest tier was against the wall and the others descended forward toward the center. The tiers were sectioned into thirds by two waist-high petitions.

The elders were seated in the middle section, all in black. A mix of hoods and veils covered their faces. Donavon wondered if Muma was among them. The kaharpynn, the war chiefs, were seated to their right. Straight faced and in war paint, they filled all four rows from floor to wall. Scarchief sat on the foremost tier, though his face bore no paint, only burns. The section to the left of the elders was empty. Donavon and Notalk were directed to sit alone in the front row.

Gwyntahpynn Choroqua entered through an archway behind a raised platform, on which sat his throne. A great sculpture of a raven loomed overhead with wings extended. Two masked shamans assisted the high chief to his throne under the wings. Once seated, he raised his staff and opened the forum.

The deliberation began with the elders. An old man, stood up, pulled back his hood, and addressed Choroqua. Notalk quietly gave Donavon an overview of what was said—that the water level of the lake was dropping and that the peace stealers planned to house their forces in the holy grounds of the Lake Savior.

The elder pulled his hood forward and sat down. The floor was then opened to the kaharpynn. One by one, each war chief spoke. Donavon could not understand their ancient dialect, but there was no mistaking the fierce conviction in their tones. Once every kaharpynn had his say, Choroqua led the council in discussion. From what Notalk conveyed, the question was not if they should go to war, but when and how. Opinions were not unanimous, however, and at times Choroqua had to temper the debate.

"*Sach hayem!*" he would shout. Stand no more.

The debate carried on for some time. Notalk whispered key points of discussion, but his summaries were hard to follow, and Donavon became increasingly perplexed as to why he was even there. At last, when the words became nothing more than a stream of sound, Choroqua raised his staff and ended the talk.

"*Sach nahee brethule Meguntoc,*" he said, looking at Donavon.

Donavon snapped out of his trance and turned to Notalk.

Notalk stood up. "Gwyntahpynn wants to know what the son of One Talon has to say."

"What?" Donavon said.

"You must stand, Wulfwynn. You have been given the floor to speak."

Donavon stood up and scanned the council. All eyes were on him, elders and kaharpynn alike. What could he possibly say that would not humiliate him? Confusion strangled his thoughts. He felt cornered, like a wild animal ensnared in a trap. Looking at the elders, he saw a hunched woman in a veil gesture with her hand. Muma? A warmth on his left wrist drew his gaze to the blue crystal in his guntoc; it shimmered in a light of its own. The etching of the one-eyed wolf in the leather reminded him of the fountain in Wulfhaven Square and the hard lessons issued there.

"Raise the lake," he said boldly to the throne.

Silence followed, giving Donavon ample time to consider what he had just said.

Choroqua spoke again.

"Gwyntahpynn asks you to clarify," Notalk said.

"The pogies have dropped the lake so they can work the bridge pylons," Donavon answered. "All we need to do is raise it so they can't."

One of the kaharpynn stood. "*Salhue?*"

How? That word he knew. "We go to the Weirs and convince them to close the gates."

Another kaharpynn stood and voiced his obvious dissent. Others nodded in agreement.

"What did he say?" Donavon asked Notalk.

"Kaharpynn Nayechi challenges your wisdom. He say the weirmen have no honor and sell their souls for peace-stealer money. Such a mission would fail and only disperse our strength."

Good point. He stared at the elders while he gathered his thoughts. It was a long shot for sure. Only a guess really. Who was he to assume that the chief boatman had learned his lesson? Even if he had, what authority would the brute have to close the gates? He faced the assembly of war chiefs and spoke slowly, giving Notalk time to translate.

"The war chief is right," he said. "Good warriors should not be wasted on a hunch. And no, I am not of the wise. I am here because I listened to a crazy old man who talks to his chimney. As for the warriors, my pack as you call them ..." He turned to Choroqua. "I ask that the High Chief command them to remain in Gwyntahlynn. If not, they will follow me. Every one of their guntocs is worth a hundred pogie necks!" He looked back at the dissenting kaharpynn. "I will go alone. Time is what I need. Let me find the one who defiled the Mother's pool in Wulfhaven. The one whose own blade I had at his throat. Give me time to find out why the Mahocpynn commanded me to let the weirman chief breathe another day."

A hush closed in on the hall. The kaharpynn gave no further sign of appeal. The silence continued until it seemed that the water behind the walls would burst through the stones. At last, Choroqua raised his staff in summons. Scarchief stepped forward and bowed. More words were exchanged that Donavon did not understand, and then Scarchief returned to his seat. Choroqua stood and addressed the entire assembly. His tone was stark and surprisingly powerful for a feeble old man. Donavon did his best to understand what he said, though he caught only certain words. *Luhn*— moon, *kahar*—war, *maha gaila*—mountain flower, and of course, *Wulfwynn*. Then, just like that, the council ended. The Gwyntahpynn was assisted back through the shadowy archway below the wings of the raven. The elders left through a separate exit, followed by the war chiefs. Last of all, Notalk stood up from the bench.

"Come, Wulfwynn, we leave temple now."

"That's it? What did he say? Did he hear my request?"

"Yes, he hear, and no, he not accept."

"Then I will go anyway," Donavon said. "I am not a prisoner. He cannot keep me here."

"That you will, Wulfwynn, but not alone. Gwyntahpynn commands your pack to stay intact. He also assign Kaharpynn Swalhula to serve as your wisdom advisor on mission."

"Scarchief?"

"Yes. He grant us one moon to raise lake. If water still down when mountain flower bloom, then war he declare on peace stealers."

"One moon," Donavon said. "That shouldn't be too hard."

The owl nodded, and they left the temple.

20
Pogie Day

The Yellow Wagon was one of Wulfhaven's oldest heirlooms. A priceless gift and token of peace from the Fatherland, the relic was a treasure to behold. The closed coach was made of sturdy hand-carved hardwood finished in gold-flecked enamel that beamed by day and sparkled by night. Impressive shoulder-high wheels, embossed in brass, revolved around massive spindles mounted on lancewood axles. The interior was fit for royalty: six seats upholstered in the finest crimson felt and hemmed with golden satin. Ornate windows adorned the chassis, as if portals to another world.

Traditionally, stewardship of the Yellow Wagon was bestowed on the residing lord baron of the time, Augustus Mitterhal the last of six. Mitterhal, a son of Toricia, recognized the significance of this symbol, this tie to the Havens' fatherland, and prided himself on taking meticulous care of the prized chariot. In the growing unrest of his day, the Yellow Wagon served as a reminder to the people of the Three Havens that their heritage was noble, and something to be proud of.

Heinrick von Krutzwig raised his glass to the chief engineer. "Building codes are like taxes, Barbarus. They're only as good as the guns that levy them."

"Point well taken, Constable," Barbarus said. "Though I dare say it took more than taxes and span charts to build the Silvermine Bridge."

Marlin Barleycopp took a sip from his glass before chiming in on the chat. "By the light of the Haven, have I just heard the chief engineer suggest that the bridge was built on a prayer?"

"Not at all, Mayor. In my field we prefer to call it reasonable deduction. I merely point out that calculations only go so far on a structure without prior model."

"Ah yes, spoken like a true master," Barleycopp said, raising his glass. "Here's to sophisticated guesswork."

A young woman with a dark native complexion approached with a tray full of sweets. Krutzwig eyed the server in her dainty white skirt, tempted to grope for more than a truffle. Why else would the mayor hire these simple-minded half-breeds to work his state-run cocktail parties, if not to be toyed with?

Barleycopp beat him to the prize. "Thank you, madam," he said, removing a truffle from the tray. "Be sure to send my compliments to the kitchen."

The young lady smiled and bowed.

What a shameless gentleman, Krutzwig thought, barely able to mask his disdain. He watched the mayor return the bow to his heathen slave as if the transparent act might compensate for the fact that he was nothing more than a bygone crony posing as a figurehead for the masses. Yes, how pathetic, standing there in his outdated war regalia, chewing on his truffle, as rigid as one of those decorated nutcrackers he kept on the shelf in the main lobby. The mere sight sickened Krutzwig and forced him to down his cocktail.

A shift in the masses drew his attention to the ballroom entry. The man of the hour had arrived. Brigadier Douglass Wittworth, Rankwall's number-one military pick, sauntered through the pillared archway, handing his white gloves to one of several officers in his entourage. Krutzwig sized him up, having yet to meet the illustrious war hero. His hair was sterling silver—no doubt a wig—and his fleshy face wore a painted grin. Not quite what Krutzwig had expected, but facts were facts. The brigadier's decisive victory at Altamar was nothing to scoff at.

Krutzwig stepped forward as Wittworth approached, determined to beat Barleycopp to the introductions. "Welcome, Brigadier. I am Chief Constable Heinrick von Krutzwig. I look forward to working with you."

"Likewise," Wittworth said, and turned right away to Barleycopp. "Unless history deceives me, you must be Marlin Barleycopp, the famous captain of the goat-hyde pipers."

Barleycopp shook hands with the brigadier. "The same, though I am happy to say a mere servant of the people now. It is an honor, Brigadier, to make your acquaintance."

"The honor is mine, Captain. If not for your stand at Spaulding Pass, we might still be bowing to the red. It is good to meet at last."

Another server arrived with a selection of cocktails. The officer who had been handed the brigadier's gloves stepped forward and selected a glass. He drank from it, paused, and then handed it to Wittworth. The commander promptly raised his glass as if to praise the ceiling. "Here's to victory, both past and present."

More toasts, full of pomp and circumstance, were made, as Krutzwig fought for his moments to cast a witty word. The small talk went on and on until the brigadier, after his second cocktail, steered the conversation to a more poignant subject.

"Tell me, Captain. As one who was there, are the rumors true? Was Mitterhal, in fact, mad when he gave the order to sack the pass in toxic smoke?"

"Madness is a relative term, Brigadier," Barleycopp said after a swallow. "Easy to misconstrue in battle. But I do say in my judgment he was more than lucid when the bales were lit. It was the aftermath, I believe, that sent him over. None of us knew what the wulfweed would do when combined with the accelerant. The intent was to soften the enemy's perceptions, not to commit a blanket slaughter."

"Ah, yes, I can only imagine the guilt. It's not an easy business we are in, is it, Captain?"

"Not at all," Barleycopp said. "I find politics much more palatable."

Krutzwig stepped in, seeing his chance to derail the mayor at his own game. "Politics indeed, Mayor. Could it be that your policies might still be tied to that of the colonel's? Let us not forget that he was the one who unilaterally ordered the bombardment of the bridge, the very reason for which the brigadier and his troops are here in the first place. I would hate to think that a servant of the people might share the same empathy for heathens."

Barleycopp maintained a polite expression. "A crude suggestion, Constable, one that I would not typically entertain. However, in light of our present company, I will say that my sentiment toward heathens, as you call them, merely reflects that of the Haven's majority. It is not the bridge per se that the people object to, but the mines. That and the failure to honor a promise. The Gwyntahmahoma are as tied to this region as we are. War would be a terrible blow to both sides. As for the colonel, I regret to say I would be hard pressed as mayor of the people to act on his direction even if he were inclined to give it."

The native woman appeared again with her tray of truffles, perfectly timed to take the punch out of Krutzwig's assault. A little too perfect, perhaps. Krutzwig seethed while the brigadier reached for a truffle and eased the tension.

"You are right about war, Captain," Wittworth said. "Let us hope for the sake of all parties that the bridge can be repaired without incident and that our presence in your city amounts to nothing more than a deterrent to those who would impede the project."

Ignored again, Krutzwig stood hopelessly stranded with his empty glass, waiting for the right moment to break away. Where was Glockstoff anyway? He scanned the statehouse ballroom in search of Rueger's replacement. He found him mingling with the guards at the rear exit.

"Excuse me, Brigadier," Krutzwig said with a hint of urgency. "I regret to cut this short, but it seems I must tend to a pressing matter at once."

"By all means, Constable. I will see you in headquarters at the briefing tomorrow."

Krutzwig strode to the rear entry and addressed Glockstoff. "Quick, act like you have something important to tell me."

Glockstoff stiffened and saluted. "Actually I do, sir. We found out that the boy who wrote the play at the opera also led the children in the tenth hymn on the day we made the arrest at the cathedral."

"Really. His name?"

"Only Barusta. He is an orphan at the abbey."

"The abbey. My, my, what a splendid discovery. I believe an interview with the young chap is in order, Captain."

"Right away, sir. I will issue the subpoena at once."

"No! No subpoena. Tell the monks we wish to honor him for his success at the opera and that he should report to Pogetsa headquarters to receive his award."

"An award, sir?"

"Yes, for good citizenship. Now let's get out of here. Make it look urgent."

The next day, Krutzwig left the briefing room at Pogetsa headquarters with a nagging headache. The briefing had been everything he'd expected, a show of posture more than anything else. The brigadier spent nearly the entire meeting grinding out a rote list of military protocols and contingencies. It was all Krutzwig could do to stay awake.

Harriet Simpleton, the office clerk, hailed him from the lobby desk as he beelined for the stairs to his office. "Excuse me, Constable. Before I send the master copy for next week's parade to the print shop, I want to make sure it meets your standards."

"I have more important matters, Miss Simpleton. I'm sure whatever you come up with will be fine."

"If I may trouble you for just a moment, should we call it the Pogetsa Day Parade or the Haven Day Parade?"

He paused. "Hmm. I never thought of what to call it. Pogetsa has a ring, doesn't it?"

"For what it's worth, I think the Haven Day Parade would appeal to a broader audience."

"Perhaps you're right. Make it so. Wait! Make sure you mention in the flyer that the Yellow Wagon will be leading the cavalcade."

"Shouldn't we clear that with the mayor first?"

"Just do as I say!"

"Absolutely, sir. Oh, I almost forgot. Captain Glockstoff said the boy from the abbey will be coming here to pick up some kind of award. The captain said you know all about it. Would you like me to give it to him when he arrives?"

"An award, that's right. No, no, that will be fine. Send the boy to my office when he arrives. Only him, mind you. Nobody else."

Krutzwig seized the bowl of candy on Miss Simpleton's desk and darted for the stairs. On the way he stopped at the display of arms mounted on the lobby wall. His eye locked on a twenty-caliber single-shot flintlock. "This will do," he said, snatching the pistol off its wall mount.

An hour later, the boy arrived. Krutzwig welcomed him and invited him to take a seat.

The boy surveyed the office with his sharp little eyes and then made for the chair across from Krutzwig's desk.

Krutzwig stood and pointed to the couch. "Actually, why don't you sit over there? Help yourself to some of that candy on the table."

The boy did as he was told, though he took no candy. He simply sat on the edge of the couch cushion, back straight, his hands in his lap, as if waiting to receive a lesson on grammar.

"No, really," Krutzwig said. "Take as much as you'd like. You deserve it."

"No thank you, sir."

"Hmm, very well. Tell me, young fellow … uh … Barusta, I should say. Before I give you your award, what inspired you to write such a marvelous play?"

"It wasn't that hard, sir. The story was already written. All I had to do was tell my friends what to do."

"Now, now, don't sell yourself short. I'm an enthusiast, you know, when it comes to the arts. In all my years I have never seen an audience so taken. Trust me, you are quite the young master. But now that you bring it up, where did you hear the story? As charming as it is, it doesn't seem like one they would teach at the abbey."

"It isn't. The fountain lady told us."

"The fountain lady?"

"Yes, she's very smart. She knows lots of stories."

"I see. I take it you see her often."

"We all do. Miss Rafferty lets us go there after midday prayer. We're supposed to stay at the fountain, but I don't always follow that rule."

"Yes, well, rules are like taxes, young man. They are only as good as … Anyway I digress. Does your good pastor know of these visits to the fountain?"

"Pastor Marcus knows everything. Why are there footprints on your floor?"

"What?"

"Over there. There's black footprints leading from your desk to the shelf."

"Oh, that. It's just a silly bit of décor to liven up the office. Thank you for noticing. Now, getting back to the pastor, am I to understand that he bestowed on you the honor of leading the children of the orphanage in song?"

"He doesn't like that word."

"What word?"

"Orphanage."

"That's not the p—" Krutzwig loosened the collar around his neck. He had forgotten how much he hated children. "Of course he doesn't. Nobody does. Such a sad-sounding word. Let's pretend I never said it. So did he or did he not assign you to lead your friends in song?"

Silence.

Krutzwig, out of habit, went to the decanter on the shelf. No doubt the wily little rat was onto him. So much for candy and compliments. Time to up the ante.

"Speak up, young man," he said after downing a double.

"I don't think I should respond to that, sir."

"And why not?"

"Because Miss Rafferty said no matter what I think, I must mind my manners."

Krutzwig picked up the single-shot pistol from his desk. He pulled back the hammer one click and faced Barusta, keeping the barrel pointed to the floor. "All the more reason to answer my question."

Fear widened the young boy's eyes. Krutzwig drew back the hammer a second click and walked close to the couch. Ever so subtly, Barusta nodded.

"Ah, yes, much better. Miss Rafferty would be so proud of you. Now tell me, Barusta. On the day you and your orphan friends sang in church, did Pastor Marcus make arrangements prior to the service that you would sing a hymn from the Old Tome?"

Another nod.

"Excellent. That wasn't so hard, was it? You have been most cooperative and well mannered, I might add." He held the gun out to Barusta, handle first. "I want you to have this as a token of your fine achievements. It's an old sea-service pistol, a fine flintlock. Great for shooting squirrels."

Barusta took the gun.

Krutzwig smiled. "So much better than a useless plaque, don't you think?"

"Can I go now?"

"Of course. Take care of that gun. Someday you'll get the uniform that goes with it."

Barusta made for the door, eyeing the black footprints along the way.

"Oh, Barusta, one more thing. I suggest you keep the details of our discussion to yourself. Remember, every friend you tell is one we will have to question. Not all the Pogetsa are as nice as me. Besides, it would be such a shame to take back your award."

Barusta nodded, tucked the pistol in his trousers, and left.

Three days passed and Miss Simpleton once again intercepted Krutzwig as he escaped the briefing chamber. "Excuse me, Constable. Several monks from the abbey came here while you were in session." She picked up a parchment from her desk. "Marcus Poulakis has submitted a formal appeal regarding the quartering of Lakwynnian troops in the abbey dormitories. The document is strongly worded and he demands that the Pogetsa rescind the edict at once."

Krutzwig strode to the desk and snatched the appeal out of her hands. "Give me your pen," he ordered. With barely a glance at the contents, he drenched the quill in ink and smeared his answer in large letters over the gold clergy seal. DENIED.

"There you have it. Are there any other pressing matters, Miss Simpleton? I really am busy."

"Yes, as a matter of fact. The mayor refuses to authorize the chartering of the Yellow Wagon for the parade. He says it is a symbol of peace and should not be used to lead a military cavalcade. The gesture would only fuel civil unrest."

"Ah-hah! At last that pompous nutcracker shows his colors. Once Wittworth hears of this, Barleycopp will finely get what he deserves."

"Actually, sir, I believe the mayor informed the brigadier first. He concurs with the mayor."

Krutzwig sneered, suddenly taken by a fever. He grabbed the vial of ink on Miss Simpleton's desk and cast it at the lobby wall. The missile shattered on impact, leaving an ugly black scar on the stucco by the weapons display.

"Oh, my," Miss Simpleton said, both hands to her face.

"Shut up!" Krutzwig shouted. "I'm going to my office. When I come back that wall better be spotless. Understood?"

At her shaky nod, the chief constable stormed up the stairs to quell his fit.

21
High Time at the Weirs

Hector Xavier was as notorious as he was big, even among the sketchy circles in the Weirs. The Weir port provided the perfect arena for him to flex his muscle. A brutal shipman through and through, he had arrived at the Weirs as an escaped convict, having spent the majority of his formative years in a Toricean prison. As such he thrived on competition, and never balked at the opportunity to stomp the life out of his rivals. Those of like ilk, who did not pose a direct threat, he recruited with pitiless indifference into his ever-growing fleet of marauders. Yet for all his swagger, it was not status he lusted, but freedom. So he stayed to the waters even when his dealings on the mainland became firmly entrenched among the top wharf lords in the Weirs.

Donavon tossed a pair of gutted coneys over the fire and into Tiptoe's lap. "Here I am. The master of the hunt returns." The boisterous boast snapped the pack out of their mantras.

Tiptoe held up one of the dead rabbits and pointed out the fang marks on its fur. "With two-leg novice," he said, nodding to the wolf.

Laughter swelled in the camp. Even Scarchief cracked a smile at the jest.

Donavon smirked while the others threw in their jabs. To think he once thought the grim warriors were humorless. The pack fell back into silence while the rabbits roasted on skewers. When the time came to divvy the game, Tiptoe made sure to serve Scraggs first. He had left a choice portion uncooked.

Donavon chewed on a hind leg while he gazed up at the stars and tallied their nights out of Gwyntahlynn. It had taken eight days to cross the lake. The squally weather had forced them to keep their longboat close to shore, rather than battle the whitecaps over the broads. They had packed light for speed with only the basics: weapons, buckskin cloaks, wool blankets, and a store of lupini wrapped in goat-hyde to fuel the mission. Jesting aside, Donavon knew the warriors were grateful for the wild game he returned with every evening. Only once, when the day's squall had soaked them to the bone, had he and Scraggs failed to furnish the fire with a kill. That was three nights ago. Now at last they were here, at the fringe of the Weir port, in search of one of the most notorious characters in the province.

"So the way I see it," Donavon said, "tomorrow morning we shed our face paint and head straight for the waterfront. Someone's gotta know something over there. We'll act like trappers. Yeah, that'll work. From Multynhaven. We'll say we got business with Hector Xavier. A boatload of wolf pel—" He looked to Scraggs, digesting his dinner in the fringe of the firelight. "Eh, mink pelts. That's it. Fur for fish. Perfect."

"What we do if chief boatman not in port?" Pickpack asked.

"Then we wait until he is."

"What if he not want fur?" said Nosebleed.

"That's not the point. I'll lay out the real deal once we have his ear."

Blue struck next with the inevitable. "What is real deal, Wulfwynn?"

"I, ah … I'm still working on that. If anybody asks, just say you don't speak Toricean. Leave the talking to me."

Tiptoe raised his pinky finger, most untrapper-like. "Do we say that in Toricean or Gwyntah?"

Donavon spat into the fire and looked to his wisdom advisor for help. Scarchief's fixed jaw said it all. No doubt the plan needed refinement. Donavon decided to cut his losses and meditate. It was, after all, what a warrior did. Tomorrow would bring a fresh perspective.

They broke camp the next morning with few words. In short order they loaded the longboat and set out to oar. Scarchief still had yet to utter a word since last night's debacle at the fire. His stoic silence gnawed at Donavon. The veteran war chief was, after all, the wisdom advisor. If ever there were a time to give advice, now would be it. Donavon rowed on, consumed by his task, too proud to ask.

The traffic was light coming into port. Donavon bristled at the moored ships that bobbed like stark black buoys in the morning fog. It felt as if the silent vessels had eyes. Scraggs must have felt it too. His nose strayed to every scent that crossed the bow, first a sniff and then a growl. The longboat glided into an open slip midway on the wharf, where they were hailed by a gnarly old dockhand.

"Aye, visitors from the east by the looks o' ye. What brings ye Haven folk to the Weirs?" His shifty eye hung warily on the wolf.

Donavon tossed the coiled bowline to the old man. "We're trappers from Multynhaven. Looking for a sea cap by the name of Xavier. Hector Xavier. Have you seen him?"

"Oh, yes, me sees him," the old man said, tying off the rope. "Quites a bit we do. But big Hex don't take kindly to surprises. A wee bit nasty he gets with the unannounced. What's your freight?"

"The finest highland mink in the province. All in the winter molt. Where can we find him?"

"Aye, I'd be a fool to tell you that direct. You could try one of his water holes if you dare. You might get lucky. Or unlucky, dependin' how ye fare."

Not a bad idea, Donavon thought. Last time he'd tipped back a tankard was at Crown Tavern, the night before Old Mitt sent him across the Haven. Adman had organized a rousing send-off, where Serena Schonhauser had given a good-bye performance that Donavon would never forget. Neither would half the scrappers on the mountain. The fond memory made the dockhand's suggestion all the more tempting.

"Where's his hole?" Donavon asked.

"He gots a few. I'd start with the Gut Hatch, but don't let him on I told you. Keep the water on yer left until you pass the ol' works. Follow yer nose up the hill from the gaff shop. The alleys get narrow up that way so watch yer step. If I were you I'd—"

A shout came from a three-masted cutter farther up the wharf. "Where's that dock rat? We're heading out!"

"Hold yer fire, ye pushy bastard!" the old man shouted back. "Gots ta go, trapper," he said to Donavon as he hurried off. "Enjoy yer stay at the Weirs."

Donavon waited for him to get out of earshot before laying out his plan to the pack. "Okay, you guys heard the buzzard. Hector's in port, so our chances are good. We'll split up. Notalk, Scarchief, and Blue will stay at the boat with Scraggs. The rest come with me. He can't be that hard to find."

Scarchief stepped forward and spoke for the first time that day, addressing Notalk in Gwyntah.

Notalk nodded and turned to Donavon. "Karharpynn Swallhula say he cannot give you wisdom from boat. He go with you to city. Tiptoe stay with us."

Donavon swallowed back his disappointment. Scarchief in a bar?

"Fine," he said with as much sincerity as he could muster.

Instincts were like guardians, ever present, always alert. Donavon had learned to trust them a long time ago. Not in a conscious way, initially that is. As a child he simply accepted them, in the same way he accepted that rain would fall when the sky got dark. Most of his premonitions made perfect sense and hardly qualified as a mystery—but not all. There were days when he felt the rain long before a single storm cloud darkened the sky. Or what about the fresh deer tracks he knew he would find in the moss behind a hemlock in a stand where he had yet to be? Or perhaps more recently, serving as deputy in Cotton Crown, when he could tell by the scent of Gilly's sweat that the caged scrapper was going to feign compliance, only to throw a right hook the instant he cleared the cell? How did he know these things? Was it magic? Divine providence perhaps? Not until Hector Xavier baptized him in the pool of the fountain Goddess did he ever give his instincts much thought.

The grim group walked the seedy side streets—Donavon, Scarchief, Pickpack, and Nosebleed, all in their buckskin cloaks, hoods up. The smells of lake fare loomed as they came upon the Gut Hatch. It was indeed a hole, an old fish-grinding mill by the looks of it. The main entrance sank below the cobbles, down a set of granite steps lathered in fermenting puddles of who knows what. Donavon scanned the right side of the brick building in search of other exits. He spied a single iron door halfway down the alley. A row of window basins lined the lower lane, all fashioned with metal bars.

"All right, listen up. We gotta blend in best we can. That means relax, act like you're enjoying yourselves, not too much, just enough to keep the dogs off. Once we're in, let down your hoods but keep your guntocs covered. If things get messy, try not to use them. Understand?"

"Crack to jaw," Nosebleed said.

"Yeah, you got it. Just like the pogies at the bridge." Donavon looked at Scarchief. "No offense, Chief, but I think you better keep your hood up."

Pickpack translated the command and Scarchief nodded. The pack descended the steps.

The space inside was unexpectedly open, the air a mash of scents. Tables, chairs, and barstools were scattered across the dingy floor, below a high ceiling supported by a cluster of exposed pipes and thick metal girders. It appeared as if the entire ground floor had been gutted to allow headroom for a giant. A row of windows lined the red brick walls two stories up, though only the lower sashes had bars. Daylight filtered through the smoke that hovered over the tables. The serving bar started on the right wall but then extended perpendicular into the middle of the saloon, branching into an L shape that split the interior in half. Barstools lined both sides of the counter like bone spurs on the spine of a monstrous lake carp.

Not even noon, Donavon noted, and the place bustled. He scanned over the motley lot to an empty table against the wall, ten running steps from the iron door that led to the alley. "Over there," he said. He let down his hood and his dreadlocked hair fell to the sides of his face. The pack made it to the table without encounter. Donavon directed Scarchief to the seat closest the wall, the one most shielded from the light of the window. How odd to tell a kaharpynn where to sit.

Six ruffians sat at a table two windows away. Donavon gauged their stares and knew they were sizing up the newcomers. He had done it plenty of times himself, upholding the pecking order at Crown Tavern. He also knew that first impressions meant everything; the slightest show of weakness in a place like this would be a disaster. Confidence was critical.

"All right then, here we are," he said, striking his open palms on the table. "First things first. Bartender! We're thirsty. Send us a round of your finest."

A squab man with bushy sideburns acknowledged the order from behind the bar. Donavon returned the nod. So far so good. The six ruffians went back to their conversation. Donavon made small talk with Pickpack and Nosebleed while he continued to assess the lay of the establishment. The two warriors nodded, trying their best to play the part. All the while Scarchief stayed quiet in his corner, hood up, still as death.

The bartender arrived and set the order on the table, one shot glass at a time.

"There you have it, stranger. The best the Gut Hatch has to offer." He spoke it loudly enough to turn the heads of the party of six. Donavon couldn't miss the sly exchange of glances. "You're first timers," the server went on with a forced grin. "First rounds on the house."

Donavon lifted his shot glass as the bartender walked away. One sniff revealed his first mistake. The vapor stung his nose. At Crown Tavern, "the finest" always meant ale. This was more like paint solvent. No matter. Not the time or place to hesitate. And so, in one gulp, Donavon made his second mistake. Pickpack and Nosebleed followed his lead, true to the warrior code.

The fire went down like acid. Donavon's howl escaped before he knew what hit him, something between a yelp and a war cry. The other two slipped soundlessly into their altered states, as if shot in the back by arrows.

Laughter erupted at the bar. The bartender returned with two loaves of hard bread and a pitcher of water. "Aye, welcome to the Hatch, mates. You survived the first rite. Congratulations. What brings you to the Weirs, if you don't mind me asking?"

Donavon rubbed his eyes to clear the tears. "We're trappers. Looking to do business with Hector Xavier."

The table of six became quiet again.

"You must have a lot of pelts to be dealing with Hex," the bartender said.

"Finest mink in the province." Donavon focused on the bowl of ground pepper next to the bread. "All in the winter molt."

"I see. Well, best o' luck on that. Speak'n of luck, you know you impressed our lovely lady at the bar with that howl of yours. I think she'd like a dance with you."

Donavon rubbed his eyes again and looked to the bar. Sure enough, an alluring woman surrounded by brutes puckered her lips and blew him a kiss. The sight compounded his headiness. Why not? Out of impulse he obliged the request, making his third mistake of the day.

"Sure, send her over."

He regretted his words the moment she arrived. She was attractive, for sure, and crafty. Smart enough to work a crowd, but not so clever as to shed the scent of her used body. She tried with perfumes, balms, and oils to mask the whiff of her profession, but for all her exotic seasonings, it was like sniffing spoiled game to Donavon. He did his best to hide his revulsion and play the part of a skin-craved trapper, even as she sat on his lap and pressed her half-bare chest to his face. He had too. She was a pro. That much was clear, capable of whipping the regulars into a rut mentality. A flat-out rejection would spur every scab in the hole to be her hero.

The woman untied the top tethers of his cloak and rubbed his chest. She kissed him on the cheek and then hopped off his lap to undo her own outfit, one lacy garment at a time. The rest of the pack barely acknowledged her, showing more interest in the bread and water. For all their discipline, Donavon concluded that Gwyntah warriors made horrible actors, Scarchief in particular. He sat motionless like a forlorn phantom behind his untouched shot glass, cast in an aura of contempt. Thank the great Goddess his hood was up.

The whore had shed down to her lasts when she thrust one leg up onto the table and flashed him a sight. She faced him expectantly, holding a small leather purse under his nose. In that wide-eyed moment, Donavon realized his most profound mistake of the day. He had no money.

"Put it on my tab," he said with as much nonchalance as he could muster.

The purse disappeared, and then the leg. For that he was grateful. Yet barely had he breathed a sigh when he saw her break down in tears in front of her entourage at the bar.

"Damn." He looked across the table at Pickpack and Nosebleed, still engrossed in the bread. "Listen up. We're gonna have visitors. Let me do the talking. On my signal we make for the alley door and back to the wharf."

Company arrived as predicted, seven men led by a bald-headed bull covered in tattoos. Three moved in behind Donavon while the others sneered in the wake of their lead dog. The six ruffians stood up from their table for a better view. All of them carried single shot pistols. Not good, Donavon thought. Not good at all. His senses tingled. Chairs and stools slid on the floor in all directions. Stale breath behind him, ripe sweat in front.

The bull glowered with witless brawn. "You made my lady feel unwanted."

"That was not my intent," Donavon answered.

"I didn't ask for your intent. You better lay out some silver, lady's boy."

Donavon stood up. "I left my money back at the wharf. We'll have to go get it."

"I don't think so." The brute shoved him back in his seat.

Nosebleed started to rise.

Donavon stopped him with a command in Gwyntah.

"Well, well, what do we have here? Lady boy speaks the tongue. And look at these pretty little flowers pinned to his chest. I think they'd look a lot prettier on our lady, don't you?"

The brute reached for the silver brooch Sheriff Hoffman had given Donavon the night of his recruitment at the colonel's manor.

What followed had the feel of a dream. Maybe it was the firewater, or maybe something else. Donavon growled, and snapped at the outstretched hand. The bite went deep. The bull snarled and drew back his fist to strike, but the blow never came. Pickpack threw pepper in his eyes instead. The thug thrashed wildly at the seasoned air and the rest of his rabble closed in. They were met by Nosebleed's mirage of jabs.

Donavon sprang up and struck the blind bull in the gut, folding him over at the waist. He felt a sting in his shoulder but ignored it to finish his work. An uppercut to the jaw did the job; the bull went down. Then another sting, this one deep in the lower back. He turned around. Too late. Weakness ... Vision jarred ... The last thing he saw was Scarchief's empty seat.

There was a place Donavon went to as a child, before the days of Fergus Rankwall, when Muma still ran the house. It was a special place in a grove of hemlocks beyond their horse fields in Wulfhaven. He had witnessed the birth of a fawn there, though he never told Muma for fear of being punished for wandering so far from home. He did tell Enyalda, and even brought her there on occasion when the spirit so took them. It was the closest he ever came to pure peace.

Donavon's nostrils flared at the scent of stale urine. He kept his eyes closed, not quite ready to leave his special place. How nice it was to prowl the hemlocks again and listen to Enyalda's songs. The trees dissolved into brick—cold, moldy, stinking bricks. His eyes opened. An oil light flickered outside the vertical bars. He felt a hand on his shoulder—Pickpack's. He was chewing something.

"Move slow, Wulfwynn," Nosebleed said. "Pickpack fix you."

"Where are we?"

"Basement."

Pickpack removed the herbal mash from his mouth and rubbed it into the wound on Donavon's shoulder.

"Ahh, that hurts. What happened?"

"Big fight happen," Nosebleed said. "When you take knife in back, Kaharpynn Swalhulah act. He not trained in crack jaw like us. Many talon strike he give. Then men with barrels fire shots in ceiling. They hold gun to you and say stop. We obey. They take us down stairs to metal bars. No more we know."

"Where's Scar—" Donavon spotted him cross-legged in the corner of the cell, hood down and covered in blood, head to toe. "Are you all right, Chief?"

"*Sach ni yahi!*" came the vehement reply. Speak no more.

Donavon quickly surmised that the blood on the war chief's body was not his. He shrugged and turned to Pickpack. "How long ago did—"

"*Sach ni yahi!*" the chief said again.

"What's your problem?" Donavon growled back, surprised at his own tone.

Scarchief burst into a rant, uncharacteristically wordy. When he was done, he crossed both arms over his knees and stared at the wall.

Donavon looked to Pickpack for translation. By the look on his face, it was not going to be good.

"Kaharpynn Swalhulah say you not worthy of answers. That you make mockery of mission by drinking fool water and let woman work you like ass." Pickpack paused, appearing to struggle over how to phrase his next words. "He say you bring shame on self and insult those who believe in you." His gaze fell. "You owe pack apology."

Donavon looked at Nosebleed, who also stared at the floor, and then at Scarchief, cloaked in his cold silence. His lower back throbbed. He put his hand to the tender spot and felt the sinews on the sutured wound. How could they possibly understand the reasoning behind his behavior? They were warriors, masters of their discipline; he was not, plain and simple. What could he say? There was nothing left to do but accept Scarchief's scorn.

"Fine, how do I say I'm sorry?"

"No word," Pickpack said.

"Then how do I apologize?"

"Apology made in deed, not word."

"All right, what do I do?"

"Nothing."

"Then what's the point of an apology?"

"That is point, Wulfwynn. You must live now with debt."

Nosebleed stepped forward and bowed before Donavon. "Lucky for Wulfwynn, we no collect."

"*Nish hayem sahun huru!*" Scarchief shouted at the warrior.

Those words Donavon knew: No more soft talk.

Nothing more was said. Pickpack went back to cleaning the wound on Donavon's shoulder. When it came time for the sutures, Nosebleed pinned him to the floor while Pickpack tied the sinew. Donavon bit down hard on a strip of buckskin, determined not to scream in the presence of a karharpynn.

The procedure felt like hours, though in truth it only took minutes. Pickpack was quick with the needle. Donavon lay slumped in a cold sweat, recovering from the ordeal, when he heard a door swing open somewhere down the corridor. Many steps approached. Lantern light bounced on the granite walls outside the cell. Donavon sat up and summoned the strength to mutter a single sentence before they arrived. "Let me do the talking."

They came into view in a cluster, all six ruffians from the table upstairs, still sporting their holstered pistols. The seventh one who towered in their midst seized Donavon's attention. He was large, extremely so, his face the very essence of thug. A thick crescent scar began in front of his left ear, arced downward across his muscular jaw, and terminated at his cleft chin. Donavon knew the face, though he could hardly believe it. There before him stood Hector Xavier.

"Well I'll be a naked laker," Hector said, glaring through the bars. "You're right it's him. All done up in dreads, but I'd recognize those pretty red locks anywhere." He looked at the others in the cell. "Which one did the killing?"

The ruffian nearest pointed to Scarchief. "That's the one there, Hex. He done did the slice'n."

"Did he now? Hey, you, Smiley! What's your business here?"

Scarchief remained motionless and silent, staring at the wall.

Donavon approached the bars, shirtless in his sutured wounds. "He doesn't speak Toricean. He's a kaharpynn."

Hector's eyes widened. "You mean to tell me you got a Gwyntah war chief for a chaperone?"

"Yeah, I guess I do."

Pause.

"All right, that explains the bloodbath upstairs. I got another one for you. What are you doing here? And don't tell me mink pelts."

Donavon wavered, feeling the eyes of his pack on him. The moment had come at last. He knew they were just as eager for the answer as their captor. That it was only their faith in a power outside themselves that had brought them to this urine-soaked cell, and for whatever their reasons, they believed in him. Yes, this was the moment he had spoken about at Mother Temple. The time was now to cash in on his hunch. No game, no strategy, no plan—just a simple answer.

"We need you to close the weir gates so Rankwall can't fix the bridge."

The six ruffians broke into laughter. The sound sickened Donavon. That and their sideways smirks, like toothless devils screaming failure. But Hector Xavier squashed their amusement in an instant.

"Shut up! I'm not done yet." His jaw clenched, and the crescent scar on his cheek pulsed in the light of the lantern.

"That's hefty business you're talkin', mate," he said to Donavon. "Why would I want to draw Ranky's muscle to the Weirs? The other wharf lords would never agree to that even if I did. Top Dog says we drop the lake, we drop the lake. That's how it works around here."

Donavon looked at Scarchief and then back at Hector. "There's plenty of good fishing around the Awshaws. I'm sure we can work out a deal with the Gwyntahpynn."

The lame bid dropped into a long silence.

"I hear they be fish made a silver out that way," one of the ruffians said. "That would be the catch. Don't you say, Hex? From what I hear them mines be teeming with—"

Hector grabbed the chatty rogue by the jaw and squeezed until his tongue popped out. "When I say shut up, I mean shut up!" He let go and turned to Donavon. "You don't have a clue what you're doing, mate, do you?"

"I know exactly what I'm doing."

"Yeah, well, in case you haven't noticed, that doesn't seem to be working."

"I think it is. I came here to talk to you and that's what I'm doing."

A change came over Hector; subtle, like the air after a storm. They faced each other, reading silent signals through the bars, one pack leader to another. What was it? Acknowledgement? Admiration perhaps? Whatever it was, Donavon knew at the very least he had secured the weirman's respect. Anything from here on in was possible.

As if to confirm that revelation, Hector broke eye contact with Donavon and barked his orders to the man at his right. "Open the cell. I want Redlocks out. The others stay. Make sure they get some grub and water."

"You want him in shacks, Hex?"

"If I wanted him in shacks, I would have said so. Hurry up!"

They walked down the corridor, Donavon and Hector, to a steel door mounted in the granite at the far end. Hector opened the door, gesturing for Donavon to go in. It was an office of sorts, with a big table, surprisingly ornate. The air smelled of tobacco. It reminded him of the conference chamber back at Crown Tavern, only smaller and without a hearth. Several oil lamps hung from hooks along shelves adorned with a mix of treasures.

Hector closed the door and latched it. "All right, it's you and me now. Let's cut the horseshit. First you paddle in here with a handful of heathens claiming to be a trapper and tear up one of the roughest holes in port. Then you tell me in all seriousness that you want me to go head to head with the top dog in the province just so I can throw a line in your side of the pool. You either got the guts of a gun-less rumrunner or you're dumber than chum. Now I counted you out once before and I got this scar to show for it. So I'm gonna put my dumb theory on hold until I know what you're really getting at. But I'll tell you right now, it better be better than fish."

Instincts. They flowed like water. What was their source? Not until the fountain had Donavon ever given much consideration to the divine. He had always depended on himself for strength, neither blaming nor praising the powers that might be. It all changed in that breathless moment when the Goddess spoke to him in the pool. *Open your eyes,* she had said. The rest flowed together like an easy mountain stream.

And so it happened that as Donavon looked into the eyes of the man whose life he had spared at the feet of the Goddess, he saw a glimmer of hope in a soul lynched by shadow. The colonel's words came to mind—*Your manners have failed you, weirman. You are in need of a sunset.* Call it instinct, or maybe just a hunch. Whatever it was, Donavon knew Hector Xavier had not forgotten those words. With that in mind, he delivered his terms.

"At the fountain when you took the colonel's pipe, he told you that you needed a sunset. I'm offering you that now. You won't find a better deal anywhere else. Sign up with the Old Mitt and he'll give it to you. Just like that. You owe him your life as it is."

Lantern light flickered in Hector's eyes. Donavon saw it, a soft shimmer, but only for an instant. A blink and Hector's hard gaze came back, though his voice had another tone.

"You got salt, mate, I'll give you that. But your plan's got more holes in it than a cutter in a cannon fight. Now listen up. That war chief of yours killed nine rats upstairs with those wrist hooks. The locals are gonna want to see him swing. Now I always make good on a debt, so I'll tell you what's gonna happen. We're gonna get you and your mates out of here. It'll cost me. Four of those rats he carved up there were mine, but the other five make things expensive. From here on in we're even, you got that? As for your offer, we're gonna have to work on that. In the meantime, I want you to tell your tribe buddies to keep their meat hooks to themselves until we get them on my schooner and out of port. Got it?"

Donavon got it. Mission accomplished.

22

In the Name of a Father

"Blessed Father, forgive me for I have sinned."

"Then you have come to the right place, my son. I beseech to thee under witness of our Great Father, creator of heaven and earth, that through me he may hear your plea and you may know his mercy. What is your sin?"

"I have climbed the highest mountain."

"And that is your sin?"

"I shot and ate a sacred goat."

"The Great Father does not hold to such myth. The shooting of a wild mountain goat is not a sin."

"My father came down from the high peak and shared from the goat with me."

"Again, it is not a sin to feed yourself. You and your father may rest easy."

"My father told me to leave the mountain. I stayed with the goat for four days. Then a storm came and I left. I didn't want to, but I did. Now I am lost."

"You will never be lost in the Haven, my son. Your service in the Guard was noble and the land is indebted to you. By the grace of the Great Father, we will find you a home in Wulfhaven."

"Thank you, blessed Father, but there is one thing you should know."

"What is that, my son?"

"Musket doesn't like people."

Brother Michael's feeble knock said it all. Marcus opened his eyes and focused on the blanket on the wall, savoring the fading moments of solitude in his prayer chamber. He looked into the eyes of the goat woven on the mountain, the celestial wings of the butterfly draped over its horns like a great canopy. A second knock on the door. *Blessed Father*, he prayed. *Give me the strength to remain calm.* He rose and walked to the door, his black travel robe already on. Brother Michael stood in the hallway, pale and defeated.

"Your appeal is denied, Father. The children have to go. Krutzwig grants the abbey two weeks to make arrangements."

Marcus felt his pulse pound. The news was not surprising, though to hear it now, so final, was infuriating. The children ... What was Krutzwig thinking? The mere notion surpassed all limits of decency, even for Krutzwig. How could he possibly expect to get away with this? He took a deep breath. Must remain calm, no time for dizzy spells.

"Come, Michael. It is time for us to take a walk."

"Where are we going, Father?"

"To the state house."

"Through the streets?"

"No, put on your wings. We are going to fly like butterflies."

The monk flinched at the sarcasm. "Is it safe?"

Safety was the last thought on Marcus's mind as he slammed his staff on the mosaic floor. Together they marched to the exit of the north transept, where he freed his hand of the swinging scepter and thrust open the door with the unholy power of a ram.

"I am done with channels, Mayor. The children are at stake! The time for appeals is over. Either you do something or I will!"

Mayor Marlin Barleycopp stood up behind his desk. "Please, Pastor, close the door behind you and try to remain calm. Ears are everywhere, even here. My hands are tied on the matter. The order came from Rankwall himself. His reinforcements must be housed somewhere. He assures me that the children will be returned to the dormitories once the permanent barracks are built for the soldiers."

Brother Michael jumped as Marcus slammed the door shut.

"Then you have failed utterly at your role as mayor of the people," the pastor exclaimed. "These are children, Marlin. The very fabric for which you and your brethren fought. You of all people should understand the magnitude of this action."

Barleycopp strode the length of his office, stopping at each of the three windows to latch their sashes snug to the sills. A full-length mirror stood near the third window. Barleycopp looked into it and adjusted his war medals, making sure the brass medallion around his neck hung perfectly centered on his chest. When all was just right, he placed both hands behind his back and advanced on the holy men, stopping within an arm's reach of Marcus.

"Think what you will about my acceptance of this outrage," said the mayor, his voice a fierce hush. "But know that even as we speak, there are good men at work who have devoted their lives to the Haven. For their sakes, I must insist that you keep your voice down while in my office."

The mayor's tone had a sobering effect. Marcus had rarely seen Barleycopp so ominous. Even during the war, when events changed in a blink, the stately captain had always maintained a good-natured air. What he said now made absolute sense, and Marcus knew it.

"Forgive me, Marlin. I should not have questioned your commitment to the people. All this madness with the Pogetsa has made me a fool. There must be some way to prevent this. The abbey is the only home the children know."

"There is not, Marcus. If Krutzwig will not listen to your appeal, he most certainly will not listen to mine. However, there is a fund that may help ease the burden on the children." He glanced to Brother Michael. "Can the monk be trusted with sensitive information?"

"He is my successor and confidant," Marcus said.

"Very well. After Spaulding Pass, Mitterhal approached me before he ... went to his rooftop, so to speak. A vast cache of his father's wealth had been stored in a chamber below his manor. The fifth flue, he called it. He ordered me to remove anything of monetary value and set up an endowment for all the children of the men who fell at Spaulding Pass. There is still a significant sum left. Considering the colonel's intent, I see no reason not to extend the endowment to the orphans in the abbey. At the very least, we can insure that they are fostered and their basic needs are met."

"A more than generous offer, Marlin, one not to be taken lightly. But this is not about basic needs. It is about continuity, security, sense of family. The dormitories are their home, soon to be seized by soldiers. What will come next? The schoolmaster's lodgings? The infirmary? The library? The very cathedral itself? Krutzwig has lost all sense of boundary."

Again Barleycopp glanced at Brother Michael, and then his tone dropped to a murmur. "Plans are underway to insure that what you suggest will not happen. Recent events have upped the Guard's numbers substantially. Mitterhal will do everything in his power to avoid bloodshed in the Haven, but if need be, he will drop the hammer hard on Krutzwig. That is all I will say for now. Tomorrow I will tally a list of the families willing to house the children. Now you must go. It was dangerous for you to come here on foot. For your safety I will have the office guards escort you back to the abbey. Do not trust them to anything more than that."

"What are you up to, Marlin?"

"This is not the time or place, Pastor. We will contact you via confessions. When Krutzwig questions me on your visit, I will be sure to let him know your sentiments. Hail, Gahenya, Father."

Barleycopp opened the door and called for the guards.

A moment later, two armed soldiers appeared.

"Hitch the Yellow Wagon and see the good pastor and the monk back to the abbey."

It was midafternoon when the wagon's team of ponies cantered through the archway and into the square. Marcus gazed out the window at the throngs of onlookers who watched him pass. He couldn't blame them for gawking, considering the last time the Haven's famed Yellow Wagon had graced the sacred grounds. Most of the fountain folk would have been only kids at the time. How strange it must be for them to see it now—stranger yet when they discovered who was inside. Had Marcus been in a better mood, he might have played up the scene at the cathedral steps and blessed the plumed ponies. Instead, he simply bowed curtly to the driver and ascended the steps to call an ad hoc meeting of the monks.

The meeting proved utterly hopeless. None of the brethren had a solution, not even a suggestion. Krutzwig's audacious decree had caught them all by surprise. The only motion unanimously agreed upon was to adjourn the meeting and reconvene the next day after second prayer. Marcus stepped out of the cathedral, desperate for fresh air. Demoralized, he leaned on his staff and recited his prayer.

"Blessed Father, confide in me your wisdom so that I may strengthen the hearts of your children. Grant me yet one more day that I may serve this pledge with heart, body, mind, and soul."

From the chapel door, he peered out into the square—the gardens, the walkways, the statue. Not since the war had he dispatched his plea with such weight. He watched a thrush hop the tops of budding trees. Then for reasons not entirely clear, he descended the steps and made straight for the fountain.

"Good day, madam," Marcus said to the fountain lady.

"Good day, Pastor. What a delight to see you."

"Thank you, my lady, but I fear I will not live up to your expectations today. There is nothing delightful in what I have to say."

"Then say no more until you give your sorrows to the butterfly. The children cannot afford to see their pastor so glum."

Marcus looked up at the statue, the serene face of the goddess and the butterfly on her outstretched arm. "These are dark days, madam. The children of the abbey are about to be shuffled out of their home by soldiers who intend to make war on your fountain's makers. What would the goddess's butterfly do with that?"

Madam Hume smiled and looked wistfully into the pool. "The Vahegan butterfly would take your concerns to the highest meadows in the Haven and sprinkle them over the wildflowers, to which they would then rise up from their rest and splash the mountains in color."

"A glorious sight indeed, but would it solve the problem? Would the children still have their home?"

The wrinkles around the old woman's eyes tightened. "Maybe, maybe not," she said, suddenly grave. "That is a matter for the wolf."

A shadow came over her, as if her black shawl had absorbed the light from the day. Marcus regretted his despairing remark. Seeing her so stark reminded him of her first days at the fountain, when she had left her home in Tufthaven after the war. So dark and chilling, lashing out at the statue in her anger and grief, her husband and four sons lost in battle. Not until a year later, when her sole surviving son walked out of the woods and arrived at the abbey, did her mood lighten. And with that came her tales. For though her battle-traumatized son had no recollection of who she was, he would sit at the fountain's edge and listen to her stories with his musket on his lap. In time, others came to listen, children mostly, to hear her inspiring words.

"Yes, a matter for the wolf," Marcus said, his gaze on the wolf at the feet of the goddess. "Thank you, madam. You offer a fresh perspective. I see why the children find your stories so inspiring."

The shadow passed. "It is you that inspires them," she said, cheerful again. "Stories are just stories without the faithful hearts that listen. You have been their father in a very real sense. Look around you, Pastor. What do you see? Musicians, street performers, dancers. The first wave of children you took into the abbey after the war, now a grown community of faith. They have their father to thank for that. And that did not change when they left the abbey."

Another dizzy spell coming on, Marcus felt the need to sit. They had been occurring more frequently of late, without warning or obvious cause.

"Are you all right, Pastor? You look pale."

"Yes, I'm fine. Just give me a moment."

The pure pitch of a flute passed over the pool while the spell ran its course. The sweet melody pumped the vitality back into his veins. All around him, he saw his children, now adults, many of whom he'd known as infants. Some had stayed with the church, others gave their devotion to the fountain. He loved them all the same.

"Where do they go when they leave the square?" he asked.

"That depends on the season. They make do however they can. They are very resourceful."

"Yes, yes, but where are their homes? Where do they rest their heads at night?"

"Wherever need takes them."

"That is not enough, madam. A community cannot subsist on faith alone. They need a roof and walls, just like the children. A safe place to keep warm and fed."

"That would be a wonderful place, Pastor, though more than their earnings could manage. Who would have the funds to entertain such a notion?"

Marcus sprang from the bench, his strength suddenly restored. He rapped the cobbles with his staff and looked up to the butterfly. "We do, my good lady. Please excuse me. It has been a delight."

Like the shadow of a cloud sweeping the square, Marcus stormed back to the cathedral, hailing the musicians along the way.

The proposal was done sometime after midnight, drafted in his own hand and ready for the mayor's desk. "Thank you, Great Father," Marcus said, dropping his pen on the signed document and rubbing his eyes. The revelation had struck like thunder in the evening, just prior to supper, while he was in his prayer chamber. He barely remembered hurrying out of the north transept and locking himself in the scriptorium. It made perfect sense, really. The silver forge on the harbor's edge down in the old port: a reasonable walk from the abbey, spacious, well built, and abandoned when the mines shut down—an ideal facility.

He went to the tray of food Brother Michael had placed on a table full of open reference books and scrolls. The starchy rice had congealed into a hard lump; it was like chewing mortar. Exhausted, Marcus laid down his fork and left the scriptorium. The full moon stretched his shadow on the garden path back to the rectory. He felt alive despite his worn-out state, suspended in a dreamlike trance. Not a single dizzy spell since leaving the fountain. He heard a shuffle from behind the statue of a saint and then a voice.

"Forgive me, Father, for I have sinned."

"Who is there? Show yourself."

A patrolman stepped out from behind the statue, armed with a musket, his polished bayonet glistening in the moonlight.

Marcus seethed at the outrage. "You have no business here, soldier! The abbey was promised two weeks before Krutzwig's cursed order takes effect."

"Who is Krutzwig?" the soldier asked.

Odd question, thought Marcus. "Who are you?"

"I am Willis. Have you forgotten?"

"Willis? Yes, yes, of course. I recognize you now. It has been years, my son. You have grown. What brings you back to the abbey?"

"I have a confession."

"Then you have come to the right place once again. What is your sin?"

"I know where Master Schnites is."

"Sebastian Schnites is dead, Willis. What do you know of that?"

"He is not, Father. Master Schnites has gone to the Mountain, Musket as my witness."

"A terrible crime was committed on him, Willis. Did you or your musket have anything to do with that?"

"You don't believe me, do you? You don't believe in the Mountain."

"What I believe is not relevant. It is the salvation of your soul we must focus on now."

Willis raised his gun and took aim on Marcus. "Let Musket take you there, Father. To the Great Mountain Montayega. You can see for yourself." A single metallic click. "It's a peaceful place with fragrant flowers and lots of rabbits and butterflies. I think you will like it."

Marcus pushed the musket aside with his staff. "I have dire matters in the Haven, Willis. The children need a home, just like you did after the war. Do not think for a moment that I will leave this world before my work here is done. If need be, I will call down the wrath of the Great Father himself to melt your musket with my staff."

The barrel went down at once. "No, Musket," Willis said sternly to the lowered weapon. "He is not ready yet. Know your manners. Very well, Father. We will come back again when you are ready. The next full moon when the gahenya blooms." Willis disengaged the lock and vanished into the shadows behind the saint.

Marcus awoke, face down in the scriptorium. Was it another faint or had he actually slept? Hard to tell these days. Someone's hand touched his shoulder. He pushed his head off the desk. It was Michael. Or was it a dream? Hardened rice still on the plate. In a panic he searched for the document and found it directly under his nose, solid and real, perfectly intact. Thank you, Great Father.

"Are you all right, Father?" Michael asked. "I was concerned when you were not at first prayer. I have brought you breakfast."

"Thank you, Michael, but there is no time. I must get this to the mayor's office at once."

"Father, you look worn. Allow me to deliver it."

"Nonsense!" Marcus said, making for the door. "I've never felt better. In fact, the fresh air will do me good. I want you to stay and lead the brethren in second prayer."

"But, Fa—"

"Do as I say."

Outside the scriptorium, Marcus livened at the sweet scent of cherry blossoms. He made straight for the east exit, around the cathedral and into the square, hailing again the musicians as he passed through the gardens. At the fountain he paused to catch his breath. The children had gathered around the pool for story time.

"Look, it's Pastor Marcus!" one of them shouted. They all turned and waved. He trudged onward toward the two great pillars, propelled by their flapping little hands. Three steps out of the square he heard a voice behind him—Barusta.

"What's the big rush, Father?"

"Hello there, my boy. No time to chat. I have errands to run."

"Is it true that we're getting kicked out of the abbey?"

"Where did you hear that?" Marcus said, not slowing his stride.

"I have my sources," Barusta replied, trailing close behind. "If you answer my question, I'll answer yours."

Marcus stopped. "That is not the way it works and you know that. Mind your manners."

"I'm sorry, Father. When do we find out?"

"Find what out?"

"When we get kicked out of the abbey."

"I never said you were getting kicked out."

"You never said we weren't. Why else would you be racing down the Promenade?"

"I don't have time for this, Barusta," Marcus said, at a brisk pace once again. "Go back to the fountain."

"Why?"

"Because I am not taking you to the mayor's office!"

"Why are you going there?"

"That is not your business."

"Why not? We're the ones getting kicked out."

"Because you are …"

"I am what?"

Brilliant. Marcus stopped again, suddenly fighting for breath. Barusta's face wavered in and out of focus.

"Are you all right, Father? I think you better sit down for a minute. You're sweating. There's a bench in the shade over there."

Barusta grabbed his hand and led him to the bench. Marcus barely made it, his balance askew. On the bench he closed his eyes.

"Are you there, Barusta?"

"I am here, Father."

"Take the document in my hand. If anything happens to me, you must deliver it to the mayor. Only him, nobody else. Understand?"

"Sure. Why are you saying this?"

"Just let me rest. It should only be a moment."

They sat in silence while the spell ran its course. Marcus concentrated on the chirping birds over the footsteps in the crowd. At last, he opened his eyes. "There, all better. Thank you, my boy. I am glad you were here."

"I was worried, Father."

"Worry no more."

"Do you want the document back?"

Another assessment—the birds, the breeze, the fragrance. "No,

Barusta, hold on to it. I want you to present it to the mayor."

"What is it?"

"It is a proposal for a new home."

"Away from the abbey?"

"Yes."

"An orphanage?"

"No! Absolutely not. Barusta, look at me. Do not ever call it that. Do you understand? You must think of it as a school. Like that place you wrote about in your play. A facility to live and learn."

"I can do that."

"I know you can. More than anyone. Now help me up. Smell those cherry blossoms."

"Father?"

"Yes."

"You look much better."

They continued on the Promenade at an easier pace, and then detoured down a seedy side street that Barusta insisted would cut their walk in half. Marcus raised his staff to the waves of vagrants, many of whom addressed Barusta by name. By way of the narrow alleys they bisected the upper precinct and so arrived at the mayor's office in good time.

They climbed the steps and entered the lobby. Barusta was instantly enamored by the grand space. He gawked at the lines of wooden soldiers holding vigil on the shelves. Two guards approached, the same two guards who had escorted Marcus back to the abbey in the Yellow Wagon. Marcus held up his staff and told them he knew the way. Both shrugged as he strode past them and up the wide stairs. Barusta tagged wide-eyed by his side. Marcus stopped at the polished oak door at the top of the steps.

"Remember, Barusta, this is for your friends and family. Best behavior. Be sure to look the mayor in the eye when you speak. And at all times, mind your manners." The young boy nodded as Marcus opened the door without a knock.

Inside the office, Mayor Barleycopp sat alone at his desk. He stood up quickly. "So, Pastor, two visits in two days. Why am I not surprised?"

"I have a proposal for you, Mayor. But first, there is a young man here I would like you to meet."

Barleycopp went to the balcony at the far end of the office. He took a deep breath of fresh air before closing the door. Turning to the full-length mirror, he adjusted his war medals and then approached his visitors.

Barusta stepped forward and held out his hand. "Hello, Mister Mayor, I am Barusta."

"Ah, yes, Barusta. The famous playwright." Barleycopp knelt down to eye level and took his hand. "Captain Marly will do, my boy. It is an honor to make your acquaintance. You made history in the opera house, you know, and have earned your place in the veranda."

"Thank you, sir, but there's not enough room up there for all of us. I'd rather just sit with my friends."

The mayor stood up. "Well noted, lad. And what do I see in your hands? A script for the next play perhaps?"

"It is a proposal, sir, for a schoo— eh ... I mean, a place for us to stay."

"Is that so?" The mayor held out his hand. "May I see it?"

Barleycopp scanned the first pages. "Hmm, the silver forge. How interesting." He turned a few more pages and studied them at length. A long string of grunts and mumbles followed while he sifted through the details. Finally, after what felt like hours, he fired a sharp look at Marcus. "An ambitious plan, Pastor. And a significant expense, I might add. Not only in money but sweat. It is the latter that I am afraid we cannot afford at this time."

"There will be no shortage of willing hands, Mayor, I promise you that. Once the facility is established, it will sustain itself through the arts."

"I see." Barleycopp glanced at Barusta, who had wandered to the plaster model of the Three Havens on the table. "More plays for the opera house, I trust."

"Yes. Among other disciplines. Perhaps a place where young pipers might refine their skills."

Barleycopp's eyes widened. "I've never known you to be such a salesman, Pastor."

"I've never had to be. These are trying times. To think that independence could lead to such reckless disregard of the innocent."

"I could not agree more, though I dare say that even this too shall pass. A land founded on solid principles will not wither under a passing shadow." Barleycopp looked again at Barusta. "The young master here made that quite apparent in his play."

Barusta snapped out of his survey of the model. "I'm sorry, sir, were you talking to me?"

Barleycopp strode to the table. "So you like my model. Come, let's have a closer look."

"It's like being a bird," Barusta said, waving his hand over the plaster peaks. "Look at those mountains. They make a perfect circle."

"That would be the Awshaw range in Gwyntahlynn. The Great Ring. A very special place, indeed." Barleycopp picked up a thin stick and pointed it at Wulfhaven harbor. "Look here, my boy. This is us on the south shore of the harbor. The Awshaws are what you see when you look across the water to the north. You know, there are some who believe that all those mountains you see once formed the base of a single mountain. One that scaled so high, it could take you to heaven if you climbed its peak."

"Montahyega!" Barusta shouted.

Barleycopp laughed and looked at Marcus. "What are you teaching these children at the abbey, Pastor?"

Barusta put his hand to the plaster and traced the range with his fingers. "The fountain lady tells us about the Great Mountain all the time in her stories. She never said it was real though, right here in the Haven."

Barleycopp suddenly crossed his office to the door. "Reality is like a sunset, young man. It comes and goes in many colors." He swung the door open with jarring force. One of the guards from the lobby stood outside with his back to the threshold. "Ah, there you are," Barleycopp said to the surprised man. "How convenient. I was just about to summon you."

"We wanted to make sure the Pastor was safe," the guard said.

"Yes, of course, good thinking. Do me a favor and show this young lad the archive room. He has a love of maps and should find the experience most rewarding. In fact, why don't you take him to the hall of portraits first?"

"Right away, sir."

"All right then. Hop to it, young man," Barleycopp said to Barusta. "Enjoy the tour. When you come back, I'm going to quiz you on the dates of the portraits."

Barusta left, thrilled at the prospect. When the door closed, Barleycopp turned to the pastor and shed his pleasantries.

"Krutzwig's spies are everywhere, so allow me to be brief. I am deeply troubled by Rankwall's latest move. It is not for lack of options that he has chosen the abbey to quarter his troops. There are plenty of places in Wulfhaven that would have sufficed as barracks for his men. This is a calculated decision. He is reverting back to his ways as a general, positioning his forces for the best advantage to wage war, with no concern for public outcry."

"And inciting the Haven to the point that even his own supporters will question his motives is the answer?" Marcus asked. "What military advantage could he possibly attain by housing his troops in the abbey?"

"Protection."

"Protection from what? The lightning strike he deserves?"

"In a sense, yes. He knows what Choroqua is capable of doing when pushed to war, which will most certainly include late-night raids on his men. And while the Gwyntah are no match against Rankwall's cannons and guns, he fears what they can do under the veil of night with their guntocs. He also knows that the tribes consider the cathedral to be the watcher of their everlasting spring, and they will not risk desecrating the holy grounds. That includes the abbey as well as the square. For once Rankwall has done his groundwork on tribal custom."

"If what you say is true, Captain, then the battleground will shift to the streets of Wulfhaven. The Pogetsa will be forced to declare martial law."

"They will. And that I also believe is part of Rankwall's plan. What better way to spank a society that refuses to honor him? Unless, of course, we spank him first."

Marcus walked over to the plaster model. He suddenly felt sick. "Not again, Marlin. Not so close to home."

"War is already on us, Pastor. Rankwall has seen to that. The time has come to take up arms again."

Marcus leaned on his staff, flat and depressed with nothing to say. The mayor's statement pressed on his spirit like a heavy wool robe drenched by a downpour. Cold and clammy, he wavered in doubt while his empty stomach croaked for nourishment.

Barleycopp squinted at the gastric rumblings. "We go back a long way, Marcus. Perhaps we might shed our roles for a moment and talk frankly, man to man?"

"By all means, Marlin, speak your mind."

"It is with my heart that I speak. You know that after Spaulding Pass we had little to celebrate. The rest of the province hailed the battle as a glorious victory. I never bought that. Neither did the few who made it back. Yet even in our darkest hour we still found joy. It had nothing to do with victory. It was the simple joy of knowing we were not alone. I believe that all stems back to you, Pastor, and the colonel."

Barleycopp strode back to the model and rapped the mountains in the lowest southern quadrant with his pointer.

Spaulding Pass, Marcus noted. The southmost fringe of the Haven. His stomach growled again. No dinner or breakfast or lunch.

"Something extraordinary happened there, Marcus. That much we all know. What exactly is anyone's guess. We all have our theories." He slid the pointer north to the lake, to the Haven's three harbors. "You know we still quote the arguments you and the colonel used to have. We ran bets on who would be the first to buckle on a point. Mitterhal or Poulakis—who would it be? The Mountain or the Father? Hearing the two of you go at it made everything else in the war seem like child's play. You did some of your best preaching when you were furious."

Marcus swallowed back his hunger. "I'm glad to know the stubborn old goat brought out the best in me."

"For what it's worth, I think it went both ways. Anyway, I bring this up so you know I mean no disrespect when I tell you it is time to slow down. You have devoted your life to the hearts of others, and I think it best now you start paying attention to your own. Perhaps a sabbatical to manage the stress."

"A sabbatical, at a time like this? What kind of advice is that? Politics has softened your edge, Marlin. What happened to the steadfast war captain I knew?"

"With all respect, Marcus, a good war captain knows what inspires his men and does everything he can to uphold that. If telling you to stop running yourself ragged is what it takes to maintain the morale of my troops, then so be it. Even a soldier baptized in fire knows when to jump the flame." The mayor retracted the pointer and placed it back on the table. "That is the end of my sermon. Do with it what you will. As for your proposal, I will forward it to the mountain for review."

"Time is of the essence, Marlin. This is for the children."

"I am aware of that, Pastor. You will have your answer by first light tomorrow."

It was long past dawn the next day when Marcus stormed into the rectory hall, furious at himself for oversleeping. "Michael! What is the word?"

"None yet. Did you sleep well, Father?"

"I slept fine. More than fine, in fact. You were supposed to wake me at first light."

The monk bowed. "I thought the sleep would serve you well. Forgive me. Will you be leading the brethren in second prayer, Father?"

"No, I have important matters to address. You lead them."

"As you wish."

Alone, Marcus paced back and forth in the rectory hall. Why the delay? Barleycopp was famous for his promptness. Why now, of all times, did he falter? Could the answer be that bad? Had something happened? Every hour was precious time wasted. Marcus pondered the alternatives to his proposal. Perhaps the vestry could accommodate the youngest? No, the children had to stay together, all or nothing. What about the cow and goat sheds behind the abbey? Ridiculous! Or the Schnites farm? No, not after the tragedy.

On and on Marcus racked his wits while the morning crept toward noon. Defeated, tired, and frustrated, he left the hall to prepare for the scheduled meeting with the monks. Halfway there, he realized he'd forgotten his staff. Brother Michael met him on the walk.

"Father, a group of men await you at the front steps of the cathedral. They bear the mountain flower."

Marcus rounded the cathedral and found them sitting on the lowest steps. Brawny they were, and dirty. Bloodshot eyes in faces black as soot. They all stood up and hailed him. Twelve, he counted. The leader stepped forward and knelt, prompting the others to do the same.

"How may I serve you, my son?" Marcus asked the man.

"Forgive the delay, Your Grace. I am Lawrence P. Grycco, reconnaissance. The furnaces took longer to dismantle than we anticipated."

"Please, get up," Marcus said. "What furnaces are you talking about?"

"The forge. We needed to clear the first floor to make room for the kitchen and dining hall."

"By the grace of the Great Father! Are you telling me you have already started?"

Grycco got up. The others followed suit. "Yes, last night. The order came direct from the mountain. I have been assigned to lead the renovation." He held out an envelope.

"What is this?" Marcus asked, taking the soot-smudged envelope.

"It is a permit, signed and sealed by the mayor to begin work immediately. All expenses shall be forwarded to his office. If the Pogetsa question it, he asks that you refrain from engagement and direct all inquiries to him. He also said that you have promised to provide able hands. We need them now."

"Of course," Marcus said, stunned. "Allow me a moment to get my staff."

"By all means, Father."

23

Goat Licks

Short of honey, few things refreshed Cornelius Mitterhal more than a healthy gulp of wild goat's milk. Raw and unfiltered, fresh out of the teat. It was the only way to take it as far as he was concerned. The domestic stuff, for all its grand fuss, was for children. Granted, his options were limited after the war. Had not the mountain herd arrived when it did, he would have been forced to supplement his honey diet with nothing but the roughage that the tavern's sneaky barmaid stole into his root cellar every so often.

Yes, without question wild goat's milk was a prize to be praised, all the more for the hazards involved in getting it. Convincing the spirited nannies to allow their teats to be touched was no small task. Even the ladies had horns that packed a wallop. Not until the colonel had refined his techniques with the use of highland honey did the rewards warrant the risk.

Indeed, the goats loved honey, particularly in the early half of summer when the lush lupine blossoms burst into bloom. The herd was extra receptive at these times to the chimes that Mitterhal had hung inside his stock house door. The melodic tinkling never failed to lure the wily beasts away from their picnic in the gahenya.

The routine had long been established, dating back to the early days on his rooftop. After sounding the chimes, Mitterhal would walk a narrow gangway along the back wall on the outside of his stock house and smear honey on the goat licks, as he called them—a line of dismantled barrel staves mounted horizontally along the waist-high gangplank in front of makeshift yokes. The yokes consisted of three thick boards, one of which Mitterhal could pivot around the necks of the frothy-mouthed beasts and lock them into position by their horns. Most of the goats didn't mind the confinement so long as there was plenty of honey on the staves to keep them occupied. With the beasts in position, Mitterhal would step off the gangplank with a tin bucket and attend to the ladies while they slurped up their sweets. Though he had learned the hard way never to turn his back on the bucks that still waited their turns at the licks.

Mitterhal caught his breath after sliding open the doors of the stock house. The effort exhausted him. He had considered asking Enyalda to fetch Francis from the village, but decided not to. The doors were just doors. Why make things complicated?

An easy mountain breeze wafted through the entry, tinkling the chimes overhead. The pretty tones roused his spirits and inspired him to grab the pitchfork from the wall. With both hands on the prongs, he swung the handle at the chimes, careful not to twist his ribs. The wind picked up and assisted him.

The deed done, Mitterhal rehung the fork and, with several jars of honey stuffed in his vest pockets, hobbled to the goat licks at the back of the building. It had been a while since he last tended them—so much nonsense in the Haven. A horse approached while he smeared honey on a stave. It was Francis riding hard from the manor. Good, young arms to close the doors.

Francis drew his steed to a halt. "I have an urgent message, sir. Captain Marly is at the tavern with the cipher. He hopes to discuss important matters with you in chambers."

Mitterhal scowled at the stave while he pondered his options. Of all times to have a chat. What about the herd? To ring the chimes and deny them their sweets would be an inexcusable break in etiquette. Not to mention hazardous. Unlike their domestic cousins, these goats had tempers capable of cracking barn boards.

"Tell the fool I'm busy."

Francis shrank in his saddle. "Ahh ... I ... Maybe if—"

"Use your words, lad! You sound like a dribbling tot."

"Sorry, sir. I was just thinking that maybe you should ... go anyway?"

"I just rang the chimes. I'm not going anywhere. He'll have to come up here. Tell him to leave his horse at the manor."

"Right away, sir."

"Wait! Before you go I need two bushels of oats and three bales of hay spread out around the licks. And be sure to shut the doors when you're done."

***

The herd arrived later than expected. Probably distracted by the swollen buds of gahenya that had already started to sprinkle the knolls. To think in only a week's time the pastures would be splashed in blue.

Mitterhal sparked a bowl of greenbank as he took tally. Forty-eight goats. They came in three-single file lines, each led by a brawny buck. The colonel sighed. He hadn't seen Old Smoker since the last rut. Just kind of wandered off one day and never came back. Had enough of the rut, he supposed. Such was the way of the breed.

Mitterhal stabbed the ground with his cane and returned to task. The goat licks could accommodate twenty-four goats at full capacity. Only the first five staves were outfitted with yokes. Mitterhal stood in front of them, cane ready, directing the ladies to their places. It was more of a ritual than anything else. Most of the bucks had been well conditioned over the years to mind their manners, though on occasion some of the younger ones needed a hard cue to the skull.

With the ladies in position, Mitterhal secured them in their yokes and got to work. He started with the fifth nanny from the end. From the very start he could tell she was a giver. Her stream hit the pale with a ping.

The bucket was singing when the horns of every goat outside the licks went up. Mitterhal kept to his task. Marlin Barleycopp strode into view, winded by the walk from the manor. He seemed distracted by the bucks that eyed him in their frozen poses.

"Don't worry, Captain. They are reasonable creatures so long as you don't break the rules. Just act yourself and they'll stick to the oats and hay."

"As you say, sir. Hail, Gahenya."

"Right. How goes the project at the forge?"

"All goes as planned, sir. Grycco has the reconnaissance team working round the clock in shifts. He said Poulakis almost fell over when he told him they had already dismantled the furnaces."

"So the pious old soul was awestruck. Serves him right."

"That he was. Though I must say I'm concerned for his health. He looks worn. I fear he is pushing himself to the grave. I suggested a sabbatical."

"Aye, a sound piece of advice, but you know as well as I that idleness would drop the stubborn fool faster than a talon strike. Grab one of those buckets over there, will you? My hands are full."

"Right away, sir." Barleycopp strode to the far end of the gangplank where a stack of buckets teetered on the edge. He removed the top bucket, and all the others plummeted off the plank. The ears of every goat twitched at the clamor.

"Easy does it, Marlin. You're stressing the ladies."

"Sorry, sir." He held out the bucket to the colonel.

Mitterhal looked at him as if he had two heads. "What are you doing now?"

"I'm giving you the bucket. As you asked."

"I have my bucket."

"I see that, but y—"

"Go to the third lick from the end. Set your pail under the good lady just like I have here. Press up on her teats when you squeeze. It's as easy as that."

"But, sir, I—"

"That's an order, Captain. And take off that floppy tunic. I don't want your road dust in the milk."

Barleycopp moved to his assigned duty, two goat licks away from the colonel's. After positioning the bucket, he removed his tunic and draped the dusty garment over the gangplank, making sure it was a fair distance from the honey-drenched stave. His compliance wavered, however, when it came time to kneel alongside the slurping nanny. He remained upright instead, adjusting the war medals on his vest.

"Quit playing with your chest chimes, Captain. You'll do fine so long as you mind your manners. Now hurry up and get to it. We have business to discuss."

Barleycopp set to the task. Milk trickled lamely into the bucket.

"Put a little smack in that grip! These are mountain goats, not house pets."

The mayor squeezed harder and the stream struck with authority.

"Good, now tell me. Why the visit?"

"It's the men, sir. There's unrest in the ranks. Quite frankly I can't blame them. They trust you to no end, but to extend their faith to the Torics is asking a lot. Not all the old war wounds have healed. If Harthmocker proves false, then the Guard will be surrounded at the stables without an out. Rankwall will be more than thorough at exploiting the advantage."

"You are right about that, Marlin. And the men have good reason for concern. But Rankwall's southies must be drawn out of the city so Choroqua's wolves can do their work. It's essential to the plan. Declaring our stand at the stables is the only way to get their big guns out of the city. I would remind the men not to forget the lessons learned at Spaulding Pass. There are no guarantees in war. Every guardsman accepts that when he gives his oath."

"That is not in debate, sir. The men just need something, anything, to assure them that the risk is valid. And that should the Torics not show, there will be a fallback in place for them to leave the world in grace."

Mitterhal raised his bucket to the gangplank and released the nanny from her yoke. He peered out thoughtfully into the gahenya as she slipped away. "Yes, of course. What a fool I've been. Peacetime has made me soft, Marlin. Once again your attention to practical matters have proven invaluable. The pipers need a tune to play."

"Actually, sir, I was thinking something more in the lines of—"

"Yes, a war hymn. How could I have forgotten? The men need a war

340

hymn."

"Sir, if I may—"

"A song that speaks to their souls."

"Sir, I—"

"Worry not, Marlin. I know just the tune. You must find Willis Hume."

"Sir?"

"You heard me. Willis Hume, son of Johan. Find him. You told me yourself, he's a living, breathing man."

"I know that, sir, but he's not in a condition to—"

"To what? Project his voice? Where does it say in our code that a soldier with a torn soul can't sing? Trust me, he can weave a tune. I've heard him myself. So have the Torics."

Barleycopp's nanny let out a snort that caused him to flinch.

"At ease, Captain. She's just letting you know she's there. The ladies don't like being ignored. Just keep the hands moving while you talk. So what do you know of the lad's whereabouts?"

Barleycopp resumed his milking. "I fear he will not be easy to find, sir. Not since he left the Schnites compound. He just wanders the woods now."

"When did he leave the compound?"

"It's been about two years, I'd say … That's right. The fall before last."

"And he hasn't been back since?"

"Only once, in the summer just prior the weirmen's rout at the fountain. He marched right into Wulfhaven Square and told the fountain folk that Pogetsa patrol boats were taking surveyors to the Awshaw mines. Made a big to-do from what I understand. The Pogetsa were quick to arrest him, along with some others who started chanting hymns from the Old Tome. Krutzwig charged him with possession of a loaded weapon in the city proper."

"Not inciting unrest?"

"No. That's curious, I agree. They locked him away with no trial in sight. Krutzwig claimed he was insane and a risk to society. I issued a pardon on the grounds that he was a war veteran. That and the public outcry forced the constable to set him free, provided he stayed out of the city limits. Shortly after that, Sebastian Schnites was murdered in that alleged Gwyntah raid while on harbor patrol. I've often wondered about the timing."

Mitterhal scowled. "Schnites was a hobby-farm investor. What was he doing on board the patrol?"

"The Pogetsa said he wanted to assess the damage on the bridge in person before putting money into the project. Krutzwig sent him out with a crew of six, all of whom were found beheaded on board the boat. Schnites was the only corpse left intact. A classic Gwyntah execution."

"Classic maybe, but not authentic. Were the pogies in uniform?"

"I would assume so. Why do you ask?"

"The Gwyntah believe all souls are sacred, even the enemy's. Only the mind and body corrupt. Lopping the head of a rotten apple frees the jarred soul of its pickle. Why would Gwyntah raiders take the time to liberate the spirits of the six pogies and not the passenger?"

"I don't believe that question has ever been asked."

"I suspect not, especially if the Pogetsa are running the investigation. I assume as mayor you have access to the records of the inmates they got crammed in the pogie house."

"I do."

"I suggest you start there. My guess is you might find a few missing. Krutzwig had to get the bodies somewhere."

"Are you suggesting he staged the raid?"

"I am. And that he's a murderer on seven counts. We'll have to use that to our advantage. Which reminds me, what became of that Rueger fellow since Rankwall demoted him?"

The nanny snorted again, followed by a kick. Barleycopp patted her on the rump to settle her down. "He still keeps contact with the ranks from what I understand, more as an advisor than anything else."

"That's it, now rub her shoulders, you're catching on quick. And his replacement?"

"That would be Chadwick Glockstoff, one of Krutzwig's cronies," Barleycopp said while stroking the goat's back. "A real stickler for the rules. Though I dare say he's broken plenty on his own."

"Excellent. We will use that to our advantage as well."

"Your pardon, sir, but I'm not sure I see your point."

"That's because I haven't made it yet. By the way, your lady is empty. Undo her yoke if you would. Just pop the peg and lift up the top board. Make sure you put the bucket on the gangplank first, and stay clear of her horns when she pulls out."

"Sir, I'm not sure if this is a good—"

"Just do it. You wanted my point, didn't you?"

Barleycopp nodded as he placed the bucket on the gangplank.

"Hoffman says Rueger was a lead player in the counter offensive on the Torics in Altomar," Mitterhal went on. "A hands-on commander from what I've been told. That means he's got friends. The kind you don't lose from a slap in rank. It also means he's got the respect of the regulars. That is where our advantage lies."

"Colonel, I must point out that Rueger is as straight as they get. He will never betray his own men, whatever his feelings toward Rankwall."

"All the more reason to sign him up. Now quit stalling and lift up on that yoke. Your lady is getting antsy."

The board went up and the horns came out. Barleycopp pressed himself against the gangplank to give the nanny room. She left the lick without incident and the mayor sighed with relief—only to have his ease turn to angst when her imposing replacement stepped in. An enormous buck blocked his escape, horns forward, eyeing the vacated goat lick with beastly intent. Barleycopp straightened and expanded his chest, as if the sight of his shining war medals might ward off an attack.

"Easy does it, Captain," the colonel said. "Follow the rules. First and foremost, maintain eye contact. Do not look away under any circumstance. Understand?"

Barleycopp made a throaty noise that Mitterhal interpreted as yes.

"Good. Now you must get up on the gangplank to replenish the lick. There's a jar of honey on the shelf under the eave. Keep your motions fluid and natural. Remember, eyes on the goat at all times, even on the gangplank. If you turn around to get the honey, Little Three Legs will send you nose first into the barn boards with a horn in your ass. You'll have to feel your way to the jar. I'll guide you to it."

Mitterhal kept his instructions simple and clear, and Barleycopp followed every word to the tee. Only once, after a particularly threatening snort, did the colonel address the goat directly.

"Easy there, big fellow," he said with calm assurance. "That's my best captain you got locked in your sights. You'll have your sweets before you know it."

With the goat lick ladened with fresh honey, Barleycopp picked up his tunic and walked the gangplank in stately fashion, leaving the three-legged buck to its treat. He had a no-nonsense look in his eye as he descended the steps of the gangway and approached Mitterhal.

"If I may, sir, I would pose a question."

"Speak your mind, Marlin."

"At the Pass, when the goat-hydes called in the cavalry and the infantry was ordered to fall back to the high ground, some from the third line managed to escape the smoke. Most succumbed shortly thereafter, though not all. A few remained coherent long enough to report what they saw. Or heard, I should say. Hooves, they reported, like horses only different. Something in the pace, the rhythm, the shaking of the earth. Then a breeze, they said, and the scent of musk, and great shadows passing overhead in leaps and bounds through the fumes."

"And your question, Marlin?"

"My question, sir, simply put, is could there be any validity in what our dying men reported?"

"What you're really asking is if the myth of Montayega's herd is real. I'm surprised at you, Marlin. I always thought you favored the pastor's preaching."

"With all due respect, sir, what I favor is irrelevant. It is my job as captain of the Guard to speak for my men, especially those who died in service. I believe my question is valid regardless of whether or not the myth is."

"Ah, Marlin. You are a captain of captains. What would I have done without you? You just answered your own question, my good friend. But I'll add to it by saying one man's myth is another man's reality. Scramble it up enough and you'll never know the difference. That's a good thing to keep in mind as a commander. But I'll have you know that if it were my boots on the line and the order came to charge, I'd take hope over realism any day. That said, I'll pose a question back to you."

"Absolutely, sir."

"You told me that Johan Hume was our best piper, a true scholar of the Old Tome. That's why you assigned his brigade to the east ridge. As such he would know the importance of maintaining the link. Why would he jeopardize the lives of our troops by directing his pipers to a different post? Either he was a traitor or he was convinced beyond doubt that the codes would not be compromised."

"Johan had five sons on the line, sir. Whatever his motives, he was not a traitor."

"Very well. So where does that leave us, Captain? We all heard the music, there's no denying that. Facts are facts. That is the one constant that runs true in everyone's account, whether in the smoke or not. Even the enemy heard it. And so I ask you the question of all questions: Who or what convinced Johan Hume to forgo his assigned post on the east ridge?"

"I don't know, sir."

"That makes two of us."

The buckets stayed silent. Both men stood still, letting loose the reins that tugged at their thoughts. Even the nannies kept their snorts to themselves, despite the lapse of attention. All around the licks horns went up, as if an inaudible note had piped over the gahenya and pricked at their ears.

Mitterhal was the first to stir from his trance. "You know your new friend over there was the only goat born in the spring following the drought. A real loner at first. The herd leader took him in anyway, despite the deformity. Showed the little guy the ropes. Seeing him now in the rut, you'd never think he was born a cripple. His teacher is gone now, wandered off to die. Too bad you never met him."

"Something tells me I already have, sir."

"Eh. Politics has made you a shameless liar, Marlin, but an honest one."

"Given the times, I'll consider that a compliment."

"Consider it more than that. The Haven would be a sad state if not for your due diligence. You've done well."

"Thank you, sir. I best be off. I don't want to leave Jeziah alone too long in the tavern. If I may make one last request, I would send him to

344

your root cellar."

"Ah, yes, I expected as much. The pastor's project is costing more than you anticipated?"

"Actually, sir, it would be a deposit, not a withdrawal."

"A deposit?"

"Yes, Poulakis gave me the Old Tome in light of Rankwall's move to the abbey. He thought the fifth flue the perfect place to keep it safe. Just a precaution."

"Did he now? Well, let's not disappoint him. By all means, Marlin, send up the big lamb."

24

Dancing Ripples

Days passed and the old silver forge bustled with purpose. The reconnaisance team had executed their orders with flawless efficiency. Grycco, in addition to being a competent engineer, proved masterful at organizing labor. The team of twelve had no shortage of support. Many of the volunteers from the square turned out to be quite skilled and were recruited to assist in the more complicated tasks. Even the soft-handed monks had demonstrated an unexpected propensity for hard labor. Yet for Marcus, the most astounding moment came when a host of Wulfhaven's vagrants funneled out of their alleys from the upper precinct, led by none other than Barusta. The ragtag lot offered whatever services they could, even if only to bring water to the workers.

And so, by nothing short of a miracle, the old forge was converted. Though it was only as functional as the two-week time frame allowed, it was adequate nonetheless; not only for the children of the abbey, but for the fountain folk who promised to care for them as their own. The mayor himself came to christen the facility on the day of the deadline. The twelve members of the Haven Guard, including Grycco, were not present, however, and were honored with a moment of silence by the celebrators. Marcus, for his part, had kept a low profile throughout the project, making only periodic visits between dizzy spells. He did step up to the podium near the end of the event to confirm the report that Rankwall's troops had entered the abbey.

The following days proved full of challenges and adjustments. It was indeed eerie to hear the crunch of marching boots on the holy grounds while the monks chanted their morning prayers. Rankwall's forces kept to themselves and to their credit, turned out to be reasonably well mannered, as if to compensate in some small way for an arrangement even they found questionable. Many were young, fresh from the south, and probably had children of their own—somewhere.

The highland lupine came into bloom that week, splashing the mountains in blue. The sight delighted Marcus and inspired him to relax. Somehow he knew the Haven would be fine, even when Krutzwig's mercenaries sailed in from the Weirs and anchored their ships in the harbor; even when, a day later, the work barge was towed to the bridge by four steam-powered patrol boats from South Bay. In fact, Marcus had the pulpit moved outside the cathedral so that all who held vigil in the square could join him in celebration of the great bloom that reflected off the harbor. They sang hymn after hymn, many of which were taken from the Old Tome, though the book itself was never present.

His dizzy spells had intensified, but it made no difference to Marcus. He simply waited them out and went about his business, passing them off as old age. His right arm had gone numb after a particularly severe episode, forcing him to carry his staff in the left. Nobody seemed to notice. Or if they did, they didn't say. Though Brother Michael had become exceptionally clingy of late, always there to help when a spell struck.

And so it came with the most gentle intent one calm evening, only days shy of the full moon, the worried monk put his hand on Marcus's shoulder as he ate his rice in the dining hall. "Forgive the interruption, Father. Gwyntahpynn Choroqua has declared war on Rankwall and all who stand for his cause."

Marcus finished chewing his rice and went to his prayer chamber to fight off the ensuing spell. Within the hour, Michael returned with more disturbing news, though not at all surprising. "Father, the large man from the Guard is back to make a confession. He awaits you in the penance chamber."

Marcus changed into his black travel robe and went to the chamber alone. The echoes in the hall lifted his hollow steps. "We meet again, my friend," he said, after opening the door. "Let me guess. You are not here to tell me your sins."

Jeziah McCaskel turned away from the archangel in the window and lowered his hood. "Your presence is requested."

"My presence? That's it? What statement could I possibly make that I have not made already? Perhaps you could tell the good mayor to paraphrase for me and save us the trip."

"It is not the mayor's request."

"No? Whose is it then?"

"The men have mustered at the stables to declare their stand on Rankwall. They request your blessing."

"I see. I take it the carriage is outside the infirmary?"

"Yes."

Marcus lurched up and down in the darkness, listening to the wheels rattle on the cobbles. He wondered if this was how a baby felt in a mother's womb when set to vigorous motion. The turns were the same as before; he remembered every one of them. Eventually the cobbles turned to gravel. A hymn came to mind from the Old Tome—"On My Way to the Fairgrounds." One of the more upbeat chants. He scrolled through the verses in his mind.

By the third verse he heard galloping horses. Not in his mind, but real. They came from behind the carriage and got progressively louder. A lot of them by the sound of it.

"Halt the wagon!" a voice boomed.

The carriage rolled to a stop. Hooves closed in on all sides.

"What is your business?" the same voice demanded.

Silence.

"By Krutzwig's order, I said state your business!"

"I go to the fairgrounds," Jeziah answered calmly.

"With a closed carriage late at night? I don't think so. In fact, I am more inclined to suspect you're going to the stables. It has become a popular place of late. We wouldn't find any arms in that carriage of yours by any chance, would we, big man?"

"I carry no arms."

"You seem like an honest fellow, and as much as I would like to take you for your word, I must insist we see for ourselves. Open the carriage!"

Marcus brooded in the darkness. This was nothing like a mother's womb, he concluded. A direct tie to the resistance would undermine everything: the abbey, the forge, the church. Krutzwig would have a field day with it. He heard a low rumble from above, barely audible at first, like a roll of thunder before the air-rippling crack.

"Off the carriage, wagon man, and open the door. Now!"

The rumble grew into a chant. It sounded familiar. Marcus felt the springs in the chassis give as Jeziah made his descent. Where had he heard it? The penance chamber, that was it. At his first meeting with the hooded giant when he chanted to the archangel in the window. Marcus looked up, his revelation confirmed by the sound of sliding links on the ceiling of the carriage.

"He has a chain! Seize him!"

What followed had the unworldly quality of a cataclysm, as if the very sinews of the earth had been called to rise. Jeziah's chain snapped in answer to the unsheathing of many sabers. The violence jarred the carriage. Lash after lash, the mighty cipher smote his justice on man and horse. Out of habit Marcus clasped his hands in prayer for the departed, appealing to the Great Father and his mercy every time he felt a body break against the carriage. And even after the horses scurried and the chain fell silent, the storm persisted. Cries of agony were severed by what sounded like branches snapping. At last, the destruction waned and Marcus heard a single horse race away from the ruin. Silence reigned for a moment, and then deep labored breathing and footsteps approaching the carriage. The springs in the chassis compressed. A single loud snort, and the wheels rolled forward again.

The remainder of the trip was swift and rough. Marcus pressed his staff against the ceiling to reduce his jostling. When the carriage stopped abruptly, he heard the stable doors slide open and Jeziah's command.

"Our position is compromised. Reinforce the perimeter."

A jolt and the carriage moved forward again, amid shouting voices and horses' hooves. Another stop, and Jeziah ordered someone to take Marcus to the chamber. The carriage door opened. Lantern light poured in. Blinded, Marcus felt two hands grab his arm—powerful hands. "This way, Father." He knew the voice. It was Lawrence Grycco.

"Wait," Marcus said. He looked up to Jeziah hunched on the carriage bench. "Are you all right, my son?"

The giant turned and grimaced, his breathing heavy. He ignored Marcus, turning his fading gaze onto Grycco. "I said get him to the chamber. Now!"

The effort consumed him and his head dropped, compressing his braided beard to his chest.

Marcus felt two more hands on his other arm. His feet left the ground. "No! By the light of the Great Father, I will incinerate every one of you if you do not put me down."

The hands let go. Marcus rushed back to the carriage. A red stream poured off the bench and soaked the straw below. Enough blood for an ox. How could any one man withstand such a drain? "Get him down!" he shouted to the men.

Grycco and six others hoisted Jeziah off the carriage bench and laid him on the straw. His shredded torso heaved up and down with every labored breath. A pail of water was brought to his side, and one of the guardsmen started to sponge his wounds.

Jeziah clamped his hand around the soldier's neck. "Let me rest."

"Step back!" Marcus ordered, waving the men off with his staff. He knelt beside Jeziah. His black eyes were open but far. Marcus knew the look—the winding down of the body as the soul prepares to depart. There was nothing to do now but be a pastor. "Rest easy, my son. You have put in a long day."

"I am tired, Pastor."

"Yes, and for good reason. You have served the Haven well. Now it is time to rest."

"It is dark."

Marcus paused, his protocol on hold. What to do, what to say? It always came to that in the end—the darkness. The giant wanted rest; he had made that clear. Was it fair to direct him to a place where the glory of God would shine on him for eternity? Surely he deserved it, but was it really what he wanted? The decision made him dizzy. Another spell. Of all times!

"I am jealous, Jeziah," he said, fighting his own swoon.

Focus returned to Jeziah's eyes. The light of the pole lantern flickered in their depths. Marcus wavered in the swaying reflection. So much to say, so little time to say it. He had to be quick, his own spell pressing. "Rest now in the shade of your Great Mountain, my son. Go back to the womb from where you came. *Yan shahuna maha na geshiva kutchu.*"

The last breath of a dying soldier was nothing new to Marcus. Some left the world with ease, others fought hard to the bitter end. Yet nothing he had witnessed in the war had prepared him for the passing of Jeziah McCaskel. In one final surge, his torso heaved upward and out like the great bellows of an iron forge. Long it stayed elevated, suspended by air, until at last it sank to a depth that blew his breath out of the stable.

Marcus felt his own beard rise as if the potent draft had erupted from a timeless basin in the earth. The burst made him heavy, light, and then heavy again. Around the stable his vision spun—the stalls, the purlins, the straw. A great hall of crystalline walls. What? Canyons of ice withering in molten rock, snapping in fire and steam. Blurring, spinning light. *Where am I?* Hands tied in terrestrial knots of silver veins. *By the light of the Great Father, end this madness!* Peace ... darkness ... rest.

Marcus awoke. It was late, the full moon bright on his pillow. Somebody stood next to his bed. A boy, a feather ... Barusta. "Where am I?"

"You are in the infirmary, Father. It's been two days. The doctors said you were going to die. I knew they were wrong."

"What are you doing here? You should be in bed."

"I could not sleep, Father. The moon is full. I had a dream about a soldier, only he was young, just a little older than me. He kept poking me with his musket and waking me up, telling me to get up and go to the harbor. It happened again and again, so I snuck out of the forge and went down to the dock. Another soldier was there, a real one, like the one in my dream only older. He just sat there in a rowboat singing to himself."

"Did he speak to you?"

"Yes, he said he liked my feather. I told him where I got it and he showed me his musket. He said the colonel gave it to him when he was a boy just like me."

"Barusta, listen to me. I do not want you talking to that man. He is dangerous. Do you understand?"

"I really don't think he's bad, Father. He told me of a beautiful place with rabbits and mountain goats the size of oxen. And butterflies so large they could carry you off into the stars like a winged wagon. I wanted to get on the boat and see it for myself. I asked him if I could, but he refused. He said that you would melt his musket if I did."

"At least he was right about one thing. Did he tell you why he was there?"

Barusta wiped his cheek with his hand, suddenly somber. "He said he was done teaching the army at the fairgrounds his song and he came to take you to that place with the butterflies."

"Ah, yes, the butterflies, of course. Well then, you best help me up. We have a long walk ahead of us and I'm not as spry as I used to be. Be a good boy and fetch my robe and staff over there by the hook. We will go out the back way so nobody sees us."

Outside of the abbey infirmary, Marcus took a deep breath of the fresh midnight air. It felt good to be outside again, under the stars. He scanned their patterns. "Barusta, I have a task for you. Do you know where my prayer chamber is in the north transept?"

"I do."

"I want you to go there, as stealthy as I know you can be. You will find a blanket on the wall. Bring it to me. I will meet you at the dock behind the forge. Be sure to avoid the guards at the dorms." He smiled. "I don't expect that should be a problem for you."

The wily boy beamed at the challenge and darted off into the shadows.

Marcus watched him disappear and then left the abbey grounds, making for a side street that led through the old port to the harbor. He got there sooner than he thought. Not a single dizzy spell. His staff swung comfortably in his right hand, the numbness gone. The rowboat was tied to the dock, bobbing in the moonlight. A man-like shadow sat in its stern. Marcus felt the blood in his veins flowing strong and unrestricted, as if he were young again.

The shadow shifted as he approached the dock. "Are you ready, Father?"

"Not quite. Let us wait and enjoy the air."

"As you wish."

Barusta showed up shortly thereafter. "Here is your blanket, Father," he said, carefully handing it over. "It looks just like the one that Colonel Cornelius gave the church that day, only smaller. Where did you get it?"

"I have always had it. Now be a good boy and help me in the boat."

Marcus sat in the bow, adjusting his robe on the bench and laying the blanket over his lap. "Well, then, there we have it. Nice and cozy. A great night for travel. What is the matter, Barusta?"

"I wish I was going with you, Father."

"Now, now, do not wish for that. Not yet. You have an academy to run. No time for silly trips to mountains. Untie the boat, will you? Wait, I almost forgot." He held out his staff. "Take this and put it somewhere safe. It will help you make good decisions."

Barusta took the pastor's staff and untied the boat.

"Very good. Now go back to the forge and get a good night's sleep. Tomorrow your mission begins. Stay true to it."

Marcus looked back over his shoulder to address the shadow in the moonlit stern. "Let's go, Willis. I am ready. Show me this great mountain of yours."

The oar split the surface. Marcus watched the ripples dance.

25
Mother's Blessing

"Muma?"
"Yes, little one?"
"Where does the flower go when it dies?"
"It does not die, child, it sleeps."
"Do all things sleep?"
"All things that live, yes."
"So I should not be sad?"
"There is no harm in sadness, only in despair. Now be a good little girl and bring me the lupine ester. Your brother has been acting up again. It is in the blue vial on the shelf by the amaryllis."

Word of the passing of Marcus Poulakis spread like wildfire over the Haven. Enyalda received the news in the tavern kitchen while making butternut biscuits. The men had been in session all morning discussing dire matters. Francis came to her before dispatching his somber report to the others. His eyes were swollen and red. At first she thought it due to the wind from his ride up the mountain. Then he hugged her and she knew.

He went to the meeting chamber, and minutes later Sheriff Hoffman made an unprecedented appearance in the kitchen. He took off his hat and nodded to Madam Hornpout, then directed his attention to Enyalda. "The colonel needs to know, madam. I think it best you tell him."

Enyalda stayed on the carriage road all the way up to the manor. The gahenya was in bloom and she knew it would be impossible to walk through the fields without crushing the pretty blue blossoms. If only the goats would be as considerate. Not likely, she thought, watching them gorge on the buds up on the knolls.

She found the colonel at his beehives, napping by the dormant smoke pit with both hands atop his cane. Cautiously she approached, so as not to jar him out of slumber. His breath was deathly still, almost none at all. She drew her nose to within an inch of his to make sure it was not just the breeze that ruffled his mustache. Then to her horror, his eyes snapped open, blue as the lupine in bloom.

"What in blazes are you up to?" he said, wide awake.

She leaped back and spun several times to cast away her fright.

The colonel chuckled as he packed and relit his pipe.

Enyalda seethed where she stood. What a deplorable man! She made a mental note to put an extra dose of the ester on his turnip that night.

"Now, now," he said. "Why the long face, my dear? It was just a little scare to get you dancing. No reason to get locked in a twist."

She held back her anger, reminded of the mission. The colonel was feeling playful. What a shame to shatter his mood. What words could she possibly use to break the news? Not a single rhyme came to mind. Straight talk would have to do.

"He has left," she said.

"Who has left?"

"Your brother. The infirmary."

"My brother?"

Aghast, she pressed both hands to her lips. Did she really say that? She could have sworn she said pastor. So much for straight talk. In a panic she hurried into verse.

Hold me not to what I say.
Sadness clouds my thoughts today.
The man I mean is dear to us,
The good pastor, Poulakis.

"Marcus?"

Enyalda hid her eyes behind her hair, preparing for the worst. She peeked out and saw nothing: no twitch of the brow, no tremor in hand, not even a dribble from the lower lip. How so very uncolonel-like. Surely Pastor Marcus must have meant something to him.

"When and how?" he finally asked.

"Last night, a boat out of harbor paddled. The boy with feather you gave saw leave."

Again Enyalda peered through her hair; again dead silence. Mystified, she kneeled to a cluster of gahenya that bloomed by the wall. Maybe the blue blossoms knew something she didn't. Then, as if to confirm her suspicions, the colonel suddenly burst into laughter.

Enyalda gasped in midwhisper, appalled at what the gossiping grasses were suggesting. Not once in all her years on the mountain had she ever questioned the colonel's sanity. Now for the first time, she was put to the test. She thought she had prepared herself for anything, yet joyous laughter simply never crossed her mind. It was pure joy, in fact, the kind that seizes a child without an ounce of malice. He carried on as such until she feared he might unravel completely. Yet for all her healing skills, she could not think of a single blessing to quell his fit. The fever spread to the clump of gahenya in front of her, then to the other flowers in the field. Even the steadfast lichen on the stone wall began to giggle. Finally, when it seemed the entire pasture had lost its senses, she raised her arms high to the sky and commanded it all to stop.

"*Nish hayem!*" she shouted.

All became silent: the grasses, the lichen, the flowers. Even the colonel, though the joy still flickered in his eyes.

"That sly old fox," he said. "He devotes his entire life to his Great Father, only to leave the world like a pagan. Leave it to Marcus to get the last laugh. Come, my dear," he said, hoisting himself up by the cane. "A celebration is in order."

The colonel was exhausted by the time they made it back to the manor, and so the ceremony was put on hold until after a nap. Enyalda tucked him into his leather chair next to the hearth. There she lit a fire so that he would wake up to the merry sounds of the crackling pops. As he slept, she searched for other things that might lend to the festivity. She set candles on the mantel, to make it appear as a cake, and placed a mason jar full of honey front and center. Then to her solarium she went and brought up pots of morning glories. The vines had yet to bloom, but their spade-shaped leaves gave reverence to the room, especially around the bricks where she hung them from shelves alongside the mantel.

At one point the colonel stirred, and she promptly sang a lullaby to send him back to dream. Everything had to be just right before he awoke. When all was almost ready, she looked upon her work. A lovely sight, she thought, but something was still missing. What was it? Music, of course! That was it. What was a celebration without music? She could sing to him, but that would limit her chores in the kitchen. She still had cookies to bake.

One of the vines on the shelf spoke up, pointing out the blue box under its leaves.

Yes, what a great idea—the colonel's favorite song. The perfect tune to celebrate the life of Pastor Marcus. Carefully, she lifted the heirloom from the shelf and whispered to the vine, thanking it for the suggestion. Then she set it on the nightstand next to the colonel's chair, opened the lid, and turned the little brass handle on its side. The music flowed as pure as the day when he gave her his mother's necklace. Satisfied at last, she broke for the kitchen, singing with the tune on the way.

Mountain lupine in full bloom,
Flowing blue on meadow's tide
On yellow wagon you and I,
To the Haven we will ride
Upon arrival at lakeshore
We will open wagon's door.
By her fountain we will be
Blessed in love eternally.

From the fountain we will cross,
Love's reflection on the lake
Wagon carry us away
Sea of crimson in our wake.
And in the moonlight's subtle glance,
We will watch the ripples dance.
From our wagon we will see,
The land we love, the love we leave.

Celebration, song and dance,
See the wagon's ponies prance,
Beneath my tapestry receive
Your mother's blessing.

In the kitchen Enyalda scuttled this way and that to gather the ingredients for the batter. Most of her culinary tricks she had learned from Muma, though the dance moves were strictly hers. It had always been that way, and Muma never seemed to mind. She put an extra pinch of black horehound in the mix to spice up the celebration. That particular trick she had learned at the tavern. The cookies had just gone in the oven when she heard the colonel humming in the hearth room. Happily she slipped out of the kitchen to join the fun.

The colonel sat upright in his chair, still a bit groggy. He held the open box on his lap and turned the hand crank, slow and steady.

"Such a pretty little thing, isn't it?" he said, gazing into the rich blue enamel. "Made in Toricia of all places. Imagine that. It wasn't just war we were good at."

He shifted his gaze to the crackling fire and stared into the flames, spellbound by the music. A log settled in the coals and brought him back to the party.

"You know the Torics hung my father right here on the mountain, from that big old beech you climbed as a girl." The colonel paused again. "At least that's what I've been told." He shut the lid on the music. "I don't remember much of that, only dreams now and then of swinging boots. I remember this box, though. My mother would sing to me whenever I turned the crank. Funny how that sticks."

"Funny yes. Fun, Fun, fun," Enyalda said. She arced her arms over her head and twirled throughout the hearth room on her toes. The party needed a boost. Every so often she looked through her hair to make sure the colonel was watching her.

"In Toricia they told me my father was a traitor. An infidel who succumbed to the seduction of a heathen witch."

Enyalda faltered in her steps. What a horrible thing for them to say.

His gaze shifted to her shadow on the wall. "They never told me the witch was my mother."

Terribly horrible. Time to check the cookies. "Hold that thought for another day, cookies and chamomile on the way!"

Back in the kitchen she prepared the tray: two teacups, a plate full of cookies, and a pitcher of tea to share. How she wished her brothers were there. Even Adman's political spouts would be a welcome diversion. Anything to spice up the event. Spice! Yes, that was it. Some pretty blue petals in the tea perhaps? Why not? The lupine was in full bloom. Muma never said anything scary about the blossoms, only the seeds. Neither did Pastor Marcus, for that matter. Perfect! She sped down the stairs, through her solarium, and out the door to fetch a stalk of gahenya from the wall.

Halfway across the terrace she froze. A man-sized owl stood by the hedge of laurels, staring at her. Only it had arms where its wings should be. Another one stood at the other end of the hedge, his face mottled in red. Nothing owl-like about him. Both had bows, spears, and a quiver of arrows. Too scared to scream, she bolted back to the solarium and up the stairs.

"Where are the cookies?" the colonel asked as she beelined to his chair.

"Men!" she blurted, grabbing his arm.

"What men?"

"Scary men in laurels, painted faces!"

In an instant the colonel was up with cane in hand, making for the front parlor. He stopped in the entry to face Enyalda before opening the door. "How many did you see?"

"Two, they be."

"Stay back. Not a peep out of you until we know their purpose." He swung the door open and stepped onto the stoop. "*Huru ay etsa!*" he commanded—Speak your peace.

Enyalda was shocked. She never knew the colonel spoke Muma's language.

The two painted faces approached from the hedge. Both stopped at the foot of the steps. The owl man spoke. "We bring word to Mahocpynn from Wulfwynn, son of One Talon, the one called Donavon."

Enyalda lunged out the door, hearing her brother's name. He was alive! Not a day had passed since he'd left last fall that she did not whisper a prayer for him in the solarium. Eager to hear more, she stormed past the colonel and down the stairs without the slightest care to civility. At the base of the steps she locked her eyes firmly on the owl man.

Purpose is as purpose does
Now dally not and tell us of
The word you bring this day in spring
Lest wulf in bloom make owl sing!

The owl man turned to his cohort. "*Dahu gwaheen ahla Wulfwynn,*" he said, and both dropped to their knees.

"It is an honor to meet the sister of wolf spirit," the owl man said. "He speaks of you always and loves you like stream loves rain. My pack name is Notalk and this is Nosebleed."

Misunderstanding, Enyalda gently pinched the red warrior's nose and recited a blessing. It was a well-established routine at the tavern, especially when the Grange boys got to scrapping. Both warriors maintained a respectful silence throughout the ritual.

"All right, that's enough hocus-pocus," the colonel said. "I'm sure you lads didn't cross the Haven to get your sniffers squeezed. What's your business here?"

The warriors got up and faced the colonel. "Our council is with Mahocpynn," the owl man said.

The colonel struck his cane on the stoop. "Call me whatever you want, but I'm in the middle of a ceremony of my own, so I suggest you make your point quick."

The warriors looked at each other, obviously shocked. In an instant they were back on their knees, bowing so low the arrows nearly slid from their quivers.

"What are you doing now?" the colonel demanded.

"You are Mahocpynn. Forgive us."

"I do not want your apology. I want to know why you are here. Now quit dirtying your knees and get inside."

Enyalda hummed a pretty melody while she brought the platter of cookies and the teapot, along with two extra cups, to the hearth room.

"*Su gahwynn,*" the warriors said, accepting the gingerwhips and tea.

Enyalda decided she liked them, especially the owl face. He had a gentle soul and good manners. But how strange to be treated with such reverence. She also decided that Donavon must be fine, for surely their demeanor would have been different if otherwise. Still, she was eager to hear of his tidings. The colonel, for all his initial urgency, sat in his chair, more occupied with his pipe than anything else.

The red-faced warrior, the one called Nosebleed, sat cross-legged by the fire, engulfing the dainty teacup with his strapping hands. "Wulfwynn say you sing to stars of Sky Father and speak to roots of Mother. Your voice he hear in wind between leaves."

The owl man named Notalk, who also sat cross-legged by the fire, placed his teacup on the hearthstone and reached into his satchel. Something sparkled in his hand as he held it out toward Enyalda. "Your brother want you to have this. He say his home now in Gwyntahlynn."

Enyalda gasped. It was the badge Sheriff Hoffman had given him that first night when they all had dinner together. She could not stop her hand from shaking as she reached out for the silver brooch.

Notalk put his hand over hers as she took the brooch. "He also say he run like wolf across water if you call." The warrior's assuring grip calmed her.

"All right then," the colonel said, encased in a cloud of his greenbank. "Now that we are on the subject, what else did the lad have to say?"

The owl nodded. "We secure pact with boatmen. They agree to assist our cause. Weir ships that come to harbor make false alliance with peace stealers."

A plume of ash erupted out of the colonel's pipe. To Enyalda's shock, he leaned forward, gagging. Only a handful of times had she witnessed his smoke get the best of him. That it happened now in the presence of others at such a crucial time added to her concerns. She watched him gasp for breath, debating whether to intervene. "How?" he finally managed to ask between hacks.

Nosebleed answered. "Wulfwynn take war pack to Weirs and find boat chief. He remind him of lesson taught at fountain."

The colonel finally gained his composure and looked at Enyalda. "Go to the village, my dear. Find Hoffman and tell him to get up here at once. Do not let anyone know of our visitors, not even Hoffman. Tell him the hammer found the anvil. Also, have Madam Hornpout prepare provisions for a sortie to ride at first light tomorrow. Tell her it's a three-day ride and to pack for speed. Go, Enyalda. Run."

The outburst kicked the colonel into another coughing fit. Enyalda did not feel comfortable leaving him in such a state, so she decided to administer a blessing. No sooner did she lift her arms than the old man raised his cane. "I said run!"

Enyalda charged down the carriage path, wondering what it was about politics that made men so testy. So much for celebrations. All that effort for nothing. Not once was Pastor Marcus even mentioned. The shadows of the blue blossoms stretched to the east. It would soon be mealtime at the tavern. She quickened her pace, hoping to catch the sheriff before dinner. He tended to be so much more attentive when he wasn't digesting.

A slow waltzy ballad wept out of the windows as she approached the door. Inside, the tavern was more crowded than usual, the common room packed with village folk lamenting the death of Pastor Marcus. Even the Grange boys were on their best behavior.

Enyalda panted on the threshold, searching the room for the sheriff. Someone charged across the dance floor. It was Francis. He cut through the crowd, deep concern in his eyes.

"Are you all right, sister? Why are you out of breath?"

"Word I have of ..." She stopped just in time, remembering the colonel's order. "Word for sheriff." She pinched her lips tight with her fingers.

Francis got the hint and nodded. "He's in the chamber with fighters from Multynhaven. Can it wait?"

She turned her head back and forth like an owl.

"I didn't think so. Come on. I'll see you in."

He swung open the chamber door, the squeak of hinges topped by a round of metallic clicks. Enyalda saw a grim group of men with their pistols drawn, all pointed directly at them.

"Sorry, I forgot to give the code," Francis said, hands up high. Another round of clicks and the guns went back in their lanyards.

"What is it?" Hoffman asked from the head of the conference table.

"Enya's got news that can't wait, sir."

The smoke hung thick around the table, not a breath of festivity in the air. Hoffman was the only man she recognized. The others were stern and bearded, with eyes locked in the shadows of their scowls.

She wavered. The moment had come to deliver the message. How easy it would have been to weave it in melody, to give the colonel's words that extra punch. But such were the limits of her options in the conference chamber. The amendment to rule seven had spared her once of Madam Hornpout's wrath, but to count on chance again was a stretch. No, it had to be words, tuneless and clunky. She did her best to convert her lyrics to straight talk and prayed that her mouth would oblige.

"From manor I have come command on urgent run to bring a word that none shall hear the colonel wants the sheriff's ear. Go the sheriff must at once to manor no delay, for the hammer found the anvil is to him what I must say."

The look on Francis's face said it all. Apparently her mouth hadn't cooperated. The grim men seemed equally confused. Their eyes searched the ceiling as if the meaning of her outburst were encoded in the knot patterns of the timbers. It was Hoffman who cracked the code.

"Hammers and anvils. You heard her, boys. Let's go!"

Every man nodded and charged the back wall to fetch his musket. In an instant, the entire lot was out the door, led by Hoffman in his wide-brimmed hat. Francis and Enyalda stood alone in the deserted chamber, having barely escaped the stampede.

Enyalda went to the kitchen to deliver the second half of her message. Madam Hornpout was chopping carrots and Brewmaster Garrison was stirring up a pot of wart for the brew. "It's 'bout time this kitchen had somethin' pretty to look at," he said as Enyalda sped in.

"You won't be looking at anything pretty when I dunk your head in that wart," the madam said. She turned to Enyalda and asked what she needed.

Once again Enyalda dismantled the verses in her mind. "A three-day ride awaits at sunrise speedy riders take provisions we must lightly make to get them where they go."

Madam Hornpout took only seconds to decipher the message. "I see. Well, let's get on with it then. Be a good girl and mince me up some jewel weed." She fired an order to Garrison, who was less quick with the translation. "We need a pot of boiled sheep's lard on the double."

"I'm busy with my wart."

Hornpout reached for her rolling pin mounted on the back splash.

"I'm going, I'm going," the brewmaster said.

Enyalda spent the bulk of the evening assisting Madam Hornpout with the preparations. Brewmaster Garrison did his part with only minimal complaint. At one point, Serena Schonhauser came in to catch a breather and asked Enyalda to hold her post at the bar. The frazzled barmaid was quick to say that only the regulars remained. Madam Hornpout nodded approvingly and Enyalda went out the door.

The counter itself was thankfully bare, only a few belly-uppers. Most were scattered about in conversation. In the far corner the McGregor brothers were fussing with Patrick Grange and his cousins over a round of darts, their backs to the bar. Others lingered in the common room where a lone lute player plucked out a ballad. At the hearth Francis sat with Gildryn and Angus, engrossed in discussion.

"I would have given half the flock to see the cipher do what he did," Gildryn said, his mug raised high to the tablet of rules. "Seventeen mounted pogies with nothing but a chain. Not to mention six horses. What a way to go."

One of the belly-uppers stirred. His glassy gaze followed Enyalda's hand as she wiped the counter. "So what ye know 'bout all dat fuss?" he asked. "I han't seen Hoffman move like dat since dem pogies hit da Mitt's place."

"Now why'd she go and spill da beans to a crusty old drunk like you?" the man next to him said. "Whatever it tiz, we'll be hear'n it soon enough, won't we, madam?" He favored Enyalda with a lopsided smile.

She smiled back politely and wiped the foamy dribbles off his chin with her bar rag. Men as a whole were so easy to read. Most just blurted out their questions without the slightest care to temperance. Some tried to work their magic by taking her side while others made dubious statements designed to loosen her tongue. The smarter ones used the ignorance of others to work their agenda. Those were the ones to watch out for. Yet even they could be defused with a well-crafted compliment. With her thoughts no longer scrambled by urgency, the words flowed smooth and clear.

"Wise you are," she said, "to wait and see what tidings have in store for thee."

A commotion flared up in the dart room. "What do you mean!" Patrick Grange shouted to Seth McGregor. "We took 'em once, we can do it again. All we gotta do is lure 'em off those boats so we can plug 'em."

"Don't be an idiot, Patsy," Seth retorted. "The weirmen will be armed this time. We're not gonna beat their pistols with our fists. We also had half the square backing us up last time."

The evening tarried on until the front door of the tavern slammed open, sending chunks of wall plaster to the floor. In the doorway stood Hoffman with his brawny forearm still extended. The drafty lamplight cast more shadows than light over the crags in his face.

"Everybody in the chamber now!" His gaze fixed on Enyalda. "I want Garrison and Hornpout there too."

Enyalda headed for the kitchen, but the cook and brewmaster were already on their way. She stood by the hearth watching the other patrons funnel into the chamber behind them. The grim fighters—the ones Francis had said came from Multynhaven—strode through the tavern entry and seated themselves in the common room. She covered her face with her hair to avoid their scary eyes.

"Enya!" Francis shouted from the meeting chamber. "Hoffman wants you in here too."

She darted from the hearth, thankful to escape their watchful glares.

Hoffman paced the chamber with both hands on his hips. Not a soul was sitting.

"Everyone listen good," he said. "The colonel is making his move. Timing is everything." He pulled an envelope out of his overcoat. "Seth, I want you, Gildryn, Patrick, and Dugan ready to ride at first light tomorrow. Take the fastest steeds in the village. Go to Spaulding Pass and give this to Harthmocker."

Seth took the envelope, and Hoffman looked to Hornpout. "Murtie, make sure—"

"Already on it," she said.

"Good." He shifted his attention to the brewmaster. "Garrison, we need to get the uniforms from the mill to the train depot at once. Load them in barrels and send them on the mule. Make sure you weigh them down with rocks and mix them in with the real kegs."

He removed his badge and strode over to Angus, who towered above the two belly-uppers that had been at the bar. "You're in charge now, Angus," he said, handing him the badge. "I'm going with the boys to make our stand at the stables. I want a live musket at every window in the village. Nobody gets through. Understand? It's open season on pogies now."

Angus nodded, his jaw clenched tight.

The sheriff then looked to Enyalda at the door. He seemed about to say something to her, then stopped. Instead he took a deep breath and addressed the entire assembly. "All right, that's it. The rest is common sense. There'll be plenty of time for yarnin' once this is over. Until then, keep your gossip on the mountain. Any questions? Good. Hail, Gahenya." Then just like that he was out the door, leaving all in the chamber stunned.

Enyalda nearly broke down in tears. Something wasn't right. So many empty faces, like flowers when their petals wilted. How could this be? She had to think fast before it was too late. No, not think. Do! The sheriff was right. Timing was everything. And so with no further plan than that, she darted out of the meeting chamber and into the common room where the scary men were strapping on their muskets and making ready to leave. She wove through the group like a speedy grass snake, noticing the owl man and the red-faced warrior standing under the tablet of tavern rules. At the door she turned around and lifted her arms, making herself as big as she possibly could.

Everyone froze, even the sheriff, only strides away. The others came out of the chamber and did the same. Enyalda faced her audience and felt their burdens fall heavy on her heart: the empty faces, the scary eyes, a tremendous weight, like a dead limb pressing. Still holding out her arms, she imagined herself as an enormous butterfly bearing their weight. And though the load was grave, she knew she had to be quick and flighty, just like her days in the beechwood. The times had changed, but not the options. What should it be? A whisper, a riddle, a rhyme perhaps? Then it dawned on her. The song from the blue box. Why not? It worked on the colonel, it could work for them, especially with the gahenya in bloom. What better way to christen the colonel's mission than with his own mother's blessing?

And so, as the yarn was later spun: Enyalda McFadden, daughter of the One Talon and sister of wolf spirit, light as the seed of air, bestowed her blessing upon all in Cotton Crown Tavern. And though the days ahead were sure to be a challenge, not a soul left the tavern that night with a heavy heart.

363

26
Law of the Lake

Hector Xavier's fleet was twelve ships strong: four schooners, three cutters, and five smacks. He claimed they were fishing vessels in spite of the fact that every one of them had been refurbished with enough firepower to sink a galleon. Hector insisted the arsenal was meant strictly as a deterrent against unethical lake rats who might be tempted to pillage his honest living. That was his story and he stuck to it.

Donavon sat on the prow of Hector's schooner, chewing on hazelnuts while Scraggs sniffed at the harbor breeze from the crux of the bowsprit. So many things had transpired since their arrival in the Haven three days earlier. The mountain flower had come into bloom and Choroqua, true to his word, had declared war on Rankwall. The arrival of the weirmen coincided perfectly with the qwyntahpynn's declaration—all part of Hector Xavier's scheme. Krutzwig had been quick to accept the weirman's offer to keep the harbor clean of heathens, and had even given an advance for the first hundred scalps delivered.

In the meantime, Scarchief, Tiptoe, Pickpack and Blue had gone upriver to convene with the council of kaharpynn at the Gwyntah war camp. Notalk and Nosebleed were smuggled into Wulfhaven so they could carry word of the weirmen's false alliance with Krutzwig up Cotton Crown to Mitterhal. It tormented Donavon not to go himself and see his sister, but Hector insisted he stay on the schooner as insurance in case the savages had a change of heart. For now, Donavon was stuck chomping hazelnuts.

"Looks like that wolf of yours finally got his sea legs," a hard-cutting voice said from behind. It was Hector, one massive tattooed arm braced against the head mast.

"He likes the air," Donavon said, spitting out a bit of shell.

"I bet he does. How'd you get him?"

"I found him on the mountain. Both his parents shot. The litter was denned up in an outbuilding at the Old Mitt's place. A badger got every one of them except for him. Barely an ounce on him and he still fought like a weasel."

"Sounds like a real buster." Hector ducked the jib and crossed to the prow rail. "That's a fine quality for a first mate. So where you going after this? Have you thought of fishing? I could use a guy like you on board."

"I'm a hunter, not a fisher. There's no chase in fish."

"It's not about the fish, mate. That's just what we do to pass the time. You make the real money on the side jobs."

Donavon spat out another shell. "Yeah, well, you're not getting rich on this deal. What's in it for you if it's not the money?"

"I'll tell you what's in it for me," Hector said, looking to the broads. "Freedom. I spent fifteen years locked up in Altomar. Everything changed when Rankwall attacked South Bay. Those Torics never knew what hit 'em. That and whatever stunt your boss pulled off out there in the hills. Every one of 'em crinkled up like cheap sails in a gale, prison guards and all. We busted out even as Ranky's boys were storming the streets. Found ourselves some schooners moored out in the bay and off we sailed into the sunset. First one I'd seen in fifteen years." Hector peered across the harbor to the cathedral in Wulfhaven. "You know, you haven't seen a sunset until you sail the broads."

"Try the mountains sometime."

"No way, mate, not for me. Mountains have roots. When this deal is done, I'm out of here. Nothing beats floating on the open water when it's all lit up. It's like sneaking through the back door to heaven—only way for a scab like me. Fishing gets ya out there. Trust me, there's a lot more than just hauling nets and rigging sails. You do your job and nobody bugs you. And if they do, you just give 'em a poke or two with your dagger. Out here, the laws are what you make of 'em. You'll fit in just fine. You got the salt for it. Stick with me and I'll show you how to write those laws. I'll give you first mate's share of the profits. After a season or two on my boat, you'll be ready for your own. We'll set you up on a smack and you'll be calling the shots before you know it. You can bring on those heathen mates of yours, too, if you want. What a crew that would make, eh? And if you like the chase, there's no shortage of ladies in the ports. What do you say?"

"I still don't see how siding up with us gets you anymore freedom than if you stuck with the pogies. Either way, you get to do all the fishing you want."

Hector laughed. "You don't miss a beat do you, mate? I like how you think. I'll tell you why, but it stays between you and me. If I find out you get loose lipped with the boys, I'll hang you on the sloop by those pretty red dreads of yours, got it?"

"Sure."

"You know I've been called a lot of things by a lot of people. One thing I've never been called is a countryman. That colonel of yours caught me off guard with that one. Looking ahead, I don't see any future with Ranky. He's a scab just like the rest of us. Once he gets his bridge built, it'll only be a matter a time before he moves in on my turf. When you showed up with those savages, I decided right then and there to put my money on your boss. At least he's got salt."

"Yeah, I guess he does."

A shout came from the crow's nest above. "We gotta clipper come'n in from the broads, Hex. They're signal'n they got somethin'."

"Send 'em in," Hector ordered.

The man in the nest pulled down a rope that sent a green flag soaring to topmast. In the meantime, Hector resumed his spiel to Donavon on the prow. An hour later the clipper dropped sail and latched alongside hull, towing a dory. The ship's captain left the helm and hailed Hector from the rail.

"Aye, Hex, we found this 'ere floater out in da broads," he said, pointing to the boat in tow. "Not a ticker in her but sure's got a crazy mix o' loot. You gots ta see."

Hector invited Donavon to come along, and together they walked the gangplank and boarded the fishing ship, along with several other curious crewmembers. Scraggs stayed behind and whined from the rail, not quite willing to maneuver over the water on the narrow board.

The captain of the clipper directed them to a tattered old sail laid out on deck. His tar-laden grin all but split his scruff. "We spotted her just after da rise. Nothin' special 'bout da boat, but gets a look at this." He grabbed a corner of the sail and flipped it back.

Donavon nearly fell over at the sight. Stretched out on the deck was a blanket, just like the one in the loom at the colonel's manor, only smaller. Next to it, lying on an animal skin, was a brass-stocked musket. "Let me see that thing," he said, grabbing the gun. Sure enough, the name was engraved in the brass, exactly as he remembered it—Gen Simon Harthmocker. "I can't believe it! This was the Old Mitt's gun. And that blanket! He had one just like it on the mountain."

Hector knelt down and poked at the pelt with his dagger. "Well, I'll be a naked laker. That's one big rabbit," he said, flipping over the folded ears with his blade.

"Aye, Hex, tain't no fox I'd know make that catch," said the captain of the clipper. "That thar lil' bunny be da size of a dog."

Donavon spun the stock, his thoughts racing. "We gotta get this to

Gwyntahlynn. The elders will know what to make of it."

"Not so fast," Hector said, snatching the gun away. "This musket's worth something. It stays on my boat. You can do whatever you want with the blanket and the bunny."

"Fine. I need a boat to get upriver."

"Slow down, mate. We'll get you back to your pack, but you're gonna have to wait till dark. We don't want Krutzy's boys getting nosy. In the meantime, I got an idea for you to take to your tribe friends. It'll take some gutsy spears, but if we pull it off it'll shut down this bridge for good and get us a fine prize to boot." Hector looked to the captain. "Good job, Shanks. You just doubled your wage for the month. Now get this catch over to my boat and have your boys grab a barrel of the good stuff out of my brig. Leave the dory with us."

"Aye, aye, Hex," said the captain.

Later that evening, Donavon tossed the sheriff's combat pack over the rail of the schooner and into the dory. He descended a rope and then signaled the weirmen to send down Scraggs in a net. The wolf snarled the entire way down, reeking of fish. Donavon untangled his humiliated friend and set the boat to oar.

Above, Hector leaned over the rail and called down instructions. "All right, mate. Just hug the bank and keep an eye out for the smack on the other side of the bridge. They got some fresh arms to take you upriver. Don't miss 'em or you're gonna have a long fight with that current. Let me know if the plan's a go and I'll set another date with Krutzy."

On into the shadows Donavon rowed while Scraggs lapped furiously at the fish slime in his fur. They stayed close to the harbor's edge past the cliffs to where the land flattened and a great stand of oaks absorbed the moonlight on the westward shore. He paddled past cove after cove, always keeping a wary eye on the tiny lights that flickered on the work barge far out in the harbor. Eventually he passed under the bridge where the trusses towered high at the entrance of the mines. Shortly thereafter he spotted the weirmen's smack anchored not far from the rampart.

He paddled to the boat. Three hopped on board the dory with extra oars to assist in the scull upriver. They all smelled of whiskey. One of them was Captain Shanker from the clipper ship.

The current increased considerably where the mouth of the river converged. They arrived at the Gwyntah war camp in the dark hours of the morning, every one of them spent. Painted warriors met them at the embankment with torches and led them to a glade where clusters of skin-lined yurts had been erected. The three weirmen were led to one and Donavon was granted a tent of his own, away from the rest. He immediately dropped to the earthen floor and fell fast asleep between Scraggs and his loaded pack.

He awoke after a dreamless sleep, not sure where at first, only that both the sun and Scraggs were up. The wolf whined at the interior flap in the dim light of the yurt. His tail swung back and forth, eager to get outside. Donavon untied the flap. The light poured in and Scraggs dashed out.

He peered outside. Five warriors sat cross-legged in the sunlight, shielding their faces from the wolf's slobbering tongue. Donavon hailed his pack. "When did you guys get here?"

They all rose, except for Notalk, who could not get the wolf's paws off his shoulders.

"Wulf give Notalk crack jaw," Nosebleed said, holding up his arms in mock defense. The others laughed.

Donavon charged at Nosebleed. "I'll give you crack jaw!"

The staunch warrior didn't budge until the last instant, then blocked Donavon's playful sparring with ease. He followed up with a blinding series of jabs that knocked the breath out of Donavon. Scraggs relented on the licks and growled at the rough play. All five warriors nodded respectfully to the wolf and resumed their stoic expressions.

"We did not expect you last night," Notalk said, getting up and wiping the paw prints off his tunic. "We made ready to send you word of war council with kaharpynn."

"That's good." Donavon sneaked a solid shot at Nosebleed's jaw. "I saved you a trip then. How's my sister? Did you give her the brooch?"

"We did. You right, Wulfwynn. She have voice of priestess. Powerful blessing she gave on mountain." Notalk looked to Nosebleed, who nodded while rubbing the swelling on his lip. "We also met with Mahocpynn and discuss many things. He send us back with war plan. His chief is in river camp now meeting with kaharpynn. They call you to council."

"When's council?"

"As soon as you rise from sleep."

"Oh. I'll strap on my guntocs."

Donavon munched on an apple on their way to the war tent, his guntocs snug to the arms. It felt good to be in his tribal garb again, natural. Three weeks had passed since the pack had shed their colors at the fringe of the Weirs.

He and the other warriors—except for Tiptoe—passed through the clusters of yurts and made for a large circular tent midway in the glade. Many Gwyntah warriors sat cross-legged outside their yurts with their eyes closed in a state of meditation. Calmness abound, contagiously refreshing. Those who were not entranced simply nodded or raised a guntoc as they passed.

Tiptoe waited for them at the entrance to the tent and immediately admitted them. The space was surprisingly vast, more so than it seemed on the outside. Round poles supported a cloth shell encrusted in musk oil. The war chiefs sat on skins in a semicircle around the center pole. Animal skulls of every sort were mounted on the thick shaft.

Donavon scanned the gathering of kaharpynn, and he immediately saw the wide-brimmed hat amidst the painted faces. "Sarge!" he said, unable to restrain his surprise.

Sheriff Hoffman rose from his spot next to Scarchief. "Good to see you, Donny. You are missed on the mountain," he said, rubbing the circulation back into his thick legs. "Swalli here says you're fitting in just fine. That was quite a move you pulled at the Weirs."

"I guess I broke the ninth rule on that one, didn't I?"

"I would say so. I'm sure Hornpout will forgive you." He turned serious. "The crunch is on, Donny, we need to get to business. How sure are you about this Xavier fellow?"

"Who knows? My gut tells me we can trust him."

"Enough to run weapons for us?"

"I guess. What weapons are you talking about?"

"No guessing. We have to know for sure if he's with us. Secrecy is critical. We need Rankwall's long-range muskets. He's got a cache at the docks on board the *Lyssia*."

"And you want Xavier to hop the *Lyssia* to get them? I don't think so. Whether he's with us or not, he's not stupid."

"Deck hopping won't be necessary if the colonel's plan works. First we get Xavier to broker a deal with the pogies. Have him tell Krutzwig that for a price, he'll send his mercenaries upriver to shake up the tribes. To do it he'll need riffled muskets and some light artillery to shell their longboats. In the meantime, we'll keep our forces massed at the Haven stables. Krutzwig will see his big chance to wipe us out for good. With the weirmen putting pressure on the Gwyntah, he'll be more inclined to point his big guns on us. All we got are flintlocks. We'll hold the perimeter a lot longer if we have Rankwall's long shooters."

"That's the plan?" Donavon asked. "To hold up at the stables while Rankwall's southies hit you with everything they've got? Even with the long shooters you'll be cooked meat. What kind of a plan is that? You got no out."

"We've got a regiment on the march from Toricia. The last thing they'll expect is to be outflanked at the fairgrounds. They'll be the ones dodging the flame."

"Torics!" Donavon said, astounded. "The Old Mitt's signing up Torics?"

"It's a long story, Donny. No time for it now. But it turns out he's got family ties there."

"Wouldn't have anything to do with Harthmocker, would it, Sarge?"

Hoffman's jaw clamped down like a vice. "That's top secret. Who told you that?"

Donavon nodded to Pickpack, who came forward with the sheriff's combat pack. "That's a long story too. Just take a look at this. Weirmen found this stuff in a dory out in the broads. A flintlock musket was with 'em, but Xavier kept it. Harthmocker's name was engraved in the brass."

Another nod and Pickpack removed the blanket and pelt from the pack. The entire ring of kaharpynn, who up to that point had remained utterly still, jumped to their feet with their eyes fixed on the rabbit skin. Even Scarchief appeared stunned.

"*Hulu heim nar kunna!*" he shouted—What dark magic is this? Then he turned and addressed the assembly, speaking too fast for Donavon to decipher. Though he did hear the other kaharpynn mention the name Poulakis many times.

Notalk put his hand on Donavon's shoulder. His eyes were solemn. "I am sorry, Wulfwynn. The pelt comes from Great Mountain. Your chief shaman has passed. He was taken there by Talking Gun."

Donavon looked at Hoffman. "Pastor Marcus, dead?"

Hoffman nodded. "His heart failed. He was laid up in the infirmary for two days. Doctors said he was a goner. Then three nights ago he just got up and left. Walked down to the old port and paddled off in a boat. Some child from the abbey saw him off. Apparently he gave the boy his staff before he left. No mention of a gun though. This is news."

The council continued long past morning into the afternoon. Many things were discussed, not the least of which were the findings in the dory. Hoffman did his best to keep the discussion centered on the practical aspects of battle. At one point Murdock Shanker, the weirman captain, was admitted into the tent and the plan laid out for him. How strange, Donavon mused, to see the outlandish pirate in league with tribal war chiefs.

The plan itself was simple, though risky. And as Donavon listened to Hoffman methodically grind out the details, it became increasingly plain to him how the Old Mitt had beaten the Torics at Spaulding Pass. Brilliant, really. Just bait the enemy with a false sense of confidence until you get them exactly where you want, and then yank away their prize in one fell swoop.

The only caveat came when Donavon presented Hector Xavier's suggestion on strategy. In many ways the boatman's shrewd plan would have combined nicely with the colonel's had the kaharpynn been willing to surrender their trust to the weirmen. Hector's scheme was equally simple in concept: Stage a battle upriver with the Gwyntah, then bring the heathen captives to the Docks as if to cash in on the bounty. Tie their bonds with loose knots and allow them to storm the wharf when the weirmen handed them over to the pogies. Donavon thought the scheme risky but plausible and at least worthy of mention. But such were the limits of the tenuous alliance that day.

By the end of the council Hoffman was eager to leave. He had spent more time than he wanted away from the stables. At the river he shouldered his combat pack and spoke to Donavon.

"Xavier's plan would have worked fine, Donny, if we could trust him. He already knows enough to cripple the colonel's workings. Getting the Gwyntah to lay down their weapons and act as prisoners was asking too much."

"I know, sir. It was a long shot. At least we'll get the weirmen to run the guns."

Hoffman squinted in the afternoon sun. "Why do you trust him, Donny?"

Donavon looked westward, high into the towering Awshaws. Soon the sun would move behind the white peaks and cast the river bank in shadow. "Hard to say. I think he appreciates a sunset."

Hoffman nodded. "That's as good a reason as any, I guess."

"I thought there's no guessing, Sarge."

The sheriff cinched the straps on the pack Donavon had returned to him. "You know, you inherited your father's smirk. That reminds me. Your brother has taken his stand with us at the stables. He got there within the hour that Choroqua declared war."

"Adman?"

"That's right. He took the oath this winter with Seth McGregor. He's proud of you, you know."

Donavon felt a contraction in his gut, like a tight knot twisting. "Sir?"

"Yeah."

"What happens if the Torics don't show?"

"Then we're cooked meat," he said matter-of-factly. "Thanks for my pack back, Donny. Hail, Gahenya."

27
Walking the Knolls

"*Nahun alnoc vahana fwynn,*" Enyalda whispered to the perennial vine. Death takes varied form. So Muma had said. There were four fates in total: death of body, death of heart, death of mind, and death of soul. A body's death was obvious; organic sinews came undone. Less so were the others. Their threads entwined as one. Death of the heart was dire, though it often went unnoticed, whereas the mind's unraveled fabric merely floated in bliss unbound. Yet for all the forms that fate might take, the death of a soul was most tragic. For that, alone, was final. So Muma had said.

She added another whisper to the vine in the solarium; its purple blossoms were beside themselves in grief. Enyalda reached into the soil below. Some of the annuals had run their course and lay wilted in their beds. The morning glories wailed in despair as she uprooted their dear neighbors. Enyalda assured them that the annuals had lived a blessed life in the garden and all their souls were the better for it. She hummed a tune to cheer them up, just as Muma would have done.

She sighed. Still nothing. The glories agonized in grief; such was their way. What could she possibly do to console them? Something new, something absurd, something so odd, it would shock the purple out of their petals. The colonel came to mind. What would he do? What would he say?

The idea struck like lightning. Yes, that was it!

She puckered her brow just like the colonel would have done and shot up from the soil with both arms crossed over her puffed-out chest. "Happiness is having a reason to get up!" she exclaimed in straight talk without an ounce of whisper.

It worked. Better than she'd thought. Not only for the glories, but every other living being in the solarium, bugs included. A wasp rose to the occasion and buzzed at the glass to embrace the day. Enyalda clapped her hands in delight. What a wonderful discovery—to bless without tune or whisper.

The door at the top of the solarium stairs opened. "Are you all right, Enya?" It was Francis. "What's going on down there?"

If he only knew. But that was best kept a secret, like so many other things. Even so, she thought it might be fun to try out her newfound powers on her brother. She charged up the stairs and nearly barreled him backward into the mop closet.

"Love is the power that puts purpose in your puff!" she shouted, her face inches from his.

Silence.

"Right. What's for lunch, sis? I'm starved."

Enyalda backed off and lowered her arms. So much for straight talk. "Plan I have not time to make if said you were to be here."

"I know," he said. "Sorry about that. The colonel has me running all kinds of crazy errands today. He even showed me how to milk his goats. Can you believe that, Enya? I actually milked a wild mountain goat."

More milk, why? There was already enough for a nursery. She stepped around him and swung open a cabinet door. Four brown bottles of vinegar were in the back. A good start, but not enough. She would have to send Francis out for more. Quickly, she spun a rhyme to sweeten his mission.

Go you must to tavern fly
My vinegar is in short supply
To Hornpout's cupboard if you please
So I may turn the colonel's milk to cheese.

Francis blinked. "I take it that means no lunch."

Apparently her instructions needed more sweetening. She grabbed a three-day-old ginger bun she had saved to feed the birds and stuffed it in his mouth.

Hurry, brother, don't delay
The milk won't last another day!
Don't stop for lunch, don't stop for ale
Until curds and whey float in the pail!

She hurried him out the kitchen with as much love as practical and saw him to the parlor door. She shook her head while he descended the front stoop, still mumbling his protests through the stale bun. What was it about men and their stomachs? Which reminded her. It was lunchtime for the colonel.

Enyalda skipped toward the stock house with a basketful of goodies. The building was not nearly as scary as it used to be, not since she'd introduced Nicolas to the dead grass. She slid the track door a crack and peeked inside. Nobody. She smiled at the haystack, remembering her chat with Nicolas, and then resumed her search for the colonel outside. Rounding the corner to the goat licks, she again saw nothing. Not even a goat. He must be at the beehives. She scampered up the hill.

At the hives, she found plenty of buzzing bees but no colonel. Where could he be? She looked out into the knolls of the south field where the goats grazed in the gahenya. The mystery unfurled. He was walking amidst the herd, just a speck on a hill. How odd, she thought. Yet at the same time how perfectly natural. Like squirrels and birds at a feeder.

The sight made her giggle and softened her disdain for the goats. How nice of them to include the colonel in their travels. He seemed so distant of late, ever since the politics got nasty in the Haven. A pleasant outing with the herd would be the perfect diversion. He still needed to eat though, especially if he planned to walk the knolls. Enyalda waved good-bye to the bees and set out to deliver her treats.

On her way she passed the spot where Nicolas had found her weeping on the hill back in the spring. How she missed him dearly. He had promised to come back again to chat in the dead grass, but first had work to do in his new blue uniform that bore the mountain flower—the same uniform that Adman now wore. It put an extra skip in her step to know that he and her brother would be working together.

As Enyalda approached the herd, a musky goat with twitching muscles and horns the size of scythes came down to investigate. The colonel was out of sight, beyond the adjacent hill. The buck was big and white with a brown patch that draped its back like a saddle. It strode up to her without a mince of civility, spooky eyes fixed on the basket.

Enyalda hid the basket behind her back and flapped her free hand at the rude beast. "Foo, foo. Away!"

The buck kept at it with more nerve than before. Enyalda considered screaming, but then thought better of it. Something told her not to let the brute know she was scared. Rather she swept back her hair and looked directly into its eyes. It worked, to a degree. Its horns went up and its nostrils flared, though she could not help feeling it was looking through her. Its expression unnerved her, until she turned around and realized it was not her the beast was snorting at.

Another buck had taken interest in the basket. This one was just as big and nasty, only it lacked a rear leg. Like the other, it glared through her as if she were made of glass. Enyalda did not feel safe between the two glares, and gingerly stepped out of line. The collision of the two goats echoed like gunfire over the knolls.

They carried on while Enyalda jumped like a startled chipmunk at every ugly smash. The goat with the brown patch seemed to be having its way until the other one got fancy. The three-legged billy barreled in at full gait, only to weave just prior to impact, rearing on its sole back hoof above the head of the first beast and driving down hard with its horns. The direct wallop to the top of the skull dropped Brown Patch in an instant.

Enyalda stood aghast, clutching the wicker basket. She was relieved to see the stunned goat rise on its own strength and stagger away, apparently only its pride wounded. The three-legged billy held its position, its eyes steady on Enyalda and showing no interest in the basket. Enyalda concluded the goat was much better mannered than the other and so, feeling at ease, thanked it for its service and continued her quest for the colonel. Her horned escort trailed behind at a respectful distance.

She cleared the crest of the second hill without further incident, and saw the colonel sitting on a boulder amidst a cluster of stones. Goats looked up as she hurried down to him. The three-legged billy remained at the crest.

"Ah, what a lovely surprise," the colonel said, lowering his pipe. "I was wondering what all that hurly-burly was over the knoll. It's too early for the rut."

Enyalda proudly held out her basket. "Your lunch."

Mitterhal accepted. "Thank you, my dear, as always. I'm amazed your basket made it through the herd. You are truly a daring young lady."

She lowered her eyes at the compliment. Doing so, she noted the circular arrangement of wide flat stones on the ground in front of the colonel. Nine of them in total, each with a pan-sized basin carved into their surfaces. She knelt down and rubbed one of the basins with her hand. The stone felt smooth and hard, as if polished by centuries of wear.

"They are the grinding stones of my mother's folk," the colonel said. "This is where they processed the lupini. Long before a single Toricean ever set foot in these mountains."

Enyalda's thoughts raced back to the winter following the year of the drought, when barrels of gahenya beans were harvested by the villagers and sent down the mountain to Wulfhaven on the tavern's delivery cart. She remembered the bitter taste of the lupini mash and Donavon's incessant complaining over having to eat it. And the rats he would trap in the tavern's basement to supplement their family's diet with meat. Such a harsh winter it had been. That had been the year the colonel almost froze to death on his rooftop.

"She was a priestess, you know," the colonel said, breaking Enyalda out of her musings. "A high one at that. That's a no-nonsense position among the tribes. They told me she could speak in dreams."

Again, Enyalda's thoughts raced. Her dream in the solarium came to mind, and the sad woman with the enchanting necklace in her bed of vines. *Su gahwynn*, the beautiful lady had said as she faded. Thank you for what? Enyalda always wondered.

Greenbank smoke swirled about the stones. The colonel spoke after a long exhale. "Choroqua had just been made High Chief of the Ring when they found me. I was in my command tent, fresh from the south wars, acquainting myself with the new terrain. I awoke with my face on the map, my music box open. Then I heard a growl outside the tent. I put the box in my pocket and grabbed my musket. Outside I saw nothing, not a soul. Dark woods, that was it. Then a voice, beautiful, singing. I followed it into the forest. Miles it seemed. The singing stopped and I was alone. Tired. I lay down in the moss. I awoke to Choroqua's band of kaharpynn with their guntocs at my throat. They took me to Gwyntahlynn as a prisoner."

Enyalda kept her eye on the grinding stone, not daring to look up. Why was he saying this? He hardly ever talked about his past; it only made him sad. There was plenty for him to worry about in the present.

"That was the last time I ever wore the red," he said. "I stayed in the Ring three years learning their ways ... and mine. When the war heated I—"

"*Nish hayem!*" she shouted. "In tree your dream she speaks to me." She covered her mouth at her outburst. She knew better than that. Nobody interrupted the colonel. She kept her eyes locked on the ground.

"What did you say?" the colonel said after a pause.

Enyalda tried to clarify. "The dream you speak of voice in trees I hear the same within their leaves."

The colonel stayed calm, poised. Not even slightly miffed by the interruption. If anything, he looked forlorn—like her glories before they mourned.

"Funny," he said. "I knew a chimney who spoke of whispering leaves once. I actually accused it of being delusional. Imagine that. Accusing a delusion of being delusional. What a silly song that would make."

How sad, Enyalda thought. The colonel's dearest friend reduced to nothing more than a figment of his imagination. Granted, the chimney had never said a word to her, but it never had to. It was there for the colonel—steadfast on the rooftop, very real, doing precisely what a chimney does. And she knew beyond a doubt that it had paid attention to every word of her whispers and every blessing in her songs. How else could the colonel have settled his score with the wulfweed? Honey fortified the body, but not the heart, mind, and soul.

The colonel opened the basket and took out a gingerwhip. He held the wafer aloft as if studying a gold coin. After a bite he looked sadly at Enyalda. "You make a fine cookie, my dear."

Enyalda dared a glance into his eyes, and through his leathery shell she saw his suffering. His heart was broken. Of course, how could it not be? He needed a song, just like the days on the rooftop when he mourned the loss of her father and all those men. What song could possibly rise to the task? What tune could mend his damaged heart? Her glories came to mind, and the song she sang on occasion to comfort the purple blossoms after a dark night in the solarium. Why not? If it worked for them, it could work for him. The thought inspired her to glide into a dance. Around and around the ancient grinding stones she went, rolling her arms and weaving her spell.

Good morning, my mornings,
How are you this morning?
Your glories are blooming,
Sun's on the vine.

Good morning, my mornings,
No mourning this morning.
Robins are singing,
Dawn's on the rise.

Come waltz in my garden
Come swing on my swing.
I'll blow you a whisper
If you promise to sing.

We'll dance at the birdbath
Rejoice when I spring.
Together we'll dance
Like birds on the wing.

Good morning, my mornings,
How are you this morning?
Shadows are shrinking,
Sun's on the rise.

Good morning, my mornings,
No mourning this morning.
Your colors are blooming,
Your glory divine.

Enyalda concluded her dance with a magnificent spin followed by a low curtsy. Yet when she looked into the colonel's eyes she saw tears. Not the slow drizzly kind easily absorbed by a sleeve. It was a downpour, the likes of which would make her mourning glories seem giddy. Not once in all her years in the beechwood had she seen him in such a state. She grabbed his shaking hand, concerned that her blessing had done more harm than good.

When at last he had composed himself, he relit his pipe and peered into the distant view. "I miss my chimney," was all he said.

Muma's words flowed through Enyalda's lips before she had the chance to stop them. "*Nahun alnoc vahana fwynn.*"

"How right you are, my dear. *Su gahwynn.*"

28

Runnin' Guns

Being the boss was a mixed blessing for Donavon. The opportunity had seldom presented itself before, growing up under the reign of his brother. Adman, after all, had inherited the role of rule maker after their father died. The competition was fierce, especially in the raw days after the war when Fergus Rankwall commandeered control of the family. It only made sense Donavon would assume the role of rule breaker.

Recklessness had its advantages, despite the inevitable bumps and bruises. For one, he could call his own shots. That meant a lot to Donavon. Pain became nothing more than a string of consequences to be endured with tight-lipped resolve. Perhaps the assurance of knowing his sister would always be there to sing her songs fed his fearlessness. Whatever it was, he learned at an early age, through the hard-hitting tutorage of Fergus Rankwall, that pain and fear worked hand in hand. To claim mastery over one was to be the master of the other.

"I can't do this anymore!" Donavon shouted to Notalk, startling Scraggs out of a nap. "Another day of this and I'll be gnawing on my own guntocs. If we're gonna fight, let's do it."

Meditation had its limits for Donavon. Two days had passed since the war council had adjourned and already the idleness tormented him. Hoffman had said the Toriceans would most likely be setting out from Spaulding Pass within the week and would rendezvous north of the depot three to four days later, depending on the weather. In the meantime, Shanks and his men had returned on the dory to report back to Hector. The kaharpynn were instructed to sit tight in the river camp until the Mahocpynn gave word to attack. The prospect of paddling longboats across the Haven and dodging cannon balls at the harbor's edge did not sit well with Donavon. Hand-to-hand combat was the Gwyntah's chief advantage, and he could not help thinking that Hector's plan to ambush the *Lyssia* at the Docks would have made much better use of that. Yet what nagged him most was the grim realization that his brother could be facing a line of loaded muskets, even in that very moment when he sat idle at the river camp.

"That is not our call to make, Wulfwynn," Notalk said. "Mahocpynn tell us when to attack."

"When isn't good enough!" snapped Donavon. "My brother is at the stables. They need those guns now."

"That depend on meeting with chief boatman and peace stealers. If he succeed, then maybe we bring guns to your brother tonight. It best now to relax. Keep mind clear until time to act."

As if sensing the need for a diversion, Scraggs sprang on Donavon and nipped at his dreadlocks. Donavon seized the beast by the scruff, sending both down in a swirl of dust and fur. The commotion stirred several warriors out of their meditations. Many in the river camp closed in for a better view of the spar between man and wolf. By the end of the match, Donavon sat panting in the dirt while the wolf licked traces of war paint off its fur.

Later that afternoon, Scarchief approached Donavon, handing him a leather bladder full of liquid. As usual, he spoke in the ancient tribal dialect that Donavon only partially understood. Notalk translated.

"The war chiefs call for your service in smoke tent. Kaharpynn Swalhulah will escort you there himself. Time presses. You must wear your guntocs and drink honey water on way. Wulf stay with us."

Donavon and Scarchief walked through the camp to the skull-filled yurt. They stopped long enough at the entrance for Donavon to finish the contents of the skin—strikingly similar in taste to the sweet water he'd been given at Mother Temple. A deep chant emanated from within the circular tent. They walked through the thick skin flaps, which were immediately secured shut after them. Two masked Gwyntah escorted Donavon to the central pole, where a single torch burned. Looking at the base of the pole, he saw the rabbit pelt and blanket from the dory stretched out on the earthen floor. The air was still and pungent. Smoke hovered in eerie layers, suspended in space, just like at Mother Temple.

Scarchief disappeared into the chanting shadows as a shaman approached with a smoldering urn in hand. His bloodshot eyes glowed like flames.

"Weirmen find great power in lake. We send wolf spirit to mountain to learn story of rabbit. Watch for light on guntoc. It bring you back to river camp."

The shaman raised the smoking urn to Donavon's face and blew.

His head swooned, his thoughts becoming tangled. *Bring me back? From what? Where is my choice in all this? We have a war to fight. No time for this. What about the guns? My brother needs the guns! Why can't I speak? Where is my mouth? It's dark. What am I doing here? My fingers … they tingle … How do I—*

Blackness.

Dreams and visions were nothing new to Donavon. He'd often had them as a child, especially when Muma gave him a sip from the blue vial to settle him down. But to dream without vision was altogether different and took him to an uncharted place. He knew his eyes were open, so why couldn't he see? His nose still worked. The smell was wretched, like tar in burning grass. The reek seared his lungs. He had to get out of there, and fast, but where? He looked up. A glimmer from above, a speck of light in an ascending tunnel. That was it.

He climbed upward in the smoke, straight for the light, his lungs burning. When it seemed the fumes would take him, the speck widened into a prism of green, gold, crimson, and white. Just like that he was out, gasping for air in a brilliant field of sunlight, surrounded by flowers of every size and sort imaginable. He dropped to his knees, his hands at his throat, and the sweet fragrance of the blossoms cut through the tar in his labored lungs.

Long he lay until the gasping subsided. As his senses returned he caught a whiff of blood and the sound of someone weeping in the distance. A rabbit—a large one, like a mountain cat with ears—slinked out of the flowers not far from where he stood. It was injured, dragging one rear leg. The sight was sorrowful, and he thought to snap the neck of the pitiful creature for its own sake. The rabbit, as if sensing the sentiment, lunged toward the vast bank of smoke that loomed just beyond Donavon. He watched the wounded creature disappear into the fumes.

He followed its blood trail up through the shoulder-high blossoms and heard the weeping yet again. Stepping out of the wildflowers, he saw a young boy seated on a rock at the base of a wide grassy knoll. The boy was in uniform; a musket lay on his lap. It was the soldier from the dream on the mountain, but he was nothing like Donavon remembered. His spirit was broken, void of all fight, surrounded in the stench of his own excrement. The boy raised his head as Donavon approached. His eyes were blood-red with pain, though he bore no evidence of a wound.

"Why are you crying?" Donavon asked, sitting next to him on the rock.

The boy wiped the tears off his soot-stained face. "I am lost."

"Lost from what?"

He peered across the meadow at the bank of black fog the rabbit had plunged into. "My brothers. They are somewhere down there in the smoke, holding the line. I need to find them, but I am afraid."

"I wouldn't go in there," Donavon said. "You'll be cooked meat for sure. If I were you I'd find a stream upslope and get yourself cleaned up. Your brothers won't want to see you like this."

A shadow passed over the soldier's face and swept across the grass, prompting Donavon to look up. An enormous osprey circled above on black wings that fanned the sky. "Now there's a sight you don't see every day," Donavon said encouragingly to the boy. "A lakehawk in the mountains. They usually stick to the water."

Both he and the soldier watched the majestic bird circle until a single high-pitched note piped down from above. The boy's eyes lit up. "Father?" he said, looking to the ridge. In that instant, the osprey folded its wings and dove into the smoke, talons out.

The goat-hyde pipe sounded again in the distant clefts, soon accompanied by another. Several more joined in haunting harmony. The boy beamed at Donavon. He suddenly seemed encouraged, almost elated, as if a great burden had been lifted off his soul.

"That's the call to fall back and retreat to the high ground. They did it."

"Did what?" Donavon asked.

"They drew in the bear. My brothers did it!"

Distant thunder rumbled. Mystified, Donavon looked to the sky. Not a storm cloud in sight. The ground vibrated, as if the mountain itself had a heartbeat. The tremors grew until it felt like a mighty landslide had let loose from above. He scanned the cliffs for the source of the quake and saw them. Mountain goats, cresting over the knoll. Lots of them, charging over the top of the hill and down the slope. Just like the ones in his dream at Mother Temple. Donavon and the soldier ducked behind the rock as the giant beasts passed on both sides, leaping over wagon-sized boulders in single bounds. Horns down, they stampeded into the smoke bank, crushing the meadow on the way. When all had passed and only a scattering of bent flower stalks remained, the osprey shot out of the smoke with the rabbit in its talons. Up and up it soared, beyond the high peak, until it was a speck in the sky.

Donavon looked down. The soldier had left, leaving his musket on the rock. Scanning the slope, Donavon saw him already halfway up the knoll.

"Hey! You forgot your gun." He picked up the musket and set out to follow.

A cry came from below. He recognized it—a Gwyntah war cry. He turned around and saw Scarchief standing at the edge of the smoke bank in the trampled flowers, only he had no scars. He appeared young and strong, at the peak of his prowess.

"*Ni katte nahun!*" the war chief shouted. Do not chase the dead.

Donavon hesitated. The music still piped from above and the soldier was beckoning him from high atop the knoll. How tempting to follow the boy and listen to the music carry on the wind. So many sights, smells, and sounds just waiting to be explored. The mere thought made him feel like a wolf again, so free and strong. He took several steps upward, ready to bound, the fur already sprouting on his arms.

"*Ni katte nahun!*" Scarchief repeated.

Again Donavon turned around and held up the musket. "But I have the gun," he shouted down the hill. He felt a pulse on his wrist as Scarchief dashed back into the smoke. Looking at his raised hand, he saw the crystal in his guntoc flicker like a blue beacon before it burst into shards of splintered light. Blinded, he dropped to his knees and held tight to the musket, submitting utterly to the white.

Wet nose on face. Donavon opened his eyes and realized he was outside the smoke tent. Looking up, he saw Scraggs closing in for another sniff, followed by a lick. Next to the wolf stood Scarchief. The real one—or at least the one Donavon was familiar with—the scar tissue on his forehead softened by the light of the setting sun. Behind the warrior loomed the shadowy peaks of the Awshaws. The sight empowered Donavon to rise in spite of the splitting headache. Something was in his hands. He looked down—a Toricean flintlock.

"Where did this come from?" he asked, gawking at the weapon.

Notalk stepped forward, followed by Pickpack, Nosebleed, Tiptoe, and Blue. "Chief boatman come to river camp shortly after you go to smoke dream," Notalk said. "He succeed in deal with peace stealers and bring their long guns in boat. He also give us this gun. He say it cursed and not want it anymore. When you shout about gun in jahacco huru, Kaharpynn Swalhulah take you out of smoke tent. We give you brass gun and you rest easy. Now you back. Drink this." Notalk handed him the bladder of honey water.

After a long swig Donavon looked to Scarchief. "What now?" he asked, ignoring his headache.

Scarchief spoke and Notalk dutifully interpreted. "We load long guns on flat boat tonight, then escort boatmen to depot. Scouts on way now to give word to Hoof chief across Haven."

"Excellent," Donavon said. "We leave tonight then, just like you said. I never should have doubted you."

"No, Wulfwynn, Kaharpynn Swalhulah say you must stay at river camp and tell war council of your dream."

Without hesitation, Donavon looked into the eyes of the war chief. "*Harpa mit yegan ni geshiva hutzspa.*" I lead the pack and fear no pain. The ancient words simply came to him.

The other warriors shifted uneasily. At last, Scarchief nodded and addressed the others. "*Huru hai Wulfwynn,*" he said. The wolf spirit speaks.

Pemiboats had come to the Haven long before the age of the rail. Sturdy and simple, they were designed by thrifty pioneers to pick up cargo along the uncharted tributaries of the Pemihawynn River. They would transport the raw freight down stream to the larger trade ships in the harbor. Their wide flat bottoms made them ideal for hauling heavy loads in shallow water. What they lacked in speed and maneuverability they made up for in stability.

Donavon crouched in the bow of the pemiboat, staring at the lights that shimmered in and out of the harbor's mist. Somewhere out there loomed the work barge. Behind him four wide oars stroked the water in synchrony, each one manned by two men: Pickpack, Nosebleed, Tiptoe, and Blue on one side, Shanks and three other weirmen on the other. Scarchief and Notalk hummed a barely audible chant, just enough to keep their scull in sync. Hector Xavier stood atop the rear cabin, piloting the vessel with the long rudder pole.

The moon cast a shrouded light over the misty water. They moved at a steady clip, even with their payload. The river current ran strong in the narrow side of the harbor, which certainly helped. The return trip would be another matter.

A distant light appeared off bow. Far out in the harbor, the beam blinked in and out of the mist and then disappeared. Donavon put a hand on Scraggs. The wolf's ears went up, followed by a low growl. Both listened. The sound was faint yet steady, hard to pinpoint over the splashing of the oars.

"Stop your rowing," Donavon ordered.

The oars stopped. Sure enough, the sound came from the direction of the flickering light: *Shh—psst, shh—psst, shh—psst.*

It was one of Rankwall's new-fangled steamboats from the South Bay. Donavon felt for his hunting knife. "There's a steamer out there," he reported to the crew. "I think it's coming this way."

Strange that nobody else seemed to hear it. He looked to Hector on the top of the cabin, scanning the darkness, then to Scarchief, silent as death. It suddenly dawned on Donavon that he had no idea what to do. A pogie patrol was one thing, but this was a steamer from Altomar built for war, equipped with a bow gun and most likely a crew of armed southies. A clammy sweat broke out. He felt naked, powerless, paralyzed by indecision. He stared into the eyes of his pack. *They call me their leader,* he thought. *What kind of a leader does nothing?* The mist shifted and the light of the incoming boat became visible to all. The faint chatter of the steamer's paddle wheels further slapped at Donavon's doubts. At an utter loss, he looked to Scarchief.

384

"What do we do?"

The veteran war chief spoke. Though Donavon understood only a few of his words, there was no mistaking the authority that backed them. The rest of the pack jumped to action. Nosebleed and Pickpack shed all but their loin covers and guntocs. Blue and Tiptoe took the extra arrows from their discarded quivers and hurried to position among the weirmen. Notalk addressed Hector even as Scarchief, Nosebleed, and Pickpack engaged their guntocs and lowered themselves into the cold black water off stern.

"You must steal time for warriors to swim around steamboat," Notalk said. "Keep their attention on pemiboat. When fight begin we hit them with arrows while others strike with talons. Kaharpynn Swalhula say no guns fired by your boatmen unless last choice."

Hector nodded in agreement and looked to the oarmen. "You hear that, mates? It's all daggers and sabers. Keep the pistols quiet. What about you two and the wolf?" he asked Notalk.

"We go in cabin and wait. When they open door, we attack. Silence is our goal."

"Yeah, survival might not be a bad idea either," Hector said. "Have at it then. I'll do what I can to soften 'em up. Keep your ears to the gunnels."

Notalk turned to Donavon. "Come, Wulfwynn. We go in cabin now."

Donavon obeyed. He felt light, relieved of command. They entered the cabin; darkness closed in as Notalk latched the door. With his back to a crate, Donavon removed an arrow from his quiver. Scraggs growled. Donavon patted him and told him to be quiet. He heard the quick snap of Notalk's wrist blades engaging.

"Let me drop one with an arrow first," he whispered in the darkness. He set the arrow loosely in his bow and listened.

The patrol boat hissed on the lake. *Shh—psst, shh—psst, shh—psst.* The cyclic release of steam topped by the steady cadence of the paddle wheels. Donavon felt his own heart thump with every hiss. Eventually the wheels stopped just outside the hull and the hissing simmered to a wheezing gasp. Donavon took a deep breath to ease the pressure in his own chest. He felt a metallic thump on the deck followed by a tug, as if a grapple had latched the hull and drew them tight to the steamer's gunnels.

"Nobody move! By order of Rankwall, identify yourself and state your business on the harbor."

Hector was quick to answer. "Aye, Captain. We are from the Weirs and our business is with Krutzwig. We are patrolling the harbor for heathens, as directed by the Pogetsa."

"In a pemiboat?"

"It's our cover. The savages are on to our schooners and smacks. They won't expect us on a river flatty."

Silence ensued. Donavon stared into the blackness of the cabin, his senses heightened. Beyond the door he could smell suspicion brewing outside.

"Your hull is low in the water," the officer finally replied. "What is your freight?"

"Aye, I thought you might ask that. I'd rather not say, if it's all the same to you."

"What?"

"I said I'd rather not say. It's confidential."

The officer lowered his voice as he apparently gave commands to his crew. Donavon clearly heard the distinct double click of musket hammers in their locks.

"Prepare to be boarded, weirman. Keep your crew still. Anyone who moves will be shot."

"Now, now, why so pushy, Captain? We're all in on the same fight. If you gotta know, I got twenty barrels of the finest whiskey from Meridia on board, and a payment in full waiting on the east bank. What do you say we talk this through? Krutzy barely pays a stitch for heathen scalps. What's wrong with a little privateering to supplement our dirty work? It only makes your job easier. Get your boys to lower their shooters and we'll talk some real business. And I don't just mean the angel's share."

Another pause followed, along with the hushed exchange of words among the boat's crew. To Donavon's amazement, he heard the musket hammers unlocking.

"That's good," Hector said. "We'll give you a finder's share of the profits on our return from the drop."

"We don't want your money or your whiskey, weirman. Only to be sure what you say is true. Have one of your crew open the cabin for inspection, and then we'll leave you to your business."

"That's mighty righteous of you, mate, but I'm all about a clean deal. I count fourteen of you in total. Your two boys on the prow by the swivel gun could use a swig or two by the looks of 'em. And the three on stern with their muskets still drawn I'm sure would appreciate a good stiff shot, if you get my drift."

Donavon heard the crew on the patrol boat laugh at the witty remark. How unnerving to realize that even the enemy had a sense of humor—and how sad. Donavon drew back the arrow and faced the door. The pemiboat rocked as the southies boarded.

Hector ordered Shanks to open up the cabin and give them a barrel of the finest for their troubles.

"Come to think of it," he added, "there's four of 'em coming over for a look. Why don't you give 'em two kegs to make it worth their trip?"

Donavon did the math. Four on the pemiboat meant ten on the steamer. Did that include the captain? No matter. It was the four at the door he had to worry about. Hopefully Shanks would have the sense to get out of the way when he opened the door.

The wily pirate suddenly spoke, as if to answer Donavon's question. "Right this way, fellas. Just a little twist on the ol' latch and I'll be out of your way in a jif."

The door opened and a stream of lantern light poured through. Donavon made out the silhouette of a man with a cap. *Thwap*. The arrow pierced the southie in the shoulder. The wounded soldier started to raise his gun, but Scraggs was already on him, jowls to the neck.

Notalk leaped over the downed man and spun out of the cabin in a whirlwind of arms and blades. Donavon was quick to follow and discovered that Shanks had already dropped one with a dagger in the back. The third southie fell to the deck, sliced in the neck by Notalk's talons. The fourth dropped the lantern and fumbled for his gun, only to fall victim of the same fate.

How fierce, how quick, how deadly, Donavon thought. He had never seen Notalk in his death dance. Not in all their training exercises in the Ring had he witnessed such lethal precision in the warrior.

Several splashes drew Donavon's attention to the patrol boat. Already a deathly stillness haunted the deck. Three ghostlike shadows crossed the flickering light of the swinging hull lanterns. Scarchief, Pickpack, and Nosebleed combed the steamer's deck, making sure the dead were actually dead. It dawned on Donavon, as he spotted the two slumped forms in the moonlit prow by the swivel gun, why the Old Mitt had gone to such lengths during the war to win the trust of the Gwyntah.

A groan from behind caught Donavon's attention. It was the soldier he had shot in the shoulder. Apparently Scraggs had not finished him off, though by the sound of it he was not far from joining his comrades. The arrow in his shoulder swayed with every labored breath. Donavon moved in for a closer look. He could not make out the face in the darkness, but he got a whiff of ripe urine mixed with fresh flowing blood. Another gargled mumble. The southie was trying to say something. Donavon lowered his head for a better listen, ready to plunge his hunting knife into the dying man's ribs should he suddenly spring to life. Again the pitiful groan.

One of the weirmen raised a lantern and Donavon saw the soldier's face, ravaged beyond repair. He was a young man with the remnants of what was once a neatly trimmed beard—just like Adman's. The soldier coughed, clearing his mouth of blood, then forced out a word. This time Donavon heard it. "Mercy."

Hector's booming voice cut into the cabin. "Step aside, mate," he said, squeezing through the door. "What we got here?"

"He lives," Donavon said.

Kneeling down, Hector put his hand on the soldier's heaving chest. "That he does." As casually as smearing butter on bread, he slid the blade of his dagger across the soldier's neck. "Sweet dreams, mate."

Donavon watched as the last spark of life left the soldier's eyes. Appalled, he followed Hector out of the cabin. "Why did you do that!" he shouted at the weirman's back.

Hector turned around and glared at him. "Listen here, mate. You got me into this. If you don't like the way I operate, then you never should have signed me up. We gotta a boatload of guns to get to your friends. I'm not gonna let a half-dead southie slow things up."

"The fight was over."

"Is that what you think? Do you have any idea what Krutzy will do if he finds out we were behind this? You and every one of your wild boys can kiss your cause good-bye. If I were you I'd get your mind where it belongs." Hector spun around to address his men. "Come on, mates. Fire up the lungs on that steamer. We'll tow the pemi to the drop. It's all about time now. And leave the dead on the boat. When all is said and done, this has to look like a Gwyntah raid. Hurry up, get to it!"

The weirmen jumped to task. The towline was attached to the bow of the pemiboat and the steam engine stoked. Donavon sat alone on the flat boat, unable to get his mind off the dead soldier. Scraggs was the first to approach once the boats got moving. Yet not even the assurance of the wolf at his feet could shed the last look of the dead man's eyes. How he craved in that moment to hear his sister sing. Only Enyalda's songs could make him forget the dying eyes—just like they did with Fergus Rankwall.

A hand on the shoulder stirred Donavon out of his rue. It was Nosebleed, uncharacteristically gentle. "Ease mind, Wulfwynn. Chief boatman act with wisdom. No time we have for crack jaw."

Donavon knew the warrior meant well. Why then did the sentiment enrage him? The resulting left hook struck without warning, sending Nosebleed careening to the deck. In an instant Scraggs was up, snarling at the violence.

"There is no wisdom in murder!" Donavon shouted at the downed warrior. The wolf curled its jowls to within a snout of Nosebleed's face, ready to snap at the slightest hint of retaliation. Nosebleed backed away on his hands and knees and then got up and staggered back to the pack, which watched from the bow of the pemiboat.

The steamer made it to the drop in short order. Fighters of the Guard met them at the bank to unload the cargo. Not a moment was wasted with words. One of the hooded men approached Donavon once the guns were off the boat. In the moonlight he shed his hood. It was Adman.

"You did it, brother. You did it."

They embraced only for an instant before Adman covered his head and sped off to follow the loaded carts.

In the meantime, the weirmen transferred the four dead southies from the pemiboat onto the steamer and sent it out to drift at slow idle. The oars were taken up once again on the pemiboat, and they rowed north along the eastern bank to where Gwyntah longboats waited to take them upriver. Donavon sat alone at the stern, watching the moonlight ripple around the oars.

Notalk approached just before they reached the rendezvous point. "Kaharpynn Swalhulah send me to give you his wisdom."

"Yeah, I'm sure," Donavon said, still staring at the ripples.

"He say when you first cross Haven he think you young with much to learn. Now he see you have much to teach. You have heart of fierce warrior and mind of just chief. He is honored to serve in your pack. He also trust your faith in boatman and will stand for his war plan at council." Notalk walked away, leaving Donavon alone with his thoughts.

Shortly thereafter four Gwyntah longboats sliced through the moonlight off the east bank. The weirmen chopped holes in the hull of the pemiboat and the tired crew quickly transferred over. A swift course was set upriver, as the flatboat bubbled to its grave. Donavon felt his body and mind relax for the first time that night. He looked up to the stars in the sky. What a relief to know that Adman was still alive. His hand dropped to Scragg's back and he felt the wolf's rough tongue on his fingers.

"Good job, boy."

29
Big Dreams, Little Bugs

Chief Constable Heinrick von Krutzwig hated bugs. Bugs were small. Bugs bit. Bugs slinked about in shadows until the lights went out, and then crawled under bedsheets to jolt the unwary out of dreams. Not that dreams were anything special. In fact, Krutzwig hated them as well. Most of them, at least. Occasionally one would come along that made him feel big, almost invincible, but they were few and far between. Gin dreams were altogether different. He wasn't sure if he liked them or not, for he could never remember them once he awoke; only that he had them and they occurred in the darkest hours of the night after he'd paced the floors. In that sense he liked them because it meant he actually slept. Whether he slept or not made no difference on how he felt about bugs.

Complications were like bugs. They were small and bit and came out of places least expected. The big ones were manageable, easy to target and crush. It was the little ones that bothered him and kept him up all night. Like the reports of citizens taking potshots at Pogetsa patrol squads from the rooftops in the upper precinct. Or the mysterious decline of protestors at the square. Granted, the fountain heretics were busy tidying up their new home in the old port, but why the sudden change of heart?

The standoff at the Haven Stables was another puzzle. Mitterhal's rebels were actually putting up a fight, though that was not the surprise. The fact that they had accurate guns with three times the range of standard issued flintlocks was. And though he knew it was only a matter of time before Wittworth's cannons flushed the vermin out of their trenches, it vexed him nonetheless not to know where they got the guns.

The briefing room at Pogetsa headquarters was packed with officers. Brigadier Wittworth stood amidst his staff of southies, discussing maneuvers over a map of the fairgrounds laid out on the conference table. A stifling air hung about them. Krutzwig strode through the door with Captain Glockstoff, annoyed that the meeting had apparently commenced without him.

"Brigadier," Krutzwig said curtly.

"Constable," Wittworth answered.

Krutzwig seated himself at the empty chair at the head of the table. "Gentlemen, have your seats. Shall we begin?"

All sat except Wittworth, who continued to eye the map.

"Now then," the constable said, looking to one of the field lieutenants. "Tell me the good news from the lines."

"We've surrounded the stables, sir. Nobody is getting in or out."

"Yes, yes, that was yesterday's news. How far have we advanced since then?"

"The rebels have dug pits within their defensive perimeter and piled rocks, sir. Many of the pits are covered and fixed with spikes. We can't mount a full-scale charge until the fields are swept. The riffled muskets they have are making it tough on our sweepers."

"So in other words, nothing has happened. Is that what you mean to say?"

Wittworth stepped in. "What the lieutenant is saying is that our position is secured around the enemy and there is no need to squander the advantage by taking unnecessary risks."

"And so we do nothing until the infamous Haven Guardmen decide they've had enough of this spineless engagement and simply throw down their guns out of boredom? Is that the plan, Brigadier? I remind you that the bottom line here is the re-establishment of the rail. Every day these rebels hold out bolsters the confidence of this godforsaken place to resist progress. Already citizens have taken up arms. Nothing the Pogetsa can't manage, mind you, but why let their hope linger when we can crush it in one swoop? The sooner you do your job, the better."

"Allow me to remind you, Constable, that every man in my brigade is doing his job, and it is my job to make sure they continue to do so. We have the clear advantage and therefore options." Wittworth looked down at the map. "As it stands, the rebels are entrenched around the main structure. Our first course of action should be to sever the link with their supplies."

The brigadier tapped his finger on the map, and Krutzwig stood up for a better look. He saw a succession of red circles drawn around a black square.

"It's a simple matter of getting our long guns in range," Wittworth said. "The highest point of elevation is right here on the northwest side of their perimeter. We'll set up the battery here and commence a controlled assault to cover the sweepers. We will advance one trench at a time until the cannons are in range. Once in position, we'll fire incendiary shells on the stables. The rebels will be stuck between us and an inferno."

Krutzwig savored the image. "I like it. How soon can you get your guns in range?"

"Very soon if we concentrate our attack from the high point. There is one consideration, however. The topography of the land on that side—"

The briefing room door slammed open. Barrel locks clicked as every southy in the room pointed his pistol at the broad-shouldered seaman on the threshold.

Krutzwig could not believe his eyes. Of all times, of all people. It was Hector Xavier, alone, without escort. The tactless brute was obviously displeased about something. The vicious scar on the right side of his face glowed white on his sun-scorched skin.

"Put your guns down, he's with us," Krutzwig said. "What is it, Xavier? We're in the middle of a military briefing."

Xavier strode toward the table, ripe with sweat, churning the stifled air with his musk. "Then I'd say my timing's perfect. I got a boatload a heathens stinking up my brig and I aim to cash in now. I lost half my crew upriver gettin 'em. It's gonna cost you double if you want 'em live."

"Prisoners?" Krutzwig repeated. "We never said anything about prisoners. Your orders were to kill on sight."

"Fine, we'll scalp 'em then. But I want half down now and half on delivery, and two dozen barrels of the finest whiskey in Wulfhaven to calm the nerves of my men. Not that horse piss you gave us last time. I want the kind that burns blue when you light it." Xavier scanned the line of southies standing by the map. His menacing gaze stopped on the brigadier. "You in charge of this fight?"

"I am Brigadier Wittworth."

"I don't care who you are. I wanna know if you're in charge of the fight. Cuz if you are, you're gonna have a long march with those savages. They're not like that fish chum you're going gun to gun with over there on the hill. They gotta whole different way of killing. Times gonna come when they get a hold of some of your boys. And when they do, you're gonna want to have some bargaining power. I'll tell you right now that won't happen with a crateful of scalps. If I were you I'd consider my offer. It's money well spent."

"Just how many prisoners do you have?" Wittworth asked.

"Enough to pack the brig of my biggest cutter. Sixty, maybe seventy. I'm sure a few have knocked off by now. I'll only charge you double for the live ones."

The brigadier looked at Krutzwig. "Constable, what is the capacity of the detainment house?"

"None. The cells are full."

"Then I suggest you empty them and find this man his whiskey."

Krutzwig stood up and slammed his fist on the table. "Brigadier, I remind—"

"I remind you, Constable, that General Rankwall has put me in charge of military operations. If you have issue with that, then take it up with him."

Furious, Krutzwig sneered at the towering weirman. "Since when do savages surrender?"

Xavier took two steps forward, engulfing Krutwig in body odor. "Since now."

"Well, I don't buy it. Those are wild pagans with no regard for life, not even their own. They would kill themselves before capture."

In a blink Xavier's hand clamped around Krutzwig's lower jaw. "I don't like your tone, Krutzy," he said, ignoring Glockstoff's pistol pressed against his head. "It sounds to me like you're trying to squeeze out of a deal."

"That's enough!" Wittworth shouted. "You'll get your money, weirman."

Xavier turned a fierce eye on Glockstoff, who still held the pistol to his head. "Anybody ever tell you you look like a rat?" He let go of Krutzwig's face and addressed the brigadier. "I want half the money and all the whiskey on the Docks by noon tomorrow. I'll send in a couple smacks to pick up the loot. If my mates like what they see, I'll park the cutter on the wharf. Not a heathen leaves until we strike a price."

A simple nod from Wittworth and Xavier made to leave.

"Weirman," the brigadier said.

Xavier stopped at the door.

"The chief constable raised a good point. How exactly did you obtain the captives?"

Tension mounted in the silence. When Xavier spoke, his tone was subdued though his eyes were no less deadly.

"We set the bait the night before, where the river bends. Moored a few of my schooners right out there in the open, far from shore. Next morning the savages hit the brook in their long boats aiming to spark us up with their fire arrows. They didn't expect us to have those long shooters you gave us. We waited till they got well in range and opened fire. By the time they realized their mistake, my smacks were on them from around the bend. We closed in on all sides and ripped their boats to shreds with twelve-pound grape shot. Didn't want the profits to float away, so we hauled 'em up in nets. A few cut loose on my boat and wreaked havoc on the crew. Meanest bunch of animals I ever saw. Had to kill every one of 'em. The rest we tied up tighter than boom rigs and made sure to beat the fight clean out of 'em. By the time you get 'em, they'll be two days in the brig without food. Good and broke for sure."

Another silence.

"Very well, weirman," Wittworth said. "Commend your men for a job well done."

Hector Xavior scowled. "Spare me the sweet talk and just make sure the goods are at the Docks. The cutter's not moving until my mates sample every barrel of that whiskey." He gave one last parting sneer to Krutzwig and was gone.

The briefing ended shortly thereafter. Krutzwig sped the proceeding along, seething in his seat. He wasn't sure which was worse, being man-handled by a thug or having his authority usurped by the brigadier. All he wanted was a drink and a quiet place to nurse his pride. So it was most unfortunate that Harriet Simpleton approached him as he left the briefing room.

"Pardon me, Constable, but Miss Annabelle Rafferty of the weavers' guild is waiting in the main lobby to see you. She has a petition denouncing the Pogetsa's claim that Poulakis was a heretic."

"Tell her we are in the middle of a state of emergency and I have no time for such matters. In fact, short of the brigadier himself, I do not want to be disturbed by anyone. Is that understood?"

The clerk cowered at the outburst. "Very much, sir. But she did insist that I tell you that the document will be immediately submitted to the supreme pontiff in Altomar if you refuse to see her."

"The pontiff! How long is the petition?"

"It appears to be quite lengthy."

"Send her up to my office. No, wait. Tell her I have pressing matters and to return in an hour."

"As you wish, Constable."

Two doubles later, Krutzwig lay back on the couch in his office watching the afternoon shadows creep across the walls. In time he heard a buzz below him, somewhere behind the couch. He got up to investigate. Sure enough it was a wasp crawling atop the baseboard. He pushed the couch aside and moved in to squash it with his shoe. It was a glancing blow that only maimed it. It gyrated on the floor, making a hideous noise. In a panic, Krutzwig grabbed a couch cushion and smothered the creature with all his weight. He heard a knock on the door. Had it been an hour already? He picked up the cushion. No wasp anywhere.

"Where the hell is it?" he said aloud.

Again came the knock on the door. "One moment!"

He scurried behind his desk and grabbed his pen, calling for the knocker to enter as he read the inner jacket of a random file. The office door opened and in walked Miss Annabelle Rafferty, her pepper and gray hair pulled back in a bun.

"Please have a seat." Krutzwig gestured to the chair across his desk. "Time is pressing so we must be quick."

"Thank you, Constable, I prefer to stand." Her tone was sharp, annoyingly refined.

Krutzwig closed the file. "Very well. I understand you have a petition you would like to show me."

"I do indeed. With sincere hope that we might settle the matter here and now before it escalates to the greater province. It is, after all, a regional matter."

"I take it you are referring to our charge that Poulakis was a heretic?"

"Yes. As well as a conspirator and inciter."

"Lady, one look at your pastor's history is all it takes to validate the charges. Have you forgotten the year of the drought when he ordered every highland village to harvest the gahenya and give the excess lupini to the tribes? Or perhaps something more recent, such as instructing orphans to sing a hymn from the Old Tome in open defiance of provincial law officers. Or the pagan tapestry he had hung in the cathedral's narthex. Or even the fact that his very name is pagan. And then to top it all off, he establishes a new orphanage to be run by known heretics and then paddles off in a boat to die like some ancient heathen chief. The facts are the facts, Miss Rafferty. There is nothing fabricated about them."

"Yet you waited to charge him posthumously. Forgive the suggestion, Constable, but the people find your timing slanderous at the least."

Krutzwig leaned back in his chair with both hands behind his head. "The fact that his health failed at the peak of a rebel uprising in which he himself was instrumental makes the crime no less severe. As I am sure you are aware, madam, the tribes have declared war on the province. Live or dead, Poulakis collaborated with the enemy. That is treason."

Miss Rafferty reached into her carry bag and removed a stack of papers that she placed on his desk. "These are the signatures of people who have agreed to testify on his behalf. Of course, the petitions from Multynhaven and Tufthaven have yet to be tallied since the harbor has been closed to common traffic. However, we anticipate the same results. Simply stated, Constable, every parish in Three Havens disagrees with you."

Slowly he picked up the stack. The paper felt heavy and dense. He thumbed through the pages and thought he recognized a name, then another, and another. Dark thoughts entered his mind. To think that a woman would dare to march into his office and attempt to coerce him with a list of scribbles. Who did she think she was dealing with? One simple nod could make her disappear. The thought empowered him.

"I understand you are a weaver by trade," he said.

"I am."

"If I may suggest, and of course this is only a suggestion, you should go back to doing what you do best. I'm sure your quilts are lovely and it would be a terrible shame for the Haven to be deprived of your fine work. In the meantime, I will hold on to this enlightening list of suspects and give it very, very thorough consideration. Thank you for your cooperation and I look forward to never seeing you again. Good day, madam."

Miss Rafferty turned to leave, outrage in her eyes. She paused at the door and took a deep breath. When she looked back at Krutzwig, her anger was gone. "You know our blessed pastor came to the abbey as an infant and was given his pagan name by the monks. They felt it appropriate that he be named after the fishing vessel that found him in the broads. How ironic that the crew of that ship came from the same port as your mercenaries. May God have mercy on you, Constable."

She left, closing the door quietly behind her.

The rest of the constable's afternoon proceeded free of hassle—uncommonly so. Harriet Simpleton, for all her female flaws, could at least follow orders. Glockstoff was the only one who made it past her, which was just as well. The visit was brief. He simply needed a signature on a document that authorized the Pogetsa to confiscate whiskey out of every local establishment in Wulfhaven. A decision was also needed on where to put the heathen prisoners once they were dropped at the Docks. Krutzwig decided, for several reasons, that the wine cellars at the abbey would make the perfect prison. Let Wittworth deal with them.

Once Glockstoff was gone, Krutzwig bypassed the empty decanter on the shelf and went straight to the private stock he kept in a corner cabinet. With a sigh of relief he leaned back in the couch cushions and partook of his first swig of many. Soon this would all be over, he assured himself. After six years, the bridge would finally be underway and the fruit of his schemes ripe for the picking. How convenient, he thought, that the elusive Haven Guard would come out of hiding to make their futile statement. It was almost too easy. Almost. Krutzwig watched the fading red light that filtered through his window, imagining the Haven stables engulfed in flame.

A few more swigs and he lit the lamp by the couch. He followed the black trail of footprints on the floor to his desk, then returned to the couch with the list of names that the snippy lady had provided. He leafed through the contents, one page at a time. By the fourth page, the letters became blurry and he closed his eyes to ease the strain. Then he left the conscious world, christened by the gin.

When Krutzwig opened his eyes he found himself seated on a high throne in the briefing room. "How did I get here?" he said, glancing down. At least the list of names was still on his lap. Looking back up, he saw a bizarre gathering mingled about the conference table. At the head of the table stood Cornelius Mitterhal with his red-haired plaything tossing petals by his side. He also saw General Rankwall, Brigadier

Wittworth, Captain Marlin Barleycopp, Hector Xavier, Miss Annabelle Rafferty, Captain Hans Rueger, and Barbarus Haunch, the chief engineer. Glockstoff stood next to him with his pistol drawn, aiming at the big red circles on the bridge plans.

"Glockstoff! What are you doing?"

Barbarus Haunch answered for him. "The damage is extensive, sir. It's as if Mitterhal knew precisely where to direct the ordnance. He certainly knew his masonry."

"Shut up!" Krutzwig shouted. "I was not asking you."

General Rankwall stepped forward and knelt before the throne, hands together, almost prayer-like. "Forgive him, Your Eminence, but it is such a splendid time of year to enjoy the Haven. Can't we all just be friends?"

"Fruit!" the colonel said from the head of the table. His bouncy companion spun like a ballerina near a group of children playing in the corner of the room.

Krutzwig heard a fierce buzzing at his feet. It was the maimed wasp leaving a trail of red circles on the floor. "Kill that thing," he told Rankwall.

"But I am afraid," the chancellor said.

"Fruit!" the colonel shouted again.

Miss Rafferty addressed all at the table. "Good evening, ladies and gentlemen. It is with sincere privilege that I present to you Wulfhaven's promising young talent. The children of the abbey have put together a wonderful skit to entertain us during the briefing. Please sit back and enjoy."

"Absolutely not," Krutzwig said. "Keep those little heathens quiet!" He started to get up but realized he was naked from the waist down. He sat back down and covered himself with the petition of names.

"Fruit!" the colonel said.

A sharp-eyed boy stepped out of the group of children and drew his pistol, aiming at the throne. "Who are you and what is your purpose?" the boy demanded.

Krutzwig shrank back. It was Barusta.

"Allow me," said Marcus Poulakis, stepping out from behind the throne and bowing to the boy. "This man has no name or purpose," he said, glancing at Krutzwig. "But the time is nigh for your friends to leave the crib. A school will be needed where they can learn to speak."

"How the hell did you get here?" Krutzwig asked Poulakis.

"I don't like your tone, Krutzy." Hector Xavier strode forward and kicked Rankwall, who still groveled before the throne, trying to kill the wasp.

"Get up," Krutzwig said to Rankwall. "You're not helping."

"Fruit!" the colonel shouted.

The wasp continued to buzz. Xavier stooped down to seize it, backhanding the chancellor out of the way. Fearlessly he pinched the bug by the head and brought the writhing torso to within an inch of Krutzwig's nose,

---

its wings droning in frenzy. "Look at that thing go. It's gonna cost you double if you want it live."

Aghast, Krutzwig opened his mouth to summon Glockstoff, but all that came out was a womanly scream. He covered his lips with both hands. The stack of names slid off his lap.

"Good heavens," said Miss Rafferty as everyone in the room gawked. "May God have mercy on you, Constable."

"All right, that's enough," Brigadier Wittworth said to the traumatized gathering. "There is no need to panic. It's a simple matter of getting our long guns in range." He turned to Krutzwig. "Constable, I suggest you step down from that chair and allow me to take over."

Captain Barleycopp approached the brigadier and pinned a war medal on his chest. "I could not agree more. On behalf of the good people of Wulfhaven, I bid you welcome, Brigadier. I trust your stay in the Haven will be a fruitful one."

"Fruit!"

Krutzwig glared at the colonel. "Shut up, you old coot! Everybody just shut up!"

A hand seized his jaw and pried open his mouth.

"In you go, little fella," Xavier said. "We don't want the profits to slip away."

The thug shoved in the bug.

Krutzwig awoke with a terrible jolt. His fingers immediately went to his tongue. Nothing. Just a dream. Dawn's light barely glowed in the office window. He rose to the reek of gin. The bottle had tipped over in his lap and soaked his clothes as well as the petition of names. He went to his closet and removed a long overcoat. It would have to do until Miss Simpleton fetched a new uniform. On the way to his desk he found the wasp from yesterday lying lifeless by a black footprint. The details of the dream had already faded, but the sight of the wretched creature was no less threatening. A stomp of his foot squashed it into a formless mass.

Captain Glockstoff arrived shortly thereafter. By the looks of him, he had been busy throughout the night. "The whiskey is on the docks, sir, and the abbey wine cellars are ready for prisoners. The brigadier said he cannot afford the men to guard the cells, so he left that up to us. His forces set up the battery last night at the stables and will commence the assault at first light."

Krutzwig looked out the window, as if by chance he might hear the first shots fired. "What's the status in the upper precinct? Have the snipers been neutralized?"

"We shot three last night, but they died before we could interrogate them. Shall I assign another squad for search and seizure?"

"No, we need them at the Docks to transfer the heathens. We will deal with the civilians once the prisoners are settled."

"I think a lockdown would be prudent, sir. Masses are gathering in the streets. For all we know they could be screening the movements of rebels."

"A good point, Captain. Close down all streets to public traffic and vending. That includes the Promenade."

"By your command, sir."

It was past midmorning by the time Harriet Simpleton got the cleaned uniform to Krutzwig. Looking haggard and overworked, she went on and on with a list of excuses for the delay. Krutzwig snatched the breeches and waistcoat out of her hands, heedless of her chatter. At last, he left his office, only to be assailed in headquarters by a flurry of questions. The entire first floor swarmed with officers scurrying about like ants. Most of the procedural issues he deferred to Glockstoff, though the ones of a more sensitive nature he handled himself—such as what to do about the monks who incited unrest in the square by chanting on the cathedral steps. The squad leader grimaced when Krutzwig ordered him to arrest them.

Just before noon, several of Wittworth's southies arrived on horseback to deliver an urgent message. The rebels had requested a parley and a cease-fire had been ordered in the fairgrounds. Krutzwig's attendance was part of the terms. The rebels also insisted that Hans Rueger be present. A curious request, Krutzwig thought, but no matter. Soon the Haven Guard's mystique would be forever dispelled.

The ride to the fairgrounds was quick, the southies accompanying Glockstoff and Krutzwig. Time was of the essence. The brigadier wanted plenty of daylight to commence the attack should the parley fail. From what Krutzwig gathered, the cannons were almost in range. No coincidence that the desperates chose now to call the cease-fire.

The parley point was to the east of the stables at a watering trough at the fringe of the fairgrounds. The smell of combat lingered in the air. Plumes of spent ordnance seeped out of the earth like pylons under a ceiling of haze. Wittworth's troops stretched across the battlefield in straight lines, their colors stark in the matted grass.

A culvert extended away from the trough and funneled into a stream lined by fieldstones. Brigadier Wittworth stood to the right of the culvert next to Hans Rueger, surrounded by a dozen mounted officers. A dour glare passed between Glockstoff and Rueger as Krutzwig dismounted. An officer next to Wittworth waved a signal flag upon their arrival. The stable doors opened and two rebel soldiers started across the battlefield on stocky mounts.

As they approached, Krutzwig could see that one of the rebels was substantially younger than the other. Both were dusty from their days in the trenches. They dismounted. The older one, who wore a wide-brimmed hat, spoke first.

"I am Sergeant Jarvis Hoffman. This is First Officer Adman McFadden. On behalf of the Haven Guard we offer terms."

"I am Brigadier Douglass Wittworth. On behalf of the Lakwynnian Army, I will listen."

Krutzwig, feeling slighted, stepped in. "And I am the final authority on this matter. I suggest you state your terms quickly, Sergeant."

Hoffman nodded to his first officer, who produced a parchment out of a pocket in his jacket sleeve.

"'In the interest of peace in the land that we love,'" the young man read, directing his attention to Wittworth and then Rueger, "'the Haven Guard will refrain from the use of force so long as the following terms are met: One—That Captain Hans Rueger immediately and without condition be reinstated to the rank he rightfully deserves as an honorable war commander. Two—That the Pogetsa step down and a new police force be appointed under Mayor Marlin Barleycopp. Three—That Heinrick von Krutzwig be dismissed as chief constable of Wulfhaven and supplanted under witness of the Haven Guard by a constable ad litum until a new chief is chosen by election of the populace. Furthermore, that the right of first refusal of said position be granted to Captain Hans Rueger. Four—That Heinrick von Krutzwig immediately be taken into custody to be tried in the Haven's highest court for conspiring to defame the good name of Reverend Marcus Poulakis, and for his involvement in the murder of Sebastian Schnites. Five—That all security forces not authorized by Marlin Barleycopp leave the Haven immediately.'"

Krutzwig was so stunned by the terms, he had yet to formulate a thought before the brigadier stepped in.

"Let me make sure before giving my terms that I have heard yours correctly," he said, looking directly at Hoffman. "You have asked us not only to lay down our arms despite a superior advantage, but also to dissolve the chancellor's security force and seize his appointed chief constable so that he can be brought to justice in an unsanctioned court. And then to simply return to Altomar with the news that the Haven Guard asked us to leave, so we did. Tell me, Sergeant, have I heard these terms correctly?"

Hoffman crossed his muscular arms at the chest. "Colonel Mitterhal is aware of the pitfalls of the arrangement and has made provisions for your troops to have a legitimate out. First, you must surrender unconditionally to the Haven Guard. Your men will be escorted back to South Bay through the borders of Toricia as prisoners of war. The colonel gives you his word that they will be treated with dignity and respect. Message will be sent to Rankwall via ship of your scheduled arrival at the border. There you will be released and allowed passage back to Altomar."

Krutzwig sneered. "This is no parley. It's the rantings of a madman. Brigadier, this farce has gone on long enough. They're stalling. If they have nothing to present, then it is time to act."

Wittworth turned back to Hoffman. "Sadly, I must agree. Sergeant, you leave me no choice. If this is all you have to offer, then return to your troops and prepare for battle. The parley is over."

"Very well, Brigadier," Hoffman said, mounting his horse. "The offer stands should you change your mind. We will watch for the white flag." He turned to his first officer. "Let's go, Adman." Together they rode through the dusty field.

Wittworth shook his head and turned to his field lieutenant, his expression grim. "Ready the men. On my order unleash hell. Let's make it quick."

Rueger, who up to that point had not said a word, mounted his horse and faced the brigadier. He saluted Wittworth and turned his steed toward the troops.

"What are you doing, Rueger?" Wittworth demanded.

"What I should have done a long time ago, sir." He snapped the reins and dashed to the open field. In plain sight of all, he addressed the brigade. "Stay your weapons!" he shouted. "I repeat, stay your weapons! The men you raise arms against are Lakwynnian soldiers. Freedom fighters. Your brothers at arms and veterans of the same war. Do not fire upon them!"

Aghast, Krutzwig looked at Wittworth, who remained frozen where he stood. "Brigadier, do something. This is beyond desertion. It is treason in the heat of battle. If you do not act, I will."

Still no response.

"Stay your weapons!" Rueger shouted again and again.

Krutzwig nodded to Glockstoff, who galloped after Rueger. Without pause he drew out his pistol, aimed at the captain's head, and fired. Rueger's body made a sickening thud as it hit the ground. His horse bolted off in a fright. Glockstoff circled once around the still form, fired another shot, and galloped back to Krutzwig.

The brigadier appeared locked in a trance. Yet as Krutzwig looked out into the field, he felt a dreadful swing in mood, as if the breeze were whispering incriminating secrets to the troops. He knew in that moment it was time to leave.

As if to confirm his fear, a lone piper stepped out of a rebel trench and blew a single note. Raspy, it sounded like the wings of a wasp. Another piper stood up from a trench closer to the stables and joined in the drone. To Krutzwig's utter astonishment, three more stepped out of the woods far up on the hill beyond Wittworth's battery of cannons.

Krutzwig blinked in disbelief. The entire wood appeared to shift behind the three pipers. A great hedge of branches came forward, out of which a banner rose—three crossed stalks of the mountain flower. All at once a song broke out, the hedge of branches fell, and an army of blue charged down the hill, their voices rising on the wind.

The song was answered from the trenches, and a second host of men charged, bayonets up. The doors of the stables opened and two lines of cavalry streamed out, each making straight for a flank.

Wittworth snapped out of his malaise and shouted his command to the troops. "Fire at will!"

The guns went off, though not nearly as many as Krutzwig would have liked. He spied a glint from atop the hill and then a great explosion amidst the cannons. Dumbfounded, he watched and listened as mayhem broke out in the ranks. Shots were fired without any attention to order. He rubbed his eyes as Wittworth's first line braced for impact. When next he opened them, he heard the haunting cry of horsemen carried by the thunder of their mounts. Though Krutzwig had never witnessed battle firsthand, he knew through a sense other than sight that this one was doomed. Without further delay, he looked to Glockstoff and snapped the reins of his horse. Together they fled back to the city.

No sooner had they left the fairgrounds and closed in on the city than a squad of Pogetsa approached, riding hard.

"We were ambushed at the Docks, sir!" the squad leader shouted. "Weirmen have seized the *Lyssia* and make to blow the barge. Gwyntah warriors stormed the Promenade and took headquarters. Longboats have landed in the old port with more savages. The city is taken!"

Heinrick von Krutzwig had never been a religious man, nor had he ever given much heed to ethics. Perhaps it was his upbringing, or maybe something more innate, like the incompatible pairing of a soul to a body. Whatever the cause of his apathy, he did manage to manifest one virtue, debatable though it was, from which he never wavered, even through his most malicious devices.

Though most would deem it blasphemous to call him a saint, it was by Krutzwig's own creed that he benefited society. For as he had often let slip in loose-lipped jests at his high-echelon cocktail parties, "A world without evil is a world without good." So it happened in the very instant when he knew his dreams had been shattered, Heinrick von Krutzwig looked up to the sky and repeated Miss Annabelle Rafferty's parting words to him: "May God have mercy."

30
Prayer on the Peak

Few things excited Cornelius Mitterhal more than a good nap. Precious timeless moments when the mind and spirit could spar together in dream. Granted, the play was not always nice. Sometimes it got downright rough. But even rough play was better than nothing. For nothing was nothing, and that just didn't make sense.

Daytime naps were especially nice. Rarely did they fail to refresh him, unlike the nighttime variety, which on occasion would set him back a spell to his bout with the wulfweed. He didn't miss those dreams, not even a bit, though he did miss his friend. Very much so, in fact. The truth was that he didn't have many, never really did. Acquaintances and loved ones for sure, even a wife once, but not until the rooftop had he ever known the comfort of a true, unconditional friend.

Bees were not friends, though he did like them. They were more like acquaintances who shared a common interest. Feisty little creatures indeed, they possessed many of the qualities Mitterhal found honorable: devotion, courage, conviction, love of homeland. He had discovered them by accident when he first returned from the war and sat down to have a smoke on what he believed to be an empty ammo crate. Whatever possessed him to turn over the crate after hearing the hum and put his hand in the hive was a mystery to him, even to this day. Perhaps it was his way of pinching himself, to prove he was still awake. In either case, he had discovered in that sedated moment, as his pipe smoke blew over the furious buzzing, that even the fiercest of bees could not resist a good nap.

The breeze picked up in the pasture; the yawn rolled over the knolls.

Mitterhal opened his eyes. The bees hunkered down in their hives. Scattered tufts of goat hair lay strewn amidst the crates. Some blew back into the smoke pit and began to smolder. Sitting on a rock, he reached down and removed a sweet nugget of comb honey from the bucket at his feet. The bees had been exceptionally generous—no shortage of pollen in the gahenya this year. He munched the raw honeycomb, keeping an eye on the mountain goats that scavenged the last vestiges of the alpine bloom. Summer was waning and most of the gahenya had gone to seed. Soon it would be time to supplement the herd's diet with hay—that and a little taste of honey once in a while to keep their spirits up.

He also noticed rabbits nibbling here and there among the stout legs of the beasts. One popped out of a burrow and raced past a billy. Funny how the goats only chased them when they ran. The sight brought him back to the rooftop and the chimney's curious fascination with the hardy little furballs. Not until now, nearly two months after Rankwall's Pogetsa had been ousted from the Haven, did he understand why the mushy stack of bricks had been so smitten by them. The memory of his good friend inspired him to reach into his vest pocket and remove the blue box.

"Here's to you, Chim," he said, opening the lid and cranking the brass handle.

The goats had lost their shadows by the time the gears dwindled to a stop. A chickadee landed on the wall and chirped up a fuss. He watched the little black cap tip this way and that until it fluttered off the wall and made straight for the beechwood. Down at the manor, Enyalda worked diligently in the gardens. She had become exceptionally engrossed by the perennials ever since their flowers had begun to wane. Barely the time to boil a turnip, it seemed. No matter, all was good.

He made an effort to get up and rekindle the circulation in his legs, but found the effort more trouble than it was worth. Reclining back on the rock, he peered across the south pasture and spotted a black coach drawn by the village draught mule. Promptly he extended his spyglass for a closer look.

"Hmm, excellent," he said aloud. Francis had the reins and behind him, in the rear seat of the open coach, sat Adman and Donavon.

Mitterhal adjusted the lens while the lads ascended the carriage road. In time he saw Enyalda shoot out of the gardens and sail over the south pasture to reunite with her brothers. Her skirt trailed behind like a tail of feathers. Mitterhal redirected his scope to the high peak, granting Uryan's children their privacy.

The four were nearly at the hives when next he looked. The snorting old draught mule stopped at the break in the wall, its muscles bulging from the climb. Enyalda was first to hop from the carriage, Francis next, and then Adman. Together the two brothers helped Donavon out of the coach while Enyalda danced about in the grass.

Mitterhal hoisted himself off the rock and in one grand effort extended himself to the highest point his bent body would allow. The pungent smoke of the goat hair still clung to his vest. He remained as such, propped by his cane, waiting for his visitors to arrive. When at last they got to within a spit of the pit he spoke, addressing Donavon first. "You look like you slept with a badger, lad."

Indeed, Donavon was a grim sight. A black eye patch decked his hardened face beneath a thick red mat of dreadlocks. The light in his other eye was fierce, and he had not an ounce of useless weight on his bones. His lower left leg was splinted and his right arm was wrapped and tethered in animal skins. Had he not arrived in broad daylight with his siblings, he could have easily passed as some tribal phantom of the woods.

"It got rough when we jumped the wharf," he said, glancing at Adman. "Some of the pogies knew how to use their sabers."

Adman laughed and nudged Francis. "Imagine that. Our little brother finally got his chance to scrap with pogies."

"How did it go through Toricia with Harthmocker?" Mitterhal asked Adman.

"Better than planned, sir. We stayed to the mountains the whole way. The Torics sang the Pilgrim's war hymn through Spaulding Pass and set the tone for everyone. By the time we got the prisoners to the border, we were more friends than enemies."

"Very good." The colonel looked at Francis. "And what of our new sheriff? Has he accepted his job yet?"

"I think he's finally coming into it. Just last week he loaded some kids from the village onto the mule cart and gave them the ride of their lives down the mountain. They got a big reception at the forge. You know they already got the pedestal set up for Hoffman's memorial down there. It really helped Angus to see it."

"I'm sure it did." Mitterhal looked again at Donavon. "You did well, lad. Getting those weirmen on board made the difference. You have lived up to your father's legacy and more. He would be proud."

Donavon bowed respectfully in the manner of the tribes. "My father still rides the Mountain in dream. I saw him in *Jahacco huru* on my first night in Gwyntahlynn. He spoke of one who made a promise." Abruptly he dropped to a knee, grabbing Francis for stability. "*Su gahwynn*, sir."

Mitterhal shifted uneasily on his cane. "All right, that's enough of that. Get up, lad. What put it in your crazy skull to go on a smoke trip unsupervised?"

"One of your soldiers who fought at the pass tricked me. He stoked my campfire with wulfweed. Said you gave him his gun. A musket with a Toricean general's name on it. The same gun the weirmen found in that boat with the pastor's blanket and a rabbit pelt."

Mitterhal nodded. "Then by the Great Mountain, you've brought better news than I could have hoped. The Little Pilgrim finally found his peace. No better man to show him the way than the good pastor."

He looked at his beehives, recalling Marcus's spirited dance with the stinging buggers. Not even the swarm could steer the old fool from his mission. What kind of faith would drive a pastor to charge an angry hive? Then again, what kind of faith would send a twelve-year-old into battle to hold the first line against a battery of cannons in an open field? Or inspire a young highlander to arrest a weirman chief while surrounded by his ruffian crew? Somehow it all fell into place. He turned back to Donavon.

"Where's your four-legged friend?"

"He's with the rest of the pack, sir. Didn't want him spooking the mule."

"Good thinking."

Francis spoke as Enyalda began an easy waltz around the hives. "There's a vigil tonight at the stables for the fallen, sir. There'll be fireworks set off the bridge afterwards. We got a spot set and ready for you next to Captain Marly."

"I have my spot right here."

Enyalda did a do-si-do around him and rested her chin on his hand that held the cane. She hummed a sad note, draping his beechwood staff with her hair.

"Keep your puppy eyes to yourself, pretty miss. I'm staying put, that's all there is to it."

She started to sing, but suddenly stopped, making her plea with words instead. "Come as family must we ride enjoy our trip down mountainside."

The colonel toked hard on his pipe and looked to Adman. "Tell the mayor I want that Barusta lad from the abbey to have my seat. And make sure your sister sits next to him. I'll make my own turnip tonight." To seal the decision, he encased his devoted caregiver in a cloud of greenbank. "Now get going, all of you. You're cutting in on my nap time."

"Absolutely, sir," Adman said. "Come on, Enya. Orders are orders. Hail, Gahenya, sir."

Tearful, Enyalda accompanied her brothers back to the carriage. Not until the mule heaved in its harness did she look back to sing her farewell.

Few they knew the box that is blue,
Cast upon brass and verse
Your father, your mother your brother the other
The family by right of your birth

In cloth be there woven a life seldom chosen,
But happy the womb from within
No tears in her nest, your mother can rest,
What ended again shall begin

Her words sailed sweetly over the fieldstone wall, carried by the rustling grass. As he watched the family roll away, it dawned on him that his job was done, his service to the Haven complete. Slowly his hand rose to his pipe. It felt old and used, like a worn-out musket. Wisps of greenbank wafted out of the burl and twisted in the breeze.

"Evidence," he said aloud as he traced the ripples in the grass down the hill, over the laurels to the manor. He eyed the beechwood, the gardens, the roof ... the chimney. Yes, why not? He'd done it before, he could do it again. Or at least die trying. Better that than to let old age gnaw at his body. So resolved, he plucked several seed pods from a cluster of gahenya growing near the wall and tucked them in his lower vest pocket. From there he set out for the old oak ladder that still leaned against the back of his house.

At the ladder he took a deep breath and put his hand on a rung. It was soft and mossy, yet firm enough to bear his weight—probably. As he pondered the velvety texture, his thoughts returned to Willis Hume and that cricket-less dawn when the torn soldier held him at gunpoint at the foot of the ladder. Why had the lad forsaken the peace he deserved? Who were these brothers of his that had sent him back time and time again to wander the Haven in rabbit pelts—trapped between life and death, shadow and light, dream and myth—when all the boy wanted was to sit on the ridge with his father and listen to him play his pipes? Whatever the mystery, one thing was certain. Marcus had to push the limits of his own stubborn faith to get the lad out of limbo. That alone was worthy of his Great Father's praise.

Not to be outdone, Mitterhal threw down his cane and stuffed his pipe in his inner vest pocket. "That's it," he said, gripping the rung like a vice. "Get up, you old fool."

Three rungs up, the pain was pronounced. The left side of his ribs throbbed with every effort. He stopped for a breather, wrapping his good arm around the side rail for support. He could still turn back. The thought only propelled him onward. Three more rungs and he stopped again. Not so long this time, for his right hand began to tingle. Upward, upward, upward he scaled, cursing the distant eave with every surge of effort. Halfway up he realized there was no turning back. Sweat poured down his face as he snarled at the pain. Three-quarters there, he lost the feeling in his right hand, which forced him to grip the rungs with his bent elbow. The awkward adjustment only worsened the hurt in his ribs. He made it to the eave, though he barely had the strength to hoist himself onto the second ladder that hooked the ridge.

The climb from that point was easier, aided by the incline of the roof. It was the traverse along the ridge to the platform that proved to be the greater challenge. He had to straddle the peak as if saddled on a horse and inch his way forward—another taxing maneuver on the ribs. Hard to believe he used to walk it standing up. Eventually he made it to the platform, though he had lost the circulation in his legs. Again, he dragged himself on all fours to the chimney, numb from the waist down.

"My apologies, Chim," he said once the wheezing subsided. "I had a little tumble that kept me away longer than expected. It's good to be back, my friend."

Silence. A long and terrible silence. He assessed his old post. The wooden crate was exactly where he remembered it, though its gray exterior was cracked and curled. From the corner of the crate a spider's web extended to the chimney's bricks. Its maker's victims hung like fuzzy white orbs in their coffins of thread. Solemnly, he prepared the ritual, placing the seedpods on the crate. He then reached for his soot scraper to crush the seeds.

"So, Chim, tell me, what did the wind have to say while I was gone? Any shapes in the smoke? The rabbits seem happy."

Still no response. What was wrong? The chimney never missed a chance to talk about the rabbits. The cold reception began to play on his mind. Perhaps it was upset and was going to make him wait? A little payback perchance.

"Listen, Chimney, I did not drag my old bones up here to babble on with myself like a fool. I understand it's been a long time, but I got here as soon as I could. There is no need to hold a grudge. Why don't we clear the air, right here and now?"

No answer. Just a pale stream of smoke.

Mitterhal peered into the plume and spied a ripple, ever so subtle. "Is that all you have to say? A puff of smoke after all these years? After everything we've been through?"

A squall picked up in the pasture and whistled over the rooftop. The wind slid the seedpods off the crate and spun them every which way on the platform. Mitterhal realized his blunder a second too late. He lunged at them, lurching this way and that to seize them. The sudden action tweaked a nerve that stabbed his already tender ribs.

He wailed as if skewered by a bayonet, cursing the wind at the top of his lungs. The horns of the goats went up. Desperately he focused on them—staunch sentinels in the gahenya. The pain unbearable, his bearings shot, the knolls began to melt before his eyes until his vision collapsed into a tunnel. Blind, he felt his way back to the bricks and succumbed to the void, shutting out all illusion.

What does the spirit do when the body sleeps? Where does the mind go when the spirit plays? Why do dreams seem so real? Who has the authority to deny them?

Questions. Mitterhal despised them. At least certain ones. They did nothing but impede decisions. He much preferred the kind with tangible answers that led to solid courses of action. Perhaps it was his training as a soldier, or his climb up the ladder in the Toricean ranks. Maybe it was the burden of knowing the war from all sides. Whatever the case, it was not until his days on the rooftop that his buried questions were given the chance to breathe.

He awoke in a black, tar-laden vapor. He had no idea where he was, only that he was sitting in a place void of all light. The seat felt familiar, like his leather chair in the hearth room. A draft picked up from behind. A small fire ignited in front of him and revealed a wall of bricks. The bricks were close, close enough to see that the joints needed pointing. Above the fireplace hung the portrait of his parents: the lord baron Augustus Mitterhal and his wife Hayalgaila, high priestess of Gwyntahlynn. Cornelius read the words etched in the brass plate below the portrait: *Yan shahuna maha na geshiva kutchu.*

Looking down to the hearth, he squinted. Could it be? More smoke cleared and the air lightened. He looked up. Yes, it was without a doubt his chimney, only without walls or a roof around it. It stood alone as a monolithic stack of masonry, immense at the base. The tower rose fifteen feet or so to a second fireplace cast within the bricks. Above that, the stack tapered inward by layers of bricks set like ascending steps on a pyramid. From there the smoke chamber extended a farther distance to the chimney's cap. How impressive to see the entire structure so exposed. How massive.

A thick plume belched out of the chimney's top and ascended the sky like a thundercloud. Darkness reigned above, yet below the noxious air began to clear, sucked up the damper of the fireplace overhead. Already Cornelius could see the ghostly shapes of cannons strewn, their ruined muzzles pointing every which way in the mist. The fog continued to lighten, and as it did he realized he was on a battlefield, surrounded by the carnage of war. Red and blue corpses everywhere, twisted in unnatural positions, their muskets scattered on the scorched earth like twigs. Not far from where he sat, a line of bales smoldered, reeking of tar. The stench of death combined with soot made him ill. Out of habit he reached for his pipe.

No sooner did he set the spark than a great surge of air descended and snuffed out the flame. To his astonishment a tremendous butterfly landed on the field just beyond the line of bales. From out of the yellow wings stepped a gray-bearded man in a black robe. With vigor Marcus Poulakis strode toward the hearth. On the way he picked up two sandbags as if they were feather pillows and stepped over the line of bales with the ease of a troll. At the hearth he stacked the two bags on top of each other near the footstool by Cornelius's chair.

"Put that pipe away, Cornelius," he said. "You are long past the point of torturing yourself."

He lowered his pipe, careful not to do so too fast. Dreams could be tricky, especially in the smoke.

"Good," Marcus said. "Do you mind if I join you?"

Cornelius nodded.

The pastor immediately made himself comfortable on the sandbags. "All right then, our time is limited, so let's get right to point. Why did you do it?"

"Do what?"

"Go back to the wulfweed."

"I miss my friend."

"And?"

"And what?"

"And why would poisoning yourself make you miss your friend any less?"

"It doesn't answer."

"Why should it? You've reduced it to nothing more than a byproduct of the wulfweed. I wouldn't talk to you either if you did that to me."

"Why would I bother? You're just a dream."

"A dream you say." Marcus scanned the bloodbath around them. "If that is what you want to call this, then so be it. In any case, what if I am? Does that make me any less real? What if a dream were to lay bare an insight you never would have known had you not had it?"

"Spare me the lecture, Marcus. I spent the entire war putting up with your nonsense. You're the one that flew in here on a giant butterfly, not me. I'd be a fool not to question the validity of anything you have to say. Just because everybody else embraced your silly words without question doesn't mean I will."

"And the story of a living, breathing mountain with fierce goats that protect its slopes is not silly?"

"The men needed a vision. It was war. Your fluffy view of heaven wasn't cutting it."

"Yet you still insisted that I bless your troops before battle. Where was the logic in that?"

"It's not about logic. It's about faith, the power within. Tap into that and the possibilities are endless."

"Ah, so now we come to it. It's okay to accept the unacceptable so long as the results are genuine. How convenient that it works for you and not for me. Perhaps we are not so different after all. And to think all this time I accused you of being agnostic."

"Keep your big words to yourself, Pastor. I did what I did because I had to. The land was bleeding and so were the people."

"Praise the Great Father! You could not have made my point any better. Think about it. How could you have inspired such faith in your men if you did not believe in the myth yourself? Look at your dearest friend, right here in front of you." Marcus extended both hands to the chimney. His black robe hung from his arms like the wings of a raven. "Your chimney is doing exactly what a chimney does—nothing more, nothing less. The reason why it will not speak to you is because chimneys do not speak. You know that as well as I. Yet that does not make the insights gained through your friendship with it any less. You would be a fool to deny that."

"All right, Marcus, for the sake of argument, let's say you are actually making sense for once. If this be more than a dream, then tell me something I could never have known if you did not tell me now."

"Ah, always the skeptic. Some things never change." A long moment passed while Marcus appeared to ponder the question, staring at the painting above the mantel. "Very well, if proof is what you need, then proof is what you'll get. The people in the portrait are your parents."

"That is old news, Pastor. You'll have to do better than that."

Marcus squinted into the fire. The flames rose high to the damper, drawing in the stench of the battlefield. A long moment lapsed before he answered. "They are mine as well."

Wary of a trick, Cornelius let the words sizzle while Marcus sat silent. As he gazed into the portrait, he thought he saw his father nod. Then from behind the frame, on the side nearest his mother, a tiny green sprout appeared. It curled out and down, and then back behind the portrait, only to appear again above it. A curious spade-shaped leaf on the tip of the sprout peered over the portrait as if it were the head of some shy woodland creature. Cornelius shook his own head to shed the illusion.

"And how exactly do you know that, Marcus?"

"By all accounts, I don't. As you said, this is only a dream." Abruptly, he stood up. "Furthermore, it is your dream and not mine. Everything I say is suspect to being something you already know. The more prudent question for you to ask is, how do you know that?"

Marcus looked to the sky, hearing it seemed, a distant call. "I believe you may have another visitor coming. I best be on my way. Pleasant dreams, my good brother."

He tightened the collar under his beard and strode back over the charred bales to the butterfly. The wings of the great vahegan flapped again and he vanished into the starless sky.

A draft picked up from behind and something seized Cornelius by the shoulders and waist. He dropped his pipe, snatched in the talons of a great bird. It carried him upward, into the black plume of smoke that towered over the battlefield. He listened to the wind on the lakehawk's tail as higher and higher he soared.

When at last he broke through the smoke, he saw the peak of a mountain that overlooked the clouds in a celestial sky. The summit shone silver in the light of the stars and moon. Then he saw her, silver as the summit of the Great Mountain Montayega—a ship of enormous girth, sailing atop crystal clouds. The lakehawk swerved toward the ship and circled her once. He recognized the enchanting figurehead below the bowsprit—it was the *Lyssia*. A great host of men lined her rails and saluted as the lakehawk passed. A piper in the crow's nest began to play. It was Johan Hume. Other pipers joined in from her upper aft deck. At the end of the bowsprit, standing on one leg with his hat on backward in trademark fashion, was Uryan McFadden. He hailed the hawk as he led the Haven Guard in the tenth hymn.

And so it happened that in the talons of a lakehawk, soaring high above the slopes of the Great Mountain, a lifetime of war was lifted, and Cornelius Mitterhal felt at last the rabbit's peace. He cared not in that moment whether he ever awoke again. As the great bird began its descent into the smoke, he heard a tremendous boom rattle the heavens. Looking back he saw the *Lyssia* unleash her ordnance, filling the sky with color.

It was nighttime when Mitterhal awoke on the platform. Colored lights sparkled over his south field—villagers launching fireworks off the knolls. Far away over the dark waters of the harbor, he saw more colored lights, though much grander, accompanied by the distant rumble of the *Lyssia's* cannons. He lifted himself up to a sitting position and leaned his back to the chimney. The bucket was nowhere to be found but no matter. The planks would do. He was grateful for it all, even the pain in his body that reminded him he was still alive.

How blessed he felt to be there, to have lived and known the glory of the rooftop for all those years—so many sunsets, storms, and moonlit nights. He found his pipe, cold and unused, on the crate. Thoughtfully, he picked it up.

"You've been naughty," he said with a stern look to the burl.

More lights appeared over the high slopes across the harbor. Gwyntahlynn of all places.

"Well, isn't that a sight."

The villagers launched another volley of fireworks in answer, and Mitterhal bowed his head in the flaring light. The silver buttons on his vest shimmered.

"Hmm. Just when you think you've seen it all."

"Colonel?"

Afterword:
The Story of the Story

This story was a gift. It came to me, quite literally, while I sat on my own rooftop. At least the colonel did. I am not a military man, nor do I claim to be an expert on post-traumatic stress. I've always enjoyed writing, but never on the scale of a novel. Had I known the labor that goes into making one, I might have found another vice to nurse my sorrows.

Now that the work is done and I am officially an author, I feel obliged to mention a few things about being one. First, the notion of an author being a recluse is a myth. Yes, there are long periods of solitary confinement in which the silence becomes so dense, it assumes a gravity of its own; and yes, there are moments when self-doubt takes the shape of a demon and strangles any attempt to create a sentence, but these are merely rites of passage. Without them, novel writing would be a cinch and we would all be authors. What an impractical world that would make. Anyway, I digress. My point is that without others to feed from, an author would have no place to go, no reason to get up, nothing to drive the pen. He or she would melt away like the Wicked Witch of the West, never having graced the world with a single insight on the human condition. Having survived my first novel, I can only conclude that an author is never really alone.

Part I of this book came at a time when I was not happy with reality, and so I made a new one up, loosely tied to the geography and history of my own locale. I had a nice little cape on the southwest face of a mountain in the historic district of Cottonboro in Wolfeboro, New Hampshire. Day after day I climbed up my ladder to watch the sun set over Lake Winnipesaukee. The mountain was named after Colonel William Cotton, a veteran of the American Revolutionary War. At some point, I began to ponder the sorrows that might afflict a war hero, and how trivial mine would seem in comparison. Cornelius Mitterhal arrived shortly thereafter and roused me out of my sorry state. In return for his service, I gave him life and a land worth fighting for; a place where he could do what heroes do and reflect on his own condition. It was the perfect symbiotic relationship. I am indebted to the crazy old bastard and will never look at a chimney the same way again.

I have another thing to say about being an author. One must have a message, whatever it may be. Without it the results are disastrous; like a soldier without a code, a builder without a plan, a priest without morality, a gardener without water. That is not to say an author can't be void of ideas. Quite the contrary. Sometimes the most profound revelations spawn in streams of absolute nonsense. Those are actually my favorite because they bubble out of nowhere and give substance to the underlying message.

Finally, the most important commodity for an author is time. Time to think, time to observe, time to process, and time to write. It is an unconventional way to make a living and requires a certain degree of compulsiveness, which for better or worse often trumps practicality. A life change in March of 2008 put me on my rooftop. By October of 2009, I had managed to sell my house on Cotton Mountain and avoid a foreclosure with all but a crumb of dignity.

My son Connor and I were blessed a month later when Titia and Gijs Bozuwa, proprietors of the Twin Farms Writer's Workshop, invited us to stay in their guesthouse in Wakefield, New Hampshire, while I searched for an affordable apartment. By Christmas they had extended the invitation eight years, to when Connor graduates high school. Not only was I granted the time to write a novel, but a stimulating place full of love and colorful flowers that my son and I could call home. Five years later we are still in the guesthouse and I consider the Bozuwas very much family. That is why I dedicate this book to them.

Gwyntah Translations

ali nahala : how would?
alnoc : take
ay : you, your
baha : wing
cha : yes
enya : seed
etsa : peace
fwynn : form
gah : air
gahenya : seed of air (mountain lupine)
gahutah : to live
gaila : flower
gelbynn vahegan : yellow wagon
gelbynn : yellow
geshank : feel
geshiva : fear
gnash : bad
gnish : good
guntoc : talon
gwyn : children
Gwyntahlynn : land of the children
gwyntahmahoma : children of the mother
gwyntahpynn : chief of the children
har : obey
havynn : haven, harbor
hulu : what
humala : everyone
hunwynn : noble spirits
huru : talk, speak
Huru Shakein : Talking Gun
hutzspa : pain
Jahacco balhalad : dream ladder

jahacco huru : dream talk
kahar : war
kaharpynn : war chief
kutchu : evil
lak : lake
Lakwynn : lake of spirits
lynn : land
maha gaila : mountain flower
maha : mountain
mahoc : music
mahocpynn : music chief
mahoma : mother
mahopa : father
mahun : great
mahunamaha : great mountain
Meguntoc : One Talon
meh, doh, cheh : one, two, three
multyn : hawk
Multynhaven : harbor of hawk
nahun gahtta : living dead
nahuntah : to die
nar : dark
ni : no
Pogetsa : keeper of peace
pogeya : to keep (possess)
prista : light
pynn : chief
sa : I, mine
sach : say, state
shahuna : shadow
shakein : gun
solam : return
su gahwynn : your gracious spirit, thank you
tuft : goat
Tufthaven : harbor of goat
vahana : varied, various
vahegan : wagon
vishwaw-myah : illusion
wulf : wolf
Wulfhaven : harbor of wolf
wynn : spirit
yakina : please
yam : name

Phrases

A Mahunamaha Montayega geh hunwynn solam. — To the Great Mountain Montayega their noble spirits have returned.

Ali nahala Muma wulf ach nahock prunus? — How would Muma feed a wolf prunes?

Ay yakina noch humala. — You can't please everyone.

Gahutah heim nahuntah. — To live is to die.

Har geshank sa guntoc. — Obey or feel my talon.

Harpa mit yegan ni geshiva hutzspa. — I lead the pack and fear no pain.

Hein shahuna a prista al gahut solam. — From shadow to light all life returns.

Hulu heim nar kunna? — What dark magic is this?

Huru hai Wulfwynn. — The wolf spirit speaks.

Mynwah yan vahegan a baha yan Havynn. — We fly on the wagon to the Haven on a wing.

Nahun alnoc vahana fwynn. — Death takes varied form.

Nahun tah guntoc. — Death by talon.

Ni katte nahun. — Do not chase the dead.

Ni wulf nahun. — Do not kill the wolf.

Nish hayem sahun huru.— No more soft talk.

Nish hayem. — No more.

Prista su hunwynn al etsa mit hutzspa. — Light your noble spirit, peace over pain.

Sach ay yam. — State your name.

Sach ni yahi. — State (speak) no more.

Yan shahuna maha, na geshiva kutchu. — In the shadow of the mountain we fear no evil.

www.ingramcontent.com/pod-product-compliance
Lightning Source LLC
Chambersburg PA
CBHW021123260626
47169CB00005B/1414